Another Alias

Greg Davidson

Enquiries should be made to publisher.
Author: Greg Davidson
Publisher: Vacartistry

Website: http://www.vacartistry.com.au
This is the website for the art genres (including this novel) of Greg Davidson.

The Facebook URL:
https://www.facebook.com/pages/Another-Alias-by-Greg-Davidson/489232107855186 can be accessed and clicked upon or copied and paste to your browser from my website: http://www.vacartistry.com.au

ISBN: 978-0-9875816-0-0

Dedication

For Christine – *fond memories*

Acknowledgements

No writing pursuit is purely solitary. Along the journey, I have been mentored, inspired and supported.

I thank and acknowledge:

Editor: Gail Tagarro
Cover artist: Shanina Conway

Contents

1 – A Serendipitous Beginning

Time goose-steps all before it.
Ultimately fate will be accused
or destiny, eulogized

The snake lay coiled in a warm swag. Unfortunately, its impending victim occupied the bedding also. An intermittent clunk of falling dewdrops woke John Bycroft; there was no need for him to peer from under the protective oilskin to know of a chill in the air. His rasping lungs sounded more like an old man's than his twenty-seven years. The weather was getting colder; so was his optimism of striking it rich.

Warm rays thawed eucalypt treetops and wildlife quarrelled. Cockatoos demanded the best positions to perch and took it; other species at the bottom of the pecking order debated amongst themselves in the lower branches. Wally Beaumont lay worn out from the previous day's work. He'd done all the manual labour while Bycroft had deceitfully staged an asthma attack.

"…Ahhhh."

Wally awoke with a jump, startled by the piercing scream. His eyelids sprang open but he lay motionless and silent, listening, hearing only his thumping heart, not sure if the cry had been his own or the sniper's victim in the nightmare he'd experienced. Sensing he was awake, the dog exited from under his master's oilskin as cunningly as it had covertly infiltrated during the night.

Thud. Thud. Thud.

"Jeez'us. What's going on?" Wally's head appeared from inside his swag. Boyish features camouflaged his experience of serving with the Imperial Camel Corps in Sinai and Palestine. Repatriated back to Australia, he'd spent two years convalescing in hospital. At twenty-four, he still looked like a teenager, not the battle weary veteran he was.

Gasping for breath, Bycroft responded, "...this. This is what's bloody going on. Have a look at the bastard." There was only one thing he hated more than snakes and that was rats, a legacy of growing up on the filthy inner-city streets of Sydney. The Bubonic Plague nineteen years previous had been the demise of both parents. From the age of eight, he learned survival meant – by any means.

Bycroft knelt upright with both arms raised victoriously. The pulverized snake dangled in one fist and in the other was the rock he'd slain it with; it was ready to come down again at the first hint of life.

"Jeez'us, you're lucky it didn't bite you."

A throbbing sensation emanating from puncture wounds in Bycroft's arse confirmed the worst. His comb-over hung limply to one side. Pale-faced, beginning to sweat profusely and now frozen in fear, he whimpered, "It did."

"When I was in Palestine..." Wally began. Bycroft listened, not knowing if Wally was pulling his leg or not, "...an army mate stepped on a King Cobra. You should see the teeth on one of those buggers; anyway, the medical officer, I can't think of his name, he lanced it and sucked on the poison."

"Did he live?"

"...Tyson, that's it, Captain Tyson – a good bloke."

"Did...he...live?"

"Yer...he spat the poison out."

Panic was beginning, hysterics not far off. "Your army mate, Big Ears, not Captain 'bloody' Tyson." yelled Bycroft.

"Naw, the unlucky bugger copped one at Rafa."

"He survived the bloody bite though?"

"Yeah, but sucking a foot is one thing...on an arse, another."

"Bloody hell, what do ya want...a medal? We're partners." Bycroft snarled.

"Then stop calling me Big Ears," Wally requested casually.

"Okay, Sunshine. Whatever."

Bycroft was certainly no Adonis. His portly build, thinning hair and hard drinking did his appearance no favour. His penchant for name-calling put people offside and yet he persisted in it; for the past month Wally was a recipient. Bycroft won the deed of title for a miner's claim in a two-up game. Wally had won a fist-full of notes in the same game, enough cash to finance the partnership the stranger proposed. Bycroft preyed on the newcomer's gullibility; those who knew Bycroft hung onto their money rather than risk it on what may have been a swindle perpetuated by the deceitful character. The

3

two men had shaken hands over the concoction Bycroft had successfully plied as whiskey.

Wally crawled over to inspect the wound. "Jeez'us," he teased, "I don't know if we're good enough mates for this sort of thing?"

"Pal, buddy, chum, cobber, of course we're mates," Bycroft enthused.

Wally apprehensively undid the buttons on Bycroft's long johns to reveal not only the victim's white arse and telltale puncture marks. "Ah Jeez'us, you got a hairy arse...this is above and beyond the call of duty," he wailed, "No, not a hairy arse."

"For Christ sake, get on with it, we'll be partners for life if ya want."

Wally procrastinated, "Partners, what's there to be partners in?"

Still kneeling upright with the rock held precariously above his partners head, Bycroft could feel anger rising. He focused on the rock and then yelled, "This." The smashed edge of the rock he was staring at revealed more than snake blood. The encrusted weapon was a substantial gold nugget. He'd kicked it aside the previous night when laying out his swag.

Between sucking on the puncture wound, spitting bum hair from between his front teeth and gasping for breath, Wally assured Bycroft his procrastination had only been a humorous prank such as those played on army pals. Bycroft thought callously, *kiss my arse, Big Ears*. It never occurred to him that Wally could skedaddle with the nugget, abandoning him to die painfully and decompose, nobody being the wiser.

4

* * *

Plagued by flies, Wally stoically moved onward following the dog. Pulling the victim on a jerry-rigged stretcher through the bush was demanding. Wally had a slight build and the task wasn't made any easier with the load whining all the time. "I'm baking back here." Bycroft shouted.

"Jeez'us. This isn't hot. You should've been at Rafa...now *that* was hot."

"I would've been...if not for my asthma," Bycroft asserted, between drags on a cheap cigar. The stretcher lurched as Wally stumbled. "Hey. Watch out. It's getting rough back here."

"This isn't rough. You should've been..."

"Yeah, yeah whatever. Hey. What about the wog women? Give me some entertainment."

Wally always jibed with army humour, both amicably and defensively. "I don't tell tales out-of-school...besides, there's noth'n to tell – I was too busy fight'n."

"Give 'em a bit of the ol' pork bayonet, eh...eh?"

In battle Wally had his sanity tested; confined in small spaces with irrational comrades also reinforced his patience. Bycroft's taunting only served to spur him onward, obscenities squawked by a murder of crows soaring high in the heat haze taunt him also. "You can say that again," he called. The bouncing momentum of the stretcher stopped as Wally propped looking into the blue expanse. He swigged from the canteen and gave the dog a drink from a cupped hand. "I reckon you should be feeling crook by now if that snake was poisonous," he told Bycroft.

"I'm slowly burning up, I got a helluva thirst...must be the toxins?" Bycroft gestured with his empty canteen for a drink also.

"Are you sure about this immobilising the victim stuff?" Wally handed him the canteen.

"Slows down the venom that's what I've heard." Bycroft took large gulps.

"Not all of it." Wally snatched the canteen back.

Bycroft dozed peacefully as the arrival of late afternoon ended the rising currents, free rides and persistent squawking. But for the distraction of the dog barking and snapping at his leg, Wally's mind drifted aimlessly in the desert sands of Rafa. Intermittently, his muttered words broke the incessant barking when the dog heeled him to reality and the direction of Gunnadoo. The settlement consisted of a dozen or so rough bush huts but mainly the tents of prospectors, although no significant finds warranted the attention the area received. If one wished to become invisible, Gunnadoo was an ideal place and many dubious characters congregated there. As night fell so did Wally. Searing pain burnt deep within his gut, reminding him of his shrapnel wounds. He buckled over onto his knees, collapsing within sight of the medical tent.

An insipid yellow glow emanated from a kerosene lamp, illuminating the worn-out Dr. Porticos rubbing his unshaven growth. His shadow danced grotesquely on the canvas wall behind him.

"When are ya gonna take a look at me?" Bycroft complained. On a bunk, he lay on his back smoking a cigar watching the silhouette performance. "Hey Sunshine", I'm the one who was bitten."

The dog lay in a corner of the tent watching the three men and a shadow. Wally was given priority; he lay fever-ridden on the bunk opposite where the doctor had dumped him, and with shirt removed the scarring was evidence of the afflictions he'd suffered. Dr. Porticos shook his head, applied a wet compress to the patient's forehead then slumped into a chair wheezing; influenza, tuberculosis and whooping cough were of epidemic proportions.

"Is he going to die?" Bycroft asked. For what he thought was an unreasonably long time the doctor contemplated the question. "Well, is he?" he sniped, "You're supposed to be the bloody expert."

The doctor removed and wiped a thick pair of spectacles, replacing them to squint at the calendar sitting on the wooden packing crate utilised as a desk. "Someday." The small dates were unreadable. "But not on…" He gave up, "…in May."

"What are you going to do then?"

"Right now I'm going to clean myself up." The last remnants, encouraged from an all-but-empty bottle into a dirty glass, disappeared down his throat. "There's nothing I can do for him that hasn't already been done before. Right, let's have a look at you…an Eastern Brown you reckon – I don't think so."

"Either that or a Taipan; the bugger's in my pack." Bycroft motioned the doctor to look for himself.

"So this is your Eastern Brown is it?" Dr. Porticos held the misidentified offender up; it was a harmless python.

The only medical treatment that could be performed was the surgical removal of the gold nugget from Bycroft's vice-like grip, and he wasn't about to let that happen. He swung his legs off the bunk and sat up stretching. "Well Doc, ya know what I reckon ... I reckon I must be one of the very few victims of an Eastern Brown left alive to brag about it." He stood up, taking the snake carcass from the doctor and held it high. The slaying of the serpent played out again. "What say we brag about it together, the drinks are on me, Doc."

"You're a lucky man indeed you are," the doctor confirmed. He removed his stained coverall and slipped into a suit jacket that was no cleaner. "That's the biggest, ugliest Eastern Brown I've ever seen."

"Come on," said Bycroft leading the way, "I've got a big thirst."

"Dehydration is a commonly found symptom of..."

They exited.

Wally's trembling lips purged forth ramblings of recrimination and remorse to anyone in earshot; hallucinations, only a veteran conjures, pervaded the stricken. Startled by the piercing scream, his eyelids sprang open but he lay motionless and silent, listening, hearing only his thumping heart, not sure if the cry had been his own or the sniper's victim. Pain racked his brain. "I'm hit." he cried out. He *is* the sniper's victim; the stench smelt is himself, the bad taste in his mouth is his own guts. A tremendous flash of white silenced the turmoil of red snow falling to a ravaged earth, and fire then consummated the union. Eyes watched skin melting from shattered bones; the final indignity, the final sight – Hell is blindly entered.

The putrid smell of Bully-beef rations boiling in muddy water should have turned Wally's stomach but he didn't have one. A bland liquid inappropriately called tea, and the tasteless rock hard biscuit ration soaked in it wasn't seen or smelt, nor was it felt yet somehow its presence registered. Wally quizzed himself: *this can't be?* Taste had vanished along with his guts; although not being able to see he knew this to be so because he couldn't feel them either. Nor could he feel his hands when clapping them together: *most puzzling* he thought. The vast colourless void was unfathomable, senseless, yet the odourless fragrance could be felt…and followed.

Wally's sniffing alerted the doctor to his patient's recovery. "Well, well, well. I'd just about given ya up for dead." Voices reverberated in Wally's head. "Let's take a look at ya." The dry cloth on his forehead was removed and a pulse taken. The silhouette figure sprayed cheap rum that dribble from a now unkempt beard. As if losing the phenomena searched for, Wally's nostrils ceased convulsing. "That's one hell-of-a fast heart rate you got there." The doctor estimated it; he had no watch. He waited for a response other than a sombre stare. "I'll tell Mr. Bycroft you're awake." The title given Bycroft never registered. The odourless scent of something unexplainable, and something never experienced previously still countermand his returning faculties.

Bycroft had made plans and many new acquaintances as he played the gold-find for all it was worth. For the past week while Wally lay stricken, he had lived on IOU's – the dog had survived on what it scrounged. Having convalesced Wally was now back on his feet listening to Bycroft's plans that were well underway.

"Get what ya need and go back out there Sunshine. Make sure nobody starts poking around on the claim," Bycroft told him, as he prepared to leave for Sydney. "I should only be away for a week or two."

"You *are* coming back?" Wally queried, handing him mail to post.

"We're partners," Bycroft reassured. "I'll be back with a pocketful of cash once our little friend is unloaded."

Wally tore the lining of his jacket and removed the last of his money handing half of it to Bycroft. "Partners are one thing, mates are another."

"Ya sucked on my arse, didn't you? If we weren't mates, do ya think I'd let ya do that?"

* * *

Rumours of the discovery soon proliferated, interpreted by all as 'nuggets bigger than your fist'. From the Dundee rail siding, prospectors converged on the Yapsly River and its diggings. The rush of horse, wagon, wheel-barrow or anything else that had a wheel and could carry a load cut a route for the forty miles of dirt track to Gunnadoo.

Thud. Thud. Wally hammered another claim-stake into the ground. Every time he did this to mark out the boundary, he carefully checked the rock he was using. "Nope, not this one either," he told the mongrel as it lay watching. "Come on, that's enough for the day. I reckon it's near enough tucker time."

In the still of evening, smoke rose like a beam of grey light to vanish in a background of luminous stars. The billy boiled and stew simmered in the camp oven placed on the embers. The bush became alive with sounds as its residents foraged for their tucker. The mongrel, all grey except for a black patch around one eye that opened at irregular intervals, lay dozing; until the heat from the fire became too much, it stretched, turned around and lay back down to cook on the other side. Under the billy, accompanied by the bush chorus of Cicadas, flames danced mesmerizing Wally as he sat in an armchair fashioned from saplings and potato sack.

Over the previous two weeks, a lean-to had become a one-room shack. Gum leaves weaved through crevices of sapling walls provided some benefit from chilly winds. A tarpaulin roof stopped the rain and a sapling bunk, raised off the ground, stopped any slithering wildlife from entering the swag; the mongrel was also a deterrent. For a city boy Wally was quite dexterous with his hands and had a creative mind. Many a time this talent had saved him and army mates from life-threatening situations...or boredom when a life-threatening situation wasn't being experienced.

Bang. The gumnut exploded. Hit by a hot ember the mongrel yelped. Hit by a flashback Wally yelped also, his trance broken. "Come here old fella. Get a hot belly did you?" he sympathised. "I know how it feels." The dog lay on its back at his feet and got a belly rub. "What say we put some tucker in it and call it a day?"

* * *

When Bycroft returned to Gunnadoo his persona had changed, his tailored appearance was that of a merchant not a prospector, the wagon full of goods confirmed it. He erected a large tent and placed a sign out the front, informing all that Bycroft Holdings was open for business. Hearing of his return on the bush telegraph, Wally left the claim and made his way to Gunnadoo. A wall of chatter from many unrecognisable faces confronted Wally as he entered the tent. Bycroft saw him standing wide-eyed and gestured acknowledgement.

"Gentlemen," Bycroft shouted, "that's all for the moment. Drinks are on me."

With that, the so-called gentlemen adjourned to the army surplus mess tent Bycroft had erected as a pub.

"What's going on?" asked Wally, sitting down in front of the mahogany desk. It seemed out of place yet added an air of authority to the canvas office. Bycroft produced a bottle from its drawer.

"Business, Sunshine, it makes the world go around...drink?"

Wally nodded. "Speaking of the world...does it still exist?"

"Sydney is like a madhouse – the place is awash with money if you know where to look." Bycroft slipped him a shot of whiskey across the polished desktop. "I've just finalised agreements with Ted White, the boss of a timber cutting gang."

"Yeah, so what?" Wally asked naively, still coming to grips with the surrounds. The whiskey burnt on the way down.

"Building supplies will be required, as will transport," Bycroft explained. "Kevin Bastock has a dray and timber jigger, and just got an injection of capital and is now Bastock Transport. One of our first projects is to get a steam engine out here to drive the timber mill."

"What timber mill?"

"The one Ted White and I are setting up," he boasted. With small investments, Bycroft had solidified himself into each of the men's lives – and, more importantly, their businesses. Bycroft poured another shot, holding it up and peering through the opaque liquid he prophesied. "There's lots of money to be made and it won't just be made out of the ground, Sunshine."

"What makes you say that?"

"History and opinion I believe." Bycroft refilled Wally's glass. "I don't know about you, but I never put all my eggs in one basket and I'm certainly not about to put all my faith in one piece of dirt. I like to spread myself around." He slid the wad of notes and Wally's mail across the desk. "That's your half of the little friend I found," he told him, emphasising the 'I found'.

Wally looked on perplexed, "What about the claim?"

"It's not about what we dig out ourselves; it's about how much is there." Bycroft gestured at the money. "I've invested my half in a couple of businesses already."

Wally picked up the wad and mumbled, "Couldn't be much of an investment, I've won and lost more in a two-up game." He perused the handwriting on the mail.

"My half wasn't the investment: that was the inducement." Bycroft lit a cigar. "Finance, it can be got if the right people are known and the right inducement shown."

"I reckon so, but where's that leave us?"

"We're partners in the claim and I've shown my good faith by this." He produced the deed of title; both names appeared on it. "Whatever comes out of the dirt, we're fifty-fifty. I made the first find, now it's your turn. Get the evidence of a mother load and we'll put a workforce together to do the digging; you'll only be there to keep the buggers working." He poured himself another shot. "Here's what I've got planned…"

* * *

A survey team from Sydney was to lay out a suitable route from the Dundee rail siding, but they disappeared into the gold-seeking population. The meandering dirt track, twisting between

14

configurations of boulder clusters, became the accepted road travelled. Upon reaching the settlement the road widened to that of a bullock team's turning circle, prime frontage along the main section of dirt disappeared as commerce and private enterprise moved in. The Commonwealth Bank arrived along with the constabulary; a sergeant and four constables escorted Charlie Roister and his Chubb safe into Gunnadoo with great fanfare.

When Irvin Browning arrived, Bycroft cunningly supplied him with a site for accommodation and an assayer's office; the temporary tent was set up conveniently between Bycroft Holdings and the pub tent. The small man with mouse-like idiosyncrasies was no match for Bycroft's posturing and was soon drawn into his growing brethren of cronyism.

Wong Foo serviced the growing oriental population. The Chinese had begun arriving in Australia in 1830s and their numbers grew until the 1880s. So did xenophobia. The colonies adopted a ban on Asian immigration during the 1890s, prior to Federation. Chinese workers, still considered as cheap labour, now made their way to Gunnadoo. Opposition to the large numbers arriving was apparent by the bigotry they received.

In opposition to Wong Foo's enterprise, Houten's General Store opened its doors for business. Along with all the necessities for alluvial mining, protection dogs were for sale as a snake deterrent and should that fail, free Bibles accompanied the purchase of picks and pans. When receiving a venomous snakebite Victims could die with a Bible in hand, if that was of any consequence. Even so, the adverse conditions didn't hold back the surge of confident prospectors.

A new era promised more than the previous had. Not since Federation had Australians shown an enthusiasm to roll up their sleeves and get on with it. Following the years of war – the war to end all wars – attaining some semblance of normality was a priority for the Government. Pursuing a brighter future, no matter where it led, was the main concern of the populous. The Outback offered salvation for some, while more turmoil lay over the horizon for others.

2 – Catherine

Unassuming love may escort
a body and spirit
to unpalatable destinations

Like a contagious yawn, the sound of sobbing began filtering down the line of mourners who were waiting for the East Street gates of Rookwood Cemetery to open at 8.30am.

Catherine stood amidst a sea of black observing gaunt faces, strangers united by the previous four years of grief. The imbalance of men to women, as great as in the Great War itself, was now accepted as the norm and would be for generations to come. The fortunate women clung to the arm of a service uniform or a frayed suit with a battalion stickpin in the lapel. The unfortunates clung to the hands of fatherless children. Wearing her Sunday best, a predominantly red tartan tunic and straw boater with matching ribbon, Catherine was conspicuously not in mourning. She was not impressed when she felt a hand touch her up.

"Beg'n ya pardon, Miss." The stranger pushed obscenely into her while smiling innocently. "Bit of a tight squeeze, isn't it?" The distressed woman on his arm was oblivious to her partner's wandering hands.

Irate but containing her temper, Catherine stopped any further abuse with a steely glare, berating him quietly with the first words that came to mind.

"If my fiancé was here ... "

When the gates opened five minutes late, the procession of agitated mourners swept Catherine along Necropolis Drive. Individuals then peeled off, heading in various directions to visit deceased loved ones. Catherine was left to wander alone through a montage of tall pillars and grandiose monuments. Still unaccustomed to the sprawling acreage of sandstone, granite and marble, she stared at the vista and thought about Gunnadoo. *It won't be long now.*

"Excuse me, Miss."

She jumped at the gruff voice, and then turned to face the scruffy man, noticing that he wasn't in uniform. Granny's confusing words reverberated in her head. *Don't trust nobody not in uniform and them that are, beware of too.*

"Yes, Granny."

"Er, who ya callin' Granny?"

Catherine blushed. "My Granny Dunn." She crossed herself and whispered, "God rest her soul."

"It's not safe for a pretty little thing like you to be wander'n around 'ere on ya own." Her isolation now apparent, Catherine quickly took a step backward. Her last recollection was of trying to take a shortcut through the labyrinth. "No, not me Miss, I'll not 'arm ya, there's snakes all 'round 'ere. Ya can't be too careful." He held forth a squirming Hessian sack while surveying the area. "Are ya comin' or goin', Miss?" A grin revealed blackened teeth as a sprig of wattle in his other hand appeared before her

18

face. "A bargain for a sixpence but for a pretty little thing like you – thruppence." He thrust it forward, pleading, "Tuppence, a penny – surely ya wouldn't be missing a penny?"

Looking into the man's sunken eyes, Catherine empathised with his plight. "It be a beautiful gesture and a bargain to be sure, but I've brought me own," she gestured to the wicker basket on her arm, "and I can't be afford'n more, for you see…"

"Please Miss, a donation," he emphasised, "the lad ain't 'ad anythin' to eat for days, show some compassion."

In the distance, an urchin stood regarding them, motionless atop a tall pedestal, the former occupant now rubble at its base.

"Ya wouldn't want to see 'im go 'ungry." Stepping in front of the victim, he changed his tone, "Or 'is old man go without a beer, would ya?"

Catherine considered her isolation and the underlying threat. "You'd not be taking advantage of me if my fiancé was here."

He came to attention and saluted her mockingly. "Well, Gallipoli-boy ain't 'ere…"

"He wasn't at Gallipoli," she declared, "he was at…"

"I don't give a damn…a donation – now."

Catherine conceded to the demand and fumbled around in her basket for her purse. "Holy Mother of Mercy, forgive…"

The urchin shouted a warning. The swindler grabbed her purse and shoved his victim backward. Catherine and the contents of Granny Dunn's bequeathed wicker basket toppled over the ornate fence and into the overgrown plot. She lay speechless, staring up at one of the many religious effigies staring down at her. The angel and accompanying cherubs morphed into an animated illusion as the March sky scrolled across the Sydney heavens. The pleasant sound of the cherub's harp strings changed into the shrill of a constable's whistle blown frantically. An aura of sunlight moving from behind a statue's head pierced her eyes, bringing an awareness of reality. "Holy Mother," she wailed, "mugged and now blinded."

The constable and pursuing crowd stopped at the unkempt plot in which she lay. Catherine looked up into their gawking faces.

"Here, Miss, let me give you a hand." The constable stepped over the wrought iron as Catherine began rummaging through the long weeds.

"I'd rather you be catch'n that scoundrel – he stole me purse." A tear at the back of her dress exposed more than it should have. The flamboyant straw boater, now crushed, epitomized how she felt. It too had seen better times.

"Awright, move on you lot...the show's over, there's nothing more to see." He sat on the grave leering at the pale skin of her inner thigh as she crawled on hands and knees to retrieve her possessions. "What would a pretty little Irish lass like you need with a French dictionary?"

Catherine felt both the chill of the constable's question and the torn dress. Realising the exhibition she was providing him, she quickly stood.

He picked up the small book at his feet. "Is this yours?" He held it out teasingly.

"Yes, it be mine and it be none of your business." She snatched the book from his hand. "But see'n you asked, my fiancé and me are…"

"And where is your fiancé?" he interrupted, and then condescendingly looked around. "I don't see him." The horny copper, who preferred 'consoling' young widows and lonely fiancées rather than pursuing villains, pulled a notepad from his jacket pocket and moved toward her. "Is he fighting for King and country?"

"He be mining for gold he is and we're going to be rich and we're going to France," Catherine retorted breathlessly, climbing back over the fence. "And it be none of your business."

The constable scrutinized Catherine as she used a safety pin to mend the tear temporarily. She bunched up the pleated material and tucked it into the rear of her tunic belt, then straightened the ribbon in her hair. He handed her the basket.

"Merci…" she thanked him smugly.

He smiled arrogantly and then held forth her crumpled straw boater. The rim was broken; the crown flipped up and down like a clown's hat. "Don't forget this," he laughed, "we don't want ya gett'n sunstroke."

The embarrassment was too much; Catherine felt her face turn red and heard her habitual French idiom resonate. "Sacré bleu," she exclaimed and briskly strutted off in a huff.

"Hey, wait up Miss Riding Hood," he called after her. Following his wolf howl when she paid him no attention, he shouted, "Stop. In the name of the law - stop."

Catherine shook her brunette mane and stood defiantly looking ahead.

"I'm the law, I gotta make a report." He eyed her thin waist, wanting to take her from behind. "I'll need a few details." She felt his breath upon the nape of her neck. It rekindled nasty memories that were best left suppressed. "Now...what's your name?" He fought the temptation to slip his fingers into her bloomers via the tear in her dress.

"Catherine Dunn...Catherine, spelt with a C." She stood as rigid as the sculptured onlookers.

"And how old is Catherine, spelt with a C?"

"Nineteen I be and wise for my age, so don't you be trying noth'n."

He moved to stand in front of Catherine, blatantly undressing her with his eyes. "This isn't too difficult, is it?"

She pretended not to watch him lick the pencil lewdly.

"Now let me get this straight. Your fiancé isn't here and you've been visiting your dead husband? How long was your husband dead before you found a new fiancé?"

"I be hav'n no dead husband," she declared haughtily when the insinuation registered, "it be me Granny Dunn I visit – to pay me respects," she added.

The copper seized upon the information. "No fiancé, no dead husband and no – more – Granny – Dunn."

Catherine's eyes glazed over, her emotion still raw from Granny's passing in January.

"Who is Granny Dunn?" His change of tactics and compassionate tone unbalanced her. He waited,

22

watching her choke, as so many had done before, and held out his handkerchief.

"It be none of your business." She wiped the tear away, refusing his offer. "I have my own handkerchief, thank you."

"You wouldn't be all alone now, would you?" He stepped back a pace, replacing the notepad in his pocket. "It's a lonely feeling not hav'n a friendly shoulder to cry on…especially in these times."

He did not receive the expected gush of tears or the soft, feminine body collapsing in sorrow against him. Instead, with the steely resolve of a marble bust, Catherine repeated, "It be none of…

"One last question then." He stepped forward and placed the pencil tip under her raised chin, forcing her to look at him.

"What?"

"Are ya a good root?"

Catherine's eyes conveyed her rage. "You be lower than a snake's belly – if my fiancé was here…"

* * *

The December heat was intolerable. Catherine had travelled from Dundee sitting uncomfortably on her trunk in the rear of the wagon rather than next to the driver on a sprung seat; his bawdy demeanour at Dundee had instigated her detachment. A cloud of grey dust billowed from the plodding hooves of four whalers pulling the supply wagon. An hour's delay while repairing an axle had put the teamster behind schedule. Under a straw bonnet, Catherine's hair was lifeless and limp; her usually rosy cheeks matched the greyish colour of her hair, her clothes and the merchandise stacked around her.

The teamster continued explaining, "…and travelling in the dark is too dangerous. I'll try and make up the lost time. It won't be too bad if we have to camp out…I got a nice warm swag we can both snuggle into."

"Holy Mother. My fiancé is expecting me," Catherine called to him, "he'll come looking for me if we don't arrive, and a terrible temper has he. There'd be a dreadful donnybrook there'd be."

"Go on, you don't say?"

"Holy Mother," she exclaimed, crossing herself, "he be a jealous man, he be. Nearly killed a man just for looking at me, he did."

"Is that a fact?"

She cleared her throat, "…arms the size…big as," she thought hastily, "…tree trunks."

"I'll be buggered. You're not having me on, are you?"

Catherine shook her head, unable to speak, her throat also now lined with the grey dust. The rigid bouncing was unpleasant, as was the thought of having to camp on the side of a bush track with the uncouth teamster.

"Why a man would leave a pretty little thing like you…"

The words raised her indignation; fatigue subdued it and she returned to the letter imploring her relocation to Gunnadoo before Christmas. Having memorised each word, she now stared at the mosaic imagery behind the letters and punctuation marks. The promise of a hot bath would be as pleasurable as lying with her man; after all, it had been eight *long* months.

From daylight to dusk Catherine had worked to repay the debts of her fiancé as well as Granny's expensive medical bills. She made the final payment on the cemetery plot before leaving Sydney and told Granny, "You can rest in peace; you'll never have the worry of eviction again."

At sunset, the wagon broke free of thick bush and they crossed open ground covered by Spinifex. A red haze crowned Gunnadoo, its northern outskirts silhouetted in the distance. Seeing some form of civilisation lessened Catherine's apprehension.

"It won't be long now, ten or fifteen minutes if we don't break an axle," the teamster laughed.

Skeleton constructions intermingled with the outlined façades of more substantial buildings such as the established businesses and private residences. Dark shapes moved around, illuminated by the lamps they carried. The wagon pulled up at the goods depot, it too under construction.

"You're late," shouted the unseen voice from inside.

Catherine stood up unsteadily. She stretched, arching her back and feeling each disc of her backbone slip into a new position.

The teamster moved to the rear of the wagon and dropped the tailgate. "Let me give you a hand, Miss," he said, arms outstretched. His hands slyly fondled each firm breast as he held her under the armpit and lifted her down. Catherine's trunk didn't receive the same courteous attention as she; it was flung aside as the wagon was unloaded. Dempsey, the clerk, stood in the doorway observing the dust storm approach as Catherine brushed her clothing clean of the grey powder.

"Have you seen Danny O'Shaunessy?" she asked naively.

"No, I haven't," Dempsey replied.

"Would you be telling me where to find him then?"

"And what does he look like, darling?"

"He not be a tall man..." she began, and was immediately cut off.

"He be short then?" Dempsey mocked her lilting brogue.

"No, he be about this tall." Catherine raised her hand to what she believed was Danny's height.

"Right. Is he of sandy complexion?"

"No, dark hair...and he's got..."

"...one eye missing."

"No. He's got the loveliest brown eyes the like you've never seen."

"I know him." Dempsey shouted. "He's missing a front tooth?"

"No. He's got a lovely smile," she corrected him.

The clerk contemplated and then gestured enthusiastically. "Come here, come here." Having her undivided attention, he then whispered in her ear, "Does he give ya a good root?"

Catherine stumbled backwards, stopped from falling as the driver's hands slipped under her armpits from behind.

"No harm meant, Miss," he whispered in her ear, "Dempsey does that to any good-lookers arriving."

Catherine shook clear of his roaming hands, regaining her balance and her independence, and picked up the carpetbag she had dropped. Dempsey nodded towards one of the larger tents further down road.

"Try the pub. You can pick the trunk up tomorrow. There's no extra charge, it's part of the friendly service."

Thick smoke lay dormant under a canvas peak. Below the delineation line, the yellow smog of dirty kerosene lamps consumed all available space; grog consumed the customers. Catherine battled to explain the situation to the barman above the noise. Bycroft watched from afar, ultimately told of her dilemma by the bartender. Danny O'Shaunessy had worked for Bycroft; booze had been the Irishman's weakness, and Bycroft had bled him dry of his earnings as soon as he'd earned them.

"No, wait," he told the bartender, "tell her nothing." He studied Catherine's feisty attitude when confronted by the unwelcome advances of two drunks. "Better still, tell her about the accident and to see Wong Foo."

"She's ripe for the picking, boss," the bartender prodded, "you should make a move on her."

"That's not ripe, that's spirited. One could do oneself a damage mounting a filly like her; she needs to be broken in. That's a job for Wong Foo."

"That's a good one, boss; Wong Foo, working for you."

27

"Doesn't it beat all," Bycroft replied, "he doesn't know he is and he's not even being paid…and if you want to keep getting paid yourself, Sunshine, *never* tell me what *I* should do."

Bycroft observed Catherine's stunned reaction as she received the unpleasant news and then watched her leave. Unfortunately, her unprosperous fiancé had died when an Eastern Brown took a dislike to him. What should have been a joyous evening would never eventuate. Two weeks prior, the undertaker had laid Danny O'Shaunessy to rest in a pauper's grave. Catherine walked sombrely south, failing to notice the folk she passed or her surroundings. The toll from Clemet's hammer upon the anvil echoed like a death bell, not the joyous bells of Christmas she had expected. With each fall of the hammer, an iron spike drove deeper into her heart.

Intimidating shadows animated on the billowing canvas played tricks upon Catherine's eyes as she entered the large tent. Obscured by supplies stacked high around him, the merchant sitting before his accounts ledger wasn't visible. His presence was only made known by the clickity-click of the abacus. The Chinese laundry enjoyed a monopoly. Wong Foo enjoyed low operating costs – his wife and seven daughters facilitated the well-known fact.

In the dim yellow light, Catherine felt claustrophobic. "Mr. Foo?" she softly enquired. The clicking ceased. She clutched the carpetbag in both arms as though it was a security blanket. "Mr. Foo?"

A voice emanated quietly from the shadows. "I have been expecting you."

Startled by the unseen observer Catherine hesitantly edged forward, "Me name is…"

"Welcome, Miss Dunn." The shadow of a beckoning hand with its long come-hither fingernail appeared on the canvas, its imagery alarming – as was the oriental inflection welcoming her. "I recognise you."

Catherine was startled, "You do?" Her eyes gradually became accustomed to the subdued light; Wong Foo's leering eyes, grotesquely magnified through opaque lenses, were another matter.

"My condolences…I am most sorry at your recent loss." He pushed the Gladstone bag, which she recognised, across the counter towards her, his hand remaining on top of it. "I have held it for you in safe keeping; personal effects – watch, compass and most pleasant photograph, of you." He shooed the sleeping cat from the stool and gestured she sit.

Tears welled up in her bloodshot eyes. "I gave the watch to Danny for his birthday…saved for two years I did. He treasured it."

"Thought behind gift is treasure – not watch." Perplexed by the statement, she opened her mouth to speak but he immediately stopped her again. "A watch stops if not wound – time does not."

Catherine picked up the thread of her unrehearsed eulogy. "The compass was a going-away present. I told Danny when I gave it to him, 'You'll always be able to find your way home to me'. "'tis the sentiment, Mr. Foo, the sentiment."

"A most valuable commodity," he empathised.

"Thank you, Mr. Foo. You're the first gentleman to show consideration, your kindness will be rewarded." She went to pick up the bag; his hand remained on it. "Again, thank you, Mr. Foo."

"Unfortunately, Miss Dunn, I am a business man. Your sadly-departed fiancé has an account to settle, not only with his God but with humble self also." The mortified look on Catherine's face induced him to add, "I too must answer to superiors."

"Are your Gods benevolent, Mr. Foo?" she enquired.

"Gods yes…unfortunately, not Mrs. Foo."

The entrepreneur's safe contained gold attained by dubious deals with illiterate customers, but he'd taken a drop in profits when Irvin Browning, the assayer, had established himself in town. Wong Foo's clientele sought the assayer's advice as to how much gold they should trade in return for the merchandise they purchased from Wong Foo. If there was a profit to be made, Wong Foo would make it.

Having paid the three pounds Danny owed Wong Foo, Catherine found the Gladstone bag still irretrievable. "As you can see, Miss Dunn, space is at a premium. Alas, most regrettably, I am forced to collect a baggage fee also."

"I've not yet found lodgings," she pleaded, holding her remaining coins in her open palm. "I've not but a couple of pennies left to me name and…"

"You have not eaten. I understand."

"I've just arrived." she retorted. "I've just found out me lovely Danny is gone," she crossed herself, "and…"

"And now you are most fortunate to meet me," Wong Foo placated.

Catherine was speechless.

30

He sharply clapped his hands twice and in native tongue snapped instructions to unseen ears. He then informed Catherine, "Your departed fiancé has accommodation. You will sleep there; daughter will take you." A servile woman dressed in black coolie pyjamas appeared, handing Catherine a Hessian bag. "You will require these necessities."

"I can't pay."

"Fiancé account closed, yours opened." Wong Foo handed Catherine the Gladstone bag. "I will see you tomorrow." Catherine was bewildered. "Goodnight, Miss Dunn." He signalled the daughter to be on her way.

No sooner had Catherine left, following Lotus-Flower, than Wong Foo received another visitor.

"Ah, Mr. Bycroft. And to what do I owe this honour?"

"Just passing."

"Just passing what? Passing time, passing wind, passing…"

"Passing your establishment," he snapped. Wong Foo knew he was under Bycroft's skin already. "How's business?" Bycroft then asked beguilingly.

Wong Foo masterfully manipulated his stooge into looking up. Oriental superlatives sprayed forth and he then returned his attention to Bycroft. "See." he pointed to the roof.

"See what?" Bycroft craned his neck further. "What?"

"Business going through roof." Wong Foo's contemptuous laughter incensed Bycroft. "I am pleased to say," he gave another chuckle, "I just hire new girl. Business at premium."

"The girl I saw leaving?"

"Most observant, Mr. Bycroft."

"She is very pretty, Mr. Foo."

"So young and so vulnerable," he replied, stroking his cheek with the intimidating fingernail.

"Stop with the games, I know who she is. She was just at The Arms. Does she know who I am?"

"Unless you tell her, why should I? Your fame precedes you maybe?"

Bycroft was out of his league with the sarcastic witticisms and he resorted to accusation.

"Do I detect jealousy? We Australians like a man to be upfront; if you got something to say, say it."

"I am a humble businessman, negative feelings most unproductive. I have no ill feeling to you, Mr. Bycroft."

In Wong Foo's safe, along with other treasures, was a land title Bycroft wanted. Wong Foo had acquired it and in so doing had become Bycroft's archrival without knowing it. Unscrupulous business was endemic to most commerce in Gunnadoo; posturing, pecking and positioning simmered below deceitful transactions. In the assayer's safe was some of Wong Foo's ore. When held at the right angle, the gold seam in one piece resembled an incarcerated dragon. Wong Foo had used it to cement a cordial relationship with Browning. Although displeased with the assayer for disrupting his profit-line, the wily Chinaman still kept up the pretence of cordiality with him. It was also a form of insurance against Bycroft.

* * *

Thin plumes of blue campfire smoke stretched unhindered to meet a new moon rising. Resembling a sprinkling of moon dust, a peace offering, perhaps, from the black abyss of a heartless God, the expanding ripples of light shimmered above Gunnadoo. The peace offering went unnoticed by Catherine. She followed Lotus-Flower south along High Street. With a Shaolin monk's fluidity, the daughter weaved and twisted her way through groups of people. With three bags to carry, Catherine struggled to keep up. Her pleas went unacknowledged; the woman refused to slow down.

They passed a row of slab cottages. Slithers of insipid lantern light confirmed the hastily laid timbers of one. Bickering voices from within another revealed hastily made plans to go gold mining. Further on, tiny mud-brick huts still under construction resembled dolls houses. For Catherine, the sapling poles spearing earthen walls conjured voodoo images. Black shapes void of front doors and windows morphed into charcoal faces screaming in terror. Whimpering, not comprehending the nightmarish images, she clasped her chest. The foreboding impressions dissipated at the southern end of High Street. Calico and Hessian tents lined the dirt thoroughfare, the silhouettes within accentuating the little privacy afforded them.

Miners, warming themselves around open fires, discussed what fortunes lay in waiting. Women cooking on red embers chattered about the outrageous prices they were paying for life's necessities. Children and dogs chased one another in and out and around the canvas metropolis. Lotus-Flower finally stopped outside a darkened tent. There, she took the Hessian bag from Catherine, placed it on the ground and removed the kero lamp. She primed and lit it, then repeated the process for Catherine's sake.

"This on, this off. You sleep here," said Lotus-Flower. She gave Catherine the lamp while lifting the tent flap for the new tenant to enter. A bucket, a blanket and the bunk Catherine slumped onto were the sum total of Danny's accommodation. She turned to thank her escort but the woman had already vanished into the night. The first tear dribbled down her cheek. She shook her hair free of its encompassing bonnet and bit her top lip, refusing to cry. The second tear fell when she looked up at the internal steeple of canvas; it resembled a cathedral.

"Thank you Holy Mother," she snivelled, "for the roof above me head...and forgive me for thinking poorly of Mr. Foo. He be a good man, I'm sure." Loud rumblings from an empty belly interrupted the sombre moment.

As Catherine hungrily devoured the dried biscuits and beans, her eyes fell upon the Gladstone bag and the memories contained within. She opened it, removed Danny's French thesaurus and fingered the pages lovingly. The image of the two of them trying to learn and pronounce words from it spooled back into her memory. "Bless you, Danny; one day I'll go there for both of us." She kissed the thesaurus as though it were a bible. "Adieu." She lifted out a crumpled ball of blue shirt and buried her face in it to reinforce the memory. Placing the bundle with the bequeathed possessions upon her knees, she opened it. "Holy Mother. I've been swindled." Cheap replacements confirmed the statement. "I'm not going to cry," she repeated.

The unwelcoming blanket lying on the dirt floor mocked the months of anticipation of lying warmly in Danny's arms. All that she had previously been taught and had believed, 'there is always someone worse off than you', became a fallacy. Catherine removed her jacket and then paused, looked at the lantern and turned the wick down, snuffing it and her silhouette image out. The wick spluttered as if gasping for air and darkness engulfed her. Clasping the carpetbag, she lay fully clothed under her jacket sobbing relentlessly into Danny's blue shirt.

3 – Lessons to be Learnt

Hindsight is attained when
time becomes a companion

Cockatoos screeched in branches, teamsters and pedestrians avoided one another by shouting obscenities and children played noisily. Catherine lay listening to all, a sadness hanging over her as heavy as the dust-covered clothes in which she lay. The thought of a hot bath intertwined with those of the events experienced the previous night. Her back ached, as did her belly. She consumed the last of the beans and biscuits while observing the surroundings. The tent was one of many in a long line; each had a small clearing at the rear cut out of the bush for any furniture that didn't fit within the canvas confines. Before setting off northward into the township, she noted the lot number marked on a tin lid tied to a sapling.

* * *

The sign read, 'Hot baths, thruppence, pull rope for attention'. Catherine did. A middle-aged man appeared from the tent smiling and bowing.

"How may I be of service, Missy?" Ying Lee enquired.

"And just how hot is hot?"

"Make plenty hot if want," he replied obligingly.

"I be wanting it plenty hot," she replied, arching her back and stretching sore muscles.

Wong Foo owned the bathhouse and, figuratively, the hired help, Ying Lee and his family. Catherine booked her tub to be ready in fifteen minutes and then headed for the goods depot. She found her keys at the bottom of the carpetbag and unlocked her trunk, hastening her selection of clean clothes when noting the keen interest shown by Dempsey. Arranging for delivery of the trunk to Lot 184, she then returned for the promised hot water.

The women's bathing tent, with only two tubs, was separate. A plump woman occupied the largest tub. Steam rose invitingly from the smaller tub as Mrs. Lee pail water from an iron pot simmering over hot coals. Under a bonnet of soap bubbles, the plump woman wiped clear two holes for her eyes to peer through, "Hello Luv...I'm Ruby, Ruby Houten."

"Catherine Dunn."

The words boomed around inside Ruby's head. "I got a u-beaut hangover alrighty. It was my birthday yesterday; thirty years old, I am. Last night Mr. Houten and I celebrated...over indulged, if you know what I mean." Ruby noticed the dust fall from undergarments as Catherine removed them. "Just arrived, eh? You'll get used to it and a lot more. I did...can't do without my hot tub though. It's the only luxury you'll find around here." In the limited confines, Ruby managed to stick her head between her legs to wash the soap from her short curly hair. Mrs. Lee gestured for Catherine to get a move on; she required no more encouragement to do so. "In you get, Luv, don't be embarrassed we all got the same bits, haven't we Mrs. Lee?"

Catherine eased herself into the soothing liquid. No sooner had she adjusted to the heat than a pail of hot water poured down upon her. "Holy Mother of Mercy."

Ruby raised her head, cocked it and listened. "Questioned the hot water, eh?" She turned to Catherine who was glowing pink. "You gotta be careful what you say to the chinks, they take all requests as gospel." She gave Mrs. Lee a warm smile. "Don't you?" The woman pretended not to be listening.

"Have you lived in Gunnadoo long?" Catherine enquired.

Ruby laughed. "It ain't been here all that long."

Catherine stared questioningly waiting for an answer.

"All right, let's see." Again Ruby submerged then resurfaced. "Six months. Mr. Houten came out ahead of me. He can drag me to the ends of the earth but I told him," she took a breath, "I am not going to live in a tent. Next thing I know we're in the hardware business and..." From then on Ruby never stopped to take a breath, information flowed freely as the Yapsly River. "...and there'll be fortunes made and lost you can bet on that. Mark my words – somebody's gonna cop one hullava blood nose." With a little prodding from Catherine, Wong Foo and John

Bycroft became the next topic of gossip. "...and watch out for that pair," Ruby advised, "that's a time bomb ticking. Mark my words – that dustup will end with more than just a blood nose."

Nodding her head in agreement, Mrs. Lee poured another pail of water over Catherine and continued to scrub. Catherine couldn't decide which pain was worse, the scalding or the harsh bristles of the scrubbing brush on her back.

"I need to find some work, I'm..."

"You please stand," requested Mrs. Lee.

"...I'm of able body," stated Catherine.

"That and a bit more, I'd say." Ruby observed the naked woman's Aphrodite like stature. Soap bubbles clung desperately to her pert breasts and then slid down a flat tummy and slender thighs. She looked down at her own body, shook her head and plunged under the cloak of bubbles.

Catherine waited for her to resurface, "...and I be smart too."

"You can't be more than seventeen?"

"Nineteen, and I can look after myself I can."

Again referring to Catherine's figure, Ruby replied, "You're doing an excellent job so far."

A final pail of water rinsed off the remaining soap to reveal the marble smoothness of Catherine's gleaming body. Shown to an area where priming could take place in the warm sun, Ruby joined her some time later.

"Before you ask what took so long...there's more of me," Ruby wisecracked.

Catherine avoided questions asked of her where possible glossing over the subject briefly or changing

39

it. Little inducement was required for Ruby to do the talking, the history lesson continued as she dressed. Catherine listened, brushing her hair; brunette locks intensified as a natural wave highlighted rich veins of copper.

"Well, you certainly keep your cards close to your chest," Ruby confided. She tilted her head fingering water in the ear, "but if you ever need a girl chat."

"A confidante."

"Alrighty, I'm sure you are but you know where to find me. We girls have got to stick together." Feeling exhausted, Ruby excused herself. "I'm not as young as I used to be – but last night I sure gave Abe, Mr. Houten, a run for his money." She left the bathhouse laughing and groaning at the same time.

Catherine dressed in a tweed jacket and matching skirt and tied her hair back neatly with a blue ribbon, looking and feeling clean for the first time in three days.

"Very nice." Mrs. Lee stood back approvingly.

* * *

Behind Wong Foo's large tent, out of view of the public, was the hub of his operation. A small tributary from the Yapsly River ran along the rear of a clearing cut from bushland. The two taller women removed and replaced washing on many lines. A stockily built teenager rushed back and forth carrying clothes in a wicker basket on her back. Three slightly younger girls scrubbed as the youngest filled their tubs with water and did the final rinse. Mrs. Foo, the largest woman turned a wringer handle and out came clothes all but dry into another wicker basket. The production line was a fine example of time and motion, the operation run from behind the abacus and accounts ledger.

Catherine stood before Wong Foo armed with information she'd received from Ruby.

"Miss Dunn, how pleasant it is to see you. You look remarkably recovered. I trust you slept well?"

"I appreciate your concern, Mr. Foo, thank you." He was mildly surprised that Catherine hadn't complained about the switch he'd pulled but didn't show it. He assumed she didn't know. He wasn't surprised when approached for a job, again he kept poker-faced. He knew that, with the vulnerable state she was in, anything might be possible.

"Payment at the end of each day worked," she requested wisely.

"As you please. When shall I expect you to begin?"

"Today. I'll be back in two shakes of a lamb's tail."

Catherine walked briskly back towards her tent. "Watch out ya stupid bitch." shouted the wagon driver. She jumped aside, recognising the trunk bouncing precariously around on top of the wagonload. To her horror and before she could catch up with the errant delivery, he'd dumped the trunk without stopping. It hit the ground with the thud of a tree felled. Pedestrians momentarily scattered and then casually resumed their travels as a dust cloud rose in front of Lot 188.

"Holy Mother. Can't you read?" Catherine protested to the rear of the wagon as it trundled off to make further deliveries. It was no easy task dragging the battered trunk back to Lot 184, assistance wasn't offered: only witticism.

"Put your back into it lass," the jester encouraged.

"And then come back for me," added the other larrikin.

Dressed in a smart tunic and apron that she believed were quite fitting to serve customers and do the odd messy job if required, Catherine returned to her new place of employment. Pleased with her presentation, she dropped the large bundle of dirty bedding at her feet and once again stood before Wong Foo.

"You look very nice," he complimented suggestively.

"I'm ready to start," said Catherine enthusiastically, "show me what you want done."

Wong Foo clapped his hands and Lotus-Flower immediately served steaming tea. There were two cups; he let Catherine believe the other was for her and at the appropriate moment, as she was about to reach for it, he instructed, "You go with Lotus-Flower. Take," he rose and peered over the counter at the bundle, "whatever with you."

To her dismay, Catherine joined the women on the washing production line, practising first on her own bedding. Upon completing the task, covered in suds and mud, she received a pair of black coolie pyjamas from Mrs. Foo. "You do good work; you wear these, more comfortable." For three hours, the new employee was in hot water up to the elbows and when she finished there, she was shown to an outside kitchen at the rear of Wong Foo's mess tent. Mountains of vegetables awaited peeling. "You do good work here too…yes? Much chop-chop you do." Catherine lowered her head, bit her tongue and proceeded with the chore. Mrs. Foo strode off to organise her daughters for their next projects.

Like most of Gunnadoo, the walls of the kitchen were unfinished although a corrugated iron roof afforded some protection from the sun. She looked up and wiped her brow. "Thank you Holy Mother for the roof above me head." Dust particles from the dirt floor danced in magnified shafts of sunlight that streamed through nail holes in the corrugated iron. Tree trunks stripped of bark and branches held the roof aloft.

From behind the potato pile, Catherine watched labourers laying sheets of roofing on the timber frame encompassing Wong Foo's office and supply tent. Work had begun that morning and labourers toiled in the heat to complete the job and then begin roofing the mess tent. From light to dark, the kitchen fires burned. Many hungry men required feeding, prospectors, miners and labourers, all with large appetites. Bread baked in the mud brick oven and two forty-four gallon drums, cut in half, contained boiling kangaroo stew, the meat so tender that it fell from the bone. Catherine stirred in her contribution of peeled potatoes as she watched Mrs. Foo ladle the contents into large pails. Under the yoke, the daughters took turns delivering the near-overflowing contents of pails to the rear entrance of the mess tent.

In what Catherine thought to be an exotic language, the women chatted and shouted at one another. She studied each of them and the roles they played within the hierarchy. She noted that Lotus-Flower, who seemed to be the favoured daughter, waited on Wong Foo's every whim.

"You plenty good worker. You now eat," said Mrs. Foo, as she filled a bowl and motioned to Catherine to join the women at the table. "My husband said you need plenty fattening up…me to feed you big bowl." Her daughters all laughed loudly at Catherine's expense.

Having not spoken since joining the workforce in the field, she nonchalantly responded, "Bon appétit."

The women immediately began chattering and nodding, looking back and forth between themselves and at Catherine. Although painfully difficult, and with her tummy rumbling from lack of food, she persisted with the chopsticks and her eating etiquette as she believed a fashionable mademoiselle would. The women watched fascinated. Catherine role-played as she had many times before when talking with Danny of the travelling they would do when they'd struck it rich. Having consumed two bowls and much bread, she delicately dabbed at her puckered lips with a jacket sleeve. "Très bon."

"French woman good eater too," Mrs. Foo stated. Catherine enjoyed the attention and didn't correct the error about being French.

"Merci beaucoup, Madame Foo."

Everything had its order of doing and its place to be put when it was done. As peasants toil in a field of rice, the women laboured in their field of washing. An afternoon cycle began after lunch and continued until another load was hanging in the sun. Kitchen duties then recommenced. Rose-Petal lit the lanterns as twilight fell. Catherine watched the same ritual as she stirred the vegetables; apparently, job allocations didn't change. Neither did the menu. Wong Foo's evening meal did, however – he received his own chicken gourmet delight. Lotus-Flower delivered the tray to his private residency beside the supply tent, while his wife and children kept working.

As quickly as the food tent had filled, it emptied. With bellies full, the patrons departed with their bowls and spoons for the pub. Six o'clock closing was mandatory for hotels in the city but that rule was not policed in Gunnadoo. The women sat for their evening meal and Catherine continued her charade. The steamed rice was a bonus. It was also hot.

"Holy Moth…" Seven voices stopped chattering and seven faces looked in her direction. Catherine immediately began tapping her chest, creatively coughing the near slip-up into a passable choking sound. She modestly sipped a cup of tea passed to her. "Sacré bleu." she stated, fanning herself and recommencing her meal; the women did likewise. After the clear-and-clean procedure, Catherine changed into her freshly washed and ironed tunic. She quickly washed and hung the pyjamas on a nearby line, said her goodnights and left to collect the day's wages.

"I am told you are a good worker. If Mrs. Foo is pleased, then so am I." Wong Foo handed her a shilling.

Catherine couldn't hide her surprise. She didn't know whether she was coming or going, Irish or French.

"Holy Mother, sacré bleu."

"Of course your expenses have been deducted; tomorrow you will earn more."

"And what expenses I be actually paying for?" she enquired indignantly.

Wong Foo opened his ledger. "One bag of necessities containing: one lantern, one…"

"To be sure I know what was in your bag of tricks…the hidden expenses if you please."

"…and two meals – I not charge for hire of working clothes or washing soap for bedding – and two night's accommodation. Tonight you can afford tenancy rental fee in advance."

"Sacré bleu." she wailed again.

"Your text book vocabulary requires enlarging, Miss Dunn. A dictionary would be most useful." She returned his arrogance with a feisty glare. "I am bilingual Mandarin. I speak five languages fluently. Is that all?" he enquired, tapping the accounts ledger with forefinger.

"That will be all, thank you," she retorted.

Wong Foo scanned his immediate surrounds then propositioned softly. "You are not French neither are you Chinese. Chinese women work hard: age quickly. You could work for me in, let's say, more comfortable surrounds – easy work, most pleasurable."

"Work never killed anybody," Catherine declared.

"No expenses, you make plenty money." He slipped beads back and forth on the abacus. "You think about it."

"There's nothing to think about," she announced on exiting. "Goodnight."

She did think about it though and concluded that the little cash shown for the laborious hours bent over scrubbing boards, washtubs and forty-four gallon drums was not for her; but no man would rule her either. Catherine conceded Wong Foo was right; she wasn't Chinese and she was sitting on her own goldmine. If the cycle of poverty was to be broken, breaking a back over the tub wasn't the way to do it; there *were* other ways and she resigned herself to accepting Wong Foo's immoral offer.

* * *

The next day, Catherine negotiated an amorous rendezvous with Wong Foo for that evening and then proceeded to the cemetery. Religious totems stood vigil in an overgrown carpet of non- denominational dandelions. Segregation applied in the outback also, as evidenced by partitioned sections for Catholics, Protestants and various other religions. To the rear, in an inconspicuous corner where Catherine headed, the paupers lay. Here the penniless, if lucky enough to be buried on a day when the undertaker was sober, received two pieces of wood roughly nailed together to resemble a cross – no matter what religion. Buried in a drunken haze, a tin lid nailed to a broken off tree

47

branch signified Danny's resting place. Upon reading the name wrongly spelt, a morose tide swept over Catherine. She collapsed on the mound, wailing like a banshee.

"You promised you wouldn't, you promised." Her hand repeatedly thumped and then caressed the bristle of new growth sprouting like a five-day-old beard.

Time stood still but the sun didn't. Emotionally and physically drained, Catherine sat up and proclaimed, "Danny, to do right by you I've got to do something I not be proud of doing but it must be done. I've nobody to watch after me but the Holy Mother and myself..." She got to her feet. "It's every man," she stopped, "it's every woman for herself in this town."

Catherine hadn't had an easy life being raised in the squalid slums of Exeter Street in the Rocks area of Sydney. Such was the stress arising from overcrowded environments that family breakdowns were common. A drunken husband and father deserted her mother and her, and then Catherine's mother deserted her. Taken in by a family on a selection at Parramatta, she performed house duties as repayment for their so-called kindness when not at school. Raped by the squatter, she told his wife and the fourteen-year-old found herself homeless again. An elderly Irishwoman yearning company took her in. It was the first time of any affection and a bond soon grew between them. Catherine had worked in a factory sweatshop and looked after Granny Dunn until her death.

"I was undecided as to what I be getting you for Christmas, but now I know." She dusted off her dress. "Of course you won't be getting it until I save enough but I know the right man for the job. Mr. Booth did Granny's headstone, a grand job he did too." She wiped dust from the tin lid with her handkerchief. "I'll not be forgetting you, Danny O'Shaunessy."

Catherine spent the afternoon familiarizing herself with Gunnadoo. She inconspicuously studied the townsfolk and their relationships with each other as they went about their business. John Bycroft was of special interest as he apparently had a finger in many of the businesses. Walking back to her tent she reinforced her resolve to carry out the evening's liaison. *If I had a pound for each time I'm called a pretty little thing,* she thought, *I'd be a rich pretty little thing.*

* * *

Catherine's anxiety increased as twilight approached. At dusk, her apprehension at her ability to go through with the liaison grew. The thought of Danny not having a headstone propelled her. She waited nervously until dark for the opportunity to be unobserved and then slipped into Wong Foo's private residence.

The décor was typically oriental: cushions, drapes and dragon statues, red, black and gold, incense waft throughout. A meal lay unfinished on an exquisitely laid table set with a pretentious candelabrum. Dressed in a silk bathrobe, Wong Foo stood with his back to her, packing his pipe as she entered. "Please be seated," he requested. She moved to the table nervously. Without turning, he told her, "Not there." There was only one other place possible. In the middle of the iron bedstead, two bronze dragons claw at each other. Catherine sat on the bed feeling the texture of the dragon scales. "Woman like you need not work over tub."

"Precisely what would it be you be meaning by 'woman like you'?" she replied, hoping the conversation would stall the inevitable.

"You are very pretty; not old and wrinkled like wife, she only good for working."

His derogatory comments about the woman affronted Catherine. She felt her nervousness overridden by indignation. She had observed Wong Foo kowtowing to his wife the previous day when an argument occurred, and believed this deceit by him was a betrayal.

"And would it be you're telling me you'll treat me better. Is that what I be hearing?"

"Young woman requires older man to teach oriental lovemaking...much pleasure given. Young woman requires..."

"Money...and this young woman requires lots of it," she said forcibly. Wong Foo wasn't impressed at her words.

Though her legs felt like jelly, Catherine stood and then sauntered up behind Wong Foo, pressing her breasts into his back and rubbing her belly on his buttocks. Her hands slowly slipped around his waist, anxious fingers undoing the silk tie; it fell to the floor followed by the silk bathrobe.

She returned to sit on the bed and stall with her eyes closed.

"You like what you see?" he asked arrogantly, without turning.

A rich girl, she repeated to herself and then looked in his direction. She was pleasantly surprised. *Thank you, Mother.* She crossed herself and replied, "What I do, very much. Is there more?"

"You come to senses but…" he paused to augment the significance of his words and then continued, "Wong Foo unfortunately may have lost interest." He waited for her pleading.

"Regrettably, Mr. Foo, so have I," she replied to his amazement, "but my visit is still going to cost you."

He turned confused and faced Catherine, an erection contradicting his previous statement. "You crazy woman, I give pleasure, you should be grateful. I not pay you one penny."

Catherine smiled. "Ooh, I be wanting much more than pennies." Now lying back on the bed with arms outstretched, she stared him down while her forefinger caressed a dragon's underbelly. In a seductive voice she then hinted, "It very well could be costing you more than what I ask."

"Like what?" he demanded.

"Like your workforce."

Wong Foo knew immediately what she talking about and what was at stake. "Wife not believe blackmailer," he replied smugly.

"To be sure that scar is certainly unique," she teased, "now how would it be a young, innocent girl like me knows about that?"

Wong Foo felt the erection collapse in one hand as the other quickly tried to cover the deep scar welt across both buttocks. His forlorn posture portrayed how he had felt when he had originally received the cane lash. His prying eyes and lustful thoughts had also instigated that embarrassing situation. Conceding that he'd misread Catherine and been outmanoeuvred, he retrieved the bathrobe and slipped it on.

"Would I be right in presuming my lustful foolishness is going to cost a pound?"

"No...I have changed my mind, it's not your money I be wanting – I'm lying on what will make me many pounds."

Wong Foo was beginning to panic. "No. That is impossible. What will I tell Mrs. Foo?"

"Now let me see," she teased, "what could...I know. What about...a leprechaun stole it?"

"How many pounds you want?" The more his voice trembled, the more Catherine gained confidence and her heartbeat slowed. "I give you money." He opened a wardrobe drawer to get cash from his money belt.

"I give you two days," she said, getting up and rearranging her attire.

"Please. I cannot do what you ask of me." Wong Foo offered her a hand full of notes.

"To be sure you can – a smart businessman like you. It's been nice doing business."

"This not business," he castigated, waving the money in her face, "this blackmail."

"Here I am leaving without so much as a penny in me hand. I can't help but feel you've taken advantage of me, Mr. Foo. Have it delivered to my abode, comprenez-vous?" she enunciated.

He stood up, a dumb look on his face.

"Oui? Do you understand?" Either he didn't, or he was reeling from the expensive consequence of his actions. Catherine experienced a sense of power like never before. "Could it be you are no more Mandarin than I Chinese? Adieu, Monsieur Foo."

* * *

Catherine lay on her bunk, staring up into her private cathedral, not believing her luck at what had happened; she also couldn't believe what she'd been prepared to do. *I don't be meaning to be blasphemous Holy Mother, but thank Christ for man's lustful ways*, she thought and then added, *and thank you for the scar on Mr. Foo's arse*.

* * *

With minor reshuffling of possessions, the dragon bed fitted quite comfortably into the canvas abode and Mademoiselle Catherine's private enterprise soon opened its tent flap for business. Within a week, her selected clientele of businessmen had grown, as had the fee for her services. Her confidence blossomed, likewise the French accent and vocabulary. Bycroft soon came knocking.

"Oh. John. You were simply très bien, magnifique, I should be paying you."

Bycroft sat on the edge of the bed pulling on his boots. Lying on her back with arms outstretched, Catherine stroked the dragon's belly. Turning to half lean over her, he dropped hot ash from the cigar held between his thin lips onto her belly.

"Ouch." she yelped.

There was no apology. "Same time, same place, you lucky girl," he said, placing two sovereigns on the ash. He removed the cigar after drawing on it again, exhaled and then she vanished into a brown haze smelling of whiskey. She felt his cold lips kiss her goodbye. "This is our little secret, right?"

"But of course."

Catherine let Bycroft think he was the one doing the string pulling. She knew where she stood and had made up her mind that he'd be the favoured client. She kept the late night visits secret as he cultivated an image for bigger quests ahead. Being servile and praising the ground upon which he walked would draw him into the net and she'd learn what made him tick.

Next morning, Catherine paid Wong Foo a visit before going the bathhouse.

"Bonjour, Monsieur Foo."

Recognising the voice, he looked up from the ledger apprehensively. Catherine's appearance was that of a Mademoiselle but her smile was that of a leprechaun. She stood there with bed linen rolled up under an arm.

"You bring much embarrassment to Wong Foo and now you bring washing too?"

"Oui. You do good job, no?"

"You send me to poor house," he complained.

"Moi is a *paying* customer, Monsieur Foo." Catherine placed a ten-shilling note on the counter. It instantly caught his undivided attention, but she dumped the bundle on top of it. "Business before pleasure."

Wong Foo was now more impressed than embarrassed. "Please accept my humble apology for previous indiscretion. Maybe you are good businesswoman. I wish we start new page in…business relationship."

Catherine held out her hand as would a mademoiselle and Wong Foo responded as would a gentleman. She smiled. "It will be interesting to joust with such an honourable swine. Pickup and delivery of course," she informed him, referring to the bundle. Wong Foo courteously nodded.

He then told her of recent bad karma that had necessitated the removal of his beloved dragon bed. Catherine feigned a surprised look to support the charade. She then informed him of her fortuitous find concluding with, "I have always believed dragons to be lucky."

"Dragon represent many things to many people, fortune, fame … fate; dragon also guardian of female chastity," he laughed. "Wong Foo loves dragon but also believe, beware dragon does not bite you in arse."

"I bow to your mythical knowledge," Catherine sparred, "but how do I know which dragon is the dangerous one?"

Wong Foo rubbed his bottom. "Female dragon of course. They have the biggest teeth." He looked pleased with the witticism delivered and began his insipid chuckling.

"I fear you have mistaken the female dragon with karma?"

Wong Foo nodded acceptingly. "You will be a most worthy opponent, and I bow to your gamesmanship."

"…Games-*man*-ship? I am a woman."

He quickly forfeited to avoid getting embroiled in another precarious debate.

4 – Come in Spinner

Two pennies, two lives – a flip of the coin
Heads or tails – fate or destiny

At the end of each month Wally routinely left the mining site and visited Gunnadoo for supplies. Visiting the bathhouse was a ritualistic first stop.

"Jeez'us. That's hot," he screamed.

Ying Lee emptied the pail over him anyway and picked up the bar of Sunlight soap. He countered, "That's what you pay for, Mr. Wally." He began the soaping and scrubbing.

"Take it easy mate. I want some hide left on me."

Having attended Wally previously, the bathhouse attendant was aware of his client's shrapnel wounds; they were still tender as was Wally's self-consciousness of the ugly welts. The first time he visited the bathhouse Ying Lee made light of it and told him, "My wife beat me too. I show you my scars some day." The Chinaman's humble awareness led Wally to believe there was more to Ying Lee than met the eye; a mutual respect for each other bonded the unlikely duo.

The pail emptied over him. "Jeez'us. That's cold," Wally hollered.

"You dry yourself," Ying Lee demanded, throwing him a towel, "I not your slave."

With the caked-on dirt washed off, the white welts on his brown skin resembled Zebra stripes. The mongrel lay watching as Wally dried himself.

"Me not wash dog too."

"No, he can do it himself. In you get."

The dog jumped at the command and sat in the bathtub with a forlorn look on its face.

"Last time Mr. Wally."

"Last time Ying Lee."

The pungent smell of sweat and dog lingered in the sauna-like conditions of the bathhouse tent. Wally sat down in an incongruously ornate, leather barbershop chair. Like Bycroft's mahogany desk, it extracted currency from the unwary.

Wally lifted his beard as the wrap tightened around his neck. "Easy there mate, it's not a noose, I'm not..." A mouthful of shaving cream abruptly stopped his chatter and he listened to the slap of cutthroat razor upon leather.

"You know where man most vulnerable Mr. Wally?"

He didn't dare answer as the razor peeled the bushy briar from under his chin. The smiling Chinaman acknowledged Wally's eyes. "Yes, many unfortunate client it has been said lose life in shaving accident; you right – but that only happen when barber talk too much and not concentrate." He flicked the residue from the blade with the skill of a Shaolin swordsman, and Wally seized the opportunity as though a quiz contestant.

"The heart because … " The blade cut short his reply.

"Ying Lee ask for answer, not explanation. Get plenty explanation from wife, bad example for children." He acknowledged Wally's astute answer by lifting an eyebrow, "but you right again, heart most difficult to protect," he paused, lifted the razor and then resumed, "only one way known. You know how eunuch is named eunuch?" Wally nodded slightly and the barber raised the blade.

"They cut off his nuts when …" The blade fell again.

"Question not why but how eunuch is named eunuch?" Ying Lee looked into Wally's soul as he pondered the question again, and then lifted the razor for an answer.

"Search me … I give up." The razor flicked within a whisker of his nose.

"You nick a little off." The barber broke up laughing and lifted the blade, "You nick. Plenty funny huh Mr. Wally … you want me give you haircut too?"

"Yeah, a little off the sides and leave me ears where they are."

From behind, Ying Lee prodded Wally's large ears. "You sure got plenty."

"Bugger off you half wit."

"Ying Lee's ears too small, cannot hear well. What you say?"

As the sunlight faded, Ying Lee lit a couple of lamps and then helped the client on with his suit coat. He brushed the shoulders, picked off a loose thread and hastily wiped the cheval-mirror of condensation as Wally inspected himself.

"You now look right dandy-man."

"That's 'ladies-man' you ning-nong."

"Whatever you wish, customer always right," Ying Lee replied, holding out a prune-like hand for the usually generous tip. He then routinely complained when receiving it, "Not enough for dog drying."

"He can do that himself." Wally clicked his fingers and the mongrel bounded from the tub shaking furiously. As customary, Ying Lee let fly expletives in his native tongue.

"See you ... next year."

"Chinese calendar says next year not for another two week."

"By my calendar it's tomorrow, Happy New Year."

"Before you go, Mr. Wally, I give you tip."

"Jeez'us, make it snappy then...Lady-Luck is waiting."

"Man with big ears – should keep eyes open."

"Confucius?"

"No. Ying Lee."

* * *

A rising moon reflected a ghostly image on the surface of the Yapsly. Strung in the Coolabah branches, lamps illuminated the riverbank and the crowd below. Men and women, standing around a circle scratched in the baked mud, drunkenly shouted obscenities as hard-earned wages were lost on the spinning coins.

Tethered horses munched contentedly on feedbags, there was little grass under hoof on which to snack. Wagons and carriages haphazardly parked in the clearing, it was a traffic jam waiting to happen. Wally pulled up next to Bycroft's new rig. "Whoa. Lightning ... easy 'ol fella."

"How's it going Wally?" asked the cockatoo.

"Jeez'us Kenny. You scared the living daylights out of me. I didn't see you sitting up there."

"You're not supposed to; I'm the one who does the seeing."

"Are you looking for anyone in particular?"

"Word has it we may be paid a visit from the sergeant and his boys."

"So you reckon Doyle might be showing up for his cut. There might be a bit of fun and games later, eh."

"It's on the cards."

"Well look sharp. I'd rather lose my money in the game than to the coppers."

"I got a book going on getaways; first back to town. Are you feeling lucky?"

"Hang on ... hey. Lightning," the horse stood with his head bowed as if asleep, "Naw, I don't like the odds. I think it might be wise to go to ground and find me a possie out of sight. See ya later, Giddup Lightning."

Wally kept moving through the scrub until well out of sight. As he climbed down, the horse immediately dropped its head as though nodding off again. Placing the feedbag in position he gave instructions to the nag, "Don't choke on it and be ready, if we're discovered we may need a quick getaway. Come on dog, let's find Lady-Luck." The dog bounded from the rear of the wagon pleased at not having to stay guarding it.

In the shadows of the thick foliage, Wally worked his way towards the glow of lamps. Hearing a musician sawing a jig on a fiddle and the laughter of dancers trying to keep up with the increasing tempo augmented his adrenaline. Not watching where he was going, the Wait-a-While bush, with its thorny tentacles, nearly grabbed its victim. The dog finally broke through the scrub followed by Wally and they joined the mingling revellers. Bycroft was standing by the grog wagon. He'd organised the selling of illicit refreshments and while his two lackeys rushed to keep up with demand, he kept an eye on the money rolling in.

"G'day," he greeted Wally. "I was wondering when you two would show up."

"Wonder no more. The bearer of important news is here."

"And looking pretty spiffy … new shoes?"

Wally rubbed the dust off each shoe onto the opposite trouser leg. "Yeah, but I wouldn't want to be playing a game of footy in 'em."

"And what's that important news you've got for me?" Bycroft enquired.

"I hear there might be raid happening. You'd better have on ya running shoes."

"Naw, Sunshine … I would've heard."

"Well, don't say I didn't tell you."

Bycroft sucked on his cigar. "Naw, I've got my sources – not tonight Josephine. So …who's the lady you're out to impress?"

"Lady-Luck." Wally rubbed his hands together. "Tonight is the night. I can feel it in my bones."

"Come in Spinner," the pit boss called.

Wally's head turned as the crowd roared again. "Are ya feeling lucky?" he asked Bycroft.

"Luck has nothing to do with it if you want to make a quid."

"Ah … a bloke's gotta have a bit of fun, I'll see you later."

"Probably not," replied Bycroft. He looked in the direction of Catherine and the followers she was attracting. "As you said, a bloke's gotta have a bit of fun."

Wally moved through the crowd. He kept hands in pockets rather than having a shyster's hand slip in to relieve him of his two-up money; the gathering of so many inebriated suckers was a pickpocket's dream. He stood and watched the pea under the thimble game. The operator's sleight of hand moved in a quick succession of figure eights. He had no idea where the pea was; the intoxicated player had no chance. Set up at a table close by, the card trickster showed his talents also. Fistfuls of notes changed hands as players tried their luck.

"Lady-Luck certainly isn't here," he told the dog. "Come on, she's around here somewhere."

There was no apparent pattern to the region's gold discoveries; it wasn't as though all the gold was being found along the banks of the Yapsly, prospectors staked out claims in the bush also and deep pits haphazardly appeared overnight. The good fortune of Gunnadoo's inhabitants didn't go unnoticed and many a visiting swindler was soon dealt with when apprehended. Court proceedings took place in the solitude of the bush, attended by the aggrieved and witnessed only by mobs of inquisitive kangaroos. The shyster, if found guilty, then silently disappeared down one of the many snake-riddled mineshafts – abandoned either through no gold or the operator having been bitten by the hostile resident. Word spread of the kangaroo courts, and conmen soon learnt – if there was any dudding to be done in Gunnadoo, it would be done only by the original inhabitants.

"Heads – come on, heads." yelled half the crowd.

"Tails, tails." shouted the other half.

"Odds it is," confirmed the pit boss, to the crowds jeering.

Having lost for a fourth consecutive toss of the coins, Wally scratched his head. "Jeez'us. Let's get out of here before I do me shirt," he told the dog. He had taken a couple of steps when the pit boss introduced the next spinner.

"Stand back and give Lady-Luck room, boys. You blokes, are you in or out? Get ya money down or get out."

Hearing the magic words, Wally stopped and returned to the game.

Catherine's attire was immaculate. From under the straw boater, her hair flowed across her partly exposed shoulders caressing bare skin divulged by a low-cut bodice. In the middle of the circle, she received instructions as to throwing of the coins.

"I'm in, I'm in," shouted Wally, holding the last of his two-up money high.

"Last bets Ladies and gentlemen … are we all in? Then, come in spinner."

"Come in spinner," called the crowd in unison, and up the pennies flew with all eyes watching them spin in flight until hitting the ground.

"… tails." called the pit boss.

"You little beauty." Wally yelled. "It's about bloody time."

"Are you going to let it ride?" the pit boss heckled before paying him out.

Wally called to Lady-Luck, "Are you tossing again?"

"No Monsieur. Once it is enough," she replied.

"Naw, that's it for me. I'll take the winnings and run."

Catherine joined him and flirted. "Monsieur is a wise man."

Wally blushed, "Thank you, Miss," his fingers tipped the floppy brim of his unrecognisable slouch hat, "I appreciate that."

She took a step, stopped and turned. "Polite and sober, you are a rarity indeed. Catherine Dunn." She held out her hand.

"Stay. Don't move," he commanded the dog. It sat at his feet. "James Beaumont." He held out his hand, with the fistful of pound notes still in it. Catherine stood looking at it.

"Is this a proposition Monsieur Beaumont?"

"No, Jeez'us, I'm not like that. I mean, not that I wouldn't but …"

"But you do not find me attractive, oui?" Catherine retorted playfully.

He quickly stuffed the winnings into his pocket and held out his hand again. "My friends call me Wally."

"Enchantée, Wally. It is nice to meet you…and who may I ask is this?" she enquired, referring to the dog.

"Stay." The dog sat looking up, tongue hanging out and tail wagging wildly. "That's Dog."

Catherine had quickly recognised there were many ways to attract a man's attention; his dog was just one. "Is Dog smart?"

"Smart enough to know we're talking about him."

"He is a rogue with a pirate's patch, oui? I can tell."

Wally bashfully replied, "He's been known to stir the pot."

"Dog?" she questioned. "Such an unusual name for a magnifique canine."

Wally stopped smiling and did a double take to see if Catherine and he were looking at the same animal. He was too polite to ask if she'd lost her spectacles. "He is … well, Dog doesn't … sit." he sternly instructed the excited animal. "His manners need polishing when it comes to women."

"Pardon?"

The mongrel received a nervous pat and Wally said to him between gritted teeth, "Jeez'us, I'm digging a grave for us both here." He changed the subject. "Naw, I mean … well … he's not gonna die of hard work, that's for sure."

"Then he is not a working dog, oui?"

"Yes, well no … depends on what you mean by working, I just haven't figured out what he does yet." Wally realised he was beginning to talk gibberish but couldn't stop. He now defended the mongrel. "Sleeps like a log, eats like a horse and lives the life of Riley he does. I guess that's pretty smart if that's …"

Catherine interrupted. "If I had a dog I would have a shiny black Retriever."

Wally was glad she'd stopped him from waffling on. He tried to listen and be able to deliver an intelligent question or answer when required – she was intoxicating. He reeled with embarrassment and chastised himself at hearing the intelligent question he asked. "And what'd you call him?"

"I would call him," she paused, thinking astutely with a finger to her chin, "I would call him … Frederick. Shall we walk and I shall observe just how smart Dog is?"

"Go." Wally commanded. The dog took off like a greyhound then realised he wasn't being chased and returned to his master's side. The trio ambled along with the crowd, Wally hoping the dog would do something intelligent and she would see it. Unfortunately, Dog did what he usually did – scavenged for tucker morsels, cocked his leg on stationary objects and surprised many a woman by sticking his nose in her crotch. Wally awkwardly tried to make conversation but then gave up, kicking at the odd rock and the playful mongrel until finally saved by the smell of a pig cooking over an open fire. "Are you hungry?"

"No, but you go ahead. I enjoy watching a man eat heartily."

He placed his order, "Two glasses of fruit punch and a bowl of the porker."

"Here, let me." Catherine took the two glasses and picked up from the conversation's high point. "Are there other unusual names in your family?"

"Naw, only Lightning, I guess." He stood facing her with bowl in hand and the dog at feet between them.

"Let me guess ... mmm, Lightning is a racing horse, oui?"

"Well, he's a horse and he's got four legs and ..."

Catherine curtseyed, "Voila." As she did Wally received an unexpected push in the back. His bowl was thrust forward, hanging momentarily on Catherine's chest and the contents then oozing slowly down the bodice of the low-cut dress, depositing in her cleavage. With a drink in each hand and an astonished look on her face, she stood frozen until being knocked to the ground by Wally falling on top of her. Another thump in the back had propelled him forward, forcing him to trip over the dog. It immediately pounced on Catherine for the tucker.

The trio lay in the path of the panic-stricken revellers running in the direction of the wagons for a quick getaway. "Cops." the cockatoo shouted, as he ran through the celebrations warning all of their impending arrival. "Fair go, Wally," Kenny panted, "no time for that, it's the constable, he's early – run for it."

In the mêlée, Wally caught a glimpse of Bycroft disappearing with the bag of cash under his arm. "This way; hurry up." He dragged Catherine in the opposite direction to the crowd rush. The dog pranced underfoot, barking at the excitement of fleeing people. Catherine lost her straw boater, trampled underfoot – as she would have been not for her rescuer. Out of breath, they stood in the shadows listening to the police whistles and watching the uniformed men round up those not fleet of foot. A copper began his search in their direction.

"Quick. Through here," Wally whispered, holding back the foliage of a Banksia bush for her to climb past. "Be careful and watch out for the Wait-a-While bush."

"What a quaint name, why is it called – Sacré bleu."

The barbed tentacles latched onto her. The more she struggled the more entwined she became. She yelped loudly and liberally. Wally placed a hand over Catherine's mouth as the lamp approached; the long arm of the law was combing the bush.

"Shhh," he whispered, "you'll give the game away."

"Hey Blue, there's somebody over here." shouted one of the constables to another.

Catherine stood frozen, her green eyes wide in trepidation as the bushes rustled. Wally scrutinized the pig remnants upon her heaving chest.

"Come out. I can see you," the voice demanded sternly.

Catherine stopped breathing. Wally pulled her closer, the waltz position – she felt more than just his heart thumping. Her knees weakened and she slumped; his grip tightened. Wally's nostrils flared like an excited stallion. A hand's width separated their mouths … their lips.

"All right, you got me," another voice replied from under a nearby bush; the sucker capitulated to the constable's bluff and gave himself up.

"Right then. Out you come. Quickly man, I haven't got all night."

Wally recognised the military overtones of the constable. He knew what the captured man could expect; an embittered provost usually handed out harsh justice. Catherine stood defiantly waiting with a hand over her mouth until she'd had enough of the suffocating act.

"Ouch." Wally stifled his own yelp by sticking his bitten hand in his mouth and sucking hard.

"I saw where you were looking," Catherine rebuked. She felt the embarrassment radiating from Wally's red face.

"No I wasn't, I was …"

"Ouch. Get me out of this."

"Stop struggling, you're making it worse, don't move," he told her. "Here Dog," the dog got a pat on the head. "Go and wake up Lightning. Go on."

Her eyes resumed the startled position as the dog bounded off into the dark and Wally methodically untwined the tentacles of the bush, carefully trying not to touch any bare skin.

"I hope Lightning is faster than you," she informed him. One obstinate tentacle had latched onto a lodged pig remnant and he accidentally touched her breast. "I asked if you'd care to walk – and that is all."

Wally was then all thumbs; he worked up a sweat until finally releasing the trapped victim. Grimacing, she rubbed her chest, the pig fat helping allay the burning sensation. Wally watched her until she caught him out again, then stood aside and gestured her forward.

"Sacré bleu. Such a gentleman – you go first," she demanded. "And I hope you get caught and I will last laugh." She paused, indignantly correcting herself. "Laugh last."

Voices calling to one another in the dark grew distant, as did their invasive lamps. Catherine took a tumble and her slip of the tongue broke the stillness of bush and night. "Shit." She lay on her back breathing deeply. Through the eucalypts, stars distanced themselves. Listening to the silence reinforced the remoteness; the rustle of leaves averted her panic. "Wally?"

"Shhh." he appeared next to her. "There's not much further to go."

"Exactly how much further is your not further?"

"There's our getaway. You can see the outline of the wagon if you look hard enough. I found a possie to hide Lightning just in case there was a raid. Pretty smart, eh?"

Catherine sat up. "Where?"

"There." said Wally, pointing.

"Where?" Rising from her sitting position, she stood up and over-exaggerated looking into the dark. "Sacré bleu. Moi is damaged." She placed a hand over her right eye then the left, declaring each time, "I am half blind."

"Jeez'us." Wally took her by the shoulders to give her support. "You might've knocked your noggin. Where are your spectacles? Put them on," he politely suggested.

"Pardon? I do not wear spectacles." She pointed. "Catherine sees your wagon but no Lightning."

"You'd better sit down."

"No, look. There is no Lightning. He has woken up and gone without us," she stated dramatically.

Wally lifted the brim of his hat with a forefinger and looked again; she was right. "Your eyesight is better than mine ... bloody coppers. And that's not funny," he said, referring to her fake blindness. He strode away, agitated, not knowing why but distancing himself from Catherine until she managed to catch up when he stopped at the clearing. She peered over his shoulder and saw the dog lying beside the horse, which was lying down also, its muzzle still in the feedbag.

"How sweet – they sleep together, oui?"

"Yeah, real bloody bonza. Come on Dog."

For twenty minutes as they walked back to town, Wally refused to talk or answer Catherine. His dead horse might have been slow but was broken in, as were his work boots, which he wished he'd worn; the pain inflicted by the new ill-fitting shoes was excruciating. The glow of tent lamps intensified along with the noise of the town's frivolities. Catherine, looking worse for the experience, strode rebelliously alongside Wally, matching her perplexing antagonist stride for stride. She had managed to keep up a verbal barrage of conversation and abuse.

"Look what you have done. My best dress is ruined, you beast." She squirmed, still discovering remnants of his dinner between her breasts. The dog trotted contentedly beside her waiting for the titbits. "That is the last time you will take Catherine for a walk, do you hear? And I refuse to let Monsieur …" she threw back her unruly mane, "… walk me home."

Wally interrupted, "Jeez'us, don't you ever stop talking?"

She squared up to him, "… and I hope next year brings you more fortune than you had tonight." She pondered whether what she'd said made sense but didn't correct herself. "Bonsoir to you." Her grand exit abruptly stopped when she turned and walked into the dog's nose. "Sacré bleu."

Catherine strode headlong into the tide of oncoming revellers. They parted like the Red Sea before Moses, each chorusing drunken greetings. The sea of drunken larrikins reunited to sweep Wally, now hobbling, along on the tide of good cheer and blistered feet.

5 – Yakka Dakka

When foundations are laid on assumption
a collapse is always imminent.

Yakka Dakka, a camel Wally had ridden in Palestine, had played games with him. Continually they had been at odds with each other, and for that reason he had named the gold claim after the troublesome beast.

At the site, a small creek flowed along the gully floor, an offshoot of a tributary that sourced its flow from the Yapsly. A pick and pan was all that was required, the auriferous sand from the bedrock of the watercourse yielded its treasure encouragingly. Overhanging the stream, high foliage made the summer heat bearable; the stream was cool to plunge into and prospecting was enjoyable.

But the winter months were excruciatingly cold; the area didn't receive direct sunlight until mid morning. Frostbitten fingers didn't make keeping a positive attitude any easier, and neither did the fact that over the previous two months decreasing amounts of the alluvial gold had been found. Wally was glad to see the last of August.

At Yakka Dakka panning for riches was now in serious jeopardy. Many individual prospectors in the region saw their claims overrun by poppet heads and stamper batteries as the syndicates moved in. They had the manpower and assets to sink shafts and tunnels, to follow elusive veins of reef gold where individuals couldn't go.

The door of the slab hut open, Wally stood stretching with the dog yapping excitedly at his feet. "No work for us today fella, come on … and remind me to get another sack of flour and tobacco. Have a look at ya. Anyone would think you haven't been to town in a month of Sundays." He hadn't. Wally only went at the start of each month for supplies. "Just as well I wrote a list for you - you won't remember."

Blackfella Jimmy had shown up one day and then become a regular visitor. For the past year Wally had traded flour and tobacco for fish and native tucker; the aboriginal always seemed to come out of the trading sessions with the better deal though. It was a two-hour trip to Gunnadoo by wagon on the dirt track, or one hour on foot via Billygoat Pass. It cut across the ridge as the crow flies.

Wally removed his coat and threw it up onto the wagon seat where Dog immediately sat on it. He continued with the last of the harness buckles. "Whew. It's starting to warm up again, eh Dog?" Equine knowledge wasn't Wally's forte and another horse replaced Lightning. He placed an ear on Atlas' chest and listened to the rasping lungs. "No more than three cigars a day," he lectured the nag. "Get over, ya mongrel," he told the dog and sat with reins in hands observing the clear sky. "Spring is in the air … what say us boys go to town." The dog agreed. "Giddup Atlas."

* * *

As the diggings flourished so did the community, the dwellings of the privileged few ostentatiously displayed ornamental statues in their front gardens. Each time Wally visited the settlement he noticed how it had grown. He sat at the top of Main Street north amazed at the amount of traffic and the number of pedestrians. "Have a look at that," he told the dog, "they'll be sticking in tram tracks soon. A bloke will have to get used to driving on the left by the looks of things. Giddup Atlas."

Bastock's goods depot and holding yard had expanded yet again. Many wagons jostled for attention; some for unloading others for consignment. Men shuttled supplies from a wagon onto a dray already loaded with heavy mining equipment, the team of bullocks bellowed as if complaining of the imposition. The driver sat impatiently waiting for his load. "Hey Wally," he called, "are ya looking for a job? I'll swap ya."

"Naw, I got my hands full with Atlas here." Atlas was a resurrection of Lightning; he plodded along contentedly.

A parcel of bush lay undeveloped next to Bastock's and further along another construction was underway. A hastily painted sign announced the coming of Radcliff's Stationer and Newsagent. On the next block, the Savings Bank appeared quite small in comparison with the new structures under construction either side.

Bounding from the wagon, the dog ran in circles frantically sniffing the surrounds, leaving

76

calling cards on any object in the vertical position. Wally observed a man and woman chatting at the front gate, their attire not that of the working class.

"Get out of it, ya mongrel," shouted the angry resident, about to kick the dog as it cocked its leg on the fence. Wally noted the man's shiny shoes; he was yet to walk the dusty street.

"Come on Dog," he grunted, eyeballing the would-be assailant then the woman. "Good morning, Miss." Her attitude was one of contempt and she looked away. Wally's appearance was that of many prospectors and miners – a mass of unkempt hair, a bushy beard and two eyes peering from under a battered hat; caked-on dirt embellished the black picture. As the wagon passed slowly with Wally eyeballing him, the gentleman apologised profusely for attempting to kick the dog. The dog disappeared from view chasing what Wally could only presume to be a bitch on heat. "Giddup Atlas, he'll find us when he's ready."

* * *

Bycroft had proposed enlarging Catherine's business. A two-storey establishment was now a work in progress. Bycroft had become a silent partner and facilitated architectural plans, labourers and financial investment. Many of the tradesmen became clients; the day-to-day operation still thrived in temporary premises on the newly acquired property. Catherine had hired extra girls and made sure they showed no discrimination. 'One man's gold is as good as the next', she would say, and the profits rolled in.

A thorny box hedge planted around the property perimeter and the beginnings of an oriental garden became priority for Chung Dow; the elderly man took great pride in his gardening. The dirt road that the box hedge fronted, known as High Street, proceeded into the Chinatown district. The house of ill repute, if located at northern Gunnadoo, would have outshone the houses of the so-called community leaders and elitists. Built on the plans of an 1850 Victorian mansion the two-story structure became an instant landmark, albeit, on the wrong side of the tracks. Logically, Wong Foo's establishments were the demarcation line where Main Street became High Street. The oriental community consumed a large quantity of opium every day; High Street reputedly got its name from the activity.

Wally's visits to town had been for business only – drop off the alluvial dust, pick up supplies and return to the claim. He didn't catch sight of Catherine even though he looked for her, and he believed she might have left town. When finally hearing the gossip of the French brunette and her dragon bed antics, he was thrown into confusion. He worked out his emotional conflict by swinging the pick from morning to dark.

* * *

As great as any gold find, the copper streaks in Catherine's hair instigated a thumping in Wally's chest. Chatting with Wong Foo, she stood with Granny Dunn's wicker basket over her arm and a parasol in her other hand. It wasn't a large smile he threw to her, it was more of a grin; enough to make his beard move. He nodded and touched the rim of his battered hat with his forefinger as Catherine looked up. Her response was disappointingly indifferent.

"Giddup Atlas," he mumbled.

Wong Foo continued, "… and next week I receive the shipment …"

"Pardon," Catherine returned to the conversation. She lightly tapped her chest and tried to pick up her train of thought.

"… from China. Your silk sheets …"

"… sheets?" she queried. She turned to observe the wagon.

"You work too hard."

"I remember you saying that previously," she again returned to face Wong Foo, "and you are right."

He smiled. "You know what I mean. I only have seven girls to worry me. How many do you now have?"

"Eleven. I must be going, look at the time. Bonjour Wong Foo."

In the agistment paddock at the rear of the farrier and blacksmith's, Wally observed four camels. He stood unnoticed, watching sparks fly as the smithy's boy pumped the bellow handle. The boy then removed the white-hot studs from the forge and Clement pounded them into an iron wheel rim. He then dunked it into a tub of water, Wally waited for the screaming hiss to fade.

"They must be the ugliest looking horses I've ever seen." Clement looked up and then in the direction Wally was looking. He smiled. "Look after me rig," Wally called to the boy, "and stick a feed bag on Atlas. I'll be hour or so."

* * *

The humid atmosphere contained within the recently timbered bathhouse felt suffocating as the pores on Wally skin opened then immediately filled with baked-on dirt.

"And how may I help you?" Ying Lee enquired of his scruffy customer.

"I'm not that bad, am I?"

"Excuse, please?"

"All right, you've had your joke."

Ying Lee acted surprised. "Mr. Wally, it's you," he felt the whiskers, "I never recognise you. Where is fat lazy dog?"

"Rooting around somewhere, he'll showup when done. Jeez'us, the place has changed." Many men sat awkwardly in small tubs scrubbing off their toil, Wong Foo had replaced the larger tubs with the cost effective option. "I see Wong Foo is expanding – shame the tubs aren't."

"You want large tub, you come." Ying Lee led Wally along a corridor then pointed to a sign on the door. "This room for Gentlemen only, I make exception for you, Mr. Wally."

A Chinese lad filled the tub with water as Wally stripped off his work clothes. "Wong Foo must be doing well; who's he been…"

Ying Lee interrupted. "I am most grateful for Wong Foo consideration," he then gestured to the lad.

"Yip Tung nephew of Wong Foo – now helps, we plenty busy."

Wally changed tack. "Yip Tung work hard, maybe open own bathhouse one day," he told the lad.

"I don't think so, mate. There are opportunities other than this," he replied with a broad Aussie accent."

"I look after Mr. Wally," Ying Lee informed him. Yip Tung left Wally with a bemused look on his face. "Him much trouble. Careful what you say in front of him; he got bigger ears than you." After much scrubbing, scissor work and cut-throat razor expertise from Ying Lee, Wally lay back in the tub with a hot towel on his face, listening to the last of what his reliable news source had to say. The conversation ended with the usual: "You towel yourself, I not your slave." The white scar welts were again visible with the dirt removed.

"Now I recognise you," Ying Lee teased. The dog showed up, sniffed out its master and scratched at the door. "Go away fat lazy dog, can't you read?" The ritualistic dressing of his customer took place as Wally stood before the cheval-mirror. "You right dandy man again," Ying Lee informed him, picking at the same loose thread.

Ying Lee received the usual payment and a generous tip. Wally stopped with his hand on the door handle. "And what does the wise man have to say today?"

Ying Lee pondered and then replied, "Generosity is also of mind."

Wally mulled it over. "Yours or Confucius?" he asked.

"Yours ... if you want, Mr. Wally."

He opened the door. "Go on then." The dog immediately jumped into the slurry at the bottom of the tub. Wally gave the dog a whistle as he walked down the corridor; the dog bounded down it following him. Ying Lee's colourful language trailed after the dog.

The aroma was overpowering; there was something special about Mrs. Foo's culinary expertise, a result that Wally couldn't accomplish when cooking roo stew. In front of the food tent, he stood watching as a syndicate's mine equipment lumbered south; the teamster's abusive language cussed the ears of his bullock team and all within hearing distance. A beast of burden felt the stinging lash of bullwhip on its hide; the other fifteen strained so they wouldn't. They bellowed loudly as the next threatening crack above their heads forewarned what would happen if the teamster spotted a loafer not pulling his weight. Wally then joined the queue of hungry diners as Mrs. Foo slopped the meal into their bowls. With no bowl or spoon, the deposit and hiring fee was, of course, extra. Wong Foo didn't miss a trick.

* * *

Dr. Tubber had arrived along with all the other enterprises flooding into Gunnadoo. Dr. Portious, the original practitioner, was now only capable of working as an undertaker. His drinking qualifications had secured the position; his first job had been to bury his alcoholic predecessor. Dr. Tubber's qualifications and ethics were a bonus for the community, albeit, he'd come out of retirement. Influenza having left him a widower, his marital status was much discussed among the older women.

Catherine sat in the doctor's waiting room looking out the window. She recognised the black pirate patch on the dog chasing a bitch and immediately began patting her chest. Approaching from the opposite side of the street, Wally wasn't far behind the frolicking animals. Catherine breathed deeply, placing a hand firmly on her chest as she turned in her seat. She readjusted her hat, picked up a two-week-old newspaper, waited … and waited. Realising he wasn't about to enter the practice, she stuck her head out the door and saw him about to enter Houten's.

Catherine returned to her seat and sat down. Picking up the newspaper, she paused and then threw it on the table, calling to the doctor as she hastily left, "I just remembered, I must see Madame Houten; bonjour Dr. Tubber." She returned just as quickly for her basket. "I will come back later."

Crouched behind a wagon having timber planks unloaded, Catherine observed Wally and Abe Houten talking outside the storefront. She readjusted her attire, placed a hand on her chest and looked skyward, *Holy Mother,* she thought, *it's now or never.* Without looking where she was going Catherine nearly walked into the lengths of planking carried on a labourer's shoulders.

"Watch out," the boss shouted.

"Pardon Monsieur," she replied. The progression of men delivering the timber blocked her path. Catherine ducked under the bouncing end of one length and marched forth. Wally and Houten were no longer there; Wally wasn't anywhere to be seen on the street. She pinched her cheeks and made an entrance into the hardware store.

"Bonjour, Ruby." Catherine greeted her in a louder than usual voice, her eyes not leaving Ruby's smiling face.

"Hello Luv." Noticing the red cheeks, Ruby stopped stocktaking and stated, "My, aren't you glowing. Is there something you're not telling me?"

"I feel wonderful. Spring is sprung, oui?"

"Alrighty," Ruby warily agreed, "if you say so."

She moved to the counter at the rear of the store with Catherine following. Their relationship had grown to where Ruby felt that she played the part of a confidante. Her booming hangover when they had first met assisted Catherine's change of nationality from Irish to French. Ruby accepted the transition without a second thought. "Now … what can I do for you today?"

Catherine hadn't planned on the visit and was stumped. She tried to look past Ruby's bulk, through an open door behind the counter into the small office and storeroom. Ruby's expression changed to that of intrigue. She held out her hand. "Your shopping list?"

"… my shopping list? My shopping list. I forgot it. Let me think, what do I require?" She wandered around casually, not seeing what she was looking at, searching for what hadn't been forgotten. Customers came and went. Catherine finally ended up in the medicinal section near the counter. She pretended to read labels on lotions, potions and elixirs.

"Can I get Mr. Houten to help you there, Luv?"

"No, I do not wish to disturb Mr. Houten's conversation," she replied craftily.

Ruby defended him. "I'm sure he is becoming senile – but he's not talking to himself yet."

Catherine raised her voice. "And how is your husband?"

"Mr. Houten is …" the voice interrupted, "… fit as a fiddle." Houten appeared in the doorway.

"And I hope he hasn't been up too no good." Ruby added.

"Please. Do not let me stop you from your conversation," Catherine stated innocently.

Ruby turned to him. "Who've you got in there with you?"

"Nobody."

"Are you sure?" She took a quick look and returned. "There's no one there," she told Catherine, "Are you feeling all right, Luv?"

"Pardon, but I thought …"

Ruby leant on the counter and interrogated her. "You thought what?"

Catherine could feel the rest of her face catching up with the pinched cheeks. She quickly passed the bottle clutched in her hands to Ruby. "I have found what I require. This will help my tummy upset."

"Are you sure you're all right, Luv?" Ruby held up the bottle and read aloud, "Dr. Winn's Equine Remedy – Guaranteed Cure for Colic and Flatulence.

I'm sure we have something else that will do the job and isn't so severe."

Embarrassment camouflaged confusion; Catherine felt the heat radiating from her blushing face. "I just remembered ... I have a doctor's appointment I must keep, bonjour Ruby."

Ruby waved the mixture in hand. "I hope it's nothing serious," she called to the exiting customer.

* * *

Bycroft sat behind a new cedar desk with his back to the window, twirling a cigar in one hand and a whiskey in the other. Wally sat opposite observing the man's ever-changing persona. Behind Bycroft's old desk sat his new accountant, Joseph Billings. Wally didn't receive an introduction and the accountant didn't lift his head once from the ledger in front of him.

"Sinking shafts, you're talking big money, it's a flaming big gamble," said Bycroft, "by my calculations we're ahead ... just."

Wally looked around the office at the comfortable setup. "You seem to be doing better than 'just'."

"Never put all your eggs in one basket, Sunshine, I told you that." Cigar ash fell on the desk. He paused and casually flicked it onto the floor. "I tell you what, I'll stick with you for a while longer," he leant back with his hands behind his head, "if the potential can be shown." Wally looked over Bycroft's shoulder and saw Catherine leave Houten's. Bycroft continued, "And it's got to be high grade. It's not worth the trouble of digging it out if it aint."

"Yeah," Wally replied, his mind now on other matters. "I'll get back to you."

"By the way, is your Neddy still alive?"

It was a well-known fact, except to Wally, that Bycroft had flogged the nag off to the saleyard for dog meat. There, the auctioneer had given the nag a belly full of dope to keep it alive until it was sold. Wally was the unfortunate sucker to buy it – a local bookie was giving odds on the nag's longevity.

"His name is Atlas and ..." Wally paused as Bycroft began choking on a lung full of cigar smoke.

"At – At ...," he tried to get the name out, laughing and gasping, his face turning red. "At ..." Bycroft thumped the desk until he caught his breath. He then thumped his chest and wiped tears from his eyes. "Damn. Don't do that again," he reprimanded Wally, "you'll kill me before Neddy."

Wally rose defiantly to his feet. "Atlas. And he's still kicking."

"Kicking eh, the bastard will be biting soon."

On the street, Wally casually looked for Catherine but could only see the dog. He gave it a whistle and headed in the direction of the bathhouse.

The consequence of a childhood illness had left Catherine with a weakened heart. The murmur would sometimes leave her breathless and a lethargic period would follow, but overall Dr. Tubber's check-up suggested her health was fine. Catherine now joined two other women in the doctor's waiting room. Shouting first alerted them to the fray outside. She did a double take, pulling a muscle in her neck as she looked out the window. The dog again caught her attention, this time fighting. Rolling beneath a hitching rail, the brawling canines panicked tethered horses. Pedestrians scattered in all directions as horses and hitching rail headed south towards High Street. Catherine rose to her feet as Wally came into view but quickly returned to her seat remembering the previous embarrassing incident at Houten's. As the hot flush rose she placed her hand on her chest, and then on her neck, massaging the pulled muscle. The doctor suggested liniment.

* * *

The dog stood bolt upright in the wagon barking commands at the approaching bullock team, the teamster matched the dog's hullabaloo with his swearing. Wally was on his way out of town, supposedly leaving quietly rather than risk antagonising the community any more.

As Catherine approached the commotion, her palpitations began, so too Wally's. Out the corner of his eye he saw the parasol open and begin twirling. Catherine tried to act nonchalantly and not crash into other pedestrians or poke out an eye with the whirling parasol while observing Wally. She wished him not see her observing him. Likewise, Wally acted irrationally too.

"Giddup Atlas," he shouted loudly, making sure Catherine would hear, look in his direction and see that he was paying her no attention."

Unwilling and now irate participants in the folly yelled in unison, "Watch out." as Wally nearly collided with a passing wagon. Catherine received the same warning when bumping into a hawker plying his wares on the sidewalk: merchandise toppled. Her embarrassment multiplied as contents from the wicker basket fell out when bending over to help retrieve the hawker's merchandise. A couple of bottles of disinfectant broke and personal hygiene items for the girls littered the footpath. Wally and Catherine each contained their humiliation by not daring to look in the other's direction.

* * *

A small tributary running behind the scrub reserve marked the rear boundary of the brothel. Aided by moonlight and a cloudless sky, an unfit Bycroft preceded along the well-trodden path, the trek was tiring, helped little by the large cigar and the constant drinking from his hip flask. Private stairs at the rear of the near-completed establishment, assuring anonymity, accessed Catherine's boudoir.

Each Wednesday she accepted the unsavoury rendezvous as an unavoidable chore. She stood on the small balcony observing the red glow of the cigar approaching. This evening, the chore was more difficult and she felt uneasy. Seeing Wally had raised suppressed feelings. The relevance of being 'a rich girl' seemed a high price to pay for the turmoil she experienced. Bycroft eventually joined her.

"How's my girl tonight?" he enquired.

"I am fine."

"You seem a little reserved. Are you sure?"

"Oui, I am sure," she responded lethargically.

"Then show me, I'm the one who did all the work getting here."

Catherine placed her arms around his neck and did as requested. Bycroft shuffled her straight to the dragon bed, as always. She'd learnt not to postpone the inevitability of the liaison. Besides, the lacklustre act never took long and it was then he unwittingly divulged snippets of information while bragging of his business acumen.

* * *

"Now, how do you feel?" he requested, lighting a cigar.

"Much better, merci. As usual, you were magnifique," she lied. "It is me. I need a holiday."

"Tell me about it." he cut in.

Catherine didn't have the chance to. Bycroft began relating the hardships endured with the people he had to deal with, Wally included. He always painted the bleakest of pictures.

"Whiskey?" she asked, at the first opportunity.

"Is the Pope Catholic?" he responded.

6 – Welcome to 1921

All that is seen may not be so -
when the game is not played by the rules.

Wally had sunk an exploratory shaft at Yakka Dakka. Above the shaft head, he had built a windlass to raise ore and mullock to the surface; this made life a little easier, although climbing down the ladder to fill the hungry bucket and back up to hand-wind the windlass was still demanding.

With a bridle in hand, Wally had chased the troublesome camel across the sand dunes of Esdud; he now chased a troublesome gold-seam underground with a pick in hand. When the ugly beast was cornered and all but bridled it would lash out and try to bite him – so too the cantankerous mine, alluring and wild with a tame-me-if-you-can attitude. Many of the corps caught 'the mange' from their camels, an exasperating itch followed. The mine resembled that festering irritation, which, likewise, couldn't be ignored.

With a routine and the reclusive lifestyle, days and months sped by. Wally looked forward to the big two-up game held annually on the banks of the Yapsly. He crossed the days off the calendar until December 31 was finally marked with a cross.

* * *

All residents of Gunnadoo were invited to attend a grand opening to celebrate the completion of the house of ill repute and New Year's Eve. At the imposing entrance, two large cedar doors with ornate gargoyle doorknockers stood open. Beside them stood Catherine, dressed in a white designer evening gown and long, matching gloves. Her hair was stylishly swept up and the single pearl earrings swung freely. From the choker necklace adorning her mannequin neck hung a golden dragon, various gemstones gripped in its claws. Catherine's emerald green eyes outshone the diamond lustre of the beast's eyes. "Entrée vous si'l vous plaît," she purred, with a breathy inflection on the 'play'.

A new bevy of beauties waited inside for introductions and then, like lambs to the slaughter, the patrons followed their escorts to the rooms of pleasure above. Curious townsfolk, there for a gander only, soon parted with their finances when introduced to Bycroft's rotgut whiskey. He had had it rebottled and labelled as authentic Scotch; the first couple of drinks were free, the following cost dearly.

A magnificent chandelier glittered above the tiled foyer, and an equally impressive polished cedar staircase rose to the many rooms of pleasure above. On the ground floor, twin doors either side of the staircase opened to reveal the drawing room styled in the indulgent Victorian influence. A fireplace and shiny brass fittings confirmed the former was yet to see a flame. Decorative figurines, vases and miscellaneous items cluttered the mantelpiece. A large mirror with ornate carved frame reflected light from a smaller chandelier hanging from the high ceiling. Velvet curtains fringed with bobbles hung heavily from window pelmets. Photographs littered the walls. Occasional tables and chairs draped with embroidered cushions and antimacassars added to the clutter. The wallpaper pattern appeared to ooze from the walls and continue into the carpet, sucking all those who trod upon it into euphoric claustrophobia.

From the balustrade above the staircase, Venus, the Goddess of love, observed patrons as they ascended to her world. Mrs. Chang joined Catherine who was standing beside the life-sized statue. The middle-aged widow had been with the establishment since its inception. She excelled at organising the kitchen, had risen through the ranks and was now indispensable as confidante and second in charge. Catherine was baffled as to how she managed to control the household staff and keep the girls in line without so much as a stern word.

"It has been a great success, oui?" Catherine confided.

Mrs. Chang nodded agreement. "It will soon be twelve o'clock."

"Merci, Madame Chang."

Catherine joined Ruby on the balcony. Below, on the lawns, revellers waited for the promised surprise. The atmosphere was that of a church fête, with groups of people mingling under lanterns strung in surrounding trees. Ruby slipped her arm through Catherine's. "Well, Luv, you certainly proved you can look after yourself." She waved to a face she recognised below. "I feel like royalty. Your castle is mighty impressive alrighty. And look at you; you *look* like right royalty, I reckon." Catherine smiled politely. "Are you feeling all right, Luv? You seem preoccupied."

"Just a little tired, it has been a big year," she replied. Her eyes surveyed the faces below.

"A little tired." exclaimed Ruby, "I wish I had half your get-up-and-go."

Catherine gave Ruby a cheeky smile. "Are you applying for a position?"

Ruby's tummy bounced as she laughed heartily. "There's enough of me for two positions. Oops. That statement could be…"

"Could be what?" Houten asked.

"Never you mind – Catherine and I was talk'n women's business." She turned to face him. "Where have you been anyway?"

Wong Foo's chattering preceded him. "This going to be plenty good," he informed all excitedly. "Much Chinese know-how presented for your delight."

"We certainly got the best seats in the house…" Ruby stopped, "What are you up to, Abe? Houten and Wong Foo were giggling between themselves. Any opposition they may have had in business hours wasn't being displayed as the countdown to midnight began.

Ruby took Abe in her arms as the sky lit up with fireworks supplied by Wong Foo Importers. Catherine stood alone watching the explosions and flashes pierce the night as oohs and aahs chorused in unison from the spellbound crowd.

Wong Foo manically clapped his hands, telling her, "Who knows, maybe it will catch on and I have monopoly on fireworks too."

Catherine's loneliness intensified as the strains of Auld Lang Syne heralded another year. Her lips moved but she choked on the words.

"Big finish," Ruby shouted, "…for the sake of Auld Lang Syne."

Houten and Wong Foo looked at each other quickly and then to the steeple of the garden pagoda. A Catherine wheel lit up and slowly increased intensity as multi-coloured sky rockets shot forth.

"That's a lovely surprise, Abe," Ruby hugged him, "why can't you…"

The exploding rockets cut short her compliment and sent the crowd scurrying for cover. The wheel abruptly ceased rotating and toppled over, dispersing the remaining projectiles all at once into the mêlée.

Wong Foo raised an eyebrow at Houten. "Gunpowder mixture is…" he paused. Another surprise began spurting orbs of colour from its strategically placed position atop a eucalypt. "…not quite right." The spectacular grew in intensity until it too self-destructed with a loud explosion and a flash. Silence followed as the stunned crowd edged forth to stare up at the burning phenomenon. Those of a religious persuasion fell to their knees and crossed themselves.

Catherine smiled at the irony.

* * *

All participants at the two-up game on the banks of the Yapsly stopped to watch the fireworks display over Gunnadoo. Wally watched silently as others drunkenly yelled salutations. A cold shiver ran down his back; the distant explosions and flashes of light conjured up the Beersheba barrage and preparations for the ensuing battle. An intense loneliness pervaded him. He was glad when the display finished and the game resumed, although within fifteen minutes the wad of notes he had won was again lost.

"Come on Dog, Lady-Luck isn't with us tonight." His thoughts immediately flashed back a year to the raid, to Catherine, and to the long walk back to Gunnadoo. He now accepted the hollow feeling as loneliness for the woman and yearned for the long walk again. "Come on, Dog, let's find Lady-Luck."

Unlike the previous year, wagons and sulkies were organised in neat lines for a quick get-away if required. Wally pulled up his wagon on leaving the cutting.

"How'd ya do?" enquired Kenny. He jumped down from his perch. A chair strapped in the branches made the position tolerable.

"Naw, I did the lot...should have stopped while I was ahead."

"If I had a quid for every time I've heard that said tonight ... "

"You'd be a rich man," added Wally.

"Until the miss'us took it off me." Kenny gave Atlas a scratch behind the ear. "Let me give you some advice, Wally."

Hearing the word 'advice' triggered what Ying Lee had previously advised – 'generosity of mind'. It now made sense to Wally. "Damn." he blurted out.

"Yer women. Damned if ya do, damned if ya don't." Kenny nonchalantly slapped Atlas on the neck and then rubbed the nag's chest cunningly giving it the once-over. "They'll send ya 'round the twist if ya let 'em."

"I'm a bloody fool," Wally thought but said aloud.

"We all are mate but that's what they do to us." Kenny casually slid a hand under the horse's belly. "First it's around the little finger and then it's around the bloody twist I tell ya." He listened to a rumbling in Atlas's digestive tract as would a plumber searching for a blocked drain. "Can't live with 'em and can't live without 'em." He waited for the flatulence that never came. "That's my advice for what it's worth."

Wally hadn't heard a word of Kenny's advice, only Ying Lee's words of wisdom. "Wise words indeed," he muttered.

"No problems…glad I could help – Happy New Year Wally."

"Yeah, Happy New Year. Giddup Atlas." Wally's heart rate picked up at the thought of seeing Catherine. He encouraged Atlas to pick up speed with a slap of the reins on the rump. Atlas lifted his head only: not the speed.

The celebrations were still in full swing as Wally pulled up at the box hedge. He watched as folk, some in anticipation of good times ahead, entered for an entertaining frolic while others drunkenly exited with a belly full of repercussions. He then thought twice about leaving the rig where an opportunist too lazy to walk could pinch it, and instead wisely continued to the bathhouse. Ying Lee was sitting out the front of his tent watching the passing clusters of inebriated pedestrians amble along High Street, some leaving Chinatown, others heading towards it.

Wally climbed down from the rig. "How 'bout putting your watching skills to good use and keeping an eye on these two?"

"I full-time babysitter," he gestured to the tent, "why not another two." He stood up and stretched. "Ying Lee soon grow feathers like Emu."

"Well, don't go getting 'em ruffled...you just sit there and keep the eggs warm."

Wally joined the boisterous crowds on the street heading south.

Well, it's now or never, he told himself, gathering up the courage. He then joined a group of men at the box hedge gate so he wouldn't feel isolated when entering.

Wally found an out-of-the-way corner in the crowded drawing room and surveyed the scene while looking for Catherine. Revellers sang bawdy songs at the tops of their voices around a red-faced musician; with sweat pouring from under a bowler hat, he thumped an upright piano. As soon as his glass was empty, patrons refilled it; the room was stifling. Wally felt a hand on his shoulder. "Are you looking for a girl?" The young woman looked as though she was ready for bed – to sleep.

"Naw, I'm looking for a special lady...Lady-Luck."

"You mean Lucy." She perused the room, spotted Lucy and called her. Lucy pirouetted through bodies with form and grace. She then did a high kick in front of Wally, coming to rest with her ankle on his shoulder. Her big toe rubbed his big ear.

"You are not Lady-Luck, I'm afraid," Wally whispered in her ear.

"And you are not a lucky man," she replied.

He watched as she moved off to another client, whispered in his ear and left with him, laughing. After ten minutes of discomfort, Wally considered that it might have been a bad idea. He began moving toward the foyer and then caught sight of Catherine as she entered the drawing room. The congenial host moved through the crowd making conversation; Wally was cornered, he looked for another way out – there was none. The thumping piano accompanied the thumping in his chest. His legs were like jelly, his mouth dry, his nerves contorted. It was the same sensation, the same adrenaline surge, as marching into battle. When the barrage stopped and the whistle blew, soldiers left the safety of the trench and entered no-man's land; Wally was there now.

Catherine was all but upon him when Wong Foo stopped her. They exchanged words and left the drawing room. Wally pushed his way through the crowd to see Catherine and Wong Foo climbing the staircase together. The pain now was worse than that inflicted by battle. He departed the establishment cursing Catherine, Wong Foo and 1921.

* * *

"I want my money back," the irate customer complained to Catherine. In the bed next to him, the young woman lay fast asleep snoring. Wong Foo politely entered the heated discussion.

"Could it be embarrassed client may be in need of an aphrodisiac? If so," he lectured the quarrelsome man, "ginseng should be consumed, woman never fall asleep in your presence again." Once he'd registered the statement, he took it as an insult but before he could act upon it, Catherine pacified the man.

"I suspect Monsieur is too virile and you already give too much pleasure. You tire her out, oui? Could this not be?"

Lucy and a couple of other girls and their clients now stood at the end of the bed waiting to hear the answer.

"Yeah well, maybe... all right," he lied, while quickly slipping on his trousers.

"I'll get you another girl to wear out," Catherine assured him.

As the sun rose, Catherine, Mrs. Chang and some of the girls raised their coffee mugs, toasted the start of another year and then retired for a well-earned rest.

* * *

A couple of weeks later, Catherine, Wong Foo and invited guests stood on the balcony watching brilliant fireworks explode over the Chinatown shanties. The sky lit up once again as the Chinese New Year celebrations commenced.

"We Chinese have much to crow about," Wong Foo informed Catherine, "This year – year of rooster."

Catherine saw the humour and took his arm. "I have a surprise for you, come."

She walked him along the long passageway, at the end of which were her private quarters. With each step taken, his heart rate increased. They stopped at her door.

"Close your eyes and don't open them." Wong Foo heard the door open and Catherine entered the room and began what sounded like bouncing on the bed. His heart raced, pumping blood to all extremities of his body. "Now you can open them – Happy New Year." It wasn't the dragon bed she was lying upon but an Edwardian four-poster. The dragon bed leant against the wall stacked and ready for return to Wong Foo.

He wiped tears from his eyes. "I have a confession to make." Catherine crawled down to the end of the bed and knelt before him, waiting for it. Instead of expressing his lewd fantasy, he thought better of it and made another confession. "Mrs. Foo not told of bad karma bed. I told her bed sent back to China to be blessed by Shaolin priest so that we may have another child."

"So what is the problem?"

"She not believe eight lucky number for Chinese … she says if bed comes back…she will go."

Catherine threw herself back on the lush quilt. "I love my new bed."

Wong Foo stood beside his treasured possession. "I too love my dragon bed."

"It is yours," she told him.

"And what am I to offer you in return for such a generous undertaking?"

"I have not yet decided," she said playfully, "I'll let you know when the time comes."

* * *

In February, Wally discovered a small pocket of reef gold. Bycroft begrudgingly assigned him three workers to help dig a tunnel off the main shaft and continue with the search. Four months later, as winter closed in, only breakeven results showed for their efforts. Wally was on Bycroft's case, calling in promises made. He reckoned if the Yakka Dakka gold mine was to show results, investment capital for heavy machinery was required, as were more labourers.

Once work on the building of the pubs was completed, many of the men hired for the job then chose to try their hand at prospecting their own claims, creating a labour shortage. Bycroft managed to find labourers to clear land and tradesmen to begin building him another private dwelling out of town, but apparently there were none available to work the mine. The amicable partnership showed signs of tension. Bycroft's other wheelings and dealings were paying off handsomely and were less troublesome. He was making a financial killing as licensee of the Gunnadoo Arms and the Plough Inn. That carried favour with the masses and he was being touted as the town's founding father.

At daybreak, Wally left the three workers and headed to Gunnadoo with the dog sitting next to him on the sulky seat. "Giddup there, Buttercup," he told the spirited mare. "This is a bit better than Atlas, eh," he then told the dog. Unexpectedly, the previous month, Bycroft had surprised him with a new sulky and the Bay mare for his birthday. Atlas now spent his days plodding back and forth in a circle pulling a whim, which raised and lowered the larger ore bucket he now used.

The pale-faced accountant didn't look up as the doorbell rang. Billings pushed his spectacles onto his nose and kept writing. Abundant dandruff covered his shoulders and the accounts journal he was scrutinising. It reminded Wally of the heavy dew he'd just travelled through; the reception was just as cold. The mongrel immediately limped to the warmth of the potbelly stove and sat in front it.

"Where is he?" Wally queried.

"Bycroft Station."

"Where are the men I was promised last week?"

The bookworm stopped writing and scratched his head with the pencil, then proceeded to tally figures again. Wally didn't receive an answer and was left looking at the falling flakes.

"When are you expecting him back?"

The antagonist didn't look up. "I'm his accountant, not his social secretary."

Uncharacteristically, Wally slammed his hand down on the desk. "You may be good with numbers but your personality needs tidying up."

The accountant raised his head to stare contemptuously then pushed the spectacles onto his nose again and returned to the figures. Wally scratched his head and rubbed the burning sensation in his belly.

"Come on, Dog. There are a few things we need to sort out."

The bell rang and the door slammed. He lifted the mongrel up and sat him on the sulky seat, then rubbed his hind leg. "Arthritis, me old mate."

Houten swept the newly built wooden sidewalk that ran the length of the general store frontage; it was more a place for displaying merchandise than for pedestrians. "G'day, Wally," he shouted, spotting him.

"Ah. Just the man I want to see. Stay," he told the dog.

Each nook and cranny inside the general store was overflowing with supplies. Stock filled the rows of shelves, which rose to meet the paraphernalia hung from ceiling hooks. Wally followed Houten through the maze.

"It's not the end of the month. You're a week early," he stated.

"By the time I get to the counter to purchase what I want, I won't be," Wally wisecracked. Houten slid under the counter to reappear on the other side.

"Now, what can I do for you?"

"A bottle of liniment and a couple of bottles of that snake oil you call belly medicine...and before you ask if I'm gonna drink the liniment too, mind your own business."

"It wouldn't surprise me what anyone drank these days. I'll get it – a new shipment just came in." He went out to the storeroom.

From within the warren Catherine appeared, greeting Wally from behind by poking him in the back with her parasol, "Bonjour Monsieur Beaumont."

"Jeez'us." he yelped and turned to face her. "You near scared the life out of me."

"Drinking that mixture may well do the same." Sixteen months had passed since their first introduction; the chemistry was still there, suppressed but ready to react. "Are you not happy to see me, oui?" Catherine's words didn't register. Wally, caught unprepared for the encounter, was shell-shocked, tongue-tied and trying to stabilise his wild emotions.

Houten returned with the elixir. "Good morning Catherine," he greeted her.

"Bonjour. Is that good for a surly liver also?" she enquired.

"Dr. Lovett's Cure-All is good for everything; it's one of my best selling lines. Nine out of ten doctors recommend..." Catherine cut short the shopkeeper's sales pitch.

"... a home cooked meal. When was the last time you had one?"

"Last night," he answered obligingly, "Ruby's cooking is ..."

"Not you. Here is my shopping order, please give it to Ruby." She handed it to Houten, dismissing him, and turning to Wally. "Well, that's what I recommend. Now please walk moi to the door like a gentleman." Before Wally knew what was happening, an arm slipped through his and he was ushered from the store into the warm sunshine.

"When can I expect you then?"

"I'll have to have a bath …"

"Merci …"

"I wasn't planning on staying in town tonight…"

"Then luncheon it will be." She refused to let the opportunity pass by. "Shall I expect you at, say, midday, oui?"

"Yes, that'll be great." Wally then immediately toned down his enthusiasm. "Er, fine I guess."

"Do not look so worried…I have forgiven you."

It wasn't worry; it was confusion. Wally returned into the store punch-drunk and with a bad case of belly-burn. Catherine headed south pleased as punch at the way she'd handled the chance meeting.

The sulky skipped along High Street. Wally smiled to himself as pedestrians awkwardly moved between dirt and wooden sidewalk, and then precariously past the shopkeepers standing like vultures in doorways ready to lunge at the first hint of interest in their wares. He felt on top of the world after the conversation with Catherine and a couple of swigs of Dr. Lovett's Cure-All. Stopping at the tent next to the bathhouse Wally yelled, "Hey Ying Lee, wake up."

"Me awake." The tent flap swung back and five barefooted kids bolted from their confines. "Much work done already – I no time to sleep."

"Yeah, I can see that," said Wally, referring to the kids, as he rubbed the dog's muscle with the liniment.

"Book me in for the works; I'll be back at eleven."

"The works? Must be plenty special?"

"Mind your own business." Wally kept rubbing the dog's muscle.

"Dog has sore leg?" Ying Lee enquired.

"Naw, I got a cramp in my thumb."

The patient raised its head and moaned in ecstasy. Wally took another swig of the snake oil mixture, grimacing. Ying Lee noticed but said nothing.

The sulky skipped along the track heading to Bycroft's property a couple miles northwest of the township. "I don't know if it's the snake oil or the sprung seat but me guts feel better; how about you?" he asked Dog. Sitting upright the dog lifted its head high and sniffed at the air; they both enjoyed the wind in their faces. Wally took deep breaths as if trying to cool his hot belly. The dog took a couple of swipes at him with a sloppy tongue. "Better than walking, eh." The chilly morning was now beginning to warm up.

Bycroft stood with hands on hips. Wearing moleskin-riding britches, knee-high boots and a squatter's hat, he surveyed the circular drive at the front of the uncompleted homestead. The scene was a hive of activity as workers finished laying four hardwood logs; they were now impressive steps leading up to the veranda that ran around the permitter of the building. The 'coo-wee' called by

Wally alerted Bycroft to the visitor's arrival and he turned to watch the horse's approach.

"Welcome, welcome." He held both arms high. "Well...what do think?" The house was grandiose compared to Wally's bark hut accommodation at the claim. "Come in. I'll show you around."

"Jeez'us, a bloke could get lost in there," said Wally, lifting down the dog.

"Come here," requested Bycroft, shaking his hand. "We don't get to see each other enough these days. You still like the birthday present, don't you?" Bycroft had acquired the horse and rig by dubious means at a fortunate time for both him and Wally. He slapped the horse's rump.

"Sure. I'm still in shock, so is Atlas," said Wally.

"Yep. That nag sure fooled everyone. Eh, the mongrel looks like he's just about had it though."

"He's all right; it's just a bit of arthritis. Eh, old fella."

"Any problems with the rig, you let me know. Henderson." yelled Bycroft. A young aboriginal kid came running. "Look after Mr. Beaumont's rig."

"It's a good-looking rig, boss."

"It certainly is," he snapped, "take care of it or you'll get a good flogging."

"Yes boss."

"That bugger is as lazy as they come. I got to keep my eye on him all the time." Bycroft caught sight of two others of his indigenous workforce leaning on a stack of timber having a smoke. "Hey. You blokes, you can smoke and stack at the same time, can't you?" He returned his attention to Wally. "It's hard to find good help these days."

"Tell me about it," Wally replied.

Bycroft walked his guest through mostly empty rooms bragging that he would soon fill them with the comforts he deserved. His private quarters were already crammed with the trappings his wealth afforded him. Good taste couldn't be purchased; antiques could. The Indian carpets, Chinese paintings and Greek urns clashed, as did most of the furnishings. "I've kept the best for last," he said, opening the double doors to the study. "And this is my office, where all the money is counted. Pour yourself a whiskey and make yourself at home. I need to give some instructions, I won't be long." He left by the French doors which opened onto the front veranda.

Wally took a swig of the elixir and walked to the open doors, he stood observing the circular driveway and beyond. Shouting and boots upon timber flooring heralded Bycroft's return and Wally moved inside to sit on the leather lounge. The vast library of books caught his attention, as did another mahogany desk; a candlestick telephone sat patiently on it.

"Tonight. No excuses," Bycroft shouted, entering the study. "That's all I bloody get: excuses." He poured himself a whiskey and noticed what he interpreted as Wally's admiration for the telephone.

"She's a beauty, eh? I picked it up for a song," he bragged.

"Does it work?" Wally enquired.

"The telephone cables have to be strung first but progress is on the way and I'll be first in line when it arrives."

"Naw, I meant the desk, not the telephone."

"Always the joker," Bycroft retorted, "let's see if it does." He sat behind it.

The financial returns from the partnership hadn't been adding up to what Bycroft believed they should have been. Little profit was being shown from the Yakka Dakka claim after expenses were deducted; either the commodity was fast running out, or Wally was creaming off the top. The idea of paying men to dig gold out of the ground without any checks or balances to make sure they weren't filling their pockets was absurd. The promises to Wally were a stalling tactic until he could make a decision as to how he could make a profit from the mine; it was now becoming a liability.

Bycroft ran his forefinger along the polished timber and positioned himself for Wally's challenge. "Business is all about timing Wally, it's not just about who or what is known, it's getting the job done; that's the priority, this we both agree. How it is achieved I believe to be inconsequential as long as it is; this, we seem have some disagreement on."

Wally was straightforward. "Many of your actions leave me wondering."

"Such as?"

"For a start I don't believe in handing out floggings."

Bycroft's defence was to attack. "Sometimes it's necessary. You're too soft, Wally; you tend to let people walk all over you. I always put in a good word

110

for you and you're welcome to join my colleagues and I at our social events. You shouldn't keep so much to yourself. You live like a hermit."

"I don't feel comfortable with your friends."

"Wally, you and I, we're not just friends – we're mates. We each possess certain talents the other doesn't; that's what makes this partnership work. We've got to look after each other. There are plenty of bastards out there who'd soon bring all this down on our heads if we let them." The two men stared at each other then Wally smiled. Bycroft showed his tobacco-stained teeth in a manner he believed was smiling. He stood up and raised the near empty glass. "We'll show the bastards, won't we?" Moving to the French doors, he began shouting, "Henderson. Henderson."

Wally raised the snake oil, "…or die trying."

"What?"

"Or die trying," he repeated.

"Yes or die trying, I like that. Now about those men, its been taken care of; you'll have them within a couple days. Trust me on this."

"Yes boss?" Henderson called from outside.

Bycroft gulped down the last of the whiskey and walked out onto the veranda. "Mr. Beaumont is leaving, get his rig."

"Yes boss."

Wally joined Bycroft on the veranda as workers laid the shingle roof above.

"Another couple of weeks and you can have these blokes too. Just look at that view," Bycroft encouraged, "twenty acres of front yard and six hundred out back." Still under construction also, the stables were but a framed structure with corrugated roof. "One day I'll have a Melbourne Cup winner stabled down there."

As they strolled along the veranda towards the front steps, they could see Henderson leading the mare and rig up to the house. "Yes sir. That's a good looking rig, all right," Bycroft enthused, reminding Wally once again who had given it to him.

"Watch out." screamed a voice from above.

Wally received a shove from Bycroft as a heavy bucket of roofing nails crashed to where he'd been standing. The dog and Wally both yelped as the shrapnel flew in all directions.

"Jeez'us, that was close." Wally rubbed his calf muscles.

"You bloody moron," reprimanded Bycroft. The culprit perched awkwardly above. "You nearly killed Mr. Beaumont. Get out of here – you're fired."

"It was an accident," Wally maintained, "besides, we need the workers. I'm all right – scared shit out of the dog though."

"I only have one partner and I don't want to lose him. You," he called to the culprit above, "what's your name?"

"Robinson."

"You now work for Mr. Beaumont. Get your swag together and be at the Yakka Dakka claim by this evening."

Wally jumped into the rig; the dog sat looking. Bycroft moved as if to lift him; the mongrel snarled.

"I'll get him," said Wally, "he's a bit touchy about that hind leg."

Bycroft stood watching the sulky disappear down the long drive. "Anything you need just let me know," he shouted.

"You okay, boss?" the careless roofer asked.

He stared straight ahead, "Foresight, Robinson."

"What?"

He then tapped his riding boots. The only marks on the new leather were from the nail shrapnel. "Have you got what you need?"

"A bag full of 'em."

"You know what to do then, get going." Bycroft's mouth turned up at the corners.

* * *

Wally could feel the hot water penetrating deeply into his sore joints; the superficial shrapnel wounds below the knees stung.

"Jeez'us," he yelled as the bucket of cold water was poured over him, "I was expecting to be scalded, not frozen."

"Always expect the unexpected."

"Is that Confucius or Ying Lee?"

"Wife of Ying Lee. You scrub yourself, I not your slave, more important things to do."

Wally lay back in the tub watching Ying Lee. He took a book the size of a cigar box from his personal belongings and placed it on the table. Then to Wally's surprise, Ying Lee, washed his hands. For a man who had his hands in water all day it seemed a strange thing to do.

"Jeez'us. That must be a pretty special book."

"Man with big ears, still not open eyes. Expect unexpected."

He opened the book and removed a leather satchel from within, placing it on top of the closed book. The Chinaman bowed his head and placed his palms upon the satchel. "Ah chow wee coo, ah chow wee coo," he began. Opening the satchel and taking out a candle he then lit it and concentrated on the flame. "Ah chow wee coo, ah chow wee coo." He ordered the dog to jump up on the table. Disobediently, it sat there looking.

"Arthritis, he's getting old," Wally informed him.

"Dog not old, Ying Lee old." He picked the dog up and laid him on the table then commenced to stick in the acupuncture needles. Wally was fascinated.

"I've heard about that kind of thing; never seen it done though."

"This very old medicine. Hey." he paused to observe Wally, "you concentrate on what you do, not Ying Lee."

Wally soaped up.

"Me get more soap for big ears if needed."

The dog gave a small yelp.

"You keep an eye what *you're* do'n, not Mr. Wally," Wally mimicked.

"Ying Lee have two eyes, he keep one eye out for best tipping customer also."

"What makes you think I need it? I'm experienced."

"I more experienced."

"You reckon?"

"Ying Lee have five children. How many you have?"

Wally's head disappeared under the water; he had no answer for that one. The dog, prodded and poked until the practitioner was satisfied and the candle blown out, listened to the Mandarin chatter as it lay with the one eye opening intermittently.

"I'm through here."

"You dry yourself…"

"… I not your slave," Wally interrupted, "I know."

"Mr. Wally is quick learner – sometimes. I get suit."

Wally wrapped himself in the towel and moved to the table to study the dog. It lay there resembling a pincushion with a look of ecstasy on its face.

"Feels a bit of all right, does it?" He picked up a needle and lightly stabbed at the end of his calloused finger. "It doesn't feel all that sharp."

"Hey." Ying Lee shouted.

Wally jumped. "Ouch."

"Man with big ears also have sticky nose."

"Man with sticky nose now have sore finger. I thought you said you'd keep an eye out for me?"

"Ying Lee just done that."

"How?"

"Maybe finger now too sore to put where you shouldn't." He handed Wally the suit and asked, "Who the lady?"

"Mind your own business."

"I am. Mr. Wally good customer. Ah chow wee coo, ah chow wee coo." He began chanting again, removing the acupuncture needles from the dog as

115

Wally dressed. Wally then stood before the cheval mirror as Ying Lee played his part in the ritual of coat brushing and picking at non-existent loose threads.

"Come on, old boy." Wally went to pick up the dog from the table.

"He do it himself. Get off table, fat lazy dog," Ying Lee demanded.

Without a whimper, the dog bounded to the floor, its arse violently shaken side to side by the wagging tail.

"Jeez'us," said Wally rubbing his belly, "does that work on humans?"

"Acupuncture work on all God's creatures."

"That's for the usual," Wally told Ying Lee, placing a shilling in his hand, "and here's another for the pin sticking and chanting."

"Mr. Wally is most generous."

"Go on, outside Dog." The dog left, followed by Wally and Ying Lee. It jumped up onto the sulky seat and sat waiting. Wally climbed in and grabbed the reins. Ying Lee rubbed the mare's withers.

"Ah chow wee coo, ah chow wee coo," he began.

"Wally paused and pondered. "You're a good man, Ying Lee. Is that a Buddhist chant?"

"Not chant, kid nursery rhyme, it drive me stupid; can't get out of head."

The men sized each other up with a wary glance.

Wally winked. "I don't know whether to believe you or not. You're gett'n pretty good at pull'n a bloke's leg."

Ying Lee's ambiguous smile revealed nothing.

$$* * *$$

The heavy dew and warm sun encouraged the box hedge; it thrived under the winter conditions and Chung Dow's maintenance.

"Whoa." Wally gave the dog a head scratch and told it to stay. He climbed down, tied the mare to the hitching post and produced a feedbag from under the seat. The mare received a good nuzzle scratching, then the feedbag.

"And if you behave yourself you might get a doggy bag," he told the dog.

"Bonjour." Catherine stood with picnic basket in hand. Her appearance was that of a Southern Belle.

"Jeez'us, you scared the living daylights out of me."

"I hope there is plenty left in *this* horse." She smiled, remembering Lightning.

"What?" It went over his head.

The straw sunbonnet with what seemed like yards of white mesh netting wrapped around it amused Wally; it reminded him of the protection an apiarist would wear. The blue ribbon meeting in a bow under her chin and falling into her small cleavage was breathtaking. He succeeded in not being caught looking.

"I am wearing new shoes...he is not called Lightning, oui?"

"He is a she." Wally now cottoned on. "This is Buttercup."

"Buttercup? How quaint. I thought we might have a picnic; it is such a lovely day. Do you mind?"

117

"I know a good place," he said, removing the feedbag. "In the back, Dog."

Wally took the basket from her and placed it and the horse's feedbag in the small tray of the sulky at the rear. Catherine then sat next him under a parasol – her perfume was intoxicating. The bouncing motion of the sprung seat wasn't as acute with the extra weight. The dog stood, adding his weight with both paws on the back of the seat, his head stuck annoyingly between them. The hustle and bustle of High Street diminished as they reached the track that ran beside the Yapsly. There was no conversation until instigated by Catherine. She had observed that although Wally was wearing his good suit, he was also wearing his work boots.

"I hope your footwear is not a premonition."

"What?" It went over his head again.

"Never mind." It was as though the previous sixteen months had never existed. "I do love closing my eyes and just listening."

"Yeah, so do I," replied Wally, and did so.

She gave a shriek and grabbed his sleeve. "Open your eyes."

He laughed. "Buttercup's got two eyes; she knows what she's doing."

Catherine looked directly into his eyes when they opened. Embarrassed, he quickly shut them again.

"What do you feel, what do you hear?" she enquired. At that most inopportune time the mare's flatulence broke the silence; they began laughing.

Wally replied dryly. "Well. That broke the ice." Catherine's arm slipped through his. He blushed. "I don't know how I should address you?"

Her parasol twirled. "My name is Catherine. That is a good start. And you will be Wally again." She looked at him questioningly. "Oui?"

On both sides of the riverbank miners panned. Catherine smiled and waved to the men; in return, they gestured, whistled and shouted their approval – she was a pleasant distraction to the backbreaking toil. Wally chose a secluded tributary well away from the prospectors.

"Whoa. Buttercup. What do you reckon?" he asked.

White water babbled continuously as it tumbled over a picturesque waterfall. By the side of the stream, lush willows arched, drinking thirstily, long manes dragging in the fast-moving current.

"It is wonderful, très bon," she exclaimed, removing her shoes and jumping from the sulky; abrasive sand granules massaged between her toes. "I never knew this place existed."

"Jeez'us, you should get out more." He removed his suit coat and rolled up his sleeves.

Released from her harness and leg roped, the mare contentedly grazed as Wally filled the billy and then gathered firewood. *All right Wally,* he told himself, *don't cock anything up.* "Go on. Get the bunny," he shouted, throwing a rock into the bush for the dog to chase. *Just be yourself.*

Catherine laid out the blanket and placed cold meats, salads and dessert delicacies upon it as though creating a floral arrangement. *Stop fussing, act naturally, don't be a smart-aleck,* she told herself, and pretended to be interested in the polished pebbles she collected at the rivers edge. Wally never came near her and she returned to unload the trophies. *That will give us something to talk about,* she complimented herself, hiding them under the blanket. She then sat tapping her fingers, watching the antics of master and dog still frolicking. *Come on, come on.*

Wally finally returned laden with enough wood to build a bonfire.

"That is a lot of wood to boil water is it not, oui?" she questioned.

He stopped in his tracks red-faced, unable to hide behind the load of wood. "Er, ah…" Embarrassed, Wally rid himself of the load and blurted a plausible explanation, "I usually keep a supply here."

"So, this is where you bring all your lady friends?" Catherine bit her tongue immediately and busied herself in non-existent duties.

Wally was in no-man's land and prepared the campfire. *Go on, tell her you do,* coached the voice in his head. The laughing of an unseen Kookaburra parodied the awkward silence as he put match to kindling. *Now wander over and lie down…sit down,* Wally corrected himself, *and make conversation.*

"Jeez'us." Sitting on the egg-sized rock was like getting a kick in the arse with a work boot. Wally lifted himself off it, only to plunge his hand in the beetroot bowl. The sponge cake soaked up most of the juice and the rug the rest.

"Sorry, I'm making a right mess of this."

"Relax. I'm going to eat a sandwich, not you." She reeled at what she had just said and hastily held out the plate of trimmed sandwiches. "Bon appétit."

She doted on him, enjoying the role of mother. His unassuming persona and embarrassment at the fussing attracted her. She stole glances at him when he wasn't looking. Throughout the meal, Catherine toyed with Wally's emotions, unable to help herself when he gave an impromptu lecture on the rocks she'd collected. Her wicked sense of humour made him blush many times. She observed the perspiration on Wally's forehead and his shirt as it changed colour, soaking up his copious sweat.

He wiped his brow and began swaying. "Must be too much good cooking, I'm not used to it." He tried to get up and collapsed, falling into the food laid out on the blanket. "Jeez'us."

"Wally." Catherine placed her hand on his chest. "Sacré bleu, you are burning up."

Cursing non-stop while half-running and half-tripping over layers of petticoats, Catherine slipped one off and dunked it in the cold water. She gasped at the shrapnel welts when unbuttoning Wally's shirt to wipe perspiration from his body. The sodden petticoat brought him relief.

"I'm all right," he mumbled. The dog crawled onto the blanket and began licking sponge cake from his master's face.

"You are not all right," she replied, pulling him up by the shirt to a sitting position. "Can you make it to the sulky?"

"Of course," he replied optimistically. Wally stood, swaying. Catherine pulled his arm across her shoulders and gingerly moved towards the sulky. Sitting on the end of the tray he declared, "I'm all right now." She let go of his shirt and he fell backwards into the small tray with a thud.

"Holy Mother."

There was only enough room for his torso and his legs dangled freely. Picking up the four corners of the picnic blanket, Catherine threw it and the messy contents within into the back of the sulky. She extinguished the campfire by dropping the boiling billy into it, burning her fingers in the process on the hot handle. "And you be getting in the back too," Catherine commanded the dog. She placed one foot on the sulky preparing to climb in and then froze, "Holy Mother." The mare was still grazing contentedly. *Think, think,* she told herself, "yes." she shouted aloud.

Catherine opened the blanket and retrieved a part of the soggy sponge cake; the cream filling soothed her burnt fingers.

Wally grabbed her arm and lifted his head. "Ying Lee – bathhouse," he panted, and then passed out. Thud.

"I hope he has a hard head," she told the dog, not thinking to place the blanket under it.

Holding out a handful of the soggy treat, Catherine edged closer to the mare until plucking up the courage and taking hold of the bridle. "Your eating habits are deplorable," she reprimanded the horse as it made a dog's breakfast of the treat. She slowly led the mare to the rig, "It's just you and me, Buttercup, us girls, now help me out here." After a couple of attempts, the mare was in position and

Catherine lifted the sulky shafts. She buckled, unbuckled, and re-buckled the harness rigging, in as many configurations as she could figure out but there always seemed to be a leather strap or two askew.

"And I whined about corsets and petticoats," she complained. "What we girls go through, eh Buttercup." The mare stood quietly looking ahead while the task was completed. The dog stood on rear legs peering over the sulky seat, gripping it with front paws; he was ready for the wind in his face. Catherine climbed in and apprehensively lifted the reins.

"I be ready now. Go Buttercup, go." The mare didn't move. Catherine lightly slapped the reins on its rump. "Are you deaf? Go on, move."

It looked around at her then straight ahead but didn't move. The dog barked as if commanding it to get a move-on also, Catherine was getting cranky. She got down and checked the harness again until satisfied, then climbed back up, this time ripping her dress in the process. "Mother of Mercy," she pleaded, "be moving Buttercup or I'll shoot her meself." The dog barked and Catherine cursed again, "Giddup, you banshee."

The sulky lurched forward then stopped as though the mare had taken offence. It whinnied and shook its mane. "This be your last chance, Buttercup." She climbed down and began repeating the harnessing procedure, her burnt fingers throbbing.

Wally began murmuring deliriously. The June sun was abnormally hot and Catherine's demure appearance was suffering, flowing locks resembling the drooping willow branches as perspiration dripped from her forehead. She splashed handfuls of water over herself, dunked the petticoat in the Yapsly again and then returning bedraggled, replaced it on Wally's chest. She retrieved the sunbonnet from the blanket, oblivious to the food scraps adorning it and securely tied the beetroot stained ribbon under her chin. Hurriedly grabbing another handful of mushy inducement, she approached the mare in a conciliatory manner and gave her a cautious pat on the neck.

"I be sorry for yelling at you. I get it from me Granny Dunn, she had a temper too; she taught me how to cuss she did." The agitated mare champ on the bit and stamped a hoof, Catherine stumbled and fell backwards, "Don't you be gett'n cantankerous with me you ungrateful bag of..." The abuse stopped as she sat looking at the leg roping. "Ah, you'd be a sweetie you would Buttercup, that is what you were trying to tell me wasn't it." Catherine fought with the granny knot and the mare, as it grabbed at the smorgasbord laid out on the sunbonnet.

Without a word being uttered, the reins immediately lifted and the mare edged forward onto the bush track and began leisurely strolling back to town. Catherine crossed herself and raised her head. "I be hoping Buttercup's eyesight be better than her eating manners and her heart be stronger than Lightning's, Amen." She checked the ribbon tied under her chin, pulled down on the straw brim and yelled, "Giddup."

As if leaving the starter's gate, the mare immediately threw back her ears and took off, mane flying. Thrust back into the sulky seat, Catherine held the reins in one hand and the bonnet with the other.

Wide-eyed with terror and clasping the straw brim to her pounding heart she peered through the torn hole in the crown, mesh and lace trimmings trailing, with the dog snapping at various delicacies still caught in the mesh. Unbeknown to Wally he was receiving a good bruising bouncing around in the rear tray.

McSloy leaned on his shovel noting the dust clouds billowing. "Crikey, will ya take a look at that. Someone's in a hurry."

"Looks like she's running late for her own wedding," suggested Bedson.

"She's a bloody good horsewoman the way she's handling that rig…look at her go."

Bedson removed his hat and wiped his face, "Wouldn't mind giving her a go myself."

"You and half the town…but ya too late, she retired since becoming the Madame."

"Did you …?"

"Naw, I was too late too," he sighed, "… couldn't afford the likes of her anyway."

"Who's that in the back?"

"Dunno, whoever it is he can't hold his grog."

"Or she wore him out."

As the bush track became High Street south, the mare broke from her full stride to a trot; the yapping dog drew attention to the folly. Passing the house of ill repute, Catherine modestly waved to some of the girls partaking in tea on the balcony. They stared in astonishment at her appearance and the man passed out in the back of the sulky. They said nothing but thought much.

As Catherine had previously noted when meeting her new girls from Bastock's coach, she mimicked the driver's action. Planting her bare feet on the sulky floor, she raised herself out of the seat by pulling on the reins. "Whoa." she screeched, in a most unladylike manner as the sulky passed the bathhouse. The mare nearly had her head ripped off.

Ying Lee recognised the dog's barking and appeared from his tent expecting Wally. He stopped in his tracks, recognising Catherine, although they had never been formally introduced.

"What you do to Mr. Wally?" he enquired.

"What are you suggesting Mademoiselle Catherine did?" She struggled down from the rig, legs still shaking from the harrowing experience. "I did not do anything. One minute Monsieur Beaumont was fine and then…"

Wally lay delirious in the swamp of picnic remnants. He lifted his forearm. "Ying Lee," he moaned, as Dog licked a glob of cream from his ear.

"You broke Mr. Wally." Catherine was speechless. "Ying Lee must now repair; we get him in tent. You help; me not so young."

Kids appeared from obscure hiding places and surrounded Wally on the bunk; Catherine looked on. "You kids drive me stupid – out. You too Missy," he demanded, ushering the audience before him, "You," he gestured to Catherine, "wait outside, I call."

Catherine leant against the sulky listening to Ying Lee's chanting. Surrounded by the kids she became the object of curiosity; their merriment helped distract the anxiety.

"Ah chow wee coo, ah chow wee coo." The acupuncture needles found their mark and Wally began to resemble a pincushion. Ying Lee spoon-fed the patient foul-tasting syrup. "No more snake oil, Mr. Wally," he said, "Ying Lee have better medicine, won't fix head though." A large bump on the back of his head was the result of a punishing ride.

After what felt like eternity to Catherine, the practitioner appeared, his fingers rubbing beneath wire-framed spectacles.

"How is Monsieur Wally?"

Ying Lee leant on the sulky and stared into the tray, then exploded.

"He like fat lazy dog – eat too much. Get up fat lazy dog," he demanded. The dog lay on the blanket tangled in Catherine's petticoat and covered in what little food he hadn't yet consumed. "Mr. Wally see you now."

"Pardon?" she asserted, "See me now, will he? He is going to hear from moi too." Catherine stormed into the tent and stopped immediately. Wally lay with just a small towel covering his manhood and acupuncture needles from head to foot, the full extent of his zebra scarring visible. She caught her breath and quietly squatted beside the bunk. "How you be feeling?"

"I feel great..." he slurred, trying to focus on her, "... you're beautiful."

"And you're in trouble." She stood up. "Holy Mother of Mary, look at me, I'm barefoot and covered in dirt, had me fingers burnt to the bone I did and me dress torn." Food particles remained lodged in the tangle of wind-swept hair under the torn sunbonnet. The dog had made a meal of the brim when snapping at the titbits flying from it; it was shredded but she still wore it rebelliously. "Holy

Mother." she shrieked again, seeing herself in a mirror. "Look at me new hat."

Resembling a drunken Irishman, Wally began singing, "I'll take you home again, Catherine."

She placed her hand over his mouth. "It's Kathleen not Catherine and you'll not be taking me nowhere you will, you devil." Her mind began spinning uncontrollably. She jumped back from the bunk with both hands against her thumping chest and her Irish brogue ringing in her head. It was she who was now feeling flushed.

"Missy must go," Ying Lee informed her on entering.

Catherine composed herself and chastised the patient. "Monsieur Beaumont will be hearing from Catherine." Wally was now sleeping peacefully with a silly grin on his face. "A full apology is required, do you hear, oui?" To Ying Lee's constant chattering, she left in a huff and he followed.

The unholy configuration of the harness resembled Catherine's appearance. He stood with his back to Catherine smiling and then shook his head at the lathered mare. "This your handiwork." he chastised, "Ying Lee, look after Mr. Wally and Buttercup, you look after fat lazy dog; he unbreakable." The tail-wagging culprit had a rope from the sulky slipped around his neck.

"Sacré bleu, it cannot get any worse." She took the rope handed to her.

"Always expect unexpected Missy."

"Confucius?" she asked.

"Ying Lee." he snapped. "Why people always think Confucius? You go now. I take care of

Buttercup; you not know how, try better with fat lazy dog." He returned to his patient, leaving Catherine in a state of bewilderment.

Collecting what was salvageable of her belongings she slipped on her shoes and opened the parasol above her head. The kids watched as a shower of food scraps tumbled down like rain. "You funny lady," the eldest one told her.

Catherine turned as red as the beetroot tangled in her hair. Brushing the food out of her hair, she threw back her head, took a step and broke a heel. The mongrel strained upon the leash not allowing her to remove the shoe and squeals of laughter rang out from the young audience as Catherine hobbled off along High Street, trying her best to look nonchalant. With the airs of a mademoiselle, she greeted passing townsfolk from under the soiled parasol and dilapidated bonnet.

"Bonjour. It is such a lovely day, oui?"

Catherine finally made her way along the box hedge, her ordeal and embarrassment nearly over. As she passed through the gate, it closed, resulting in a tug-of-war with the dog on the outside. It ultimately received freedom and Catherine received rope burns to match the burns on her other hand.

7 – Evil Deeds

A snake in the grass
leaves more than just
a bad taste in the mouth…

"Ah chow wee coo, ah chow wee coo," Ying Lee chanted as he went about his business. Wally's eyes sprang open. He lay motionless, startled by the young face with its snotty nose staring down at him from the bunk above.

"Jeez'us."

"You kids drive me stupid, out."

Suddenly, Ying Lee's face replaced the one Wally had opened his eyes to – one of the identical twins. He rubbed his eyes, his mind not quite awake. "How'd you do that?"

"Ah, that very old secret Mr. Wally," Ying Lee replied, not knowing what Wally was referring to. "You feel good, yes?"

"Did some bludger mug me?" Wally asked, "I don't remember noth'n." He rubbed the back of his head and at the same time felt the bruise on his arse from the rock he had sat on. "By the feel of things they put the boot in too."

"Very long story," Ying Lee answered. He shouted a couple of words in Chinese and then returned his attention to Wally. "Most enlightening though, we have much to discuss…you good now, I keep eye out for you."

Mrs. Lee placed a bowl of rice and chop sticks before the late riser. Wally presumed it was Ying Lee's wife; he had never seen her, only the kids.

"Thank you." He nodded constantly.

For the third time within a couple of minutes of waking, another curious onlooker was staring at him. With her thumb on Wally's cheek and forefinger on his eyebrow, Mrs. Lee prised open the surrounding skin and studied the iris of his eye. She then poked him in the belly and turned to Ying Lee. Pointing to her eye and then her belly she communicated in the language only they knew. Wally ate heartily while trying to decipher the body language of the duelling couple. He finally tired of the chatter.

"My eyes were too big for my belly…Confucius, right?"

"No – Mrs. Lee say you need wife and kids. I say you need peace and quiet." The twins ran into the tent screaming. "Not kids who drive you stupid." Giggling, they hid under the bunk Wally was sitting on. His dog barked from outside.

"Ah, here comes me mate."

The dog bounded in with the rope still around its neck, pulling the other three siblings with it under the bunk. Frolicking with the kids, it paid no attention to Wally. Mrs. Lee threw her arms into the air imitating her husband's mannerisms and began chasing them. The noise increased twofold.

"Out, all get out." the harassed man cried, as he herded the kids, the dog and Mrs. Lee out of the tent.

He turned to see Wally deep in thought. "Mr. Wally. If ever you want kids, I give you mine... try first."

* * *

Small rocks and dried twigs ricocheted from under Bycroft's rig. Grey dust clouds billowed then, as if absorbing the chill, fell heavily onto the dirt track. Startled, a mob of grazing kangaroos darted from the clearing to the safety of nearby scrub. Foraging crows took flight into the yet-to-be formed updrafts. "Whoa." The matching greys stood lathered and foaming at the bit, nostrils flaring and lungs heaving. At the northern end of High Street, Bycroft stood in his rig with hands on hips, like a captain on the bridge of his paddle steamer.

"Morning, Gov'nor," the polite labourer called.

Bycroft showed no interest in acknowledging the greeting and slapped the reins down hard. "Giddup."

Houten stopped sweeping and watched Bycroft approaching. His attention then diverted to a woman and her two kids scurrying towards him from across the street. "He'll kill someone one day," she complained, struggling to climb onto the wooden sidewalk with a child in each hand.

"Good morning Mrs. O'Hara, I agree. There are too many children and old folk crossing the street these days to have these shenanigans happening," he held the door open for her. "Mrs. Houten will serve you." He returned to sweeping as Bycroft pulled up at his office.

Billings vacated the window position and scurried back to his desk on seeing the rig pull up.

"Good morning, Mr. Bycroft," Houten shouted from across the street. His only acknowledgement was a nod of the head.

Billings didn't look up as the door opened.

"That's what I like to see, head down and hard at it." Bycroft launched his Fedora at the hat rack and missed.

"Good morning, Mr. Bycroft." Billings retrieved it. "I didn't hear you pull up; I'll put the kettle on."

"Good idea, and while you do that, I'll check some figures."

Bycroft stood behind the ledger and blew dandruff from it. He quickly scanned the figures, stopping to repeat the dandruff removal exercise as he sought specific pages.

"As you like it: black."

Bycroft checked for any unwanted flotsam in the mug of tea. "Maybe I should give you a raise so you can do something about that dandruff problem you've got."

"It would be most appreciated."

"Remind me at Christmas." He placed a cigar between his smirk.

"But that's months away," Billings whinged.

"A lot can happen between then and now." Billings obligingly lit a match for him as the door swung open and an-out-of breath Houten stood panting.

"They just brought in a couple of your blokes – dead."

Bycroft sucked hard on the cigar and then blew out the match in front of his face. "There you go Billings; it seems a lot can happen overnight too." Houten hung in the doorway waiting for a reply. "Lead on Sunshine, lead on," Bycroft told him.

Outside Dr. Tubber's surgery, a crowd had gathered, chatting noisily. Boswell, one of the workers Bycroft had sent to Yakka Dakka stepped forward. "It's Maslin and Street, Mr. Bycroft. They got drunk last night; this morning I couldn't wake them."

The surgery door opened. "Move on with you. There's nothing to be seen," ordered Sergeant Doyle. "Good morning Mr. Bycroft."

"Sergeant," said Bycroft, brushing past him.

"They're in the back room. The Doc will be back in a minute." Houten followed the cigar smoke. "Not you," Doyle declared, sticking his finger in Houten's chest to stop entry.

Bycroft peeked under the first shroud and shuddered. The victim was as grey as the sheet covering him. Cigar ash landed on the cadaver's eye socket. He casually flicked it off as though chipping out of a bunker. Morbid curiosity moved him to gawk at the second body.

Wally entered. "Jeez'us. We don't need this."

"I just got here. Thank Christ it's not you." Bycroft stood holding the sheet like a schoolboy caught with his hand in the cookie barrel. "It's Maslin and Street."

"Boswell just told me." Wally lifted the shroud and looked. "Maslin …"

"Boswell reckons they were drunk and got it in their sleep."

"Dunno...I had my own dramas, I wasn't there." He moved to Street and lifted that shroud.

Bycroft was intrigued. "Where were you?"

"It's a long story." Bycroft's continuous stare prompted more. "Well if ya gotta know...I got mugged. In their sleep you reckon, well hopefully," Wally sighed, "they didn't feel a thing then."

"I don't know about that, it wouldn't be pleasant," Tubber informed them on entering. "It depends on the snake species."

"Can you tell?" Wally asked.

"Not when there are multiple bites on both bodies...never seen anything like it."

Bycroft rested his hand on Wally's shoulder. Peering at the deceased he added, "I reckon they weren't fortunate to have a good mate like I did." He made a sucking sound as though drawing poison from a snakebite.

Wally touched the hand sitting on his shoulder. "Thanks mate...you would've done the same for me."

"When you're finished here come over to the office," Bycroft suggested, "I've got just what you need."

Wally placed the sheet down gently. "Naw," he replied, "better get straight back to the site and see what's going on."

"You know what's best. Remember, if there's anything I can do...let me know – we're mates."

* * *

135

Catherine strolled northwards along High Street on her covert mission. Twirling yet another parasol, she ducked and weaved the approaching traffic, nodding politely and occasionally stopping to chat. When passing Ying Lee's tent she feigned a pebble in her shoe and stopped to remove it. Concentrating on their game of marbles the kids paid her no attention. She finally picked up one of the egg-shaped stones she'd collected at the picnic and threw it, then continued with her performance. Her projectile hit the top of the tent, toppled down the canvas roofline and fell into the circle where the kids were shooting marbles.

"What I tell you kids 'bout throwing rocks?" Ying Lee appeared from within and the kids bolted in all directions.

Catherine balanced on one leg, playing possum. "Bonjour, Ying Lee," she greeted him, "I have a stone in my shoe." He observed the collection of river stones he'd shaken the previous day from the picnic blanket scattered at her feet.

"I just have one on tent roof...kids drive me stupid."

"Children will be children," she admonished.

"That is most true." He observed the roofline and fingered a trajectory, following it to the shooting circle of the marble game. There he picked up the evidence and returned, tossing it up and down in his hand. "I solve my problem; not kids." Catherine could feel guilt written all over her face. "Mythical marble bird drop egg...I now help Missy fix her problem?"

Placing the offending footwear on the ground, Catherine wriggled her foot in the shoe. "Voilà. All gone and I must be too, adieu."

Ying Lee let her agonize as she walked a couple of paces before he stopped her.

"You want to know how is Mr. Wally?"

She stopped. Placing a hand on her chest, she raised her voice. "Ah. But of course, silly moi, I forgot to ask." She edged closer to the closed tent flap to make sure Wally heard her. "A horrible man and a horrible experience," she looked at the burn on her open palm, "and horrible dog run away."

"Fat lazy dog come back here."

"I hope Monsieur Beaumont slept well?" she asked Ying Lee. "Moi did not."

"He have good long sleep and big breakfast. Fat, lazy dog have big breakfast too."

Catherine reverted to the loud voice. "Monsieur Beaumont should be out of bed."

Ying Lee smiled deviously. "He not in bed…Mr. Wally gone. He very busy man."

Catherine glared at him in embarrassment. She tossed her mane indignantly, twirled the parasol and stormed off, leaving Ying Lee chuckling. Still tossing the projectile up and down in his hand, he listened to Mrs. Lee's statement from inside the tent and replied in a language only they knew.

* * *

Billings stood with hands in pockets behind the office window. Having heard the news of the deaths on the bush telegraph, he now watched Bycroft returning from Tubber's surgery. A passing wagon almost ran him down and the irate man stood in the middle of Main Street screaming abuse at the driver. He watched on in amusement until Bycroft began moving in his direction.

Bycroft spat venom when entering the office. "Bloody idiot, I'll have that bloke's hide one day."

"I'll put the kettle on."

"Don't bother." He selected a small key, one of many on the end of a gold chain, opened the liquor cabinet and poured a large whiskey. "Get twenty pounds from petty cash and put it in an envelope; Robinson will be calling in for it later. He held the glass up to the light. "Pity you don't drink, you'll never know what vice you're missing." Locking the cabinet, he dropped the keys into his waistcoat pocket. Standing at the window Bycroft observed Wally leaving for Yakka Dakka. He raised the whiskey in salutation and thought, *Here's to you, Big Ears.*

"What do you want me to write the expenditure down as?" Billings enquired.

Placing the empty glass on the windowsill, Bycroft pondered and then replied, "Foresight." He moved to the accountant's desk. Leaning on it with both hands he looked down on Billings kneeling at the safe. "And you don't write it down Sunshine – you chalk it up."

"To what?" he asked nervously.

"To experience and a job well done," Bycroft instructed, "Learn well; I'm not one to be double-crossed…and clean my glass, it's filthy."

Billings knew to pursue the suspicious expense no further; there was to be no transaction recorded. "Mr. Bycroft, one last question. How do I replace our recently departed employees and find the workers you've promised Mr. Beaumont if they are in such demand."

Bycroft walked back to Billings and hovered over him again. "Nobody in their right mind will want the job my colleague is offering. When you do use that," he went to tap Billings on the head but stopped short of it, "for other than just adding up two-and-two, we'll get along better…got it? I'm going back out to the property."

Billings grovelled until the door slammed and Bycroft exit, he then wiped his brow. Perspiration trickled onto his fingers and into the glass as he picked it up. He watched a kid untie Bycroft's Greys and hold out his hand for a tip. It wasn't given: abuse was.

Shortly after Bycroft left town, Robinson was standing in front of the accountant with his hand out for the envelope. Bycroft was too smart to give it to Robinson himself. Within a couple of minutes of Billings unknowingly involving himself in the murderous deed committed, he was making his way through the jumble of shanty-dwellings to his destination and *his* vice of choice.

Like Gunnadoo north, south of the Wong Foo demarcation line had also expanded. Chinatown, once secluded, was now a shantytown metropolis of fan tang gambling houses, cockfighting pits and opium dens. As the trees and scrub fell, the dwellings rose. Word of a raid always travelled faster through the labyrinth than the invasive constabulary could, although a raid only happened when the monthly kickback was late arriving in Sgt. Doyle's pocket.

The musky odour of bodies compacted together was cloaked by a sweet aroma trapped in the windowless room. Billings lay on a bunk. With each suck of the water pipe, an apparition of white swayed before his eyes on the red embers. Yip Tung, Wong Foo's wayward nephew, lay next to the accountant experiencing the same euphoria, his pipe glowing also. With each visit, Billings' knowledge of the Chinatown layout increased, as did his addiction.

* * *

On the last Sunday of each month, Mrs. Chang always had the girls up ready for church. Catherine inspected gloves, hats, handkerchiefs and paraphernalia like a regimental sergeant major inspecting the troops. Then the procession paraded along High Street like mother duck and ducklings.

The adversaries collaborated when the travelling pastor held church services. Wong Foo gave permission for Bycroft to have the old pub tent erected on his vacant block of land; Robinson borrowed chairs from various businesses and set them up. The bare necessities accompanied the parson for the service: a small wooden cross on the portable altar, the pump organ and Mrs. O'Dea, and, most importantly, the collection plate. Many of the heathens believed that, 'when the clergy turn up, you turn your pockets out.'

Pastor O'Dea's sharp features, piercing eyes and bent nose scared many of the children and intimidated the congregation, although he couldn't afford to be doctrinaire on religious issues if cynicism was to be overcome. His bean-like stature and black clothing cast a terrifying shadow, as did Mrs. O'Dea, her features uncannily similar to her husband's; two peas in a pod. Apart from the odd bushie confessing debauchery, the business community and elitists made up the bulk of the congregation – Bycroft and his cronies up the front with the storekeepers and their families. Behind them, the lower classes sat with Catherine and her girls and the Chinese community at the rear. Sister Beth accompanied the Pastor on the organ as the congregation purged the previous month's sins by singing a few hymns and listening to stories from the Good Book.

Pastor O'Dea proclaimed. "…and Noah replied, 'Yes Lord, I've done as you've commanded, I've built an ark and collected two of each animal.' O'Dae pointed to the heavens. "And then the rains began falling for forty days and forty nights."

"Well I'll be buggered," Bycroft whispered to White. "We could do with him around here in the summer months."

"The Pastor?" he sleepily enquired.

"The bloody Lord, Sunshine, aren't you listening? For forty days and forty nights it rained."

White elbowed Bycroft, "That's a bloody long piss." They chuckled like naughty schoolboys.

Bycroft topped him. "Eh, you wouldn't have to worry 'bout a feed with all that tucker aboard."

The pastor, like a cunning housemaster, concealed his annoyance and continued. "Beware. The day of reckoning shall come and the earth shall be cleansed of all sinners. Prepare to build *your* Ark...now let us sing."

The congregation rose to their feet; Mrs. O'Dea pumped the organ foot bellows. The first notes, out of tune, didn't help with the musical pitching. She then proceeded to try to drown out the off-key vocal accompaniment by playing louder. The Chinese community, many not speaking English, made a noisy attempt; kids yelled at the tops of their lungs. The pastor manically ran back and forth waving his arms to the heavens, encouraging the deafening cacophony.

"Yes. Yes. Praise the Lord, sing my children. Sing."

The crescendo was magnificent. The congregation then sat in silence, impatiently waiting to give their contribution and escape the irritating phenomena ringing in their ears. Pastor O'Dea smiled deviously as the overflowing collection plate returned to him.

Under a blue sky and warm sunshine, the women took the opportunity for social chitchat and niceties. The men lit up cigars, rolled tobacco and discussed the weather, sports and making money.

"I reckon that crack about sinners was for your benefit," Bastock told Bycroft.

Bycroft twisted his forefinger in his ear. "I can't hear a bloody thing," he wailed in jest, "I've been struck down deaf.

"I wouldn't be so dismissive."

"Sorry, I can't hear you," he replied. "Come on, who's for a Sunday drink." Although six o'clock closing was flaunted, Sunday trading wasn't and the pubs were closed. Still, there were plenty of sly grog shops for the public, supplied by Bycroft, where purchases were attainable.

White shut his eyes. "I'm blind, I can't see." Bycroft took his hand and placed it on Browning's shoulder, then commanded the assayer to follow him back to his private residence.

Catherine and the girls, as usual, climbed aboard the rented coaches for a pleasant ten-minute journey to a picnic spot on the banks of the Yapsly; some adhered to the Sabbath but tomorrow was another day.

* * *

Wally woke to the sound of running water; it hadn't stopped raining all night. He rose, made a cup of tea then stood at the open door of his shack watching Atlas and Buttercup huddled together under the stable roof for protection. The dog sat whining at his feet. "No work today," he told it, then added, "maybe not next week either."

Boswell, the surviving worker, had quit. He claimed he didn't have a death wish. Bycroft had told Billings, 'There won't be any applicants for the vacant positions,' and he was right. Wally now stood alone at the site with a mineshaft full of water. The possibility of the mine working again in the near future looked as bleak as the weather. When Blackfella Jimmy and family called in for a bartering session that afternoon, Wally worked a deal for them to look after the horses and mine site in his absence. He'd made up his mind it was time for a holiday in the city. If he was to catch the next morning's stage, he had to trek Billygoat Pass that afternoon.

* * *

Twisting the swivel chair back and forth Bycroft sat behind his desk with his feet up on the windowsill. He stared at the deluge as pedestrians splashed about in mud running from the protection of one veranda to the next. "Some day this street will be sealed from one end to the other," he informed Billings. Unrecognisable under a poncho oilskin and floppy hat, Wally approached, the dog giving him away.

"Wet enough for you?" Bycroft enquired when he stuck his head through the doorway.

He wrung out his hat and replaced it. "Cats and dogs and..." A flash of white light and a clap of thunder pierced the conversation. "Jeez'us. By the flam'n sound of things Judgement Day is upon us." A cheesy grin from Bycroft, hinting at a sinner's apprehension, supported Wally's statement. "I'll get cleaned up and come back, we need to talk." He returned to the inclement weather.

Billings looked up, "He's certainly a persistent beaver."

"If this rain continues I might have to get him to build one of them Ark things."

"A pity it's the goose and not the beaver that lays the golden egg," Billings philosophized.

"I may just have to feed the beaver a few golden pellets," Bycroft chuckled, "as an ... eggsample." The high-pitched wheezing of Billings when laughing aggravated him, "Get back to work," he snapped.

Wally kept hoping to see a mane of brunette hair as he walked to the bathhouse, but it was not to be. Heavy rain for the miners was bad news but for Catherine and the girls it meant busy times. Wally returned all spruced up to find Bycroft still staring out the window.

"How full is it?" he asked, as Wally slunk into the chair opposite.

"Full to overflowing. If there was a drought we'd make a fortune selling the stuff."

"This rain may just be what's needed."

"If you're a farmer," Wally replied.

"Well, that we aren't my friend, not yet anyway. I've been thinking ... "

"So have I."

"You go first," Bycroft insisted. In this type of situation it was one of the very few times he let others do the talking. He always hoped for a slip of the tongue and the revealing of secrets.

"The dog and me are taking a holiday."

"Good for you, it's about time," he peered over his shoulder at the rain, "timely too."

"Timely. This rain is the last flaming thing we need at the moment."

"I was thinking this might just free up some of that rock you've been trying to beaver through."

"It's certainly gonna free up the timber supports, there's sure to be a cave-in."

"That's what I mean. You never know what might fall into our hands."

"Or onto my head."

"How long will you be gone?"

"A couple of weeks, I guess."

"It should be drained by then."

"How come you're so optimistic?" Wally asked.

A lightning flash lit up the office, Bycroft waited for the thunder to dissipate. "Judgement Day *is* upon us. It's the last time, Sunshine. We either hit pay-dirt or I'm out, fair enough?"

Wally agreed. "Fair enough. One last go at it."

"What about a drink?"

"Why not," he gave the dog a rub on its belly with his boot. "We're on holiday."

Next morning the coach carefully navigated flooded causeways and bog holes, carrying its passengers towards the Dundee rail siding and from there on to Sydney.

8 – A Samaritan Gesture

*Benevolence is only such when given freely
Imposed, it will return
with vengeance.*

Bycroft held court at his small but stylish town residence. Having consumed the best of food and drink, the cronies now relaxed with port and cigars in the front parlour. The soft glow of lamps lit the room and it was warmed by the fire. Bycroft, in smoking jacket and flannels, leant on the mantelpiece.

"Gentlemen, your attention thank you." The chatter of financial matters and bragging of accomplishments ceased. "Down to matters at hand; we all know why we're here."

"To make money," Stoddard drunkenly cut in.

He had set up a dental practice and was allegedly a graduate of the Sydney dental school, albeit his graduation certificates weren't on show. The dentist not only pulled decayed teeth, he drilled good teeth and charged for the fake gold stuffed into the hole. He even replaced gold fillings with an inferior product; the practice relied on a returning clientele with gum infections. The shyster also had an arrangement with the undertaker to harvest gold from the teeth of the dead.

The other men weren't quite as inebriated as Stoddard but confirmed their support for the making of money.

"Yes, an excellent answer, I agree. And if we wish to continue making money," Bycroft informed them, "we need to protect our assets and…our backs."

This statement came from left field; they had thought it would be the usual Wednesday night banquet and drinking session.

Bycroft continued. "Up to date we've had a free run but that's coming to an end; there are do-gooders on the horizon, my friends, positioning themselves for a take-over."

Startled by the prediction, the men stared at him like wide-eyed owls, all repeating the same question – who?

Bycroft chuckled inwardly and then took charge. "Gentlemen. It sounds like we're in a barn. A little decorum if you please."

Bastock took the initiative. "And who…"

The men immediately heckled him with barnyard hoots and flapping of arms.

He collected his thoughts and continued. "…how do you know this?"

"I have my sources and they tell me it won't be long before a council is being called for."

Harrick stepped forward, glass raised. "I'll be treasurer," he stated, "I could do with a few extra quid in my pocket." He wasn't in a business relationship with Bycroft as were the other men, so wasn't manipulated to the extent that his colleagues were. The lodging house was independent of Bycroft

Holdings; he had wisely refused Bycroft's offer of capital when arriving to set up a business.

"Naw, you're too much of a ladies' man," Bastock chided, "I don't want my taxes paying for your rooting around." Roars of approval supported the statement. "I want a thrifty treasurer – I reckon Ted White is the man for that job." Polite applause supported the nomination and then everyone broke up laughing. The pittance that White paid Aboriginal workers at the timber mill was deplorable.

"I vote Mr. John Bycroft for mayor," declared Browning. The assayer was completely under Bycroft's control. Bycroft had had new premises built for him, and with Bycroft's encouragement Browning had developed a new line of business, that of a pawnbroker and jeweller, into a viable concern. His talent for repairing timepieces and jewellery produced lucrative results.

"Yes, yes, thank you for your confidence Mr. Browning," Bycroft acknowledged, "but it won't just be us doing the voting. Any political aspirations we have must be supported by the peasants out there."

"I vote for a corruptible council," garbled Stoddard.

Bycroft agreed. "We learn from history and opinion…and for that very reason when the time arrives one of us will have to hold the flag high and run for the top job – Mayor."

"I couldn't run ten feet," White conceded. "I got two left feet."

"Not me, that's not my cup of tea," Bastock stated, "I got enough problems without having peasants knocking on my door twenty-four hours a day complaining."

Everyone agreed wholeheartedly that such a situation would be untenable. Over more port, the discussions, arguments and lampooning of the idea continued until finally glasses clinked together; the men sealed the pact – when the time came, one of them *would* step forward for the good of all.

"Rug up, gentlemen," Bycroft advised. He stood at the door shaking hands with each man as they departed into the bleak weather. Browning was asked to stay back to discuss a private matter.

"Here, let me refill that for you," Bycroft offered. Browning emptied the glass, and then with forefinger and thumb wiped his top lip as if he sported a moustache. "Put your feet up, make yourself comfortable. I want you to tell me what your plans for the future are. I may have some more business to throw your way." Bycroft had previously capitalised on the man's knowledge of antiques purchased in Sydney and delivered out to the property.

Browning sat awkwardly, his balance and judgement impaired from the alcohol consumed. He ummed and aahed his way through the pitching of his alcohol-driven fantasy. Bycroft patiently waited, knowing the divulging of unfulfilled dreams would follow, as would the tears; Browning soon folded in on himself. Bycroft then picked up the pieces and began the rebuilding process.

"I didn't have an easy childhood either, you worked the mines and I worked the streets – the University of Life my friend." He lifted his glass in salutation. "Yes, I can see where a man of your intellect and knowledge would be disheartened not fulfilling education aspirations, but at the end of the day, you will be a self-made man." Browning stopped his sobbing as Bycroft continued. "What did you come to Gunnadoo with and what do you have now? Look at what you've accomplished in the short time you've been here. You're now mixing with the community leaders; not bad if I say so myself. Winners make dust – losers eat it."

Browning stopped his snivelling. "You're right and I owe it all to you. If there's anything I can ever do to repay you ..." His defences dropped, Bycroft took full advantage of the situation.

"I'm glad you feel that way; there *is* something you can do for me. What's alchemy?" he asked.

Browning immediately began a comprehensive lecture, his passion being the subject. Unknowingly he also began digging a large hole, eventually too large to crawl out of – right where Bycroft wanted him.

"Excellent. I knew I was talking with – well, you did most of the talking – I was listening to the right man." Bycroft refilled both glasses and then sat back in the reclining chair.

Browning sat back, pleased with his oration even if he had slurred or stumbled over a few words. "If there's two things I do know, its metallurgy and antiques. Glad I could be of help."

Bycroft ensnared his prey. He leaned forward stony-faced. "If you feed a goose gold pellets, will it lay a golden egg?" Browning tried to make sense of the question and then began laughing; Bycroft didn't join in. The assayer stopped laughing, thought for a moment, and then went pale. Bycroft continued, "Someone with the expertise of an alchemist would know how and where to pepper a gold vein. Maybe plant a few gold-bearing specimens that would be convincing enough for new investment capital. I'll even supply the shotgun and pellets myself."

Browning protested ineffectively. "Why take the risk? The potential at Yakka Dakka is there."

"Potential doesn't keep the wolves from the door." He emptied the remaining whiskey from his glass. "The operation requires capital to expand and here's a tip – never tie up all your own money when someone else's can be used," Bycroft confided. "I'm willing to invest a third but the investor I have in mind will demand to see something a little more substantial than your potential."

"You're asking me to risk my good standing in the community, the goodwill and trust that I've built up. I hold myself accountable for everything in my office – down to paper and pencils, and especially assayer reports."

Bycroft stood up and took Browning's empty glass. "A talented man like you should be able to..."

"Make a forgery and commit fraud. That's what you're asking me to do." Browning mumbled. He stood up swaying unsteadily.

"The document won't leave your office; it'll be our little secret. Now rug up we don't want you catching a chill." Bycroft intentionally pulled the man's woollen scarf tightly around his neck and edged him to the front door. "Relax, it'll be a mere formality," he assured.

"It's not that simple; what if…"

"Well look at that, it's stopped raining. Goodnight Mr. Browning."

The door shut. Browning felt a cold chill cut through his body.

* * *

The inclement weather disappeared over the first week of July and so too the rain-soaked ground, sucked up by the parched earth. Dust billowed once again on the streets under the movement of traffic.

Wong Foo's vacant block of land, on which the church services took place, was ideally located on the corner where High Street became Main Street; a wide lane intersected the thoroughfare and ran down to the tributary behind the town. On the opposite side of the vacant block stood Wong Foo's restaurant and beside that, his laundry and supplies store. Bycroft wanted the deed of title to the vacant block and set about scheming. If he could get it, he would then have four consecutive blocks fronting Main Street. For the next week, when strolling, Bycroft's path fortuitously crossed Wong Foo's on a regular basis. Pleasantries and short conversations took place. Banter about making Wong Foo an offer too good to refuse always followed. He kept testing the water until he believed the time was right.

Bycroft heard the clickety-click of beads on the abacus as he entered Wong Foo's establishment. "I hope that's adding up and not subtracting," he said.

Wong Foo looked up. "Good morning, Mr. Bycroft. Is this a social visit or business?"

"Both," replied Bycroft.

"I am always pleased to do both." Two sharp handclaps signalled the serving of tea and for Yip Tung who was stacking shelves to disappear. Over the beverage, Bycroft spun the tale of how the Yakka Dakka gold mine, prematurely abandoned, now exposed gold-bearing ore due to the recent cave-in. He also revealed how Wally, not yet returned from his vacation, didn't know of the discovery and the excellent investment potential at a bargain price. "Why do you come to Wong Foo?" he asked suspiciously. "Surely rich man like you could finance venture yourself."

Bycroft countered. "As Confucius says, never put all your eggs in one basket."

"Very wise man, Confucius," Wong Foo replied tactfully, neither contradicting nor agreeing with the statement or authorship. "Now I wish you to tell me real motive for such remarkable offer." He sipped his tea.

"Nothing," Bycroft replied. He picked up the teacup. "Chin-chin." His slurping was as offensive as his salutation.

"Nothing? This is most strange proposal." Wong Foo looked over the rim of his teacup suspiciously at Bycroft.

"Well, nothing for me," Bycroft confessed. "I want the deed of title but it will be for public use – a church," he added quickly.

"A gift to Gunnadoo and your God, philanthropy and homage combined, very…"

"Commendable?" Bycroft cut in.

"Clever," Wong Foo suggested politely. "Now more importantly, what is in this proposal for Wong Foo?"

"The chance to invest in a bonanza gold strike," he encouraged. "You do right by me and I do right by you."

Wong Foo thought hard; the seed now planted. "I would need to see evidence and assayer report; there is much to think about before such an undertaking."

"What about meeting at the assayer's office Monday morning?" Bycroft suggested, believing this would allow enough time for Browning to complete the tasks required.

"Until Monday then," Wong Foo agreed on rising.

* * *

Crushed ore from the larger mechanised mines was now refined on site, the gold then transferred to the savings bank vault. Individual prospectors brought their finds to Browning for the refining process. Once a month, under the protection of four constables, a wagon departed for the Dundee rail siding with its valuable commodity. Charlie Roister, the bank manager, hoped the continual rotation of constables would stop corruption. Of late, there'd been a noticeable crackdown on law and order and he hoped it would continue. From the assayer's doorway, Browning observed Sgt. Doyle marching his armed troupers towards the bank and another bullion wagon departure. The thought of incarceration ran chills up his spine as he saw Bycroft approaching.

"I've spoken with our potential investor," Bycroft teased, "and set up a meeting for Monday, ten o'clock, here." Browning sat in his chair stunned into silence. Bycroft continued, "I'm spending a couple of days at the property, I'll be back early Monday morning for the meeting."

"It can't be done. I'll need more time than that." Browning felt perspiration glands pumping out sweat and the hollow feeling of nausea permeating his stomach. "You're putting me under too much pressure."

"Nonsense; man creates his best work under pressure."

Browning swung around in his chair and threw himself upon a wastepaper basket, dry reaching into it. He then stood, wiped his face and shakily poured a glass of water from a pitcher.

Another pep talk was required.

"It's all about give and take – give a little, take a lot. You don't take but neither do you give," Bycroft waffled. "You understand what I mean don't you?" Browning listened uneasily. "Next to Charlie Roister at the bank, you and your set-up are amongst the most reputable institutions in Gunnadoo. You must be; you've got a shop full of other people's belongings and they trust you with their gold…"

Browning chimed in, "And I don't like the idea of going to jail for fraud."

"Nobody will be going anywhere," Bycroft assured him. "Have confidence, you can do it, you're the alchemist." Bycroft walked to the office door and paused. "Take charge of your own destiny. Remember: winners make dust, losers eat it."

Browning never thought to enquire as to the identity of the investor they were setting up.

* * *

Clarrie stood watching the assayer looking around the shelves. He couldn't remember the last time Browning had been in the newsagency. "Can I help you, Mr. Browning?"

"Thank you, Mr. Radcliff, I require writing paper. Good afternoon, Mr. Houten."

"It would be, if a bloke was able to get starting prices," Houten grumbled. He thumbed through the outdated *Sydney Truth*.

"Writing paper," said Clarrie, returning his attention to Browning. "Let's see. I believe we have an assortment, as we also do in our range of ink, pens, pencils, wrapping paper and string. Not to mention…"

"I take your point, Mr. Radcliff. My supplies are in need of topping up."

"Support local business, that's what I say. You should open an account here, and at the Hardware and General Store." The crusader turned to his fellow trader for support.

"Right, yes. I agree. Support the little man," Houten collaborated, and returned to his reading.

Browning contemplated the statement replying, "You're right. I am too conservative; I should be more supportive of the community that supports me." He had always purchased his supplies in bulk from the city. Clarrie was happily surprised at his about-change in purchasing policy and appreciated the new business. Browning made his selection carefully as the paper colour, texture and weight were critical. "I'll have, let's see...how many pages will I need?" the counterfeiter considered.

Clarrie did the hard sell. "It's less expensive if bought by the clip, two dozen pages to a clip."

"Then I'll have four clips." His eyes searched the shelves. "And two bottles of red and black ink – your best, and a set of those nib pens." On display, the latest model of an Imperial typewriter caught his attention. "I'll take that also," he requested.

Houten's interest was stimulated at the pricey purchase. "Planning on creating a masterpiece, are you?" he enquired.

Browning smiled politely. "You could say something like that." He picked up a newspaper and browsed through the section on crime reporting. Customers reading newspapers and magazines on display without paying for them irked Clarrie. He put up with Houten's browsing habit and now after the circumstances of opening the new account, he might also have to tolerate Browning doing it.

"Gunnadoo will soon have its own newspaper," Clarrie informed Browning.

"There's something special about reading the *Herald* with your coffee in the morning," Browning lamented. "Keeping abreast of the news is a citizen's duty."

"It's four days old," jibed Houten, checking the date. "I need a telephone, direct to the Randwick track; now *that's* keeping abreast of the news."

Clarrie passed Browning his goods and replied to Houten's statement. "A telephone...I agree but a local paper is a good start though. Organise the community; the results will follow. I'm amazed this town has functioned for so long without any formal structure."

"What do you know that we don't?" Houten asked.

"All in good time, gentlemen – let's just say the wheels of progress are slowly beginning to turn."

Browning gave his support. "I'm all for it. Make out that charge account Mr. Radcliff. Mr. Houten, it seems only fair you should get my patronage too." Browning gestured for Houten to lead the way. "After you...let's see what you've got for me."

He purchased various goods from the drapery section, chose a range of clothing including two suits and accessories from the men's emporium. The pearl-handle penknife was confirmation of his extravagant spending spree. Houten removed it from the display case. "Made from the finest Ger..." he was about to say 'German steel', then realised that Swiss steel sounded better.

Browning felt its weight and fingered the ornate scroll carved into the handle and responded, "Quality workmanship." He didn't bother to open it and feel the blade. "That's a better price than I could buy wholesale. I'll take it."

He noticed the difference in Radcliff's and Houten's attitudes. Bycroft's advice of 'give a little, take a lot' did work. "Chalk it up, Mr. Houten, and please have everything delivered." He left the store with a positive feeling, deciding he'd put the deed into practice with other traders in the community.

That evening, Browning selectively chose the ore he could match with the Yakka Dakka sample supplied. He delicately chipped away at each piece altering its shape to maximize a weight to size ratio. He then conjured each ore sample with mercury composites and acidic solutions whilst retaining the look of having just been unearthed.

The intricate work of tracing government identification seals and stamps was time consuming. Transferring reverse images by pressing sheets of paper together was difficult. With much trial and error, the ink consistencies and drying techniques were continually improved; much of one clip lay screwed up and littered the floor. By the early hours of Monday morning, Browning had five pages that he believed would pass undetected by the untrained eye as authentic. From the five, he chose the only one that would have a good chance of passing undetected to a trained eye. Inserting it in the Imperial typewriter carriage, the final step of Bycroft's deception commenced – the written confirmation of the valuable find.

On Monday morning before the meeting commenced, Browning proudly showed Bycroft the fraudulent reports and ore samples. "I'm quite proud of my work but not my actions, I believe that…"

"Excellent workmanship," Bycroft cut in. "Is that a new suit you're wearing?

"I took your advice … do you like it?"

Believing all was in order, Bycroft returned to his office and waited behind the newly painted

Bycroft Holdings sign on the window; it was now possible for him to sit and observe the street panorama without the passing traffic observing him.

Until entering and saying he was waiting for Bycroft, Browning didn't know Wong Foo was the potential investor about to be scammed: angst rose immediately. The problem was, he had written up three samples on the report, and Wong Foo would expect to see them – one of the ore samples belonged to the Chinaman. Browning could feel Wong Foo's eyes upon him as he tried to look relaxed. His anxiety increased, his hands trembled and perspiration beaded on his forehead and top lip.

"You are not looking well, Mr. Browning. Is there something wrong?"

Wong Foo received a sickly smile from the nervous assayer.

"I may have caught a chill," he explained.

Entering the office, Bycroft saw the nervous state of Browning.

"You should be in bed with that fever." he quickly told him.

"I have medicine he should take," Wong Foo advised.

Bycroft wanted the meeting to be as short as possible. "You look terrible. We won't keep you long; I hope it's not contagious." Browning began coughing to help make the sham more convincing. "Well, let's have the official report." Bycroft checked the document and then handed it to Wong Foo for perusal.

"I am greatly encouraged by meticulous report," he acknowledged after reading it. "Please show me samples." Browning felt his knees wobbling as he moved to the safe to fetch them. He placed the three samples of varying size on the desk. Wong Foo removed a large magnifying glass from his pocket and studied the gold seam in each. "Very encouraged," he mumbled. After some minutes, he placed the last sample on the desk in front of him and said to Bycroft, "You give me much to think about." He rolled up the report and slid it inside his jacket sleeve. "I consider proposal carefully. Please leave with me." Wong Foo rose and bowed to each man before leaving.

He had given no indication of recognising the ore as his own. Browning felt nauseous and wiped accumulating sweat with a new handkerchief, then sat with his head in it.

"Now, that wasn't so bad was it?" Bycroft asked. "I'll let you know when I need to borrow the samples."

Browning looked up in shock. "Borrow. You said…"

"I know what I said but it's Wally who has to make the find at the mine, isn't it?"

"No, I can't let them…"

"You don't have a choice, Sunshine. You committed yourself to this project by creating that fraudulent report, and a very nice job it is too."

Browning couldn't raise the courage or energy to tell his blackmailer of the near-fatal mistake he had made with the ore.

* * *

Wong Foo sat behind the abacus contemplating the assayer's report. His wispy moustache rose as a smile appeared; his eyes opened slowly. He quickly clapped his hands twice. Immediately Lotus-Flower appeared awaiting his command.

"Find Yip Tung."

Billings was glad to see the back of Bycroft when he left for the property. For the rest of the day he sat around in Bycroft's chair observing the passing pedestrians and traffic. After supper he left by the rear door for his appointment with the Red Dragon.

Hanging from bamboo poles, paper lanterns swayed in unison above him as he entered Chinatown. Children played around open fires as evening meals cooked; from cast-iron pots, an array of aromas drifted. Moonlight replaced the glow of lanterns as Billings crisscrossed the shadowy alleyways. Euphoric ranting replaced the laughter of children; an even sweeter temptation trounced the array of aromas wafting on the breeze.

Sitting impatiently awaiting his turn, Billings studied the faces of fellow addicts, their sunken eyes and gaunt features embellished by animated shadows when kissing the Red Dragon. Yip Tung placed a hand on his shoulder.

"My uncle wishes to speak with you."

Billings shrugged it off contemptuously, "I'm busy." He watched another face glowing and heard a gurgling of the water pipe being sucked upon. He cussed to the den master, impatient for his turn. "Come on Ho, take my money."

"Your money is worthless here," said Yip Tung, "now come, my uncle does not like to be kept waiting." Master Ho ignored the extra money Billings offered him. "You will not be kissing the Red Dragon unless your new benefactor says so."

Yip Tung moved through the alleyways that resembled the Sydney back streets of the inner city he'd been forced to vacate. Intolerant of the coolies and their servile attitude to white folk, any poor sods that were in his way received a hefty shove and reprimand. Billings followed the thug closely; the area they moved through threatened diabolical repercussions if they were separated. "Through here," said Yip Tung. He opened the door of a leaning shanty that looked as though a good wind would knock it down. Billings entered an antechamber and the door closed behind him; he stood alone in the dark, unable to see.

"You have two problems, Mr. Billings," the oriental voice stated. Billings was completely vulnerable; his panic rose. Nobody knew where he was and neither did he. "One – you have an opium addiction and two – you work for an untrustworthy employer." A match flickered in the dark, lighting a lamp. "I, Wong Foo, am your new benefactor."

Billings rubbed his eyes in disbelief. The shanty façade was but that. Inside, silk drapes and tapestries lined the walls; large velvet pillows lay scattered upon plush carpet. Incense burned in an ornate censer overhead. He'd seen Wong Foo around Gunnadoo but never dressed as he was now. Exquisite dragons embroidered with golden thread enriched his gown of purple silk and matching skullcap. Wong Foo clapped his hands. Two daughters entered through a curtain of beaded glass, one carrying a tray of tea that she placed upon a low rectangular table. Wong Foo then sat at the head of it and gestured to his guest to join him. Lotus-Flower served tea as Rose-Petal stood silently holding a marquetry box, the veneer inlaid with ivory dragons.

"It seems we have much to discuss, Mr. Billings." His long fingernail threatened from clasped hands on the table.

"Like what?" Billings asked nervously.

"Like your habit and your line of business." Wong Foo's slight nod indicated to Rose-Petal that she remove the contents of the ornate box.

"I'm an accountant...I add and subtract numbers. That's all."

Rose-Petal assembled the hookah. A dragon's head with mouth open awaited the opiate, holding Billings' attention.

"Then no doubt you would have noted your habit becoming very expensive," stated Wong Foo. "Dragons reveal many secrets, Mr. Billings. Is it not true you add and subtract numbers for yourself?"

Billings kissed the dragon and it him. He revealed what he knew. "Bycroft won't be investing capital but getting a third of the wealth should there be a gold strike."

"Let me surmise," said Wong Foo, after listening to the scam details. "Mr. Bycroft will launder my unaccountable assets, skimming funds off the top, and then use only his partner's and my investment to search for a *possible* strike."

Billing's face glowed red again, then he slurred, "That's about it – he doesn't lose either way."

Wong Foo twirled his braided moustache. "And gets valuable land title also – very cunning." Lotus-Flower responded to the handclap and his pointing forefinger. "Fetch Yip Tung. One last question Mr. Billings; when does the partner return?"

"On Thursday."

"Consider your visiting rights to Master Ho's dwelling restored. We shall talk again, Mr. Billings. You have done well, Good evening." Yip Tung responded to Wong Foo's forefinger and escorted Billings back to the Chinatown he knew.

* * *

On Tuesday afternoon Bycroft stood watching as the teamster's wagon was unloaded. Four men under the direction of Bastock rigged an A-frame pulley system, and then cautiously lifted and manoeuvred the weighty packing case onto a trolley.

"Coming through," Bastock shouted. The trolley shuddered as the men put their shoulders to it and pushed.

"Go straight through into the new extension," Radcliff instructed.

Bycroft joined Bastock and Radcliff.

"And what do we have here?" he asked.

"Progress," replied Radcliff.

"A printing press," stated Bastock.

Approaches had been made to Radcliff to join the cronies' club; he'd refused. Bycroft hadn't known why the invitation had been declined, until now – freedom of the press.

"Congratulations. What's the rag going to be called?" he asked the proprietor.

Bastock answered for him. "The Gunnadoo Advocate."

"And when does the first edition hit the street?" Bycroft threw Bastock a contemptuous glance that told him to keep his mouth shut.

"A week or so after the initial set-up," Radcliff replied.

"August, eh? Well I'm sure the Advocate will be a great success...and if I'm gonna be, I'd better do some work. Gentlemen." Bycroft departed, thinking about the ramifications of having a newspaper in town.

The following evening, after the Wednesday evening banquet, Bycroft addressed the cronies and the situation at hand. Taking his regular speaking position at the mantelpiece, he began.

"Gentlemen, precise information and communication are crucial for waging a successful mission and we have had a breakdown. Haven't we, Mr. Bastock?"

"Search me. I don't know what you're talking about," he replied, although recognising the contemptuous look. Bycroft immediately admonished him.

"If you'd forewarned us of Radcliff and his newspaper when you got the haulage contract, I would've known about the Advocate sooner than yesterday."

Bastock shrugged. "I thought you had all the sources; anyway, what's the problem?"

"The problem is – we don't run it. Unless something is found on Radcliff to keep him in his place, you and all of us," he looked around the room at the owl-like faces, "could find ourselves being front page news." All the men in one way or another had something to hide.

"We gotta discredit the bastard," declared White. "I don't want anyone looking over my shoulder."

"Me neither," Browning agreed quietly.

Bycroft leant on the mantelpiece monitoring the head nodding, chatter and drinking of his port. "Enough. Let's hear your ideas, gentlemen." Nobody spoke up. "Then I suggest until we do find a way of bringing him down, we build him up." All eyes fixed on Bycroft. "We give Radcliff what he wants – a front-page story."

"What story?" Harrick asked.

"I haven't thought of it yet, but when I do, my friends, you will be the first to know. Mr. Bastock, you are required to make amends to the brotherhood for your indiscretion."

"How do I do that?" he enquired.

"By becoming Radcliff's best mate," Bycroft told him. The men hooted and jibed as Bycroft continued. "You'll be our insider, our eyes and ears. What Radcliff knows – we know. Noth'n gets by us."

Bastock repeated, "How do I do that?"

"For a start, you can give him a generous discount on the haulage fee." The cronies roared with laughter at the imposition Bastock now carried.

"You'll still come out ahead," shouted Harrick. "We know what your rates are." The drunken laughter continued.

"…and you, gentlemen," silence fell as all awaited their fate from Bycroft, "have your cash ready also; there's a bit of investing required."

"God help us." declared Bastock.

Bycroft added, "That's the best idea you've had all night. We're always looking for new members. Send him an application form."

"God helps them that help themselves," Stoddard recited. Except for Bastock, blasphemy followed as all tried to outshine one another.

Bycroft finally ushered the cronies out the front door, reminding them of the forthcoming contribution that would be called for. An idea, seeded by Bastock's godly suggestion, was already beginning to develop into an epiphany. He refilled his hip flask, lit another Cuban and departed for a rendezvous with Catherine.

* * *

Many teamsters and their heavy drays now travelled back and forth along the route between the Dundee rail siding and Gunnadoo. Teamsters crushed undergrowth and saplings under hoof and wheel. Trees daring to block the progress of a wider track were blown apart with dynamite. Cuttings were hacked from the bush along the way for slower traffic to pull over and let the faster vehicles pass. The coach swayed back and forth as the team of four galloped along the ever-widening track. The dog lay across the

169

seat with its head pressing into Wally's thigh; he sat uncomfortably squashed in a corner, his hat pulled down over his eyes.

"Hey Wally, get a look at that." Opposite, his sole fellow traveller stared at the foreign landscape.

The hat raised just enough for him to look under the brim, "Yeah, Tom. They're called kanga-bloody-roos. Just like the mob a half mile back."

As an official photographer for the AIF, Tom Lennard had received baptism under fire attached to the First Division when he'd moved up to the line for the third battle at Ypres, Belgium. After a fortnight of rain, the allies suffered heavy losses in the bog hole. All servicemen recognised the look in the eyes of a comrade that told of harrowing ordeals. Wally and Tom had briefly discussed their experiences, many still too painful to visit; they had said enough for each to know where the other stood.

"I never want to see that much water again in my life," Tom volunteered, looking at the dry bush. He'd managed to stay free of shrapnel at Ypres only to be mustard gassed a year later at Villers, Bretonneux. Wally didn't tell him about his encounter with shrapnel, or about the rain that had fallen before he'd left Gunnadoo.

Bycroft planned to meet Wally and not let him out of his sight until the next morning, when he'd be waved goodbye to return to the mine and make the new discovery. The coach arrived at four o'clock, an hour early, catching Bycroft by surprise. At five o'clock, he ran around looking for Wally, fearing he might have left for the mine already. That would

170

undo the scam, as the ore samples were to be to be planted early the next morning.

While enjoying a second cup of tea, Wally and Clarrie, Tom's brother-in-law, watched as the photographer removed packing from a trunk.

"I bought this as a souvenir in Flanders," Tom informed the spectators, as he unfurled the blue ensign. "The boys refused to fight under the red one."

"And rightfully so," Wally endorsed, "we're Australian not British."

"Here we go…this is my baby," Tom whispered. Like removing a baby from its cradle, he took the camera out of its travelling case. "Isn't she a little beauty?"

"Jeez'us. That's a Hasselblad, isn't it?" stated Wally. "I've heard the aperture speed and lens quality make it superior to all other makes." Clarrie was surprised and impressed by the bushie's apparent knowledge of cameras. Wally then added for good measure, "Even though it is German, it's the choice of all professional photographers." For two days, he had been earbashed by Tom on the pros and cons of every camera and printing press known to mankind since its invention. Clarrie was now the butt of the repartee and Tom let Wally have his fun. "Good choice, the Platen press." He gave the wooden case a kick. "Strong and reliable – any bloody idiot could operate it."

Clarrie shook his head. "I wouldn't know. Tom's the operator. Tom?"

"Thanks a lot," Tom replied. "When we expand from a weekly to a daily I'll need a man to take over and you've got all the right qualifications," he told Wally.

"I see myself more in a consultant's role. Come on Dog, its tub time for us; you stink and my bones ache."

Ying Lee greeted Wally with the customary and escorted him to the large tub. Yip Tung filled it and then hung around until given another task to perform, leaving the two men with some privacy.

"Well, what's been happening while I've been away?"

"Not much been happening, Mr. Wally." Ying Lee told him of the pub brawl at the Plough, the raiding of a two-up game and the abnormally harmonious relationship between Wong Foo and Bycroft. He concluded with, "We also to get newspaper."

"Jeez'us. You don't say?"

Ying Lee stopped scrubbing and threw the brush in the tub. "You not dirty enough for Ying Lee's attention. As Wally soaked, he received a lecture on the Chinese and their relationship to printing and reproduction. Wally kept encouraging it by replying, "You don't say?" He'd towelled dry, dressed and was about to leave when Ying Lee finished the sermon and asked, "And what you think Mr. Wally?"

"For two days I listened to the Editor of the Advocate."

"Advocate?" Ying Lee enquired.

"That's what the newspaper is to be called. You and Tom Lennard, the editor, will get along fine; you have a lot in common."

"I have no printing experience."

"No, but you can both talk the ears off a corncob." Ying Lee pondered then began laughing heartily. Wally was also chuffed by his own wit.

"You funny-man Mr. Wally, make big-ear joke." Ying Lee put his forefingers behind his ears and waggled them at Wally.

"No. You don't get it. What I meant was…"

"Very funny, no need explanation." He held his hand out. Wally conceded, not knowing if Ying Lee was having him on or not.

"All right, it's your turn. I'm waiting, what is it?"

Ying Lee bowed. "It takes big man to poke fun at himself."

Wally held his tongue and didn't ask whose gem it was. He saw Ying Lee ready to stop the dog from jumping into the tub and so paid for the services. "See you later, Ying Lee. Come on, Dog." They all proceeded down the corridor until Wally stopped suddenly.

"You forget something, Mr. Wally?"

"Yeah," he pointed in the direction from which they had come. "In you get." The dog scurried up the corridor and disappeared, a splash indicating its destination. Wally exited followed by Ying Lee's colourful abuse.

Bycroft was beside himself with apprehension when Wally finally entered the residence; he was all over him. "Wally. Am I glad to see you…I thought you'd gone out to the mine."

"Naw, just got into a discussion on … "

Bycroft interrupted. "You *are* staying here tonight, aren't you? We have a lot of catching up to do…whiskey?"

* * *

Bycroft rose before the sun and snuck out to meet Robinson at the assayer's office. Browning, bleary eyed from lack of sleep and worry, opened the safe and handed Bycroft the ore samples.

"Don't fret, you'll have the samples back in your hands today," Bycroft told him. "Won't he?" he confirmed with Robinson.

"Sure, boss – that's the plan."

"He'd better – your life depends on it. Plant the samples and stay out of sight. Then follow him back here when he's found it. The ore doesn't leave your sight. Got it?

"Got it." assured Robinson.

"Then get going, Sunshine." The first signs of dawn were appearing as Bycroft returned to his bed for another couple of hours' sleep.

After breakfast, Wally prepared to trek across Billygoat Pass. "Next week I'll be needing supplies. I'll see you then and let you know the water damage."

"Hopefully it'll good news," Bycroft replied smugly.

* * *

To avert any communication between Buttercup, Atlas and his mount, Robinson had tethered his horse well away from Wally's camp and humped the ore the last quarter mile. He had planted it by the time Blackfella Jimmy woke and left the bark hut for relief in the bushes.

The echo of 'coo'ee' penetrating the bush woke Robinson from his slumber. From his vantage point, he observed Wally arrive. The billy was boiled. Wally's tales of buildings ten storeys high didn't impress Blackfella Jimmy, but telling him they reached the sky did. Wide eyed, he jumped about hooting, hollering and throwing his arms in the air. *Get on with it*, thought Robinson, smacking his lips together in want of a hot mug of tea himself. The camp became a social gathering as more of the extended family arrived with bush tucker and threw it on the fire to cook. They all went into raptures when Blackfella Jimmy told of the sky giants. Wally couldn't get a word in. Finally, he told Blackfella Jimmy, "You can talk the ears off a corncob."

There was silence as the men pondered the statement, which they then dismissed as nonsense and returned to Blackfella Jimmy and 'his' tale.

"Jeez'us," Wally told the dog, "talk about being upstaged."

The bush tucker aroma blew in Robinson's direction. He sat holding his belly and salivating.

"Get on with it ya stupid bastards," he said under his breath. The few dried biscuits he'd brought with him were gone and afternoon was approaching. By the time the meal had been finished and the tribe had left to go walkabout, Robinson was consumed with hunger. Wally appeared in work clothes with a lamp, then disappeared down the ladder into the shaft. The ore had been placed at the site of the first cave-in.

Robinson was tempted to do a quick raid for any leftovers but the dog was roaming the campsite. "Come on, ya blind bastard," he griped, "don't start mining now. Get the stuff and get out."

After what seemed like forever, Wally threw a Hessian sack from the shaft entrance. The dog pounced on it trying to toss the sack in the air but only managed a tug of war, dragging it backwards. Robinson knew of the discovery from the pair's antics, "Enough of the blackfella dance, idiot. Let's go, let's go." His belly was grumbling louder.

He hadn't counted on an overnight stay, but as late afternoon approached Robinson realised that that was what he was about to experience. When evening fell, he curled up under a thick bush for protection, cursing and cussing Wally, the dog, Bycroft and the day he'd been born. The next morning, covered in dew, he was too cold to say anything and simply sat watching as Wally dawdled around the site with a hot mug of tea. Finally, Robinson saw the mare hitched to the sulky. He waited until Wally threw the Hessian sack in the back. Then, in what he believed to be the first stage of starvation, he returned to where he'd left the horse. All that remained was a broken bridle tied to a fork in the tree. His cussing recommenced as he heard the galloping hooves and sulky pass along the four-mile track he was about to hike. It intersected the main route and then it was another fifteen miles to Gunnadoo.

Few wagons would stop for fear of robbery. Upon arriving at the main route, Robinson ran alongside a teamster until he was finally taken pity on. "Up ya get then, don't want ya dead on the track;

I'd 'ave to cut more bush to get 'round ya." the old bushie drawled.

Bycroft woke to a pounding on the front door of his residence. Browning hadn't slept and was near hysterical, wanting to know where the samples were. Ham, eggs and a glass of sherry pacified his anxiety. Later that morning he was greatly relieved to see Wally rush in to Bycroft's office with the Hessian sack. He'd been keeping a vigil at his window, as had a nervous Bycroft from his vantage point. A contract on Robinson's hide was all but signed.

Bycroft acted surprised to see Wally. "I thought you said you'd be picking up supplies next…"

"Look at this." Wally couldn't contain himself and emptied the sack onto the desk.

"I'll be buggered," Bycroft exclaimed, "I'll grab Browning." He soon returned with the assayer who pawed the ore like a long-lost friend. "Well?" asked Bycroft.

"I'll need to run some tests but it looks real good," Browning replied enthusiastically.

"Then run man, run." said Bycroft, hustling Browning out the door with the ore. He turned to Wally, "I guess you'll be doing some celebrating over the weekend, eh?"

"Not likely, the tunnel needs shoring up or the whole thing could collapse," replied Wally. "I aim to grab the supplies and get back there before it does."

"Good for you. Don't let me stop you, Sunshine; I'll start working from this end to get the capital together. It looks like we're in business again."

Bycroft smiled conceitedly and watched Wally head to Houten's, supply list in hand. Telling himself what a brilliant a strategist he was, he headed to the liquor cabinet, key in hand.

The next morning, before church, Bycroft collected his cronies together, telling them he had conceived the perfect story for the Advocate.

"Well, what is it then?" enquired Harrick.

"You're going to love this and so will Radcliff."

White interrupted. "You can tell him now, here he comes."

Clarrie approached with his wife Meg and their two boys, Michael and Albert. Meg had arrived with the children two weeks before Tom. Bycroft turned to greet them.

"Clarrie."

"John."

"We're all certainly looking forward to the launch," Bycroft informed him. "If there's anything we can do…let me know."

Bastock added sarcastically under his breath, "No expense spared."

"Thank you, gentlemen. Your generous offer is much appreciated but all is going to plan. Your invitations for the launch will be delivered tomorrow." Sister Beth's organ music began from inside the tent. "Must be going; don't want to miss out on a good seat."

The men dipped their hats; Bycroft went one better. "You're looking lovely, Marge. Gunnadoo weather certainly agrees with you." His lips turned up at the corners; his mind pondered whether he'd said 'Meg' or 'Marge'. She didn't correct him.

"Thank you, Mr. Bycroft. We all look quite grand in our Sunday best, don't we? See you inside." The twin boys, unwilling participants dressed in fashionable knickerbockers, were hustled into the tent.

Bycroft confided, "I'm not particularly fond of children – or their old man."

"Hey. That's Bastock's best mate you're talking about," Stoddard protested.

"Come on," Bycroft told the laughing men, "we want to get a good seat, don't we?"

The pastor delivered a more than usual fire and brimstone sermon, completing it with words few adhered to. "Listen well, my friends and remember – the good Lord frowns upon intemperance, gambling and other such evils. Amen." The worshippers echoed their agreement. "Sister Beth, if you please."

The melancholy hymn along with the preacher asked in the name of the Lord for the worshippers' generosity. The collection plate was passed along from the rear of the congregation, followed closely by the eagle eyes of the pastor. Those who tried to avoid making a deposit or preferred making a withdrawal received his wrath. Bycroft positioned himself to be the last contributor and dropped the handwritten note into the coin-heavy plate. He then held out the collection plate in both hands.

"Good Lord." the parson let slip when reading the note. The organ stopped immediately. Catherine recognised a change in his linguistics and noticed his quick recovery. "I mean, the good Lord works in

179

mysterious ways. Yes, that's what I meant." The intrigued worshippers looked on, unaware. He gestured Bycroft to say a few words.

Bycroft held a lapel in one hand and raised the other. With forefinger pointing to the heavens like a missionary preaching salvation, he began. "Ladies and gentlemen," he orated in a wavering voice, "the Lord has spoken to me." Harrick elbowed Bastock in the ribs. "He has told me to donate generously."

Bastock returned Harrick's nudge. "That's our money he's generously donating."

"Mr. Bycroft is building us a church," the parson shouted.

"I…and my colleagues," he signalled for the cronies to stand up, "will supply the building materials. Will you supply the labour?" Applause erupted, concealing various comments from the cronies.

White stood next to Browning. "Jesus Christ." he whispered out of the side of his mouth, "that'll cost a bloody penny or two."

Browning dabbed his top lip, perspiration running down his fingers. "Is it getting hot in here?" he asked White.

White answered out of the side of his mouth again, his eyes not moving from Bycroft. "When you ride with the Devil."

Composing himself, Parson O'Dea completed the service. "Until next month, God be with you and …" Sister Beth drowned him out with her enthusiastic playing of Onward Christian Soldiers.

The sunshine was bright but held little warmth. Many worshippers mingled in what they thought was a hypocritical gesture but also socially inevitable. The cronies quickly gathered to one side.

"You could have told us." Bastock complained.

White added his thoughts. "It seems redemption doesn't come cheap."

Harrick protested bitterly. "If you didn't notice, I donated five bob."

"I donated a bloody bombshell." Bycroft lashed out. "*I'm* the one who's taken Radcliff's legs from under him and saved you gentlemen from any bad press the Advocate might have had in store. Think about it, Radcliff's in checkmate for the moment ... and speak of the devil, here he comes. Don't look."

Radcliff held out his hand. "Let me be one of the first to congratulate you gentlemen on your fine community spirit." Radcliff shook each man's hand firmly. "Tom Lennard, the editor, will want an interview for the first edition, quite possibly a photo too," he informed Bycroft. "I must be going; the wife and kids are waiting. Good day, gentlemen."

The men stood staring at Bycroft. "Yes, I'm sure he meant all of us." They immediately started discussing what they would wear for the photograph. "Bastock, your best mate routine needs work; now give me one of those Cuban cigars you've been bragging about."

The pastor worked his way through the congregation, coming face to face with Catherine and the girls. His stance confirmed his disdain for the women.

"We enjoyed your service very much. Catherine Dunn," she held out her hand.

Pastor O'Dea just looked at it. "Women like you were once stoned," he informed her.

From behind Catherine, Ying Lee appeared. "He who is without sin, cast the first stone." Bowing to Catherine, then to the parson, he introduced himself. "And I am Ying Lee." He bowed to each again, "and this, "Mrs. Lee, and..." he pointed to each of the children individually, "...Ying, one two three four and five." He then pointed to Mrs. Lee's belly, "... six, may be on way."

"The Lord welcomes all Christian families, Mr. Lee."

"We not Christian family," Ying Lee confided, "we family on excursion."

Mrs. Lee, chastising her husband for not introducing her children properly, derailed the pastor from admonishing Catherine and her girls in public. The kids once again took an unruly interest in Catherine and gestured for her to do something funny, while her girls called out to clients they recognised in the gathering. Many of the men gathered up wives and children and quickly departed for fear of acknowledgement.

Ying Lee enlightened the pastor. "I make confession." The pastor towered over the Chinaman. Ying Lee gestured for him to lean down so he could whisper in his ear. "Kids drive me stupid. I bring them here for outing." Looking up with forefinger to his lips Ying Lee enticed the pastor to bend down again by speaking quietly. "Those who live in glass house should not throw stones. Shhh. This our secret."

His victim stayed in the bent position pondering whether it was something Ying Lee knew about him, or if he was the object of oriental arrogance. Ying Lee bowed again and then both men stood up, looking at each other. "I look forward to new church and what you have to say very much." Those watching the David and Goliath scenario were perplexed as to why the pastor kept bowing to Ying Lee.

Ying Lee turned and bowed to Catherine. "Missy." He departed the gathering, standing as tall as the pastor.

Catherine and the girls departed for their picnic, the cronies to Bycroft's for a drinking session and most of the congregation to keep the Sabbath, except for Robinson who was suffering a brutal cold from his unforeseen overnight campout. Bycroft had instructed him to organise the cleanup and the pulling down of the tent.

"You're a good man," the pastor told Robinson as he helped him lift the organ into the wagon. "The Lord will reward you in heaven."

"I'd rather Bycroft pay up in Gunnadoo," he mumbled under his breath.

9 – The Advocate Arrives

The written word both unites and alienates.
Honesty is appreciated only when asked for
and delivered with sensitivity.

Tom had spent the previous year in a government print shop; his service record enabled him to gain the experience required to run a small operation like the Advocate. In three days, he assembled the platen press and sorted racks of compositing letters and symbols. At the rear of the spacious room were the printing press, layout tables and associated printing paraphernalia; the front section accommodated the photographic studio. The front door could be locked when a sitting took place, with access to the studio from the stationer's by an adjoining door.

Wearing an eyeshade and an ink-stained printer's apron, Tom turned the platen handle to begin its trial run. Clarrie, Meg and the twins watched as the press fed out the simple but eloquent invitation; the launch and deadline of the Advocate confirmed for the second week of August.

"Right children, you've seen it work, back to your books," Meg told the twins. She turned to Tom. "Nice work, brother."

It had been her idea that Clarrie and Tom unite in their passion that was now coming to fruition. Meg had agreed that when she was not schooling the children, she would do the advertising pitch to potential clients for the first edition, collecting any gossip along the way. Tom would do the investigative journalism and Clarrie would back up with compositing. Meg would be the final proofreader. That afternoon, brother and sister left the Advocate office and began their appointed tasks.

* * *

Through puffy red eyes and with a hangover, Bycroft sat behind the window watching the stranger approach. As the door opened and the bell rang, he swung around in the chair and placed his elbows on the desk. Head in hands and without looking up, he began chastising, "Can't you read? No hawkers on a Monday."

"Tom Lennard, editor of the Gunnadoo Advocate."

From behind his desk, Billings watched how Bycroft would get out of the predicament.

"I've been expecting you." Bycroft looked up with a strained grin and stood to shake hands. "I hope you don't mind a bit of my humour. As you can see, I have a nasty head cold. Sit down, no formalities here. Anyone connected with Clarrie is a friend of mine. Billings, make a pot of tea."

Tom removed a notebook and pencil from his satchel. "I believe you have some news for me?"

Bycroft flamboyantly related his tale, from conceiving the concept to pleading with his colleagues. "…and I finally convinced them of their Samaritan duty." His elbows flopped onto the desk as if he'd just been lifted down from the Cross. The hangover drained him of energy and the capacity to think clearly.

"Let me just get this straight." Tom summarised, crossing the T's and dotting the I's in the process. "Well then, it's just a matter of assembling your fellow Samaritans and we'll get a photograph. I'll be in touch."

"Anytime, anything I can do to help, just holler, but not today; my ears are blocked and I won't hear you." Bycroft laughed at his own joke to confirm his humorous credentials. Head down, apparently showing no interest in the conversation but all ears, Billings snickered quietly.

"The Advocate should do a personal perspective on you and your upstanding attributes," said Tom, getting up, "that sense of humour is worth mentioning also." Bycroft walked him to the door thinking the idea sounded excellent. Tom stopped. "Let me confirm with you one last time – your colleagues are donating the materials and you're donating the land?"

Swimming in a sea of nausea, Bycroft confirmed his generosity. "That's correct."

"I must say that's going to win a few points with the man upstairs." Tom replaced his hat and handed Bycroft an invitation. "I'll be in touch," he repeated.

What Bycroft had just committed himself to made him feel extremely nauseous. "Bye," he whimpered.

"Mr. Bycroft. Mr. Bycroft." Meg called, attracting his and the attention of passing pedestrians. As she arrived out of breath, Tom enquired, "Have you met the Advocate's sales representative?"

Bycroft leaned towards her. "Yes. Marge and I are on a first name basis."

"You were right," Tom loudly interrupted for listening ears to hear, "I should never have doubted you – Mr. Bycroft *is* donating the land."

She moved as if to give him a hug but stopped short, "You don't look well?"

"His ears are blocked," Tom informed her.

Bycroft put on a brave face. "Nothing to worry 'bout…it's just a head cold."

Tom gave her a wink, "Then I'll leave 'Marge' in your capable hands. May I call you John?"

He held out his hand and removed it immediately as Bycroft put his hand out. "Sorry. You might be contagious. Good day."

Meg chastised Tom. "It's nothing but a cold, you heard Mr. Bycroft say so." She turned to Bycroft, took his arm and walked him inside. Meg also did a job on him, leaving with a signed contract for advertising space in ten forthcoming editions.

Preceded by the bush telegraph news of Bycroft's land donation, Tom moved southward along Main Street calling on all traders, introducing himself and the Advocate. Meg followed his example. He entered Wong Foo's establishment and began his pitch. "I am …"

Wong Foo bowed politely and raised the forefinger. "I have been expecting you. You are Mr. Tom Lennard, editor of the Gunnadoo Advocate." He bowed again. "We Chinese have long printing tradition – a most honourable profession. Please."

He gestured for Tom to sit at the low table. "I am Wong Foo." He clapped his hands. "You will partake in refreshments, please?"

The tea, served by the oriental beauty, was more enticing than the brew Billings had served up. Wong Foo noted Tom taking an interest in his daughter; Lotus-Flower blushed, her cheeks turning the colour of the embroidered cherry blossoms on her jacket. A glance from her father ensured she quickly withdrew from sight.

Tom began the conversation. "Mr. Foo, being the man of culture I'm sure you are, and having a printing heritage," (Wong Foo was impressed), "the Advocate requests you to be a spokesman for the Chinese community. The Advocate isn't for the white folk only; it's to represent all Gunnadoo's citizens." Wong Foo was more than impressed. "We're not like *Smith's Weekly*, there's nothing radical about this newspaper. Printing derogatory articles and cartoons only stir up xenophobia."

"Peace and harmony most important for prosperity," Wong Foo concurred.

"Education, health, law and order – there are many issues that Gunnadoo must look at. All can be exposed in the Advocate."

"I am fluent with many languages. Illiterate Chinese labourer cannot read English; many have difficulty with Chinese."

"And your children," Tom stated. "What if there was a school where they could learn to read and write?"

"Your request and your quest most honourable. I humbly accept position as spokesman."

Tom raised his teacup, "Cheers."

Foo raised his and enquired, "Who is building school? Not me I hope."

"A church is being built. With a few modifications it will also accommodate the school and public meetings."

"And where is your church to stand?" Wong Foo enquired.

"That I don't know."

"I may be of help. Let me think." He rubbed the fingernail against his cheek, a methodical succession of images falling into place. "This is how you say...off the record." Wong Foo told Tom of Bycroft's recent interest in his land. "If that is what he has planned, it would be most honourable," Wong Foo finished.

"Right in the heart of town; it would be most perfect," said Tom. He had dealt Wong Foo an ace without knowing it.

"I am but a modest business man, Mr. Lennard," he clapped his hands, "not of your faith and, as you can see, I have Lotus-Flower and six more daughters." The giggling girl cleared the table, not daring to look up; Tom was smitten. "Unfortunately," said Wong Foo, "this land must pay for shame of not having sons." Once Lotus-Flower's task was completed, the fingernail gestured for her to depart. She left, giggling even louder. Wong Foo walked Tom to the landing at the front of the shop.

"I fully understand your position, Mr. Foo. I wish you the best of luck. Whatever the outcome, I'm sure Gunnadoo will benefit. I've just had a thought," said Tom, "the Advocate should do a personal perspective on a man with such culture as your good self. I'll take a photograph; I'll be in touch." He handed Wong Foo an invitation to the Advocate's launch.

"Mr. Foo, Mr. Foo." Meg called. Tom introduced her, and then began working the other side of Main Street, heading in a northerly direction.

The sale sign announced, 'Two bottles for the price of one'. Entering Houten's store, Tom enquired if Dr. Lovett's Cure-All was good for a sore throat. Houten launched into his sales pitch. "Blimey. Nine out of ten doctors…"

"Can I quote you on that?" He held out his hand. "Tom Lennard, the Advocate."

Ruby immediately filled the open doorway behind the counter. She laughed mockingly at her husband. "There, I told you one day that snake oil would turn around and bite you."

The accused charlatan was brushed aside and Tom's hand shaken with the grip of an arm wrestler. "G'day Luv, Ruby's the name. You feel like a cup of tea? I've just read an article on tea reading; we'll give it a go."

"It's always handy to know what the future holds. Thank you."

Scones and Ruby's gossip accompanied what was probably his tenth cup that day. "I've gotta go, I mean I must go, deadlines to meet," he told her. Tom's need for an urgent call of nature dictated his quick exit. Houten joined Ruby behind the counter. They heard the first half of Tom's sentence as he bolted out the door. "The Advocate must do a…"

"Do a what?" Houten asked.

"Dunno, Luv," she humped her shoulders and put an arm around him, "dunno."

Under the lamplight, the Advocate staff discussed the afternoon's transactions. The tactical ploy of Tom being the advance guard for Meg was a huge success. He had the lead stories and many ideas for the Editorial, and Meg had signed up clients for their advertising revenue. From information extracted in general chitchat with various sections of the community, the business and social news column would also be filled.

"Let's hope the reception we got today continues," said Clarrie, sorting through the paperwork. "Do we have a candidate for a gossip columnist?"

Meg and Tom answered in unison, "Ruby Houten."

"I'll see her tomorrow and give her the good news," volunteered Meg.

Tom was satisfied with his achievements and swigged on the bottle of the Cure-All elixir. "The Advocate can do a lot of good for this community…"

"… and make a good living," Meg interrupted. She picked up the Bycroft Holdings contract.

"But we can't afford to get anyone offside yet." Clarrie added. "Let's get some infrastructure first."

She held up the contract. "Bycroft makes my blood run cold."

"I reckon Bycroft's hangover…excuse me, head cold, was big enough to photograph," added Tom.

"I haven't made up my mind about Wong Foo." Meg looked at Tom. "What do you think?"

The daughter's image came to mind. *Pretty as a lotus flower,* he thought and then asked, "Did you know Wong Foo cultivates daughters?"

Clarrie raised an eyebrow to Meg, which she mirrored. "What about him as a spokesman for the Chinese?" she asked.

"He has no problems with that. We should think about including a gardening column." Meg instigated another eye gesture to Clarrie. He got up and stretched.

"Well, that's enough for today, we all need our rest, come on Meg." Tom received a slap on the shoulder. "Good work. You get some kip too; you haven't stopped since arriving."

"You're not serious about a gardening section, are you?" Meg enquired.

"What?"

She studied him; no physical signs of stress showed. "No burning the candle at both ends. I want you to promise me you'll get some sleep.

"All right, all right – goodnight, Marge," he wisecracked.

10 – Ulterior Motives

Misrepresentation of 'the being'
leads to a life of alienation from oneself.

Houten sat on the hospitality bench in front of the general store basking in the sun. Morning tea consisted of a cup of tea, damper and a smoke, unlike his usual 'Emu's breakfast', as Ruby called it – a drink of water and a good look around. He watched Catherine cross the street and climb the steps to the boardwalk.

"Bonjour, Monsieur Houten, a lovely morning, oui?"

"Oui," he replied sheepishly. She stopped and clasped her cheeks.

"Sacré bleu. Your French is…oh-la-la, très bon."

Ruby stood out of sight in the doorway. "G'day Luv, come in. Frenchy here can look after the customers." She stuck her head out the door to him. "Oui."

The two women sat down to their morning tea in the rear office. As usual, Ruby did most of the talking. "… and the word is Bycroft's going to buy the land from Wong Foo and they are uniting to build a church. How 'bout that?"

"Are you sure?"

"Well that's the scuttlebutt…can't see it myself but mark my words there'll be something in it both them…and I don't mean salvation."

"Shop." called Houten.

"Shop," Ruby mimicked, "I knew we'd be interrupted. That man is useless…won't be long."

A wedding photograph of the Houtens hung above the desk. The bride was thin and her husband had a full head of hair. Catherine observed that Ruby retained the same look in her eyes as when the photograph was taken; she still loved her husband. Beneath her rough exterior beat a heart of gold.

Ruby returned with Meg.

"A columnist, me? I wouldn't know what to say, Luv."

"It's just chit-chat in print, I'll do the…" Meg stopped when she saw Catherine. "I'm sorry; I didn't know you had company."

"All the merrier," Ruby cackled, "it's been ages since I've had a good chinwag. There's plenty of scones and jam, and lots of gossip. I'll boil the kettle again."

The women introduced themselves.

"Meg Radcliff… it's nice to meet you."

"Bonjour, Catherine Dunn. It is a pleasure to meet you."

"Meg works for the Advocate," Ruby said.

"Our new newspaper, how wonderful."

"They want me to be a social columnist, me, Ruby Houten."

"I think that is wonderful too. Congratulations."

Ruby placed another plate of scones on the table. "I don't want to blow my horn or nothing," she tapped Meg on the shoulder, "although I do play the saxophone." She laughed jovially at her own pun, "But the recipe for these scones won the Blue Ribbon at the Royal Easter Show."

The gossip agenda twisted and turned, conversation flowing freely between Ruby and Meg. Catherine was a little more reserved with what she divulged.

"There are some things men are better off not knowing," Ruby disclosed at the end of a scandalous tale.

"I agree," said Meg, helping herself to another scone. "My father, may he rest in peace, fought tooth and nail with the university faculty so I could attend. In my last year of study I met a man, not Mr. Radcliff, and let's just say, my attendance dropped off to the point where I scraped through the exams by the skin of my teeth."

"And what did you study," Ruby enquired.

"Languages."

Ruby persisted, "Which ones?"

"I majored in French."

A piece of scone lodged in Catherine's windpipe and she began coughing violently. Ruby thumped her between the shoulder blades. The obstruction dislodged and flew across the table, landing on Meg's shoulder.

Meg quickly picked up Catherine's cup and gave it to her. She gulped at it. "Vous buvez un peu," Meg insisted. Such was the shock of hearing Meg's fluent request to drink, Catherine then had a coughing fit and showered Meg in tea. Catherine received more slapping on the back from Ruby.

* * *

Reinvigorated by having witnessed Bycroft's battering of the previous day, and a night of dragon kissing, Billings felt on top of the world. However, he still kept well out of the way of his cantankerous boss. Bycroft had spoken no more than a couple of words all morning. Relief came in the form of Tom sticking his head through the door.

"You got a minute?" he asked Bycroft.

"Any time. Come in; sit down. Billings…?"

"No tea, thank you," Tom declined politely.

"What can I do for you?"

"It's a matter of what you can do for Gunnadoo."

They discussed the requirement for infrastructure and a town council to give the community legitimate representation. The thought of legitimate power and stature was irresistible and Bycroft swooned in a private fantasy of his statue cast in bronze. Tom completed his speech by creatively implying support from the Advocate should he decide to run for office.

Bycroft lit a cigar and contemplated. "I've never given politics a thought." He leaned back and clasped his coat lapel. "It would be a challenge…God knows there's folk out there that need a helping hand."

"They need direction and from what I've heard you're the one who can give it."

"I am known for my foresight."

"If you can convince your colleagues to extend their generosity and build a school, I don't need any convincing in saying *you* should throw your hat in the ring and be a candidate for Mayor…and who knows what after that. Put Gunnadoo on the map.

"It's a lot of responsibility; I'll need time to think about it."

Tom checked his watch, "Speaking of which, look at it." He stood. "I only popped in to ask if tomorrow would be good for you and your colleagues to have photographs taken, and I'm now walking out with what may be the lead story in the Advocate's first edition."

Bycroft walked him to the door. "I'll get in touch with them. What time tomorrow?"

"Eleven o'clock. If you come ten minutes early, we'll get an individual shot of you." They shook hands.

Returning to the Advocate, Tom smiled at the outcome. Bycroft strode back to his desk smiling at what he now believed to be his destiny. "Billings, time for some exercise, on ya bike, Sunshine. Inform my colleagues we'll be meeting at my residence tonight."

After much soul-searching for a financial profit on the potential land deal with Wong Foo, Bycroft hadn't been able to find one. As he saw it, however, there was an upside – he would still get Wong Foo's capital for mining Yakka Dakka and chalk up Samaritan points at his antagonist's expense. That evening, Bycroft took his position standing in front of the mantelpiece, while on the other side of town,

Billings took his kneeling in front of Wong Foo. Under the influence of port and Cuban cigars, Bycroft revealed the approach from the Advocate. Billings, under the influence of the Red Dragon and Yip Tung, revealed Bycroft's Achilles heel.

"Gentlemen, gentlemen," Bycroft restored order. "We're not only building a church, we're building a school and a meeting hall all in one – the community can't ask for more than that. Think of it like this ..." He drew upon a cigar and with the same hand then took hold of his lapel. Holding the port glass up to the ceiling lamp, he exhaled gently, the glass disappearing into the hovering brown cloud. While the men's focus was transfixed on the levitating mass, he lowered the glass and rested his elbow on the mantelpiece. Gently blowing the cloud away, it appeared the glass had disappeared. "See." There were vacant stares only. He shook his head, realising the visual metaphor had been wasted.

White scratched his head. "I don't see noth'n."

"Exactly." said Bycroft, making the best of what he had to work with. "And, if we're not one step ahead, that's what we'll end up with – a big fat nothing."

His increasing drawl reflected the gravity of the situation. He raised the glass again. "Good times and all of us will be moved along by..."

Harrick sarcastically interrupted. "... a cloud of cigar smoke?"

The men laughed; Bycroft waited for silence, noting Harrick's recalcitrant attitude. "...the winds of change."

Bastock complained, "Sounds bloody costly." He had stuck his head up at the wrong time and Bycroft decided to make a point of asserting his authority and the pecking order.

"So how's the relationship with you and Radcliff blooming?" he asked.

Bastock realised his mistake too late. "He's an unfriendly bastard."

The men began teasing him mercilessly.

"Did you give him a good discount?" Stoddard enquired.

"That bloody printing press was no easy job. It took four men to move it."

"Did you give him a good discount?" Bycroft repeated.

"Any more and I'd be paying him. The bastard's just plain unsociable."

"Says a lot for your personality then, doesn't it?" Bycroft chortled, his witticism going down well. Browning sat forward on his chair tittering. Bastock wanted to do some pecking also.

"I don't see what this is costing you." he shouted at Browning.

Beads of perspiration immediately formed on Browning's top lip as he waited for Bycroft to come to his aid and defend him.

"Well," shouted Bastock, "what've you got riding on this?" All eyes moved back to Browning.

"My soul and career," he replied timidly. His statement had more effect on the men than Bycroft's metaphor. Silence filled the room until Bastock turned to Bycroft.

"All right, if you get the land off Wong Foo, we'll support you and build a school."

11 – Checkmate for Whom?

Deception is seen in a camera lens
Albeit not in a photograph.

The typewriter clattered non-stop as Meg and Clarrie took turns typing page content from handwritten notes. It then went to the compositing table ready for proofing and typesetting. Tom prepared the glass plates for the photographic session. At the prescribed time, Bycroft showed up in his best attire; the stiff collar and bow tie restricted his head movement, making him appear even more conceited. The sign on the Advocate's closed door said to enter through the stationer's. He did, standing unnoticed at the front counter watching the hive of activity until his patience wore thin.

"Excuse me."

"No hawkers on a Wednesday." called Tom.

"Good one." shouted Bycroft. "Love your sense of humour. Good morning all."

Tom showed him to a wicker chair and asked him to pose, requesting him to hold it as he focused the lens. Slightly angled to the camera, Bycroft imagined he was posing for an oil painting and sat frozen; he couldn't resist talking though. "I spoke with my colleagues last night."

"Chin up a fraction please…and?"

"Gunnadoo will get a church and you'll get your lead story."

Tom stopped the focusing, "You got the land."

"Well, let's just say, it's as good as in the bag."

"Excellent, that Wong Foo character is a tough nut to crack. I had my doubts you'd be able to do it." Tom continued focusing. "Left shoulder to me a little. Of course, you understand a front-page story requires confirmation. Try crossing your legs."

"I'm meeting with Wong Foo later today."

"Well, best of luck. Your chest out please, keep the chin up."

"I'll wear my lucky hat."

Bycroft watched out of the corner of his eye as Tom stopped focusing and stretched his back; he wished he could do the same.

"Calling for a council election is our lead story at the moment unless you should decide to throw your hat in the ring with building the school."

"Church, school, meeting hall – it'll be large enough for everything." Bycroft advised, "My colleagues have agreed."

"I'm impressed." Tom called to Clarrie, "How long can we hold the front page?"

"Five o'clock Friday."

Bycroft began squirming.

"Think of yourself as a statue," Tom suggested. "This Samaritan deed would be a solid platform to launch your campaign from."

"It would, wouldn't it?" Bycroft agreed.

"Now, I want you to remember the exact position you're in now for the group shot," Tom informed him, "I'll take one standing for the individual shot." Bycroft stood and stretched, relaxing from the contorted position at last. Tom removed the chair and Bycroft again took up a pose. The gunpowder cap exploded in a ball of smoke and a flash lit the subject. "There, that wasn't too painful, was it?" Tom asked.

The cronies arrived punctually and jostled for position around the wicker chair. Bycroft again took up the painful pose and waited as the pedantic photographer kept requesting slight alterations in each man's stance. Finally, with everyone in position, he took the shot.

Billings rushed back to the account journals when he saw the boss returning. Bycroft replaced him in the chair and watched the various identities – traders, gossip columnist and Chinese spokesman – turn out in their finest and proceed to the Advocate to have their photographs taken. When the photographic session was complete, Tom packed the camera in its travelling case and went on location to the very northern end of High Street to capture a portrait of everyday Gunnadoo and its residents. Alerted by pounding hooves, he swung the camera and waited with eye to the viewfinder. The horse and sulky flashed past, leaving Tom in a cloud of dust.

People who didn't know better would have thought it was Bycroft arriving in town, but he was watching from the window.

"Whoa Buttercup." Wally quickly jumped down. Grabbing the Hessian sack he strode into Browning's office. Bycroft didn't know what to make of it and sat patiently watching until Wally entered excitedly.

"This is it."

"What is?"

"We've found it. Come on." Wally returned next door, Bycroft following on his heels.

Browning bent over the new samples examining them. He looked up and informed Bycroft, "I've never seen anything like it." Perspiration was running from his lip like salivation.

Wally slapped his partner on the back, "I was just about ready to give up looking. I'm going to the bathhouse to clean up."

Bycroft grabbed his arm. "Don't say anything about this to anybody; we'll talk when you get back. There's a lot happening you don't know about. Best you do before anything is said."

"No problem." He left and whistled to the dog. "Come on, bath time."

Bycroft picked up a sample and studied it, as well as the perspiration on Browning's top lip. "You're sure about this?"

"I'm the assayer, aren't I? This is the potential I was talking about."

Browning stood watching; he said no more. Bycroft gently placed the ore down and slowly walked to the door. Then he stopped as if he was going to say something, changed his mind and proceeded to his office. He contemplated another change of plan, that of cutting Wong Foo out of becoming a partner in Yakka Dakka. Should the mine now show a 'mother load' his antagonist would get none.

When Wally returned, Bycroft informed him of the previous week's happenings. Most of it Wally had already heard from Ying Lee. He hadn't heard the news of Wong Foo's potential investment in Yakka Dakka, and when it was revealed he wasn't pleased.

Bycroft poured another whiskey and moaned, "I worked my arse off to find another partner for us."

"Never, not Wong Foo." Wally found himself declaring.

"I thought you liked them slant eyes?"

He plopped into the chair. "I got nothing against the Chins but ... " Wally then found himself questioning why he *was* against Wong Foo, finally saying, "Jeez'us, I don't trust him."

"Good enough for me, partner." Bycroft leaned back and lit a cigar. "You understand I want that land deed though?" A smoke ring rose above his head and hung there like a dirty halo. "I'll tell Wong Foo it was a false gold seam and we're not going to expand the operation. He'll be offered some cash for the deed and be happy with that – because that's all the thieving bugger's gonna get."

"I'll require help…it's too dangerous to shore up the mine alone."

"I'll get you some men but while you're in town you act pessimistic. Anything planned for this evening?"

"Naw, I might throw the pennies and catch up with a few people."

Bycroft gulped down the last of his whiskey. "Pleasant duties call," he announced sarcastically. "Wong Foo – look and learn. Billings – I won't be returning. Wally – see you for breakfast." With the partnership in the goldmining venture being withdrawn, Bycroft left the office not feeling confident about getting the deed but ready to do a deal with the devil if need be.

* * *

Like all the other businesses, the newsagency was expanding. Clarrie rearranged the large interior of the stationer's shop to include a confectionery counter.

"Jeez'us, what's happening here?"

"Just in time, give me a hand," he grunted, trying to push a glass counter to its relegated location. When it was in place, he leaned on top of it. "It's a good photograph of you."

"What is?"

"Tom will show you, he's through there."

Wally walked to the door and leaned on the counter, observing the radical change from what he'd last seen. "The press never sleeps, I hear."

Tom looked up from compositing. "Lift it up and come through." Wally joined him and immediately swung the magnifying glass on its axis so he could look at the work Tom was doing.

"I'm just checking. We don't want any slip-ups. What is it anyway?" The print being set in reverse was foreign to the untrained eye.

"That's the obituary column and my name came close to being in it."

"Go on, I haven't heard this piece of news. What happened?"

Tom showed him the photograph.

Wally stared at it. "That's a masterpiece."

The composition reeked of action. Buttercup's chest and striving hooves were aslant to the vertical because of the camera tilt, the mare's inclined head and neck embellished by a flowing mane. The bouncing sulky, airborne, projected another angle. Standing astride the sulky in a chariot-like stance, the driver held slack reins raised in one hand, looking as if he were cracking a whip behind the ear of the galloping steed. In the other hand, he was raising his hat above his head – symbol of an Australian bushman's horsemanship. The clear image of the dog levitating above the seat was a fluke, as was the delineation of dust clouds billowing into a background of gum trees and sky.

"How'd you know to set up on the back-snapper?"

"What do mean?"

"There's a depression and then a sharp rise in the track. It lifts the wheels every time if you're not careful; it so happened to lift me hat too. I nearly lost me balance jumping up to grab it."

"I thought you were posing for the camera."

"Naw, I didn't even see ya," Wally drawled, "and how'd you do that?"

"What?" asked Tom, studying the photograph.

"Get all the detail so clearly."

"By risking life and bloody limb and I won't be doing it again."

He'd said that many a time in the trenches but always did. The images and unshakable memories remained with him, blurred and fused together, like the faces of unknown soldiers he'd caught in the

207

camera lens. Their expressions were always of larrikinism, like that exhibited in the photograph he was looking at.

"I tell you what," said Wally, his voice distracting Tom from the photograph, "I got a good eye, do you want a hand?"

"I've just shown you the evidence of how *good* your eyesight is and..." Tom reconsidered. "Here's an apron, I'll show you how to typeset headlines, they're the largest letters we have. Clarrie." he yelled. "Tell Meg to set another place at the table...and one under it." The dog lay snoozing, oblivious to the Advocate's deadline.

* * *

Wong Foo welcomed Bycroft with a handclap. "Is this most pleasant occasion business or social?" The tray of tea arrived with much bowing from Cherry-Blossom, another of Wong Foo's daughters. Her black hair gleamed and Bycroft drooled at the thought of having her. He reflected on Billing's bad dandruff and flinched at the thought of his handmaiden. Cherry-Blossom quietly withdrew when given the fingernail gesture.

"I have given much consideration to your partnership offer and humbly accept."

Bycroft butted in. "Well, we've actually struck a snag...there is a small problem."

Wong Foo interjected, "Problems are for solving."

"It appears we may have been a little optimistic. The seam stopped dead. There's only solid rock."

Wong Foo replaced his cup on the table. "Has dynamite been used?"

"The place resembles the Western Front, I'm told."

"No gold, I do not understand. I have the report and saw samples."

"The gold is there – but as to how deep or how much is anyone's guess. I'd be a dishonest man if I didn't tell you the truth." Wong Foo re-evaluated the information as Bycroft spun the tale. "My partner is obsessed; no doubt he'll want to keep looking but…"

"This is most unpleasant news. I was counting on much wealth as dowry for seven daughters. You don't have daughters, do you Mr. Bycroft?"

"No time for children." He blew on the hot brew to cool it.

"Then, Mr. Bycroft, there will be no grandchildren either and they are most important."

"Not at the moment they're not."

"I disagree, nothing more important than grandchildren. How are you to leave legacy in sands of time?"

Fantasy and legacy fused for Bycroft. "A bronze statue would be very nice," he replied sarcastically.

"Very nice, until destroyed by time…" the raised fingernail stopped Bycroft from interjecting, "… or vandals. Statue can easily be melted down for commodity value."

"Well, that certainly took the gloss off the bronze." Bycroft felt as though he had the situation under his control.

"So will bird shitting on you until undignified end," Wong Foo slyly peeped over the cup rim while sipping the tea, "lineage, Mr. Bycroft, is for all time."

Bycroft was in checkmate and wouldn't admit it but believing it would carry favour with the land deal, he conceded, "You are right Wong Foo, you're a wise man. Chin-chin," he sipped his tea, "this is very good."

"I too would be a dishonest man if I did not make confession," confided Wong Foo.

Bycroft studied his patsy and likewise the fingernail, intrigued by what was about to be revealed.

"I am humble storekeeper. I am also in laundry business. Alas, I have knowledge of washing dirty clothes only, not unaccountable assets."

"Go on," encouraged Bycroft, feeling he'd gained the upper hand.

"Chinese love to gamble, game of chance most exciting. I will still gamble my unaccountable assets with you and your partner, but unfortunately I cannot gamble dowry of seven daughters."

The chance of laundering Wong Foo's dirty assets into the new mining venture was achievable; there would be no paper trail and there would be a profit for skimming. Bycroft contemplated longer than need be, playing the scene for all it was worth. "And if I should be able to accomplish what you ask?"

"I will look upon land negotiation favourably," said Wong Foo, removing writing material from a concealed drawer under the table.

"You have a deal," replied Bycroft. Not waiting to be asked, he poured another cup of tea himself.

Wong Foo passed him a sheet of notepaper. "I shall write my answer first and then you will write your offer."

Bycroft weighed up the proposition carefully. There was only one go at this kind of crazy deal, but as he saw it, the cards were in his favour. Without blatantly insulting the Chinaman to his face, he would propose the lowest figure possible.

Wong Foo didn't try to hide the three words he wrote in view of Bycroft, but they were impossible to read upside down. He carefully folded the paper in half as though working on an origami project. When completed, he slid the pen and ink to Bycroft and then sat with eyes closed.

Bycroft stared at Wong Foo, pondering the man's arrogance. *To hell with it*, he thought and penned his own insulting offer. Then he roughly folded the paper and pushed it across the table.

Wong Foo didn't look at it, instead sliding his origami project to the middle of the table. Under the intimidating fingernail, the paper stayed like a victim impaled. "We abide by our written word, agreed?" Bycroft nodded. The released paper opened up, resembling a Chinese junk raising its sail, and Wong Foo gently blew it. His reply to his opponent's offer slid to a stop in front of Bycroft. Bycroft thought the showmanship was impressive, but he wasn't impressed by Wong Foo's counter offer – 'For each daughter.'

* * *

Paddy drank at the Plough Inn, Bycroft's second pub. Here the immigrant workers congregated until the six o'clock swill – the drinkers lined up the glasses and swilled them down before being ejected from the premises at six. Paddy's salary from working down the pit went into his belly and Bycroft Holdings. Broke, he would then play at the house of ill repute for drinks. Catherine moved through the drawing room observing both customers and girls enjoying themselves. She stood and listened to the Irishman playing a melancholy version of *Danny Boy* on the piano. Certain idiosyncrasies, apart from the tooth he'd lost in a fight, reminded her of her Danny. Hearing the tune reinforced the loss.

"You be wasting your God-given talent," Catherine absent-mindedly chastised him aloud. The playing immediately ceased, the last notes resonating into the silence that followed. Patrons raised heads to look.

"Say that again?" he requested drunkenly.

Catherine blushed, the indiscretion quickly realised and corrected. "Pardon Monsieur?"

"What ya just said. T'was very good; ya sounded just like me dear old mother, God bless her soul."

"Now I am embarrassed, I cannot do it again with everybody staring," she placed a hand on her chest, "please keep playing."

Paddy returned to the ivories with more intensity. Tears began rolling down his cheeks from between closed eyes. Sobbing, he clenched his teeth together and struggled for breath. The quick intakes of air gushed through the gap of his missing tooth, producing a whistling sound that accompanied his outpouring of emotion. Catching Mrs. Chang's attention, Catherine took the opportunity to make a timely exit.

"Madame Chang, I am retiring, bon soir."

She smiled and with the slightest head movement indicated that all was in order.

Catherine entered her room to find Bycroft stretched out on the bed, evidence of his trek through the rear bush on her quilt cover. He held high the hip flask, its top swinging freely on the small silver chain.

"I couldn't find where you keep the refill."

She retrieved a bottle from the walk-in wardrobe and handed it to him. He took the hand and the bottle, pulling both onto the bed. "Now give me a kiss." Lovemaking took all of five minutes, four-and-a-half in the removal of clothing and getting it up. Catherine lit his cigar, poured him a glass of whiskey and then settled down to a session of Bycroft's self-praise.

"…Mayor Bycroft, I like it. I've always wanted a title."

"How did you know Monsieur Foo would sell his mayor title?" Catherine enquired.

"Deed of title," he snapped, "the mayoral title is my payoff for being such a nice bloke."

"What if Monsieur Foo did not wish to sell?"

"He didn't. I had to convince him it was in his own interest he should." Bycroft began laughing. "I actually feel good." He gulped down the contents of the glass. "Pour me another."

Catherine slipped her legs out of the bed and sat with her back to Bycroft. He eyed her shapely form. "Monsieur Foo is…how you say?"

Bycroft responded, "Cunning as a shithouse rat?"

Catherine gestured the jumping of tokens on a board game. "That is not what I mean, no…he is…"

"A Chin that needs taking down a peg or two."

Her hands waved in frustration. "A chess master." She handed Bycroft the glass, crawled over him to the other side of the bed and snuggled under the warm bedding.

"I was always three jumps ahead of him," Bycroft boasted, "Wong Foo was in checkmate before the game started."

"You are such a clever businessman."

His ego couldn't be contained. "I had Browning plant some ore that had traces of gold in it. We fabricated the assayer report and Wong Foo fell for it."

"And you now have two partners, oui?"

"No. Him as a partner in a mine with no gold I could handle, but with gold? Never. I just wanted the deed title."

"How do you have the deed but only one partner? I do not understand."

Bycroft related how the recent gold found by Wally changed the scam and yet he was still able to employ the new situation to an advantage. "Your so-called 'master tactician' now wants *me* to do *his* laundry."

"Pardon?" Catherine sat up. "Monsieur Foo has his wife and daughters to do his laundry."

Bycroft's ash fell on the bed linen. He brushed it aside, along with Catherine's intelligence. "Monsieur Foo's dirty money," he mocked, "will be sluice washed, never to be seen again."

"Who is this sluice?"

"No, a sluice is what miners use to wash ore," he explained caustically.

"I have never heard of this sluice, you tease Catherine, oui?"

"Wash away the dirt and you reap the reward."

He stared at Catherine arrogantly and lifted the empty glass again, forcing her to move back to his side to pour him a drink. With Irish blood at boiling point, Catherine crawled across his legs only to have her bare bottom fondled then firmly slapped.

"Ouch."

"Good breeding stock," he mumbled.

"Pardon?"

"Never mind."

* * *

Cramped conditions and many dubious characters under the one roof bred distrust and it was common for patrons to be involved in bloodletting skirmishes. Billings was now under Wong Foo's protection; Master Ho greeted him, showing him to a private room apart from the main opium den. Sweet aromas still lingered, filling his nostrils. Master Ho packed the bowl again and Billings ingested the dragon's searing breath.

"Your boss will soon move my uncle's unaccountable assets," Yip Tung informed Billings, "and when he does we must be ready to relieve him of his load."

Billings sat on the bunk swaying, his eyes heavy. "I do this because I hate Bycroft, why do you?"

"I am Wong Foo's nephew."

"Like father, like son," Billing's slurred as he lay down.

Yip Tung tried to focus his thinking. "Like uncle, like nephew," he corrected. Once he had partaken of the poppy, the present was no longer of concern. Yip Tung collapsed next to Billings on the bunk.

12 – A Deceitful Menu

*A dog's breakfast will never be other
even when rehashed by a master chef.*

A soft bed and the relative quietness compared to the
bush induced the extra hours of sleep. Wally's late
night concentration battle with compositing typeset
had taken its toll. He opened the curtains. "Jeez'us."
Sunlight streamed in. The dog stretched and
shuddered. Sticking its nose in the air and sniffing, it
began licking its lips. "Yeah, I could go half a pig and
a dozen eggs myself," said Wally, dressing quickly.

Bycroft was picking at various plates laid out in
the middle of the table. Remnants of his large
breakfast lay on a plate as evidence. Wally entered
the kitchen and sat opposite him.

"Practising for when you're a rich man, are
you?"

Bycroft slurped on a coffee. "This stuff is pretty
good. I can see why the Yanks drink so much of it."
He clapped his hands twice and the housekeeper
immediately put a mug in front of Wally, pouring the
black brew from a height. Bycroft's forefinger
gestured more instructions and plates of food began
arriving. He told Wally a fragmented version of what
would be the lead story in the first edition of the

Advocate, then an account of how he had got the better of Wong Foo. "I finally relented. He was practically pleading with me to take it," he lied. Bycroft then removed a pen and small notepad from inside his waistcoat pocket and began writing. "What do you think I offered for the land?"

"I'm buggered if I know." Wally observed the inept origami replication of the Chinese junk Bycroft created. He stopped eating. "Well, how much?"

"Old Chinese proverb says…" Bycroft slipped the information halfway across the table, leaving his forefinger on it, "…may the winds of good fortune, fill your sails."

Wally stared at the red cuticle and bitten fingernail, and the black coffee stain soaking into the paper. Bycroft raised his finger and gently blew, then a second time more firmly. On the third try a gale finally picked it up and like a kite out of control, it looped once and dived into Wally's breakfast.

"If that's the destination of good fortune," he said, staring at the increasingly soggy paper, "I hope I never have the wind of good fortune up my arse." Bacon fat and egg yolk dripped from the paper as he turned it right side up. "Confucius say…" began Wally, as he read the note, "Jeez'us, that's a good price."

"Well that's Confucius, Wong Foo and me that agree," Bycroft bragged, "what about you?"

Wally checked the price again. "No, I mean…"

"Yeah, yeah, Sunshine, I don't need it explained to me. All right, what does Confucius say?"

Wally dropped the soggy paper on the floor and the dog ate it. "Better you send message in a bottle next time." He broke up laughing at his own witticism. "Hey, that's not bad, what do you reckon?"

Bycroft retorted, "I think you made that up."

"And you don't embellish your stories any?" Wally jested.

"Well, enough of the frivolities, I've a business or two to run." Next to not making money, to be outshone in the one-upmanship stakes was intolerable. "I'm staying out at the property tonight. You're welcome to …"

"Naw, thanks all the same, I'll be grabbing a few things and getting back. That mother load is close- I can feel it. Until it's found, I don't know if I'm coming or going."

"You and me both Sunshine," Bycroft added. "Are you invited to the Advocate's opening?"

"Yeah, I'll come in."

"Bring the men in with you. They could do with a day off but tell them to keep their mouths shut or they'll rue the day they were born. I don't want news of this new find getting out."

Wally dropped off his list of supplies at Houten's then proceeded to see if Dadswell had repaired his work boots. The callus on the saddler's thumb and forefinger was as thick as his Scottish brogue. A sail maker by trade, he'd jumped ship in Sydney when the 1912 rush to Murrell Creek promised wealth for all. The slab hut and callus were evidence of his little success as a prospector.

"Laddie, join us," greeted Dadswell, "this is …"

"Benjamin Peck." the stranger held out a hand.

"An insurance hawker," Dadswell informed Wally.

"Legal representation and insurance advisor," Peck corrected, "my card."

"A newspaper and now a legal eagle," Wally took the card, "Gunnadoo's not going to know what hit it." From the conversation that followed, Wally deduced that Peck showed the natural curiosity and instinct of a lawyer. His flair with words would improve the prospects of selling insurance policies.

Dadswell dropped Wally's resurrected boots on the counter.

"Jeez'us. They were salvageable."

"Aye, laddie. They'll see a few more horizons. Mr. Dadswell, if you go with the laddie he'll introduce to you Clemet – he's an accident waiting to happen." There had been concern when a small fire ignited in the blacksmith's shop. Townsfolk quickly extinguished it but the averted calamity brought the hazard to the attention of nearby businesses.

Peck got his introduction and then Wally slipped back to Ying Lee's and changed. The smithy's boy harnessed the mare and received a tip on Wally's return. "Gee up Buttercup."

Peck was talking with a couple of potential customers in front of the vacant land Bycroft was angling to get. Wally gave him a wave and tapped his coat pocket to indicate he was keeping the business card. "You never know," he told the dog.

* * *

In the privacy of the rear sunroom, the girls breakfasted and Catherine sat doing bookwork and general business. Mrs. Chang poured a cup of tea and observed Catherine looking out the window. Where hours previously a white mist had lain over treetops, a white haze now hovered.

"It was beautiful this morning," said Mrs. Chang, sitting down. "I imagined cherry blossoms lying beneath the white mist."

Catherine turned unhesitatingly to her. "Madame Chang, how long has it been since you were loved by a man?"

The reply was immediate. "Half a lifetime."

Catherine returned to looking at her ghostly reflection in the window, wiping under each eye to leave a smudge mark on the glass. "That is a long time." Both women contemplated in silence until Catherine asked, "Was your husband a good man?"

"He was a good man."

She pawed the windowpane, her finger following the reflection of a tear as though condensation. "I am glad he was a good man but so short a time together."

"Fate sometimes plays cruel tricks." Her reply was as cold as the observation.

Mrs. Chang slid the tea she still held to Catherine, then stood and placed a hand on her shoulder. She moved off silently. Catherine composed herself, resolute about what was required but not knowing how to go about it.

* * *

Children ran screaming from Ying Lee's tent, he following closely behind. "You kids drive me stupid. I send you to Wong Foo, he put you to work."

"Bonjour," Catherine greeted him, I was just coming ... "

"You have just missed…"

"And what makes you think I was looking for – Monsieur Beaumont," she asked, and quickly made up a story, "I was going to ask Mrs. Lee for a recipe."

"Mrs. Lee," he pointed in the direction of Chinatown, "visit ill relative."

"Pardon, I hope the ill relative is better… and Monsieur Beaumont how is he?"

"Mr. Wally is fine and so too am I. And you, Missy?"

"Fine… and when do you expect to see …?"

"Mrs. Lee not be long," he tediously cut in, "she take noodle broth ... "

"Monsieur Beaumont." Catherine declared.

"Ah. He come to town next week for Advocate celebrations."

"Next week? Sacré bleu. It may be too late," Catherine took her stance of defiance. "If he is your friend, you will take me to him. I have important information. Oui?"

Ying Lee was surprised and a little more than intrigued. "And when am I to do this?"

"I do not know; but it will be soon."

"Soon, when is soon? And what I tell Mrs. Lee, she matchmaker, not Ying Lee…much trouble for husband if she undermined."

Catherine considered her response; she was becoming just as confused as he was. "Tell her, I change my mind. Bonjour." That also left him little to work with.

Knowing Bycroft was out of town Catherine was able to walk along High Street without the thought of his prying eyes upon her. Out the front of the general store, Ruby sat in the sun on the customer's bench seat with a mug of tea and a slice of damper bread.

"Bonjour Ruby."

"Hello Luv, pull up a pew." Catherine sat in the small area left vacant on the bench, self-conscious about her previous choking episode with Meg and the hasty exit. She observed the assayer's office opposite.

"I can offer you a cuppa," said Ruby, taking a sip of her tea, "but I'm all out of scones." She burst out laughing then began coughing as the liquid went down the wrong way.

"That serves you right for teasing Catherine," she quipped. She began slapping Ruby on the back then stopped to watch the assayer's office door open. Browning farewelled a customer and returned inside. "Ruby…do you know the assayer?"

Ruby's coughing subsided. "Not really, he's a nervous little fella."

"But are you not the Advocate social columnist? Should you not know?"

"Well, if you put it like that Luv, I suppose I should. He's never visited your establishment?" she queried.

"Never. Is he an honest man?"

"I hope so. We just opened a charge account for him and …"

"No, that is not what I mean."

Ruby cottoned on. "Ah, you've got a sluice jar haven't you?" Catherine's mind was now elsewhere.

She removed the shopping list from her basket and handed it to Ruby. "Bonjour."

Before enter Browning's office, Catherine quickly lifted her breasts and lowered her bodice. "Bonjour," she greeted him. Browning looked up from the safe he'd just opened. "Monsieur Browning?" she enquired.

Browning had always admired Catherine's beauty. His mouse-like character had previously stopped him from making any conversation when passing her on the street. Beads of perspiration formed on his top lip.

She placed her basket on the counter. "I shall come, how you say, straight to the point, oui. I have a juice jar."

"I think you mean a sluice jar."

Feigning embarrassment, her eyes fell to the floor and the open safe. "Pardon Monsieur, how silly of moi."

"It happens all the time," Browning replied, and felt quite stupid once he had. He immediately took refuge in the lecture on alchemy given when sluice jars arrived. A parched throat and nerves prevented its conclusion; his tongue flicked like a lizard's retrieving moisture from the top lip. "May I have a look?" he croaked.

Catherine strategically covered her cleavage with a hand. "Pardon?" She glanced at him seductively.

He stumbled around apologetically. "Er, ah … I meant the juice … sluice jar."

"But it is too heavy for Catherine to carry." His eyes followed her hand as it moved to the basket and she played with the handle suggestively. "I am not…strong enough."

"I could come around and have a look at it, if you like?"

"Merci…we shall have tea in the pagoda," she suggested immediately. "Is twelve-thirty fine with you?"

"Er, yes, that's fine. It's my lunch hour." He felt foolish giving Catherine the impression he had a boss standing over him with a stopwatch.

"Bonjour." She exited, feeling his eyes upon her.

So were Ruby's. She waved as Catherine looked in her general direction. Billings sat in Bycroft's chair, watching from behind the glass as she passed.

"Catherine, wait up." called Meg. "How are you feeling? You gave me quite a fright last Tuesday; I thought you were going to choke." Catherine didn't know what to say or more importantly, how to enunciate it. She smiled sheepishly. "We were just getting to know each other…" Meg caught sight of the sergeant. "Now he's an interesting character." They both watched as he strolled on the opposite side of the street. "I'd like to know more about him…and you; you're such an interesting person. I'm sure you'd have a few interesting tales to tell. Catherine froze at the thought of Meg's interrogation. "Well, no time to chat now, lots to do. You are coming to the launch Friday?" she enquired.

"Oui," Catherine replied apprehensively.

* * *

Bycroft stood on the veranda observing what work had been done and what hadn't. The workers had cleared twenty acres of scrub and trees; the larger species awaited haulage to the timber mill. Tree roots that were too large for extraction were set on fire.

"Henderson."

"Yes, boss."

"Where's Robinson?"

"I tell him boss … he wash up. I tell him again to hurry plenty if you want?"

Bycroft's forefinger did the talking. He returned to the study and poured another drink, replaced the bottle in the liquor cabinet and then sat behind his desk. He could hear the scurrying of boots getting progressively louder on the bare floorboards and smiled. Robinson arrived out of breath expecting abuse and a dressing down.

"Sit down, sit down. Take a load off your feet." Bycroft's good mood made him feel nervous. "What about a drink, what'll you have?" Without waiting for an answer, Bycroft rose and poured him one from a bottle of cheap whiskey on the sideboard. "It's starting to warm up. An early spring, I'd say."

"Yeah, there's talk of it."

"Yeah, there also seems to be more talk than action of late. I wouldn't like to think the coming hot weather would slow down progress any more than what I already see," he said, handing the glass to Robinson and standing threateningly close. "You told me that land would be cleared by now."

"We're short on manpower…I'm doing the best with what I got."

"Would another three workers help?"

Robinson sighed with relief; the axe wasn't falling on his head. "Sure would, boss, but where ya gonna get 'em from?"

"You know, Robinson," he paused to dramatise the significance of his words, "it's all about timing – striking at the right time. If you want the workers, there's a little job to be done first." Bycroft's principle of not risking everything on one endeavour had paid off previously. After deliberating over the evidence, the gold ore recently put before him, he considered the sole take-over of the Yakka Dakka mine an acceptable risk and wanted it all for himself, at the right price.

"What's the job?" asked Robinson, feeling the weight on his shoulders lighten, "and when do I start?"

Bycroft relit his cigar. "It's at the Yakka Dakka goldmine."

"I'm not a miner."

"Get your bag of tricks together for next Wednesday night. I don't want anyone killed though; just a bloody good shake-up will do. Release them and get out." Robinson was relieved to hear that. The last experience had left him the worse for wear and tear; his horse hadn't been found until it wandered into Gunnadoo a week later looking none the better either.

Robinson felt a sense of power about Bycroft asking for his services. He relaxed and made general chitchat. "The bush telegraph reckons you're running for mayor?"

"Can I count on your vote?"

"Of course."

"Are you enrolled?"

"Didn't know I had to be."

"When it comes time I'll do the paperwork and you supply me with the list of converts you've spoken with. I want all the votes I can get. Now I've work to do as no doubt you do. I'm staying overnight. I'll see you before I leave."

Robinson quickly finished his drink and left before Bycroft sprung any more surprises.

Throughout the homestead in secret possies small bundles of unaccountable cash were concealed, waiting to be retrieved. The never-put-all-your-eggs-in-one-basket theory tested Bycroft's memory as he collected the stashed money to pay for Wong Foo's deed of title.

* * *

Browning spiffed himself up in the private quarters at the rear of the assayer's office. He donned his second new suit, as yet unworn, and a new Homburg hat. Hanging the 'Out to Lunch' sign in the window, he left by the rear door. He moved along the wooded perimeter of the proposed church land and into the laneway leading down to the creek. Shallow pools, reeds and willows painted a picturesque setting. The smooth rocks and babbling water made it an ideal place for communal washing. Women slapped the larger rocks with dirty clothing, creating the crack of a teamster's whip flailing a bullock's back. Browning stepped across a couple of rocks then picked up some gravel. Pretending to study it, he looked downstream. The women began wisecracking.

"The only thing you'll find that way is Wong Foo's dirty water," said one.

"If you find a wedding ring, it's mine," another pleaded, "I lost it last week."

"You never know what gets thrown out with the dirty water," he replied, "I'm counting on it being my lucky day." He took a step and slipped; his new shoes received a soaking. Browning stepped from the pool and raised the homburg. "Good day." He moved off downstream.

In the clearing behind Wong Foo's enterprise, two of the daughters stopped hanging washing to observe Browning study handfuls of gravel. They soon lost interest and returned to their work. He played out the same charade when spotted by the smithy's boy tending to animals in the long yard. Browning followed the creek until he saw a chimney top and a worn path leading in its direction. He moved along it until unexpectedly bushwhacked by Chung Dow waving a raised shovel threateningly.

"Mademoiselle Catherine is expecting me, Mademoiselle Catherine is expecting me," Browning repeated as he was goose-stepped to the pagoda where Catherine waited.

"Bonjour, Monsieur Browning," she called out, seeing him approach.

Chung Dow prodded him in the back with the shovel.

Catherine closed the French thesaurus and placed it in her basket. "Please be seated. I see you have met Monsieur Dow. Thank you," Catherine gestured in appreciation to the smiling villain, and then returned her attention to her guest. "In his youth, it is rumoured, Monsieur Dow was an assassin. But who could believe that of such a lovely old man?"

"The way he wields that shovel – I could," Browning told her. He sat uncomfortably wriggling his toes in waterlogged shoes. "You have a beautiful garden."

"You like to garden?"

"Mrs. Browning liked to get her hands dirty," he bowed his head, "God rest her soul."

Catherine changed the subject. "And now you like to get your hands dirty in the juice jar, no?"

He laughed and didn't try to correct her. "It's what I know best."

"Your work comes highly recommended."

Mrs. Chang arrived with a tray of tea, placed it on the table and then left without speaking a word.

"One or two sugar?" Catherine asked.

"Four," he replied.

"Monsieur Browning has a sweet tooth, I think, oui?" Catherine led, the conversation toying with the man, gaining information each time he opened his mouth.

"…I passed my exams and then joined the government assayer's department as an apprentice." This was a different tale to what he'd told Bycroft.

"Such a position of responsibility, I think."

"One must show some degree of integrity," he boasted.

"If you could have one wish granted, what would it be?" she asked.

"That Mrs. Browning was …"

"That is not possible," she cut in, "but some degree of integrity you have had stolen can be restored."

"I don't know what you mean." His top lip began to give him away.

"I refer to your false assayer report."

Browning felt even more uncomfortable. "What do you know about that?"

"My girls hear many things; I hear everything," she informed him.

"You know about the bag of tricks then?"

Catherine had no idea what he was talking about. "But of course."

"I had nothing to do with it…it was Robinson. I never knew about their plan until Robinson had carried it out – then it was too late," he confessed. "I had nothing to do with those two men dying and that's the truth on Mrs. Browning's grave, I swear."

Catherine was shocked but didn't show it. "I believe you, Mr. Browning."

"It can't be proven though, Robinson would never testify against Bycroft. But it was just the same as putting a gun to their heads and pulling the trigger. I'm afraid when my usefulness is up a snake will be dropped in my bed too." He then revealed how Bycroft had forced him to rework the ore samples to scam Wong Foo.

"Then why leave yourself open to blackmail?" At the mere mention of the word, Browning began sweating profusely. Catherine continued. "I know the report can be returned to you and then you will not be – how you say – under the thumb."

"If only that was possible," he moaned, "but how?"

"With your alchemist's talent, of course." Catherine produced the sluice bottle for inspection. "With this and what you have already used, Monsieur Bycroft's partner will have more evidence of…"

"… a mother load. No, it's too risky, it couldn't be done again anyway; the samples have already been used once."

He neglected to inform Catherine that Wong Foo had already blackmailed him to plant the samples at Yakka Dakka a second time. The game had changed; it was now a sting on Bycroft. Wong Foo would receive cash for the deed instead of a partnership in a worthless goldmine.

"But are you not the alchemist I have heard so much about?"

Browning wiped the sweat from his lip with the back of his hand.

"The samples do not have to leave your office," she pursued.

"I've heard that one before."

"Your report can then be destroyed; Monsieur Bycroft and Wong Foo will have no hold over you."

"And you can get the report from Wong Foo?"

"Oui, Mr. Browning, I can."

"And the samples?"

"You will hold them at all times, I promise."

He opened the small leather bag and removed a magnifying glass protectively wrapped in a black cloth. He emptied some of the contents of the jar onto the cloth and began studying it. Unlike many sluice jars he'd worked on, except for Stoddard's,

Catherine's was exceptional. Browning roughly estimated its worth at fifty pounds but didn't tell her. "It may be possible but I shall need ten pounds for supplies."

"I shall require the sample to be ready for inspection by Monsieur Bycroft on Thursday."

"Nothing will leave my office. I have your promise?" he demanded.

"And one of my girls will be an additional benefit if you so desire."

Browning smiled and then asked. "What's in this for you?"

"Nothing for me but there will be a big lesson for Monsieur Bycroft and Wong Foo, oui?"

He liked the idea. Getting revenge on the man who tried to pull his strings was appealing and he could likewise see the determination in Catherine's eyes. "You have a deal."

"And you have another customer." Catherine laid the choker necklace on his black cloth. "I wish some work done on this and a valuation for insurance."

He placed the jeweller's loop to his eye and studied the dragon's diamond eyes. "South African pink – rose cut," he informed her. Clasped in the dragon's front claws were identical pearls. "These are magnificent," he studied the deep lustre. The sapphire was just as spectacular. "Cabochon cut...lovely workmanship. An excellent stone … yes, very nice," he paused, noting one rear claw devoid of a gemstone. "I'm not sure what's missing from here."

From her brassiere, Catherine removed a black opal; its lustre matched that of the white pearls. She handed it to him. "Ying and Jung," she quipped.

Browning's persona reverted to that of the apprehensive mouse. "It can't be, no ... it's a myth." He began to sweat profusely, removed the loop from his eye and wiped his face and neck with a bandana. "I don't believe it." he cried.

Catherine topped up his cup of tea, hurriedly spooning in four teaspoons of sugar. "Drink up," she implored. The memory of Wally's episode still haunted her and she didn't want the assayer collapsing.

"Thank you." He continued mumbling into the cup while drinking and then asked solemnly, "Where did you get this?" He rolled the black opal between his fingers.

"Where does one get the contents of a *sluice* jar? My clientele, of course, why?"

"And the dragon?" he enquired.

"A customer, a debt paid off...I do not remember."

"I have never seen a photograph of Roebuck's Misery and neither have any of my colleagues. Reputedly, it was a monitor dragon of the Komodo species *not* of mythology such as this." Browning shrugged, "Apprentices' folklore maybe ... but we in the trade all know about Roebuck."

"I have never met him – I would remember such a name. Who is this Monsieur Roebuck?" she enquired.

Browning had had the Roebuck tale related to him three decades previously. He'd all but forgotten it himself.

"Roebuck was an adventurer from Kalgoorlie, I heard; others say elsewhere. The poor sod was unluckily betrothed to the wrong woman." Browning placed the loop to his eye and studied the necklace again. He continued, "Legend has it Roebuck's partner had the dragon commissioned for his betrothed back in China. Roebuck killed the Chinaman and gave it to his own sweetheart."

"Sacré bleu. The poor girl," Catherine empathised.

"You know, some say diamonds are unlucky, I don't believe it." Browning fingered the dragon's eyes. "That was the start of Roebuck's problems; his fate was sealed – it wasn't enough for his betrothed."

Catherine sipped her tea. "Go on Mr. Browning your story is most intriguing."

"He went pearling on the west coast – Broome. Many a time he came close to death but once he'd found two identical pearls they were set into the front claws." Browning breathed onto the pearls and observed their changing colour. "These two are magnificent," he repeated. "From Broome, Roebuck went sapphire hunting, White Cliffs or thereabouts...lost three fingers in a shaft accident but found two identical gemstones, blood-red, some say aquatic green, and they were set into the hind claws." He put the necklace down, picked up the opal and looked at Catherine. She picked up the dragon, observing the empty claw.

"And it was finally enough, oui?"

235

"I'm afraid not. Roebuck's betrothed returned one sapphire smashed and demanded a black opal." Browning studied Catherine's gemstone. "Only then would she marry him."

"And what happened?"

"He went opal mining at Lightning Ridge."

"And did Monsieur Roebuck find his black opal?"

"He died trying; a cave-in. Roebuck was trapped for days, some say a week. His last words were, 'Woe befalls he who commissions the black pearl'."

"Woe?" Catherine enquired. "And what is this woe?" Her bemused look instigated Browning's elaboration.

"Time stands still," he declared. "It took days for Roebuck to die and time stood still, and while it did, he cursed his betrothed and…" Browning pointed to the jewellery, "his misery – Roebuck's Misery."

"You are, how you say, pulling Catherine's leg, oui?"

He handed the opal to her. "I have nothing to fear…I'm not doing the commissioning, you are."

"I only believe in fairytales with happy endings, Mr. Browning. Besides," she paused to laugh, "I am a she, not a he."

"And I am not a soothsayer but a humble craftsman." He acknowledged her determination and gestured accordingly when retrieving the opal. "I am at your service, Mademoiselle, as you wish."

* * *

13 – Who's Scamming Whom?

*One may feel short changed if led up the garden path
and then sold down the river.*

The greys were stabled at Clemet's. The smithy's boy took charge of the rig and didn't bother to make conversation with Bycroft; there was no tip in it for him. Proceeding to his office, Bycroft first called on Wong Foo to settle the transaction. The clickety-click of the abacus welcomed him.

"Good afternoon, Mr. Bycroft. Or would I be presumptuous in saying Mr. Mayor?"

Bycroft lifted his lucky Fedora. "Good afternoon to you, Wong Foo. Being a modest man, I'd say wait until the polls close but we both know one cannot afford to be modest in politics. I'll have to change my persona, won't I?" He clapped his hands twice and waited for the tea to arrive.

"Persona change good idea…vote catcher I'm sure." Before Bycroft could challenge the statement, Wong Foo continued. "You have the agreed amount?"

"I do. And you the deed of title?"

Wong Foo gestured for him to sit at the table. He clapped, and Lotus-Flower appeared with the rolled up document accompanied by teacups on a tray. Bycroft was puzzled as to why she had answered Wong Foo's signal and not his; on balance, he reasoned all handclaps sounded identical. Lotus-Flower silently poured and then served the brew. Both men drank, washing down the foul-tasting niceties they endured in the name of business.

"And now, to what you have come here for Mr. Bycroft," said Wong Foo, reaching for the document. He opened it, procrastinated and then slid it across the table to Bycroft, who pushed across the wad of notes. Each man diligently checked the goods in question. Finally satisfied with the exchange, they shook on the deal.

"I wish you well on the political path you travel," Wong Foo lied, placing the cash in the hidden drawer under the table. "And when will we do the laundry?"

"I'm going to Sydney in approximately ten days. I'll take it with me."

* * *

The ink roller wiped over the composite plate as the platen lumbered through its motions. Tom turned the large handle steadily. The sheet of newsprint ejected and slipped automatically into a drying rack. Clarrie planned the first edition to have twelve double pages, the middle pages dedicated to the election of a town council.

"Come on, put your back into it," he stirred, "let's see what she'll do flat-out."

"Steady as she goes and momentum does the hard yards," Tom instructed. "Here, you have a go."

Clarrie took over. "It doesn't look half bad, if I say so myself," said Tom, reading a page.

Bycroft stood at the counter holding up the deed of title. "It doesn't look half bad, if I say so myself," he mimicked.

"Is that what I think it is?" called Tom.

"It certainly is, my friend." Bycroft planned a visual metaphor to impress Tom and waited for his cue to throw his hat in the ring.

"Then we have our first candidate do we?

"And what's this?" Bycroft asked, as the lucky Fedora soared like a boomerang within the confines of the room. His hat unfortunately landed on the printing plate, wedged under the ink roller and disappeared into the internal workings. The platen shuddered to a stop.

"An unnecessary inconvenience," snarled Clarrie.

* * *

Catherine used the excuse of a recipe when she called on Ying Lee and found he was at Wong Foo's collecting supplies. Mrs. Lee assured her that he wouldn't be long and occupied the visitor by showing her a plethora of recipes until one was selected. She then rolled it up, tied a small blue ribbon around it, and presented the scroll to Catherine.

"There is talk of a school starting."

Mrs. Lee smiled and nodded enthusiastically; she struggled with her English, "Most important for…"

Catherine helped. "Children's education?"

"...husband's sanity," Ying Lee interrupted on entering. "Out. Be gone." The kids vanished, and Mrs. Lee took the clean towels he was carrying and left too. "Is your visit of interest in recipe or other?" he enquired astutely.

"In other."

Catherine brought him up to date with Bycroft's devious actions, and then revealed her own plan to swindle Bycroft by using Browning.

"You save Mr. Wally's hide if this so."

"And now you know," Catherine said, drinking her tea.

"And now Mr. Wally must know," said Ying Lee. "When do you wish to see him?"

"Would Tuesday be possible?"

"We must leave at dawn – not be seen by prying eyes."

She placed the recipe in her basket. "Bonjour, Ying Lee...until Tuesday."

Catherine then paid a visit to Wong Foo. "Bonjour Wong Foo."

"Come in," he welcomed, "and what can I do for you?"

She placed her basket on the counter and sat on the stool. "I have come to call in the dragon bed IOU," she informed him quietly.

Wong Foo noticed Yip Tung lurking and gestured for him to leave the stacking of shelves. "It has been long time. I thought you may have forgotten Wong Foo's debt."

"I have not. Has Wong Foo?"

"It would be most dishonourable." He clapped twice and motioned her to the negotiation table where he supplied a large firm cushion for her. Tea was poured as Catherine sat straight-backed, her knees pressed into the tabletop to stop them from shaking. Social niceties were exchanged until their cups were empty.

"Now, what is it you wish from Wong Foo?"

"The bogus assayer report," she requested.

Wong Foo camouflaged his surprise. "You don't believe in beating around bush, do you?"

"I have experienced the Wait-a-While bush, I do not believe in jumping into it either."

"Document very dangerous in wrong hands, are you sure this is what you want?"

She lied as to the real reason she wanted it. "If I want the best price for my sluice jar, I am sure it is what I require."

Seeing Catherine's logic, he nodded. "Gold can make person do evil to fellow man. You may wish to consider borrowing of said document."

"Oui, it is true what you say but once I have attained what I want, you may wish to consider repurchasing it."

"You are most clever in business." He opened the safe under the counter. "May I enquire how it is you know about report?"

"You may."

He handed her the scrolled report tied with a red ribbon and awaited the reply. Catherine thought it quaint how the Chinese never folded documents and always tied them with delicate bows. A cheeky smile was all he received.

"You very…how Australian say? Cunning as shithouse rat." He smiled broadly and bowed.

241

Catherine placed the valuable report in the basket and left with a smile. She proceeded to Houten's. "Bonjour, Ruby. Has the thread I ordered arrived?"

"Mr. Houten unpacked a delivery this morning, I'll ask him. Mr. Houten." she shouted, and stuck her head in the storeroom. "Has Catherine's ..."

"Is that you Catherine?" Meg's voice called from behind a row of tall shelves.

Catherine was cornered. "Bonjour."

"Bonjour. It is so nice to see you ... I never see you shopping at the newsagent's."

"Madame Chang ..."

"It must be lovely," Meg cut in, "to have hired help. I am having a morning tea next week. I was going to ask Ruby to invite you, now I can do it in person."

Catherine's heart was already racing when she saw Bycroft enter the store. Ruby returned to join in the conversation.

"No Luv, it hasn't arrived yet."

"Have you told Catherine of our new confectionery range?" Meg enquired of Ruby.

Ruby was beside herself at the thought of it. "French nougat and chocolates. Oh-la-la."

Bycroft approached the counter. The last thing Catherine wanted was to get involved in a conversation with Meg and have him listening over her shoulder. If she was about to be revealed as a fraud, the further away from him the better. "Come, I have something very important to tell you," she said to the women, drawing them away from Bycroft and toward the front doors.

"Well, out with it Luv," encouraged Ruby.

Catherine's mind was turning inside out as she tried to watch Bycroft discreetly and at the same time divert the conversation away from anything to do with France. The Chinese noodle recipe came to mind. "Here, look," she said, sliding the ribbon off the scroll and uncurling it. Her racing heart nearly gave out when she realised she was about to show them the assayer report. "Pardon." She quickly returned it to the basket, slipped the ribbon off the correct document and handed it to Ruby. The women studied it diligently. Catherine could feel Bycroft's eyes upon her as she rolled and slipped the ribbon back on the assayer report.

"It all looks Chinese to me," said Ruby, laughing. She handed it to Meg. "You're the language expert."

"Sorry. Chinese is not my forte."

"What's so important?" Ruby asked.

"It is an ancient aphrodisiac," Catherine replied. Both women were impressed. Catherine took the recipe from Meg, rolled it up, replaced the tie and popped it in the basket. "It is very dangerous in the wrong hands, I have been told."

Ruby was intrigued. Wide-eyed, she posed the question Meg wanted to ask but didn't dare. "Who for?" she laughed. "The man or the woman?"

"I shall tell you when the question has been answered. Bonjour." Catherine slipped out of the shop without passing Bycroft and strolled southward towards Chinatown, relieved to have survived another sticky situation.

On the southern side of Gunnadoo, three miles out of town, the Yapsly River twisted back on itself. Over millennia, the build-up of silt from the river when flooded created a fertile plain. Now cleared of flora, it was cultivated by Chinese women who tended small allotments to subsidise their husbands' meagre wages. Residents patronised the produce markets in Chinatown to purchase fresh vegetables and herbs. Well away from the gambling and opium dens, it was considered a safe environment for women

Catherine had completed her selections and was leaving when a slanging match occurred between two stallholders. A turnip was thrown, a carrot the return volley; a mêlée erupted. As feuding factions streamed in from all directions, all too willing to become involved, patrons tried to escape. Caught in an alleyway and the claustrophobic squash, Catherine could feel hands and fingers probing beneath her clothing. Her jacket was ripped and her bonnet torn off. Tossed helplessly along in the surge of people, she surfaced on High Street confronted by more opposition.

"Don't stand for any nonsense, lads," Sgt. Doyle shouted, as he and his constables weighed into the crowd with batons swinging.

Mrs. Chang and some of the girls stood on the balcony watching the disturbance as Catherine approached the safe confines of the box hedge. She'd lost dignity, clothing and a shoe but had somehow retained possession of Granny Dunn's wicker basket.

"Sacré bleu." she shouted and stomped inside to recover from the ordeal. She received due attention and related the experience to everyone's horror. "Hands were all over me; it was dreadful."

Mrs. Chang observed the state Catherine was in. "I insist one of the kitchen staff accompany you to the markets from now on," she told her, "I'll draw you a bath."

While Catherine was soaking, she remembered the assayer's report. She grabbed a robe and returned to her room, quickly tipping the basket onto the bed. It was gone. All that remained was the recipe tied in the blue ribbon. "Holy Mother." she cursed aloud, and slipped the ribbon off the scroll. Her anxiety diminished when she discovered she was holding the precious report.

At Houten's, unknowingly, Catherine had fortuitously switched the coloured ribbons and the thief had grabbed the noodle recipe by mistake. Her apprehension soon overrode her elation – who was to be trusted and who not?

* * *

14 – Another Plan is Instigated

Grass is never greener
when a man has a good woman
and – a mortgage.

Up before daybreak on Tuesday morning, Mrs. Chang had a hot tub waiting for Catherine when she rose. She had confided in Mrs. Chang and brought her up to date with the conniving of Wong Foo and the scheming of Bycroft. Not knowing friend from foe, Catherine had maintained a low profile within the security of the box hedge boundary since the market mêlée.

"Did you sleep well?" Mrs. Chang enquired.

"I had a horrible sleep – I never slept a wink." Catherine slid below the bubbles.

"Have you decided what to wear?"

"That is what kept me awake – I could not decide. Monsieur Beaumont and my apparel always clashes. I should wear a Hessian sack – it would be safer, oui?"

"You have twenty minutes, I will come back."

Mrs. Chang returned punctually and stood back admiring the chosen outfit. "A wise choice, warm, durable and most attractive," she complimented.

The tweed jacket and skirt with white blouse and necktie were reminiscent of Catherine joining a foxhunt. Mrs. Chang moved around her with the long mirror so she could view herself from all angles. "A bonnet or bowler, what do you think?" Mrs. Chang chose the bowler. "I think so too," Catherine agreed, remembering the mesh bonnet and the ensuing fiasco of trying to hold onto it when Buttercup had bolted. "I hope Ying Lee has hired a sulky, not a wagon."

"I will watch for him."

Catherine observed herself in the mirror as she brushed her hair. What she saw she liked, but what she experienced was an unhappy woman caught in her own web of deceit. Her priorities of the past year were no more. All that mattered was a man she barely knew, and for some unexplainable reason not fully thought through she was prepared to risk life and limb for him. She placed the bowler on, securely pinning it when she found the most flattering tilt, and then she adjusted the waves of shining locks falling to her shoulders.

Mrs. Chang appeared at the door smiling. "Ying Lee is here. He requests you wear this." She handed the Hessian sack to Catherine.

"Sacré bleu."

"I will make him a cup of tea while you change."

The Chinese chatter stopped when Catherine entered the sunroom wearing the contents of the Hessian sack. She bowed low. With her hair tied up under the traditional, conical coolie hat of weaved reeds, and dressed in black pyjamas, she was unrecognisable. Sandals replaced her riding boots, her wicker basket exchanged for the Hessian sack.

"We go now Missy. Keep head down, hands hidden and do not speak." Catherine turned and proceeded towards the front door. "You please stop…we go this way." He indicated the rear entrance. "Follow plait," he shook his long tail of hair, "you must walk behind Ying Lee, not in front."

"Walk." Catherine's astonishment stopped him.

"Twice as quick if we walk Billygoat Pass," he informed her, "also attract less attention."

Chinatown was awake and its residents were preparing for another day in the diggings. Smoke trails rose above the shanties as workers breakfasted on rice and dried fish. Mongrel dogs hung around open fires for warmth and any odd scrap of food thrown to them.

Still cloaked in morning fog, silhouette figures dressed similar to Catherine passed as she followed Ying Lee through alleyways. In one section of laneway, a gang of workers with shovels and picks took right of way as they scurried along it in pack formation. Those travelling in the opposite direction moved quickly to the side to avoid being carried along with the surge. After the pack had moved on, Ying Lee discovered Catherine wasn't following as instructed; she was nowhere to be seen. He backtracked quickly and found her, with head down, following a stranger's plait in the direction from which they had just come. Ying Lee followed her silently. At an appropriate time when congestion formed again at another bottleneck, he stepped in front of her. Without realising her folly, she began following him again as he led her in the correct direction.

Having traversed the heart of Chinatown, they next passed through the squalor of the Chinese underclass scattered throughout the surrounding bush. Here, addicts believed a shanty was a mansion; they slept under sheets of corrugated iron wedged between saplings. Mongrel dogs steered well clear of this area for fear of ending up in a stewing pot. A sign nailed to a tree in both English and Chinese informed all that this was where Billygoat Pass began. Like ants marching in single formation, workers climbed the track carrying picks and shovels slung over their shoulders. Upon reaching the cutting between the peaks, Ying Lee and Catherine left the formation as it descended to the mining fields. They moved along the ridge.

"We stop and rest," said Ying Lee, "easy part over."

"Holy Mother." Catherine sighed under her breath. She removed her hat and wiped her face of perspiration. Recalling Browning's unsightly lip, she dabbed her face again.

"Your expletive most interesting; you must have many Irishmen as customer."

"Pardon?" she queried, oblivious to what she'd just said.

Ying Lee did not answer. He lit his pipe and sat quietly staring in the direction of Wally's camp below. Catherine rubbed her feet, smiling; she remembered Wally's experience with ill-fitting shoes. Now her sandals offered little support and the leather bindings cut into her skin.

249

"Ying Lee getting too old to be billygoat; you may have to piggyback me rest of way."

Her smile disappeared. Catherine pictured herself collapsing at Wally's feet with the Chinaman on her back.

"Only joking. We go now Missy."

"How old are you?" she asked.

"I am half century old."

"You look younger ... I would have guessed you were no more than forty."

"With no kids I look thirty. Come, we go now," he gestured. "You may go first if wish."

Catherine looked at the thick scrub ahead and rubbed her chest remembering the encounter with the Wait-a-While Bush. "Man lead and woman follow," she replied.

The sun was yet to shine on the westerly side of the pass. Under a thick canopy of vegetation, the light was minimal and moisture dripped uncomfortably from above. The leather bindings stretched and her feet slid uncomfortably in the sandals, blisters forming. Ying Lee was right – the going down was harder. Many a time Catherine landed on her bottom, helped to her feet by the sympathetic guide. With a machete, he cut through a particularly thick patch of lantana whenever they strayed from the path.

Ying Lee suddenly raised his hand. "Shhh." he froze, listening intently.

Catherine flashed back to the constables looking for her and Wally at the two-up raid, her heart pounding just as fiercely.

He signalled they should keep moving and they hadn't taken more than a couple of steps when three

Aborigines with spears and boomerangs appeared, blocking their way.

"Holy Mother of Mary." Catherine yelped in surprise. She'd heard many a tale of a Chinamen's serendipitous ending. Whether fallacy or not, the Chinese shunned the Aborigines whenever possible; like the mongrel dogs in the poorer side of Chinatown, they too wanted to avoid the ominous stewing pot.

The Chinaman fell to his knees wailing, "Please don't eat Ying Lee…take woman, she tender, eat her."

Catherine felt light-headed and her knees went weak. She opened her eyes to see Ying Lee fanning her with the coolie hat. Behind him, the three Aborigines stood smiling and nodding, their white teeth enhanced by black bushy faces.

"Ying Lee make another joke," he told her. "This Blackfella Jimmy, he friend of Mr. Wally."

Catherine sat up ready to tongue lash the prankster but thought the wiser. "Sacré bleu. Your bon mot will be the death of Catherine."

The Yakka Dakka mine was like a tiny settlement. Wally's hut, a supply hut and sleeping quarters for the workers stood to side of the central kitchen. On the opposite side, the Aborigines had set up near the stables. When the rain was heavy, they joined the horses under the corrugated iron roof.

Wally was refilling lanterns in the storeroom. "Go on. Get the bugger," he encouraged, as the dog frantically pursued a bush rat. The Aborigines' hollering alerted him to the arrival of visitors. He stood at the door, recognising Ying Lee but not his companion following. Blackfella Jimmy and his two companions danced around the stranger, trying to look under what they called mushroom hat.

"Ying Lee...this is a surprise. Lucky you ran into Blackfella Jimmy and not another tribe; I keep these blokes well fed."

Blackfella Jimmy rubbed his belly and smiled, then prodded Ying Lee with his spear. The men chuckled amongst themselves. Catherine felt the warm sunlight thawing her shaking body; her heart was racing. With head bowed and hands up the sleeves of her jacket she stood silently, wanting to believe the palpitations as fear and the shaking the thought of the return journey, but knowing differently.

Ying Lee caught sight of two workers observing them from the windlass on top of the mineshaft. "We have much to discuss," he told Wally.

"I'll put on a cuppa. It's just about time for everyone to have smoko."

"Privacy, please."

"All right, come over to the hut, I'll fix some tucker." The procession followed Wally. "Every time I do Billygoat Pass I end up famished."

Wally opened the door and beckoned them to enter. Catherine tried to peer at her surrounds from under her hat; all she could see were the floorboards and anything below knee height. Wally stopped the Aborigines from entering. They had been about to take advantage of the hospitality. "I fatten up Chinaman, you eat later," he told them and closed the door. The billy was filled from a wooden barrel and placed on the stove. "Won't be long…we'll soon get a cuppa happening."

"You ready for next surprise?" Ying Lee asked.

"Two in one day, I don't know if I can handle it." He stoked the smouldering embers into life.

Catherine freed her hands from the restricting sleeves and removed her head camouflage. "Bonjour."

Wally dropped the fire stoker and stood dumbfounded.

Silence reigned until Ying Lee asked, "Which you prefer I make, tea or conversation?"

"Tea," Wally and Catherine answered in unison.

"I not your slave, you call *me* when tea ready. I make talk with Blackfella Jimmy, convince him not enough meat on Ying Lee's bones to eat." He left, leaving them to fill the void of silence.

Wally's emotions were running amuck. "I don't know what to say," he told her.

"Asking me to sit down would be a very good start," she replied, trying to sound on top of the situation.

Wally offered her the best chair then noticed her wet clothing. "Jeez'us you're soaked through." He threw more firewood in the stove. "I'll get you something dry."

Catherine stood and pulled a blanket off the bed. She gave it to Wally. "You hold up, oui?"

Wally held the woollen partition between them as Catherine undressed, her wet clothing falling to the floor. She then wrapped herself in the blanket. "That is much better I think."

253

He pulled the chair closer to the stove.

"Sit here, I'll hang these up to dry." He stepped from the hut, head spinning and heart thumping, thankful for the excuse to collect his thoughts and remind himself to breathe.

The Aborigines sat around the open fire with their guest.

"What this called," asked Ying Lee, chewing on the bush tucker.

"This 'em fella called goanna," informed Blackfella Jimmy, "him tender, we like him best."

Smiling faces agreed as they too tore into the reptile's flesh, oil and meat remnants remaining in their curly beards.

"Ying Lee, why didn't you come out by sulky?" asked Wally, the wet clothes still in hand.

"Missy too tired for return journey?" he queried. "Maybe Missy should stay overnight?" He noticed the pyjamas. "Maybe not – you very quick pants-man, Mr. Wally."

"The lady hasn't had a cuppa yet."

"That what I say: you *very* quick pants-man."

Wally gave up. "The billy hasn't boiled yet. I'll call you when it does."

"No hurry Mr. Wally." He tore a piece of flesh off the bone. "This most peculiar, taste like, not sure what taste like?"

The men followed Blackfella Jimmy's gesture and rubbed their bellies too. He jabbered to Wally, who replied in the native's tongue. They all laughed and hollered as Wally hung the pyjamas on a line close by.

"What Blackfella Jimmy say, Mr. Wally? Ying Lee like good joke too."

"He says goanna taste like Chinaman."

There wasn't a mirror in the hut. Catherine licked her fingers then wiped her cheeks, not knowing if there was dirt there or not. She noted her dirty feet and removed one sandal but the knotted binding on the remaining sandal frustrated her. She tried breaking it, succeeded but tripped and fell backward when it did. Wally entered to see her sprawled in a most unladylike manner on the floor.

"Jeez'us." he slapped a hand across his eyes.

"Sacré bleu." Catherine covered herself with the blanket. "Why is this always happening?" she yelled at him.

"What is?" Wally peeked through his fingers to confirm the restoring of modesty.

"It is your fault." He looked away. "Just look at me." He did as requested; Catherine then rebuked him for doing so. "No, do not look." He didn't know where to look. "I look horrible, say something."

"Jeez'us, you look all right to me."

That was enough.

"I did not bring a picnic basket...I am very hungry," her stomach rumbled. "It is your turn to feed moi."

Wally cooked eggs and listened to Catherine's tale. She divulged information of the treachery spasmodically between mouthfuls of treacle damper and hot tea. She didn't reveal the planned release of reptiles as she believed Wally's revenge on Bycroft would be adverse to her meticulous planning.

"My girls hear many secrets, I hear all from them. It is most useful information, oui?"

"Most useful but I'm buggered if I know how …"

"I have a plan," she interrupted, "would you like to hear it?"

"You bet I do." The kick in the guts from Bycroft's deceitful mateship was just as painful as the endeavour toiling in barren earth. Wally listened eagerly.

"… and when you arrive, take the Hessian bag into the assayer. He will swap it for another ore sample bag. Monsieur Bycroft's greed will get the better of him; he will want it all for himself and buy out your share." Catherine wasn't aware that was what Bycroft had planned to do anyway; if she had been, her endeavours wouldn't have been necessary. "It will be our coup d'état."

"What?"

"We win."

"And Browning is willing to go ahead with your plan?"

"To get the false assayer report he is. I have acquired it from Wong Foo."

At the mention of the name, Wally's blood ran cold. "What did you pay for it?"

"He owes me."

Wally knew it had nothing to do with him but couldn't resist asking. "What is your relationship with Wong Foo?" Catherine could sense the hostility in his voice.

"Monsieur Foo is a businessman. He pays for …"

"You?"

Catherine was astonished. The words, 'there are some things men are better off not knowing', spoken by Ruby, rang true in her ears. "Sacré bleu," she wailed, "nobody pays for Catherine."

"But I saw…"

"You saw what?" she demanded.

"You and Wong Foo …"

Wally's confession of how he'd visited the establishment and seen her climbing the staircase with Wong Foo was revealed. Torn between the joy of knowing he cared and the sorrow of realising the pain he must have felt, Catherine told Wally what he wanted to hear. She related the tale that Wong Foo had told his wife of the dragon bed's infertility curse, how she'd purchased the bed from him, returned it and how the IOU was about to be called in. Most importantly, she told him they had never been lovers. He wanted to take Catherine in his arms, but knew that if he did he would never let her go.

"Jeez'us, I'm sorry." He choked on Ying Lee's words 'generosity of mind.'

Catherine wanted Wally to carry her off, away from the life she was leading. "I too am sorry but you were horrible and paid me no attention. If not for Ying Lee…"

"Jeez'us, I forgot all about Ying Lee. Hang on."

Wally collected the dry pyjamas and then joined the Aborigines still sitting around the smoking embers. He couldn't see Ying Lee.

"You haven't eaten him, have you?"

"Him give Blackfella Jimmy message."

"Well, out with it then."

257

"Him say, he not your slave, *you* carry woman over Billygoat Pass."

Wally returned to the hut and this time knocked on the door.

"Entrée vous."

He stood patiently waiting.

Catherine waited impatiently. "Is that you Wally?"

"Yeah."

"Entrée….come in."

Wally opened the door. The dog shot between his legs to welcome the visitor by dropping the fatally mauled rat, still kicking, on her lap. In shock, Catherine threw the blanket and rat off and momentarily stood, all but naked in her French lingerie. The dog pounced on the rat and she on the blanket.

"He's a good boy, yes he is." The rat had been a thorn in Wally's side for months. He praised the triumphant dog as it gripped the antagonist proudly.

Catherine erupted, "He is not a good boy and neither are you for teaching him to do such tricks." Wally threw the pyjamas to her and hurriedly closed the door behind him. It opened just as quickly. "And take uncouth dog with you."

The dog bounded from within, tossing his new play pal in the air. Wally sat on the step contemplating the information she had disclosed. He finally decided it would be fruitless to continue digging. He said nothing to the men as he hitched up the sulky.

A young gin hung around pleading. "Boss fella Wally takes Gemma for ride."

"No can do, Gemma. You go now."

He returned to the hut. Catherine was dressed and waiting at the door to go.

"Ying Lee has gone. I'll take you back to town myself."

"I do not wish to take you away from your work."

"What work?" he replied.

"Of course, silly moi."

She put on her camouflage headdress and followed Wally to the rig. Once seated, Catherine could look from under it at the female pleading for a ride. She wasn't impressed to see a half-naked girl with pert black breasts glistening in the sunlight.

"I'll be back this afternoon," he called to one of the men as they passed the shaft entrance.

Conversation was sparse until the track met the Gunnadoo route. Catherine's jealousy of Gemma had receded, and Wally's heart rate had slowed down. She sat with eyes closed, feeling the wind funnel under the reed hat and up the back of her neck.

"You still like to close your eyes, I see," said Wally, looking under the hat.

"You remember."

"There's a lot I remember." He began laughing, feeling at ease. "But there's a lot more I want to know." The dog tried pushing his head between them. The more he pushed, the closer Catherine sat to Wally. "Who is Catherine Dunn?" he asked.

Catherine contemplated the question. Her mind raced as she contemplated who she should reveal. "My mother died and father was killed in the Boer War. My grandmother raised moi in France. She sent me to England before the outbreak of war. I had the chance to come to Australia and took it."

"Your granny had foresight. Did she survive?"

"Nothing did. C'est la guerre."

"What?"

"Such is war."

"I never got to France." The miles passed quickly as Wally related his overseas service in the Middle East. "We all thought it a lark and signed up. The band played and women waved as we departed Sydney quay. What a bunch of bloody idiots we were."

At the outskirts of Gunnadoo, Catherine requested Wally to take the turn-off to the cemetery. "I wish to introduce you to someone special," she informed him. An overhead sign above the dirt track was the only indication of what lay around the bend. "Please stop here … I wish to walk."

"That could be dangerous." She looked perturbed. "You know what happened last time we walked," he reminded her. "Stay, Dog."

Strolling under the signage, albeit spelt incorrectly, was of significance. Catherine smiled as she slipped her arm through Wally's. *Why not Rookstone or Rookgranite,* she idly thought, as they ambled along the track. Wally's last visit to the cemetery had been for the funerals of Maslin and Street – a blanket of purple sage covered their cold bones. He silently paid respects when passing the plots.

Crafted by an artisan, the chiselled headstone resembled a Celtic harp. Wally observed Catherine's tears falling onto the tuneless depiction. He then listened in amazement to her unyielding Irish accent lyrically accomplishing what rigid strings couldn't. "Danny my love, this be James Beaumont; Wally to his friends. He be a good man; to be sure you'd be liking him." Her hand withdrew from the jacket sleeve. She moistened it and wiped the white marble as a mother would wipe dirt from a child's face. Wally offered his handkerchief; it was accepted. "I've got a feeling, Danny, the time may be getting close but I'll be giving you fair warning I will." She kissed the headstone and stood with head bowed, holding back sobs. Feeling Wally's arm around her shoulders she released the pent-up sentiment. Turning to bury her face in his chest, Catherine grieved Danny's death in another man's arms for the first time.

Suppressed memories of comrades buried under tons of sand at Beersheba rose to the surface, and Wally was finally able to purge the guilt at having survived the ordeal. Between her own sobs, Catherine could feel his chest heaving. Her sobbing abated and so too the painful legacy Wally had been carrying. In silence, they stood embracing each other tightly.

Finally, Wally gave a nervous laugh. "I don't know who I'm in love with, but it's you, Catherine."

Wally's admission and the outpouring of her grief were too much. She pulled back in his arms and looked into his eyes. *Tell him, tell him,* her conscience screamed. "Me name is not Catherine, it's Christine, Christine Wingood, and I not be Irish either, I be English…with an Irish accent."

"Jeez'us." *Don't let go, don't let go,* screamed the voice in Wally's head; he didn't. "French, Irish, English, I don't care." *Kiss her; kiss her,* it now

261

advised. Before he could, the noise of the undertaker's cart alerted him to a small group of mourners following the inebriated mortician. "Let's get out of here," he whispered, replacing her camouflage. He went to take her arm and Catherine shrugged him away.

"Get going, ya silver-tongue or you be giving the game away." She fell into line behind him in her servile charade. *Thank you, Holy Mother, for send'n the mortician when ya did...I've committed enough sins without that one too.* A handful of gravel showered her and derogatory remarks followed from one of the mourners. Wally stopped abruptly; she pushed him in the back, whispering, "No, keep going." He did so under duress. Her previous assaults in Rookwood cemetery resurfaced ironically. *If my fiancé was here,* she thought.

As they approached the graveyard boundary, Catherine slipped her arm through Wally's. Her Catholicism, always more apparent in a cemetery, made her remove it just as quickly. Passing under the cemetery sign, she noticed the quasi-Latin graffiti, 'cum agen', scrawled by some larrikin for the benefit of any sinners who had partaken in lewd acts in the cemetery.

"I don't know what his rig looks like," Wally grumbled, "but I sure as hell won't be forgett'n his face. Are you all right?"

"To be sure I can throw a rock straighter than him," she tugged Wally's shirt sleeve, "but we can't be losing our temper...there's too much at stake."

"Right ... but I'm not gonna let that clown abuse *my* girl, am I," he told Buttercup. The dog agreed by yapping continuously as Wally untied the horse from the hitching post.

"He thought I was Chinese…Wally. Are ya listening to me?" She cussed the stranger's prejudices and Wally's inability to recognise the seriousness of the situation. He then offered her assistance into the sulky; she refused it. *Why do I fall for the thick ones, Holy Mother?* she thought. "Pay attention Wally. We got to be *really* careful."

"Shut up…not you," Wally quickly clarified, "I hear what you're saying. Giddup Buttercup."

Catherine let the dog sit between them. *Tell him the truth,* her conscience demanded. She opened the conversation. "Granny Dunn always said the truth is precious, so use it sparingly."

Wally pondered the statement. "I told you the truth, I really…"

She interrupted. "You'd not be playing with me?" Wally pulled on the reins. "No keep going." He did. "I believe you…so I'll tell you the truth," she paused taking a deep breath. "I'm from Sydney. Me father deserted me mother, I never knew him, and me mother walked out when I was eight. So the authorities wouldn't get their hands on me I be taken in by Granny Dunn, God bless her. She'd lost her daughter, Catherine, in the plague, raised me like one of her own; Christine became Catherine." Consciously or not, she omitted to mention the six years' child slavery and abuse. "Danny was Granny's nephew. Are you familiar with Sydney?" she asked.

"Spent a couple of days there before embarking … couldn't get out of the place quick enough," Wally replied, trying to consume the new information.

"I was born in Exeter Street, the Rocks. Not the prettiest of streets."

"Is Granny Dunn still in Sydney?"

"She died after a long illness; I couldn't get out of the place quick enough meself. I buried Granny at Rookwood and then waited for Danny's letter and followed him here." Catherine clasped Wally's shirtsleeve. "Don't you be leaving me, James Beaumont, me heart couldn't take it." A single tear rolled down her cheek. "Bycroft sure enough took Danny – I don't want to be losing you to him too."

Reaching the township, they took the track behind Houten's. It ran parallel to High Street but became impassable behind the saddlery. Catherine climbed down and looked up. "No, don't come any further, eyes be watching all the time, take care Wally. Thursday, I be looking for you." With head bowed low, she cut down the alleyway to join pedestrians where Main and High Streets joined. She heard Bycroft's voice as she approached the Plough Inn; he stepped from the doorway. Her heart pounding, Catherine stepped sideways and watched his boots pass. She then scurried past the bathhouse, catching Ying Lee's attention; he gave her a polite nod.

Chung Dow continued clipping the box hedge, not recognising Catherine as she passed him and four of the girls sitting in the garden pagoda. Mrs. Chang answered the service entrance; Catherine fooled her also until pulling her hands from jacket sleeves and giving a tiny wave.

"This way please, and wipe your feet," Mrs. Chang told her, as she did any hired help who entered by the rear door. The kitchen staff and two of the girls were oblivious to Catherine as she followed the woman upstairs. "I told the girls you weren't feeling well," she whispered.

"Merci, I shall feel better when out of these clothes."

Wally arrived back at the mine site late afternoon. Immediately, Gemma sprang from nowhere and begged to ride in the sulky.

"You git back 'ere girl." her mother Jeddah screamed. Blackfella Jimmy had recommended Jeddah, his cousin, to Wally as a camp cook and Jeddah had showed up with Gemma in tow.

"Go on, get out of here. Gemma no ride 'em today," Wally good-humouredly told her.

That evening he sat on the step of the bark hut. Long shadows were gradually becoming shorter as a near-full moon rose. The dog sat between his legs receiving a good head scratch.

Catherine had given him much to think about, but his thoughts were only of Christine.

15 – More Evil Deeds

*Venomous people rarely deliver wounds
with the clarity of puncture lesions*

It was business as usual at Yakka Dakka. Wally rose at daybreak knowing his obsession would be over at day's end. It would be out of his life for good and Catherine would fill the void. He harnessed Atlas and led him up to the whim. "Come on ol' fella, you can soon retire too." The thought of seeing Catherine the next day enabled him to keep up the charade. "Morning men. Are you looking forward to having the day off tomorrow?"

"If Bycroft's shouting the grog, it's fair enough by us," Boswell responded. He'd returned under intimidation from Bycroft. He had been assured there would be no more snakes and a pay rise had cemented the deal. "We might get our picture in the paper, eh?" he wisecracked.

Atlas began his shift at the whim and down went the bucket with Boswell and a co-worker. Everyone kept out of the unstable northern tunnel. It ran directly below the tributary stream; the porous earth seeped and sections collapsed regularly. Heavy equipment and manpower were to be used for the main shoring up procedure. It was there Wally proposed to say he had found the new ore samples. A manmade collapse would follow and he would sell out his share to Bycroft. By the time the project got up and running and no gold was discovered, it would be too late; the sting would have been pulled off. Catherine had yet to reveal to Wally the bit about the two of them sailing to France as part of the sting.

* * *

The Advocate's lamps had been burning well into the early hours for the past week. The rag was all but completed and ready for the Thursday launch. Clarrie, Meg and Tom had debated what the front page should carry; a story on the Advocate itself won. A unanimous decision relegated the story of Bycroft's Samaritan deed, his photograph and the group shot of the cronies to page three.

Clarrie pulled the page from the platen and studied it. He began laughing at the pained expression on Bycroft's face in the group shot. His seated position looked as though he was raising a buttock from the chair. "It looks as though he's farting."

"Either that or haemorrhoids," Tom suggested.

The social comment column was at the bottom of page three. Ruby had rolled her eyes in her photograph; it now looked as though she was gesturing at Bycroft's uncouth action. The column heading, 'Society Talks', supported the overall lampooning effect Bycroft was getting.

"You don't think we're pushing the parameters a little too much?" Clarrie asked of Tom.

"Naw, I can't help it if a subject pulls a face at the critical time."

Meg joined them as the men laughed at Ruby's decorum. "That's a face full of character," Meg stated.

"Full of confectionery, she's one of our best customers," Clarrie declared, alluding to the stationery shop sweet counter.

* * *

Under instruction from Bycroft, Robinson had paid the timber cutters clearing the property a bounty for each snake supplied. Over the past week, he had collected many hibernating snakes and separated them into four bags. "What horse you want saddled up, eh boss?" Henderson called. Robinson enjoyed the kid calling him boss while Bycroft wasn't around. Being at the bottom of the pecking order, Henderson knew when to call everyone boss.

"As if I'm gonna sling these nasty buggers over a bloody saddle, you idiot. Get the single axel rig." Robinson believed he was Bycroft's right-hand man, indispensable, and as his sphere of influence grew so would his own. Again, he was prepared to confirm his loyalty. "I'll be back," he told Henderson, "keep my bed warm." Robinson laughed, mimicking Bycroft without being aware of doing so – unlike Henderson.

At the town residence, Bycroft hosted the cronies, offering Cuban cigars and Cognac, and the cronies in return gave their allegiance in the usual manner. "Mr. Mayor, Mr. Mayor," White pleaded, "an interview for the Advocate, if you please."

Gushing fake humility, Bycroft rebuffed the plea, "I think we should wait until after the election."

Harrick displayed his theatrical ability. "Mr. Bycroft, Mr. Bycroft, your photograph." Simultaneously his hand touched the wall fixture lamp and he blew a fine mist of the Cognac into the flame. The resulting effect was that of a photographer's flash. The men were impressed, applauding and laughing. Bycroft hid his displeasure at seeing his fine Cognac wasted.

Bastock displayed his sarcastic wit. "An autograph, Your Holiness," he pleaded, and then went down on one knee with head bowed. Silence followed the jubilation as Bycroft unceremoniously tipped his drink over the man's head. He didn't deem this act as wasteful.

"Arise, Sir Bastock of Gunnadoo," he commanded. The cronies collapsed onto any support available. Even Browning, inconspicuous in a corner, sniggered at Bycroft's unbridled audacity. Bastock conceded defeat – for the time being.

"All right, all right, enough of the frivolities, it's all about timing – as my good friend and I just demonstrated." Bycroft delivered the low blow by putting an arm around Bastock's shoulder and giving him an insincere smile. "Tomorrow, we use timing to our advantage, eh Sunshine." The second punch also landed below the belt; Bastock had repeatedly asked Bycroft not to call him Sunshine. The cronies raised their drinks to toast the master strategist and Bycroft began explaining what would happen. "Right, Sir Bastock, you enjoy theatrics, here's a job for you. When I finish my speech, you lead the crowd with three cheers. Bastock cringed at the thought. "White, I want you to…"

For the rest of the evening, the men learnt what Bycroft's timing was all about.

* * *

Robinson turned off the main route and headed for Yakka Dakka. The cart pitched uncomfortably on the rough track even at a walking pace. Blackfella Jimmy and family whooping it up echoed through the still night. Robinson proceeded no further. This time he applied a leg rope and an extra halter; if the horse went anywhere, the tree would go with it. He slung a further precaution, a feedbag, over the horse's nuzzle and it chewed away contentedly. As the moon reached its zenith, the assassin calmly rolled a smoke and noted the changing ambience in the foliage overhead.

The smell of smouldering charcoal and the silence of sleeping residents greeted Robinson upon reaching the mine site. His neck and shoulders ached from the yoke used to carry the heavy bags. Stretching his neck muscles, he observed the intended targets and the shadowy paths that would take him there. Wally's hut, the supply hut and the workers' hut would each get a delivery. He decided against the stables; crazed horses alerting all to his visit wouldn't facilitate his silent getaway. The shaft would get the contents of the last bag. Like a foraging possum, he stealthily weaved along the trail of shadows to each destination, liberating the cranky buggers.

There was a chill in the air as Robinson briskly walked back to the rig. The ground under his feet was cold, like the underbelly of a slithering reptile.

16 – Advocate Celebrations

Seldom does the conspirator
remove dirty boots
when climbing into a collaborators bed...

Wally woke to the dog's growling. "Go on, get the rat," he encouraged as he lay in bed listening to the commotion, and then the silence. "Good boy." No sooner had his thoughts turned to Catherine and the day ahead than the commotion began again. The slapping noise upon the floor finally registered. 'That's a bloody big rat,' he thought, and lifted his head from the pillow.

"Jeez'us."

The dog was flailing the second of Robinson's silent assassins. Out the corner of his eye, Wally saw the slithering movement of another snake. Recalling the repercussions of the last infestation, he moved slowly and carefully to the door out of harm's way, calling to the dog.

Wally was half-way to the men's hut when a scream pierced the morning chill. The door flew open and three men appeared in rapid succession. Like Wally, they stood barefoot in their long johns watching the dog play with the deceased visitor.

"That's it. I quit." shouted Evans.

"What about you, Mick?" Wally asked.

"Me brother goes, I go," he replied.

"Christ, it's not even spring," Boswell yelled. "Don't bother asking me. I've had enough too."

"I know how you feel. I've just about had a gut full myself. Throw your swags in the wagon and take Atlas. Be careful, the dog got two in my shack."

Blackfella Jimmy stood holding up another. "You pay 'em like last time?"

Wally paid a bounty for collecting the snakes just as Robinson had done. Blackfella Jimmy and family began a sweep of the campsite, starting with the huts. Each time one of the mob discovered a culprit, a celebration erupted with whooping and hollering around the victorious hunter. None of the men had sustained a snakebite, albeit one of them received a bloodied hand when it got between the dog and the escaping food source. At the end of the search, Gemma received eleven carpet pythons to prepare for snacking on.

Wally gave Atlas a scratch between the eyes as the men climbed onto the wagon. "Let Bycroft know what's happened. He'll fix up your wages."

He watched the wagon veering back and forth until it was out of view. Atlas had developed the idiosyncrasy of veering to the right due to the repetitive walking in circles when pulling the whim.

* * *

The nightmare of Wally having a snake dropped in his bed had woken Catherine with a fright. She rose early, after a restless night of searching for

273

any unexpected flaws in her plan. Mrs. Chang entered the sunroom where Catherine was breakfasting and gave her the hand-delivered envelope. "This just arrived for you."

"Merci." She studied the contents. "It appears Monsieur Foo requests a meeting at my earliest convenience."

"I shall come with you. It may have been him who organised the fight in the market to try and get the assayer's report."

"No, it is not necessary…somehow I do not think it is Monsieur Foo." She finished her tea. "I shall see him on my way to Houten's." She had prearranged with Wally to be sitting on the customer's bench when he arrived with the good news of the new discovery. If all went well with the swindle samples, he'd signal her.

Catherine paraded before the foyer mirror in her foxhunting outfit. A silver cameo brooch on a choker replaced the necktie, a fawn beret the bowler hat. Her soft leather gloves coordinated with the black riding boots that climbed her calves beneath the tweed skirt. She enjoyed the feeling of wearing a vest. It accentuated her thin waist, felt snug on her lower back and emphasized her breasts when a couple of buttons were left undone. Selecting what to wear had been a contributing factor to the night of restless sleep. Pleased with her appearance, Catherine selected a parasol and Mrs. Chang opened the door for her.

"If I have not returned by midday…" she thought for a moment but could not think of anything logical to say.

Mrs. Chang hung on her words, "Yes?"

Catherine posed in a Joan-of-Arc-like stance and theatrically declared, "The bells toll for thee." Her nervous banter betrayed her hidden apprehension. "Bonjour, Madame Chang." Like a filly on parade before the start of a race, Catherine stepped out with a spring in her step. She strode down the path with skirt swaying, signature basket over her arm and parasol twirling.

As instructed, Lotus-Flower had been keeping watch for Catherine's approach. By the time she entered the store, Wong Foo was standing formally in front of the counter.

"Bonjour Wong Foo, it is such a beautiful day oui?"

"Thank you for being so prompt, Miss Dunn." He bowed lower than usual. Catherine felt an uneasiness about him as she approached. "Today, Wong Foo is not a happy man." Lotus-Flower, unseen by Catherine as she entered, closed the doors, flipped the open sign to closed and pulled down the blind. The spring in Catherine's step vanished to a lame stroll as she moved towards him, her mind racing as to what approach to take. The closed parasol became a sword and the basket over her arm a shield.

"Friendship is not to be taken lightly, would you not agree?"

Catherine went to answer but her mouth was dry; she nodded agreement.

"And we are friends, are we not?"

She repeated the gesture. She didn't see a movement of hands, but the two sharp claps penetrated her like bullets and then ricocheted off the walls. Her heart was pounding. The daughter quickly left and Yip Tung appeared, moving to his uncle's right side. Catherine couldn't think for the noise of alarm bells ringing in her head. The nephew was holding a sinister-looking bamboo switch.

"I am a man of culture." He smiled and took the switch from Yip Tung, casting it as though fly-fishing. "To be responsible for pain of fellow man pains me greatly but, I fear, sometimes it is necessary." He stopped smiling and looked to Catherine. "Would you not agree if you were in my humble sandals, Miss Dunn? Is this not so? Do I not speak the truth?"

Catherine stood speechless, a nauseating hollowness perpetuating in her belly. Wong Foo elaborated. "To be responsible for dishonour of family name I fear even greater than pain."

She didn't see the hand movement but heard the whooshing of bamboo and automatically shut her eyes. But for being frozen with fear she would have collapsed. The crack and the scream of pain fused as one and penetrated Catherine's soul. Her sword and shield didn't protect her from light-headedness and she dropped to the floor.

"Honour only half restored, Miss Dunn," Wong Foo informed her. The sentence broke apart on entering Catherine's conscious. The words disseminated into letters and all tumbled around freely, forming new words that made little sense. "My dishonourable nephew wishes to return what he stole," Wong Foo informed her.

Catherine watched as the alphabet hung together precariously and the sentence stumbled past.

"Holy Mother," she croaked, finally registering. A parched throat prevented any further expletive, and she opened her eyes. Wong Foo stood with folded arms, the weapon gripped like a sword of honour. Yip Tung knelt, head bowed, arms outstretched offering her the scroll, his torn shirt and wound testament to Wong Foo's honour code.

Catherine bowed her head graciously and received the noodle recipe as though it was the Treaty of Versailles. The bleeding rascal received a kick in the arse as he crawled from Wong Foo's sight. Catherine tried to speak. Wong Foo gestured for her not to and passed her the implement of pain. He stripped off his jacket and knelt before her, clasping the soft leather of her riding boots.

"Restore other half of honour," he commanded her.

The ankle-restricting sensation reverberated up each leg to climb Catherine's backbone. The vest sensation began embracing her lower back, rising sensually under each armpit to cup her aroused breasts. She had no sooner looked at the so-called aphrodisiac recipe in one hand and the masochistic rod in the other, than an image of Wally nearly brought her to her knees. "Holy Mother of Mary." she wailed as the orgasm shook her very foundations.

"Be quick," Wong Foo implored, "I not good at suffering." He let go of her and covered his ears. "Now, do it now."

Catherine began flailing the switch, searching for a way out of the astonishing predicament. She spotted a pitcher of water; her restricted air passage screamed for it, her Catholic morals demanded she douse the raging hormones. Wong Foo knelt with eyes shut listening to the swishing bamboo and then the sound of pouring water. He glimpsed up at his tormentor casually helping herself.

"Not water torture," he pleaded.

She drank thirstily, collecting her composure. "Nor bamboo torture, Catherine gives pleasure, oui? Not pain. Please get up. Your honour is restored."

Wong Foo jumped at the command. "I am very much relieved to hear this, and I also prefer pleasure to pain, especially when on receiving end." The scar on Wong Foo's arse was testament to his statement. He bowed, clapped his hands and the tea tray arrived. "I shall be pleased to purchase assayer report when you finish with it; not as blackmail against Mr. Browning – he is small fish, but as protection against Mr. Bycroft – he predatory shark."

"How is that so?"

Wong Foo then confessed to Catherine how he'd discovered Bycroft's original scam only by recognising the dragon rock, and how he'd then blackmailed Browning into planting the second discovery. "Mr. Bycroft greedy for everything including my deed of title, it is easy to feed garbage to shark when hungry. Deed of title is forgery also."

"C'est la guerre," Catherine replied enthusiastically. She pondered why Browning had neglected to reveal his connection with Wong Foo's scam. "There is something else you should know, Wong Foo." Catherine revealed her relationship with Wally, also how Bycroft had deceived him.

"As in life, allies most important; in business they are essential. And now that we are allies, I have something else that may be of interest to you." Conversation and tea flowed until Catherine realised the time and excused herself. Wong Foo walked her to the door as Lotus-Flower lifted the blind, allowing the sunlight to stream in.

"Merci, your offer of hospitality may be accepted sooner than later, bonjour."

Catherine crossed to the opposite side of the street rather than be caught up in the small groups of onlookers blocking the footpath. Robinson shouted orders and men threw their backs into hoisting the canvas tent on the vacant block. She smiled when she heard the ringing bell and imagined Mrs. Chang and the girls assailing Wong Foo's fortress to rescue her.

"The Advocate is coming; the Advocate is coming," shouted the town crier, "three o'clock today. Come one, come all." This approach had the desired effect and all the traders stood in their doorways as he passed. It couldn't have worked better if it had been planned, for when Wally pulled up, Bycroft was watching at his door. He saw Wally grab the Hessian sack from the back of the rig and rush into the assayer's office. No sooner had Browning switched bags, replacing Wally's with one from under the counter, than Bycroft entered.

"Morning all. Someone's in a mighty big hurry – what's in the bag?"

"Have a look," Wally replied, "I was just coming to get you; you saved me the trip."

Browning tipped out the contents and studied an ore sample under his magnifying glass. "This looks interesting."

Bycroft grabbed a sample in each hand. He studied the gold seams then began weighing each against the other. He also weighed up the new complexity thrown into the equation. "Where was this lot found?" he enquired.

"The northern tunnel, you were right about the cave-in."

"I thought you said it was too dangerous to…"

"I wouldn't try hanging a picture in there at the moment. I was just nosing around and stumbled across another part of the roof that had broken away."

Bycroft turned to Browning. "When can I have a report?"

"I could go out there over the weekend and have a look first hand. What about Monday?"

"It never rains, it always pours," recited Bycroft.

"And aren't we glad it did," Wally added.

"It may be a little early to celebrate yet," he thumped Wally on the back, "but I could do with a drink anyhow, what about you?"

Catherine watched as they left the assayer's and walked next door to Bycroft's office. She received the signal she was waiting for – Wally stopped to tie his bootlace.

"Billings, get Mr. Beaumont a clean glass." Wally didn't refuse; it was safer to drink whiskey than tea made by Billings. "I've put Boswell and his two offsiders to work on the property for the time being, they refuse to return to the mine site."

"I don't blame them," Wally replied, "snakes at this time of year – what will they be like in summer?

Naw, I need to do some hard thinking. It may be time for me to get out too."

"Well, nothing much surprises me these days but that statement has."

"There are only so many times you can push your luck," Wally stated, taking the drink from Bycroft, "and it's been pushed quite a few times out there." He took a sip; the cheap whiskey burnt.

"Not to mention the amount of times it was pushed overseas," Bycroft added manipulatively.

Wally shook his head and rubbed his belly, placing the glass on Bycroft's desk. "Nope, can't even stomach a good drink at the moment, and the belly's playing up."

Bycroft held his ever-growing circumference then burped loudly. "As I see it, nothing's going to come out until the heavy machinery goes in."

Wally sighed, "Yep, that's about it. We may have to reconsider Wong Foo as an investor."

"Well, let's not be too hasty," Bycroft cut in. "We'll know more on Monday when Browning's done the inspection. After the Advocate launch this afternoon, I'm going out to the property for the weekend. You're welcome to come out with me or use the residence. Until Monday I suggest nothing is said and no decisions are made."

"Have you seen the first edition yet?" Wally asked.

"No, it's under wraps. Robinson's putting up the tent for the launch – they'll be distributed there first."

"A captive audience eh. You got a speech ready?"

"No. I haven't been asked to prepare one," he replied casually.

Billings sniggered; he'd listened to the oration being rehearsed for the past week.

* * *

The town crier had been Bycroft's idea. Jock Mackellar, dressed in his highland kilt, wandered back and forth between the pubs at either end of High Street shouting his lungs out. As payment for services, Jock received a large whiskey each time he completed a lap. He now stood at the tent entrance swaying and ringing the bell, welcoming all. Upon entry, the townsfolk received a copy of the Advocate's first issue. Tom moved through the tent trying to take candid shots of the crowd. The explosive pop and flash of gunpowder alerted all to his whereabouts.

To many, the arrival of the Advocate represented a uniting force for progress. For others, it was insulation for slipping under a thin mattress or lining a mud brick wall. The numerous children at the event were illiterate as were their parents, but all enthusiastically took a free copy and mingled with the crowd. The headline in bold font read, *Hooray. The Advocate is here.* Below was the action-packed photograph of Wally, bearing witness to the caption. The Advocate's agenda for the good of the common man, the policy of freedom of the press and its aspirations for the coming year exploded across the front page.

Wong Foo and Ruby circulated, as did Bycroft, accepting acknowledgement of their celebrity. Wally received both acclaim and wisecracking jibes as he socialised uncomfortably. The photograph set Catherine's heart a-fluttering. She fantasised about the testosterone-charged hero as coming to her rescue and transmitted covert glances of admiration at him when their eyes met.

"I tell Missy I not your slave and she still give me note to deliver like delivery boy." Wally read it as Ying Lee protested, "I not matchmaker either – that job for Mrs. Lee."

"Hear ye, hear ye, hear ye," Jock slurred, moving unsteadily to the area from where the official speech would be made. "Ladies and gentlemen, take your seats, please."

Meg, Tom and Clarrie hung on his words. They had made a small wager as to whether the mouthpiece would still be standing to fulfil the last of his duties. Whether by habit or coincidence the churchgoers took their congregation positions and the rest grabbed what they could. Jock made his way to where the pastor usually delivered his sermon but he unfortunately strode straight into a tent pole and passed out at the sight of his own blood. Tom won the bet; Jock didn't introduce Clarrie.

"Ladies and gentlemen," called Tom, as he rang the bell, "the proprietor of the Advocate, Mr. Clarrie Radcliff." Having introduced Clarrie, Tom stood next to Meg at the side of the tent. "I'll collect later," he told her.

"Hope your policies stand up better than your publicity," shouted a good-humoured smartarse from the back. Bycroft smiled smugly as he sat listening to Clarrie struggle through his prepared speech, the audience wisecracking at every chance.

"In closing…"

"… about time," a heckler called out.

"… please thank John Bycroft and his associates for the community hall that is about to be built."

Bastock immediately began calling, "Speech. speech."

Previously offered free grog as an incentive from each of Bycroft's pubs, the drinkers soon took up the call also.

Bycroft stood and waved his arms gesturing for quiet. "Thank you, thank you," he mouthed. When not receiving the requested silence he gave up, graciously accepting the procured kudos he had cajoled from cronies and cohorts. Clasping the lapel of his jacket with both hands, he rolled on the balls of his feet waiting for silence. "My friends…"

"Where?" was the immediate response from Clement.

Bycroft copped more of a razzing. Not being the lead story and having his photograph on the front page had been brought to his attention on numerous occasions by the cronies. He'd laughed it off good-humouredly but was seething underneath. He wasn't immune to the one-liner either but he knew what lay at the end of his speech and persisted through the interruptions, "…so the timber is there, what we need now is the manpower over the next two weekends. Who'll give me their time – are you with me?"

Unenthusiastic volunteers sat motionless. "Refreshments will be supplied."

A roar of approval broke the silence. White stood up shouting, "Three cheers for John Bycroft."

The pub stooges and crowd followed White in his salutations and then they followed him to the pub for the free drinks promised. Bycroft joined them – his election campaign had begun.

Wally joined the informal celebrations for guests at the Advocate.

"Ladies and Gentlemen," Clarrie popped the cork and Meg filled glasses, "this champagne has sat unopened for the past three years."

"Are you trying to tell us it's vintage?" Houten interrupted.

"Meg, Tom and I made a pact to crack it when we launched the Advocate. I'm telling you it's been three years in the making – so here's to the Advocate." Glasses chinked and a chorus of voices echoed his sentiment. "Please look around and ask any questions you like."

Tom developed images and passed them from the darkroom. Whoops of laughter followed as they all peered at the candid shots. A recording of Dame Nellie crackled in the background. Michael and Albert took turns in changing the gramophone records and winding up the internal mechanism with its small handle. "When you've got that down pat I'll give you both a go at the platen handle," their father promised.

"It'll soon be Lennard, Radcliff *and* Sons," Wally stated.

"The sooner the better, my back is killing me," Clarrie acknowledged.

"Jeez'us, that's not a handle." He rubbed his hands together, "You should try a windlass...now that'll test ya back. Any idiot can …"

"Well, not quite," interrupted Tom. He pointed to Bycroft's ink-stained Fedora. It hung like a gutted chicken from a peg on the wall.

It had taken Tom three hours to strip and clean the platen after Bycroft's Fedora had become trapped under the ink roller. Because Clarrie had been too slow in applying the brake, the calamity had been avoidable. When Clarrie had questioned the time taken to repair it, Tom had lost his temper. He had begun his verbal abuse with, 'Any idiot can...' Their wounds were still raw.

Clarrie changed the subject. "Did you see the surprised look on Bycroft's face?"

"Which one, there were quite a few," laughed Tom.

"The one where he saw Wally's mug on the front page, not his own."

Ruby and Meg joined them. "It was nearly as good as Wally's," Meg noted.

"That wasn't surprise," Wally informed her, "it was shock."

"I noticed you kept a low profile during the proceedings. Is there something you're not telling us?"

"I was afraid some clown would call on me to make a speech," he admitted.

"I had mine ready but nobody asked for it," Ruby informed them all. She held out her empty glass to Clarrie. "Don't mind if I do, Luv."

"Wally...can I get you another beer?"

"Naw, I've a previous appointment," he slurred, "best I stay sober."

17 – The Rendezvous

The voyage of love is turbulent;
no charts are available...

Ying Lee was mopping the bathhouse floor as the last client for the evening left and Wally arrived. They immediately departed for Chinatown. "I have been told by Missy not to dilly-dally. What dilly-dally?" He produced a ginseng root from a folded piece of paper and gave it to Wally. "You eat...give strength of lion."

Wally burped. "And what makes you think I need the strength of ... "

"It also give energy, I think you going to need plenty. Now, what dilly-dally?"

Wally took the opportunity to put one over Ying Lee. "It means to stick your nose in other people's business."

"Are you sure, Mr. Wally? Give me example." Ying Lee was suspicious.

"Get a move on and stop dilly-dallying," Wally, told him.

"I confused. How I *not* stick nose in business – this job for Mrs. Lee not Ying Lee," he grumbled.

Chinatown appeared more vibrant than usual. Small boys ran through the alleyways playing buccaneers; they wore pirate hats fashioned from pages of the Advocate. The dog snapped at origami birds fluttering on lengths of cotton thread behind skipping girls.

"I guess that's one way of spreading the news, eh Ying Lee."

"That another," he said, pointing up. Wally stopped.

"Jeez'us." Large lanterns, previously torn and now restored, illuminated the newsprint shell. "Look there," he tilted his head, "I can make out me picture and that's…"

"That Chinese ingenuity," Ying Lee informed him. Wally obliviously snacked on the ginseng root like a pretzel. "You think that impressive, wait for kite exhibition. Kids go crazy…"

"Yeah but see …" he rushed to the next lantern and stood beneath it mesmerized, "look…what do you see?"

"I see Mr. Wally standing …"

"No, look hard."

Ying Lee stood close to him and studied the lantern. "What Mr. Wally see that Ying Lee does not?"

"It's more of a feeling, it's hard to explain. I know but…"

"But what?" Ying Lee queried.

"But I don't."

"How much you drink? – not good for performance."

"Naw … there's gonna be a *lot* of money made from that idea."

"How? Chinese ancestors make lantern, if *lot* of money to be made – Chinese make by now. Stop with dilly-dally," said Ying Lee.

Mutterings of agreement from the crowd broke Wally's trance. He observed the onlookers stretching their stiff necks. "There. What'd I tell ya," he gave Ying Lee a poke in the shoulder, "it somehow attracts a crowd's attention."

"Eat more," he handed Wally another piece of root, "and you concentrate on matters at hand – not show-business. We go quickly – one woman yelling at Ying Lee enough."

From a place unseen, in an area one only ventured by invitation, a woman's screaming greeted them as they crossed the shantytown boundary. "Husband unfaithful: wife unhappy," Ying Lee interpreted quietly.

"Hasn't anyone heard of street lighting down here or don't they read?" Wally joked. He tripped, stumbled and then regained his balance.

"Here, entertainment other than reading."

"Slow down, I near broke me neck on that bag of whatever."

"That not bag of whatever...don't ask."

The wailing of what sounded like a stringed instrument out of tune accompanied the woman's singing.

"Jeez'us, what's that?" The dog let out a howl of empathy. "Heel," Wally commanded, "or you'll end up in the pot like that poor bastard."

"Shhh." Ying Lee urged. "Me not agree entirely he poor bastard … but do agree fat lazy dog feed hungry family for week." He gestured for Wally to enter Wong Foo's unpretentious shanty and followed.

Strategically placed candles in the dimly lit room accentuated the positioning of Chinese artefacts. On the walls and low ceiling, shadows pulsed, creating the ambience of a Shaolin monastery. The oriental mystique increased the adrenaline and testosterone pumping through Wally's system; the incense tantalised his nostrils and heightened his imagination.

"Come," requested Ying Lee. He escorted Wally along a narrow passage and through a beaded curtain. Polished black marble underfoot reflected the flickering universe of tiny candles above, conjuring the impression of infinity. At the centre of the spectacle stood Wally's destination.

"Jeez'us, that's the biggest tub I've ever seen. Have a go at the workmanship."

Cast in iron to resemble a scaly dragon, the elaborate bathtub, supported by massive green legs protruding from its bulk, stood astride smouldering embers warming its underbelly. The five gilded claws extended onto the polished abyss giving an impression of the Imperial dragon flying; enveloping rose-scented steam added to the illusion.

Ying Lee gestured he undress.

"Two tubs in one day … this is a first."

"Maybe many firsts experienced by Mr. Wally tonight." Ying Lee collected the clothing as it fell. He exited and returned with a satin robe and ornate slippers. "I leave now, Mr. Wally, good luck. He handed Wally the last of the ginseng and then began chanting, "Ah chow wee coo, ah chow wee coo."

"What's the chanting for?"

"I plenty nervous for you."

"What have you got to be nervous about?"

"Stop with dilly-dally …"

"Ha. I got ya."

"Got me what? It my business. Eat, build up strength…focus mind. I take fat lazy dog with me."

"Jeez'us, I feel like a stallion being groomed to …"

"Now you got it. Mr. Wally slow – but sometime slow is recommended, yes?"

"They're your words. What, no wise words from Confucius?"

Ying Lee smiled. "This time Aesop's wise words should be adhered to."

"What? Now you *are* making me nervous."

"Remember hare and tortoise and who won race?" He left, leaving Wally under a canopy of stars and performance apprehension.

The dog's barking and Ying Lee's chanting merged into the ambience of Shantytown. Wally closed his eyes and drifted into a kaleidoscopic nightmare. The fragrance of incense and rose petals diminished, replaced by the pungent odour of burning oil. Suppressed memories of a soldier's greatest horror surfaced. Torpedoed. The angst of being transported on liberty ships. Refusing to sleep below deck for fear of being sucked into the bottomless pit below.

The dark underbelly of a noxious oil slick hovered above Wally as debris rotated around him in a submerged eddy. A roaring silence replaced the screaming. He struggled with belts and buckles and then the cumbersome greatcoat. Many times it had saved his frozen hide, yet now it threatened to drown him, along with the recalcitrant laces and hobnail boots. He jettisoned them all to the deep as air bubbles cascaded up from the void below. Or was it that he was sinking and the air bubbles were stationary? He didn't need oxygen now. It was longer a conundrum. Wally stopped struggling and calmly pondered another question. Before him, as if awaiting a command, Bandolier webbing, devoid of cartridges and soldier, swayed. The grandiose display of regimental lunacy cajoled him to join a great adventure, to the impenetrable fathoms of the deep. The lure was overwhelming. Yet so was the enticing fragrance that now pleaded, *don't go*. Tumbling between opposing forces Wally searched for a horizon, a reference point; a distant glow became his beacon of salvation.

Catherine was wearing a white silk robe, an aura of light outlining her shapely form. A gilded butterfly hairclip encrusted with gemstones crowned her sculptured locks. The sheer lightness of her garment overrode his inhibition to look and he digested her ravenously.

"Your eyes match your ears?" she taunted.

"Jeez'us." Wally sat up startled. He frantically covered himself, modestly scooping up the rose petals like a blushing schoolgirl. "I thought you were…"

"Oui, go on…"

"Hang on while I collect me thoughts." He leant forward, submersing his head, and then surfaced. "French, Irish, English and now Chinese."

Catherine bowed low and rose with an impish smile and a glint in her eye. She withdrew the long needle skewering the butterfly hairclip; the sheerness of her robe and the anticipation of when it would open tantalized Wally like the curtain at a premier performance. Her hair slid to her shoulders. "En garde." She thrust, parried and then raised the miniature foil victoriously in the air. "Touché."

"It seems you've caught me at a disadvantage."

"Voila, how you say – with your pants down?"

"Yeah, you could say that. Hey. Don't move, you look like that statue…"

"Joan of Arc, merci."

"Naw, the Yank…"

"Statue of Liberty. It is still French." She replaced the foil in its scabbard and tossed the hairclip aside, "Vive la France." Catherine arched her back and slowly the robe began sliding sensuously off her shoulders. Momentarily, it clung on erect nipples and then peeled from her body like a shimmer of water until it lay in a puddle at her feet. "Catherine will now wash you better than Ying Lee has." Wally naively requested she find a sponge as there was none in the tub; he soon found it wasn't required. She felt every welt upon his skin, explored every nook and cranny with her searching fingers, hands and body. When she had done, she stepped from the bathtub and held out her hand. "Come."

The interior wall silently slid aside. Plush carpet replaced marble tiles underfoot as Wally stepped into another world, the centre of which was the dragon bed. A potbelly stove warmed the unfamiliar and unchartered territory. He lay staring up at the indistinguishable ceiling. What appeared like hundreds of small candles flickered throughout the room. The dragon bed seemingly hovered in a galaxy of stars as though it were a flying carpet. "I'm dead and gone to heaven," he muttered. Catherine kneeled between his feet licking dry the tender flesh between the toes of his left foot. She nibbled on his instep and sucked on his Achilles tendon. Fingers tenderised the calf muscle and teeth tested it. "Jeeeez'us." His fingers clenched handfuls of bedding, her tongue lashed behind his knee as though sucking marrow from a lamb-shank. Wally's jaw ached from clenching his teeth, an uncontrollable muscle in his right leg convulsed as Catherine began gently blowing on his inner thigh, endorphins exploded. The hare mounted the tortoise. Confucius – Aesop – Ying Lee's words of wisdom echoed: 'Slow is recommended'.

As though his student, Wally unconsciously repeated his words, "Slow is recommended."

"To hell with your recommendations," Catherine yelled, "I can't wait." Wally opened his eyes to see her in mid flight and then landing astride him. "Holy Mother of Mary." she wailed.

His hands grasped her thrusting hips. "Jeez'us almighty." he screamed, bucking like a brumby under an unfamiliar rider. Catherine's fingers stretched fully and then her hands grasped Wally's forearms, her extended fingernails digging into his flesh like talons gripping prey. Wet strands of hair flailed his chest and face as Catherine straddled him, kicking and cussing until her loins exploded. She seized the bedstead when thrown onto her haunches; Wally mounted. The smell of wet testosterone and his gut-wrenching grunt consumed her with his every thrust. Waves of euphoria exploded to the outer extremities of Catherine's body returning to collide with an almighty big bang. Laughter followed the screams of ecstasy; the need for oxygen disrupted the laughter and both collapsed, sapped of energy. Wally's hot breath on the nape of her neck was pleasant; she visualised the photograph of Buttercup's flaring nostrils. She pulled his arm around her, vowing never to let him go.

For three days, they did not leave their surrounds. Wong Foo's daughters waited on them like royalty, fulfilling their every wish. As if making up for lost years they talked non-stop. Wally purged himself of his only sexual encounter while in Egypt. Catherine selectively revealed her past, keeping in mind Ruby's words – 'there are some things a man shouldn't know.' Bycroft's name was at the top of her ever-growing list of regrets.

Wally snuggled into Catherine's back. "Jeez'us, it's been a long three days."

"Pardon."

"Naw, I mean…I'm worn out from all the talk'n."

"And that is all you are worn out from? Sacré bleu."

"Cut it out, you know what I mean."

Catherine loved hearing his voice, his inflections and idiosyncrasies, and egged him on. "No, Monsieur Beaumont, tell me." The pressure on her back increased as Wally took a deep breath. He slowly let it out and in the silence of his pause, she could feel his heart thumping. A wave of angst washed over her and she wished she hadn't been so playful.

"I can't be any more truthful, you know who and what I am – I'm an honest man…" Guilt consumed her as another wave came crashing down. "I want to marry you." Catherine rolled over and placed her fingers on his lips. He pulled her hand away and held it firmly. "I can never be with any other woman than you." Confusion; the third and largest wave tossed Catherine on her side and she again lay spooned against him. "I'll be a cursed man until I die if you don't marry me."

Catherine struggled to stay afloat in her sea of hypocrisy.

18 – The Proverbial hits the Fan

Many a bunny is caught
with a hook, line and sinker

Bycroft stabled his rig at Clemet's then on the way back to the office stopped to inspect the work on the community hall. The floor and a frame stood awaiting walls and roof.

"It doesn't look half bad," said Wally, slapping him on the back.

"Bastock reckons the roofing iron will be delivered this week. It'll be finished next weekend," boasted Bycroft. "Maybe I should be in the construction business?"

"Maybe you should, we'd both have a change of careers. I've made up my mind; I'm getting out of the mining business."

Bycroft studied him. "What is it? – you look different somehow."

"I've had three dust-free days. It's amazing what a bit of oxygen can do. My lungs feel like they're starting to work and my guts aren't on fire."

"Good for you. Well, Browning should have had enough time to do his survey. Come on…let's see what he's got to say."

The blinds on the display window and door were still closed and the handwritten sign announced 'Re-open Monday 9am'. At the front of Browning's office, Charlie Roister and one of his clerks were in conference with White. "He'd usually be open by now," White acknowledged, "I saw him leaving town Friday morning."

"Good morning, gentlemen," Bycroft greeted the men, "Has Mr. Browning slept in?"

"He hasn't been seen all weekend," the clerk informed him.

Bycroft directed his explanation to Charlie Roister. "He was doing some work for me."

"At Yakka Dakka," Wally added. "I hope there hasn't been a cave-in."

"Is that what the withdrawal was for?" Roister enquired.

"What withdrawal?" Bycroft asked.

"He withdrew two hundred and fifty pounds from Bycroft Holdings," the bank manager replied.

Bycroft's face turned pale. "Wally. Have a look 'round back…see what's going on."

Peering through the rear window of the private quarters, Wally saw remnants of the sluice jars scattered across the floor, but no sign of Browning. He tried the door; it was unlocked. An overpowering acidic smell pervaded the room. The occupant's departure was apparent by the bare wardrobe and hangers; drawers from the oak trunk lay empty. In the shop, bare shelves and display cases told a similar story.

Wally opened the front door. "Come in, Gentlemen."

Bycroft immediately walked to the safe and turned the handle; it wasn't locked. He opened the door and removed the only piece of ore remaining – the incarcerated dragon. "You'd better get Sgt. Doyle," he told the clerk.

"Jeez'us, it looks like he's done a job on everybody."

"Except Wong Foo," Bycroft snarled.

The heirlooms and treasured possessions of residents pawned under difficult circumstances would be unredeemable – jewellery and watches never repaired. Browning had cleaned out the shop of anything of value. Roister gestured to Bycroft to accompany him into the rear room and closed the door. "You're not going to like this," he confided, "but I've the deed of title you recently acquired from Wong Foo as security for another two-fifty I gave him."

Bycroft's pale face flushed. "You what." he screamed.

Roister continued, "Billings delivered an envelope with the deed."

"Billings," Bycroft again snarled, "is he in on it too?"

"I've got no idea."

"Naw, it must be a forgery. I've got the deed in my safe...or it'd better be."

"I followed your written instructions," Roister informed him, "they were on Bycroft Holding's letterhead – I recognised your writing and signature."

"It must have been a forgery too – I never gave any such instructions."

"I thought it a larger sum than usual but didn't think twice about giving him the money. We've done this kind of thing before."

"Yeah, but I'm sure it's against banking procedures," Bycroft retorted.

Roister turned pale, "Excuse me?"

"I'll want compensation from the bank of course…it was your mistake."

Roister was tongue-tied. He would need to check the accounts for further discrepancies. He brushed passed Bycroft and the crowd gathering in the shop. The spectators congregating at the assayer's front door parted as Roister left and Sgt. Doyle entered, closely followed by Tom and his camera. Word on the street spread and it soon became evident that Browning had run up accounts with the majority of traders over the previous month; his ploy to induce them into cashing dud cheques had also succeeded. The sergeant wrote down the particulars, as did Tom.

"The amount is climbing all the time," Bycroft told Doyle.

White pulled Bycroft aside. "He got me for twenty quid and I'll bet he got the others too."

"How did he do that?"

"Concocted a story that you had gone out to the property and he was short one hundred pounds."

"For what?"

"The deed of title; I got a receipt from him saying you'd reimburse me today."

"It's a bloody scam, Sunshine. The little weasel has swindled us all." Bycroft was livid and stormed out of the assayer's office followed by White and then Wally.

Tom set up the camera. "Sgt. Doyle, can I get you to stand in front of the open safe, please?"

Billings quickly returned to his desk as Bycroft entered.

"Don't move," Bycroft warned him, and marched to the safe. The deed of title was still there. "What's this about an envelope you gave Roister on Friday morning?" He headed to the liquor cabinet.

"You mean the one you gave Browning to give to me to give to him?"

"It's getting too complicated for me. I'll have one of those," requested Wally.

White joined in. "I'll have a shot too."

Bycroft was enraged when informed of another fifty pounds that Browning had received from Billings.

"He said you said," Bycroft mimicked Billings. "Has everyone gone mad? It's my money you're giving away."

"Jeez'us, he certainly had it in for you."

White contributed. "A professional, I bet."

"That's stating the bloody obvious," Bycroft retorted. "I'll ring the little bastard's neck when I get my hands on him. Billings, get me on the coach tomorrow." To avoid further embarrassment, Bycroft didn't reveal his part ownership in the jeweller's business and the capital outlay to stock it. He also dwelt upon reimbursement of the cash he'd given Browning to repay a personal loan. The exorbitant sums he had paid Browning for antiques of now questionable authenticity and value also sent shivers up his spine.

Throughout the day, the tales of woe grew as victims came forward. Bycroft called in to see Sgt. Doyle at the police station. "Well go and get him." he told the young constable. "I haven't got all day." He sat in the sergeant's chair listening to Blake shouting in the rear yard.

"Hey Serg…Serg, where are ya Serg?"

Doyle kept his desk drawers locked so Bycroft casually flicked through the paperwork in front of him. Two desks, an odd assortment of chairs and a couple of large wooden lockers furnished the office. A picture of the King and a red ensign hung above the door to Doyle's private residence. The rear door opened onto a small quadrangle surrounded by the lockup, stables and the constables' quarters.

Doyle entered, reprimanding the new recruit. "There'd better be a bloody fire…"

"Not quite, but an emergency just the same," Bycroft interrupted. "Well, what have you got for me?" He stayed seated in the chair as Doyle unlocked the drawer and removed a wanted poster.

"I found this," he placed it on the desk. "I think it may interest you."

Commonly known as the Sweaty Swindler, Browning used many aliases. In the ambiguous photograph, he sported a large moustache to mask his sweaty lip. Shabby hair hung in rats tails from under a bowler hat; wire framed spectacles with thick lenses enlarged Browning's eyes to a frog-like stare, again protecting the fraudster's identity. In the Advocate photograph, Browning had cleverly positioned himself so that his facial features were indistinguishable; his mouse-like demeanour had enabled him to go unnoticed by Tom.

"That's the little rat," Bycroft confirmed. "Have all your documentation to me by this evening; I'm leaving for Sydney tomorrow." He stood up rubbing his bottom and walked to the door. "You need a new saddle, Sergeant."

Wong Foo stood observing the partially constructed community hall. Bycroft ambled up beside him.

"I was just on my way to see you."

Without turning, he chuckled. "And once again I meet you halfway, Mr. Bycroft."

"How much did Browning take you for?"

Wong Foo contemplated and then smiled. "Losses are less than what could have been; incarcerated dragon not taken, I am fortunate." He paused, twisting his moustache. "Mr. Browning fortunate also." He faced his adversary, "And you Mr. Bycroft?"

"No more than the usual," the forced smile told differently, "although my generosity has been somewhat taken for granted." He turned his attention to the hall. "I was heading to Sydney at the end of the week; I'm now leaving in the morning. That laundry you wanted done…"

Wong Foo interrupted. "Under present circumstance I feel it wiser to delay laundering – now is time for reviewing of situation."

Annoyed at losing the chance to skim money from Wong Foo, Bycroft mumbled, "Anyone would think I ran over a black cat."

Chinaman too quick, thought Wong Foo.

Next day Bycroft left Gunnadoo on the coach. He carried with him a police report from Sgt. Doyle and documentation from Charlie Roister for the bank officials. Arriving at the Dundee rail siding late afternoon, he made enquires and discovered that Browning had purchased a ticket to Sydney after selling the hired rig from Clemet to one of the locals. That evening Bycroft boarded the locomotive and retired to the luxury of a first-class sleeping berth.

The baggage porter at Central Railway immediately consigned Bycroft's luggage on to the Imperial. Whenever he visited Sydney, the staff of the plush hotel treated him as a valued patron. The next day he made the first of the obligatory visits to police headquarters. The report from Sgt. Doyle was received. Bycroft's request to see the commissioner unfortunately wasn't; the gruff desk sergeant told him to bugger off. Charlie Roister's superiors at the banking institution were more gracious than the police commissioner was and a meeting was hastily convened.

"Mr. Bycroft, please sit down." Clyde Dibbs didn't look up, the title on his door authorising his arrogance. "We've gone over the report and it'll be passed on for insurance investigations." He glanced up. "Until then there's not much more we can do, I'm afraid."

"Well, there is one matter," Bycroft added. Dibbs refused the cigar offered. Bycroft struck the match, drew on the Cuban and then blew a smoke ring at the ceiling. "I've recently been offered a deal to buy out my partner; his health isn't too good." Dibbs removed an ashtray from a drawer and slid it to

305

Bycroft. He then got up in silence to open a window. An audio landscape of King Street below filled the office as he settled back behind the throne of influence.

"Now where were we? Ah ha…yes." Dibbs stopped shuffling through a pile of documents in front of him. "Mr. James, Walter Beaumont and the Yakka Dakka goldmine?"

"Yes. Mr. Beaumont discovered what we believe to be a mother-load." Another smoke ring ascended until assaulted by a stiff breeze. "There's only one problem, I'm a little short on the funds at present to dig it out."

"Yes, that would be a problem," he began flicking through paperwork, "Who did the assay?"

Bycroft squirmed, rubbed his nose and mumbled into his hand. "Irvin Browning."

Dibbs looked up, "I'm sorry, I didn't hear you."

"Irvin Browning."

Dibbs smiled without showing his teeth. "That could be a bigger problem."

"The man knows his stuff – he's a genius." Bycroft watched Dibbs as he closed the files, slid them to one side and then folded his hands.

"He's a fraudster, Mr. Bycroft…do you understand?"

"Well, yes, he's that too but…"

"But nothing…this institution is well aware of Mr. Browning's activities; we've had dealings with him before."

"Well don't hold that against me."

"Mr. Bycroft," said Dibbs in a patronising tone, "let me assure you *our* decisions are made on credible facts and figures, not the creative writing of fraudulent swindlers."

Bycroft was livid but didn't show it. "I understand a refusal when I hear it." He watched as Dibbs reopened the files and began searching through the pages.

"This is your overdraft," he held up the document, "you have a large overdraft…and yet you still wish to increase it on the word of a shyster? He's a con man. Do – you – understand?"

Bycroft was now incensed. Like a naughty boy being told no, he was even more determined to get his own way. He stood up. "'No' is not in my vocabulary, Mr. Dibbs, there are other money lending institutions in this city."

"Mr. Bycroft, may I offer you some advice?" Bycroft shrugged his shoulders. Dibbs continued, now with a conciliatory approach. "At present your enterprises are making a profit and there is no reason why that shouldn't continue. The debt you're carrying is manageable. My advice to you is not to get in any deeper than you are now."

"Is that it?" Bycroft enquired.

Dibbs thought twice about continuing but did so. "There may be institutions willing to lend money now but I assure you when England calls for reparation…"

Bycroft couldn't mask his puzzlement.

"…repayment of our war debt," Dibbs informed him, and paused for the information to be acknowledged.

Bycroft retorted, "I know what it bloody means."

"Well then, mark my words," Dibbs predicted, "there'll be many entrepreneurs with their backs to the wall ... "

"...and their businesses will be for sale at bargain prices," Bycroft arrogantly added. "Expand now, I say, but if you're refusing..."

"I have refused nothing. If you wish to proceed with your request it will be put before the board, but I don't like your chances – I for one believe it an unacceptable risk." Bycroft clenched the cigar between his teeth and stared at him. Dibbs stood up. "Very well, Mr. Bycroft, I'll put your application for an overdraft extension through once you've completed the paperwork. Good day, Sir."

Bycroft had planned to spend the rest of his visit in Sydney mixing business and pleasure. He made restaurant reservations and then as usual expected the business supplier to pay the bill. Therefore, he constantly scheduled business to coincide with pleasure. The Randwick races, the cricket, boxing events and the Tivoli performances at Rushcutters Bay were his favoured haunts. Bycroft demanded nothing but the best, as he did of the two high-priced hookers that accompanied him on chosen occasions.

Cowper's Brewery, long established and held in high esteem for its philanthropic deeds, supplied Bycroft's pubs. Shipments of beer and spirits had increased over the past year and the pubs became a highly profitable outlet for the brewery operation. On previous occasions, Bycroft's invitation to the board of directors requesting them to dine with him had always been politely refused. This time it wasn't. On his last night in Sydney, Bycroft set out to impress his guests with a lavish dinner in a private function room at the Imperial.

Mr. Sloan, the elderly vice president, and Mr. Tanner, another man of similar age, had been dozing on and off throughout the dinner. Awoken when each course arrived, they picked at their plates like sparrows. Lockett and Bryant, men of middle age, contributed little to the conversation but took full advantage of the hospitality, gorging themselves on food and drink.

"…and that philanthropic venture will cost me a pretty penny, but it will be well worth it to have a house of prayer in Gunnadoo," Bycroft informed his audience. His silver tongue, solemn delivery and talent for plagiarising did Pastor O'Dea proud.

Judge O'Keefe twirled his bushy whiskers. "By jove. I'm impressed." The board chairman was long retired from the Supreme Court yet continued to use the title. "Onward Christian soldiers, eh what." His lackeys applauded. "How many children did you say you had, Mr. Bycroft?"

"Gunnadoo is my child. First I'm to build an ark; the Lord will tell me when to stock it." Tanner's snoring interrupted the beginnings of another humble sermon.

"Time we were going, no, don't get up." The judge poked Tanner and shouted at Sloan. "We'll talk again, Mr. Bycroft. By jove, I like the cut of your jib." Tanner and Sloan sleepily agreed. "Goodnight Gentlemen."

O'Keefe exited shouting for his chauffeur as Tanner and Sloan shuffled behind him. Lockett and Bryant stayed seated.

"And how many days do you envisage being at sea, Peter?" Lockett asked satirically.

"Peter?" enquired Bycroft.

Lockett's demeanour had changed from that of a subordinate. "You'll need a lot of fish to feed your many children."

"Not to mention the loaves of bread," Bryant added. "I've got four kids and all they do is eat … and the wife's talking about another."

Lockett held up his empty glass. "And the gallons of wine that will be required for the thirsty hordes – you'll be stomping grapes from dawn to dusk."

Bycroft rang a small bell for service. "I've got two pubs." He paused to smile conceitedly at Lockett and then added, "My children, let's just say my flock, won't go thirsty."

"I got three kids and a thirsty wife," Lockett added hastily, "they all suck me dry – a bloke will soon need a bloody goldmine to support them."

"It just so happens I got one of them too," Bycroft bragged. "A bottle of your finest champagne … French," he instructed the waiter.

"Then, Peter, may I suggest you fill the ark with your gold rather than bullshit." Bycroft showed no sign of surprise by the suggestion; he sniffed rebellion in the ranks. Lockett continued, "Would I not be wrong in assuming you'd rather stand on the bridge than shovel shit in the stalls below deck?"

310

"I sail my own ship, if that's what you're saying, yes."

"No, you sail your own boat," Bryant corrected.

"Boat, ship, what's the difference?"

"Size," interrupted Lockett, "it takes more than one at the helm to *steer* a ship; you don't sail it, and you *don't* rely on the unknown to make progress."

Bycroft offered the men cigars. "Would I not be wrong in assuming," he paused for dramatic effect, "you're referring to Cowper's."

"That I am." Lockett gave him a wink. "Admiral O'Keefe stands at the helm and Mr. Bryant and I stand either side."

"Holding him up," Bryant wisecracked.

The cork popped. "About time." Bycroft admonished the waiter. "Leave that, better still – get another bottle." He began pouring, "Continue, continue." Bubbles hissed on the table as crystal champagne glasses overflowed.

Lockett stayed with the theme. "You could think of Cowper's as ... as your mother-ship, Peter. Cast your net upon the waters, then at day's end return in your little sailboat to unload your meagre catch ..."

Bycroft interrupted. "Being a fisherman doesn't sound much better than shovelling the shit in the stalls."

Bryant gestured agreement and received his glass first.

"It's not for the faint of heart but such experiences are seen as ... " Lockett twirled the unlit cigar in his fingers, "mere impositions as one climbs the ladder, gangway, to the bridge where just rewards are reaped."

Bycroft slipped the glass through the tidal bubbles and Lockett raised it in salutation.

"We've both done our share of shit-shovelling," Bryant shrugged, and raised his glass.

"That we have, Mr. Bryant – that we have," Lockett agreed. "To your health, Mr. Bycroft." He burped and Bryant followed suit. Bycroft did likewise and then replenished the glasses and table.

"Hey. If points are being handed out for shit-shovel'n," he slurred, "I'll need someone to swing a bloody big shovel and load 'em into the wheelbarrow for me." He paused for breath. "Because my days of shovel'n are done – I want to stand on the bridge."

Lockett dropped the pretence. "We know all about you, John – well, Jim and I do."

Portraying a pirate, Bryant covered one eye with his hand and confirmed the statement. "Aye, that we do, that we do." He then turned to salute Lockett.

"Let me get this straight," continued Bycroft, "who's on the bridge?"

Bryant sculled his drink. "I'll help ya out, matey. There be the admiral, the captain and his first lieutenant…but soon the captain and his first lieutenant may be look'n for a new shipmate." He gave Bycroft a wink, "ya know what I mean, don't ya?"

"Fe-fi-fo-fum, I smell treasure," Bycroft parodied.

"He speaketh in a strange tongue, Captain."

Lockett placed his hand on Bryant's shoulder. "That he does, Jim, but while Admiral O'Keefe is at the helm, there'll be no virgin cabin boys on the bridge, will there?"

"Aye, aye Captain."

"Whoa, who's a virgin cabin boy?" Bycroft protested.

Lockett finished his drink and gestured with the empty glass. "Until you have a wife and family, sadly you are, my friend. Behind every man stands a good woman."

"The Admiral says so," Bryant added.

"And what do you believe?" Bycroft asked Lockett.

"On this one it doesn't matter what I think; there are some seas the Admiral refuses to traverse…this is one."

Bryant refilled his own glass and then raised it. "Davy Jones he soon be visiting."

Bycroft was finding the banter contagious and the company of his guests like that of his cronies. "If it be a mutiny we be talking 'ere," he whispered, "watch out for Mr. Tanner. 'ave ya hide, he will. He hold sway with the Admiral, he does."

Bryant immediately turned on him. "How's it you be known about 'the sway'. Are ye a spy?" The in-joke passed over Bycroft's head but not Lockett's and the two men laughed heartily.

Bryant held out a match and Lockett lit his cigar. "My mother's elder brother, Mr. Sloan, my uncle," he informed Bycroft, "holds the key and – the sway."

Bycroft treaded carefully. "I don't wish to appear rude but Mr. Tanner appears to be…"

"Just about past it," suggested Lockett.

"Aye, ready for the big sleep, the deep six," Bryant added, "and he not be taking 'the sway' with him he'll not, aye."

"The sway…I don't follow. What's the sway?"

Bryant covered his eye again. "A part of the treasure the sway be – but tha's all ya be getting from me."

"All will be revealed at the right time," Lockett assured Bycroft.

Their drinking and repartee continued until the three men staggered from the smoke-filled function room. The bell on the unattended concierge's desk received a thumping until the bleary-eyed man appeared.

"Mr. Bycroft, your bill is ready as requested." The concierge woke a sleeping porter and gestured for him to take Bycroft's bags to a waiting cab. "Your accommodation bill," he passed the envelope to him, "and the account for this evening's function. We hope you enjoyed your…"

"Yeah, yeah." He perused the bill and then pulled the notes from a gold money clip. "Keep the change." There was very little.

"Thank you…most thoughtful, Sir."

Lockett leaned unsteadily on the desk. "Here, let's have that function bill," he told Bycroft, "Cowper's will pay – we don't want any long-held traditions being broken, do we?"

Bycroft caught the cab directly to Central and immediately retired to his reserved sleeping berth. After two weeks of living the high life, he returned to Gunnadoo worn out. Dempsey greeted him as he alighted from the coach.

"Good evening, Mr. Bycroft. Did you have…?"

"Have the luggage delivered to my place."

"First thing in the morning…"

"Tonight."

"Yes Sir. I'll look after it myself."

Bycroft entered the residence in darkness. He poured a large sherry and surveyed each room while waiting for the luggage. Wally's swag was still in the spare room. When the luggage arrived, Dempsey received abuse for taking so long and then Bycroft retired.

In the morning, all conversation in the kitchen ceased when Bycroft entered. The housekeeper went about her business quietly. He gestured for coffee and sat opposite Wally. "I didn't hear you come in."

"It's a wonder you didn't, I fell over your bags – you left them in the doorway."

Bycroft's words contradicted his sentiments. "I do apologise, how thoughtless of me."

"Have a look at the bruise on me elbow," complained Wally.

Bycroft all but laughed, quickly making excuses. "I was dog tired; it was one hell of a trip."

"You went with one bag and returned with four, yup, that's one hell of a tiring trip."

"Well, what do you think?" Bycroft struck a pose and waited, leaning back in his chair to proudly show off the new attire.

It looks the same only a size or two larger, thought Wally. "Yeah, real dapper, front page material…hey, did Browning head for Sydney?"

"He certainly did and he's gone to ground, probably under a rock being the worm he is."

315

"Well he certainly wouldn't want to stick his head up around here. He's cleared out with the proceeds from many a sluice jar as well. The good folk are baying for his blood."

"That's what you get for trusting people," Bycroft grumbled. The housekeeper got the first nod of recognition when she placed the coffee before him. She also got the breakfast order and the finger gesture to get a move on. "Now, Wally…" he took a sip of the brew, "I've got a liquidity problem at the moment but I'll soon be able to have a serious discussion about buying out the partnership."

"It'd better be soon, I'm going crazy sitting around here doing nothing."

Catherine and Wally had spent the past two weeks in each other's company. For Wally, nothing had existed but the space they occupied. With Catherine's paranoia of Bycroft finding out about Wally and vice-versa, she had insisted on secrecy. When Wally questioned the need for confidentiality, she passed off her alliance with Wong Foo and his antagonistic relationship with Bycroft as being at the centre of it. She explained to Wally how there could be no connection between him and Wong Foo, not even her; their relationship must be kept secret.

Bycroft didn't want to reveal too much about his cash flow difficulty and changed the subject. "What's been happening around here?"

"Jeez'us. What's been happening, let's see." Wally scratched his head. "It seems there's been quite a few litters born with the dog's markings and…"

"Never mind," he interrupted, "I'm sure I'll read about it in the Advocate."

"Speaking of which, Clarrie Radcliff is mustering up mayoral candidates."

"Who'd be stupid enough to run against me?" Bycroft stared at him arrogantly.

Wally pondered, "Hmm, I guess you've got to have two runners or there's no race."

"You're not wrong there, Sunshine."

Bycroft left his residence in a pleasant mood. As promised by the gentlemen's outfitter, the waistcoat and flannel trousers did make him feel thinner. He strolled down Main Street doffing the new homburg, bidding all he passed a good morning and collecting their looks of admiration as though they were IOUs. As he left Houten's, Ruby commented on how dapper he looked. Standing next to her he'd never felt thinner, albeit the only thing thinner was his wallet. His amicable mood changed as he crossed the street.

"Hey. Bycroft." He turned to receive the compliment. "Ya pack'n on the pounds there, son." The emperor's new coat was no defence against a teamster's brutal jibe.

"Good morning, boss. How was the trip?" Billings enquired when Bycroft entered.

He flopped behind the desk. "How do you reckon. Do I look as though I've just had a bloody holiday? It was hard work, that's how it was. Now, what other problems do I have to deal with?"

"None that I know of," Billings smiled, "Do you want a cuppa?"

"Yes…and the paper." He swung around to put his feet up on the window ledge and missed it, the resulting action nearly throwing him from the chair.

317

"You've been sitting in my chair?" he accused.

Billings had never been out of it and thought quickly. "I moved it when sweeping up." He could feel Bycroft's eyes upon him as he prepared the brew and changed the subject. "I kept last week's Advocate for you; do you want that too?"

"While the cat's away the mice will play," he retorted.

Billings knew it was going to be one of those days and didn't bother to ask what had been the outcome of chasing after Browning. By eavesdropping on Bycroft's conversations throughout the day, he would glean enough information to give Wong Foo and receive the promised rewards. Billings delivered the tea and papers and then sat behind his desk, pretending to study figures while actually watching Bycroft's facial expressions as he read the Advocate. Lead news on the front page proclaimed the celebratory activities to be undertaken the following month. A photograph of the community hall, still incomplete but well on the way, showed the slow endeavour by volunteer workers.

"This will cost me a bloody fortune. Billings, I want the figures on the free grog," he ordered. Readers could fill out the official registration form, cut it out and deposit it at the Advocate. "And how many of your mates are voting for me?"

Bycroft smiled conceitedly at a paragraph informing the readers he would be cutting the ribbon. He turned the page. The broad smile Harrick displayed in the photograph was one of larrikinism. It caught Bycroft by surprise and his face contorted in anguished confusion. His thin lips then showed his displeasure. Billings chuckled quietly.

Although it was pretty well a forgone conclusion that Bycroft would win, various traders and businessmen had been approached to run against him. Clarrie had even talked with the brethren of cronies. In Bycroft's absence, they had decided one of them should run and keep the candidacy in the family. The cronies looked upon this course of action as a lark also, selecting Harrick to run because of his good looks. The game was to see how many women he could lure into his bed.

"Hey Sunshine. Did you know about this?"

"I don't follow politics," Billings replied carelessly.

"Who said anything about politics?" Bycroft rose to his feet, his pent-up anger also rising.

Realising the mistake, Billings quickly added, "Anything written in a newspaper is political."

Billings, the only other person available, was in his sights; Bycroft was spoiling for a fight. "Are you some kind of an atheist?" he snarled.

"An anarchist, actually." Billings looked up as Bycroft approached. He wished he hadn't replied as his mind searched for the right manoeuvre. "But when the time comes you'll have my vote," he pledged.

Bycroft loomed above him like a dog standing its ground over a bone. He clenched his fist, deliberating whether it was worth it or not and deciding it wasn't. "I'm staying out at the property overnight, give me the books."

The threatening situation passed and Billings' heart began beating again. He kept a low profile and began scheming as to what he could report to Wong Foo later that evening. Having Bycroft out of the office for another day would be worth the effort of stitching a tale together.

Leaving the office, Bycroft asked, "How many mates do you have?"

Somewhat surprised by the question, Billings looked up and answered, "Not many."

"Get some more," Bycroft advised him, "and get' em to vote for me – you'll live longer."

He proceeded to Clemet's to pick up his rig, keeping chitchat to a minimum. He'd found through a couple of previous encounters that the conversation always swung to Harrick's grinning photograph. Being told it was the face of an honest man didn't go down well but he contained the irritation. No longer able to crack the whip and leave in a cloud of dust, Bycroft showed diplomacy and sat behind a wagon as it headed out of town. He nodded, smiled and bade insincere gestures to passing pedestrians. His suppressed irritation was fast becoming an itch.

At the last moment possible, Billings sneakily dropped to the floor from Bycroft's chair. Bycroft stared at the office window as he passed, knowing of the mouse's existence on the other side. *You little rat,* he thought, *I'll catch you.* Passing the empty assayer's office Bycroft made a mental note of the available rental space. Passing The Arms, he smiled broadly, as the noise from the morning shift of rowdy drinkers foretold their fate and his fortune; while the amber fluid flowed, The Arms was another goldmine.

A swirling cloud of dust formed into a small willy-willy and the wagon ahead of Bycroft stopped as the horses reared. The good folk held down their hats, though some didn't have the chance and went scurrying after their headwear as though rounding up chickens for the cooking pot. The swirling wind caught Harrick's lodgings sign and it hauntingly swung back and forth on its chains before Bycroft's eyes. It was too much for him to tolerate – the itch now required scratching.

19 – Disparity of Agenda

Stirring the pot won't bring treason to the surface albeit, simmering tensions will rise.

Behind the vacant reception desk, the mail pigeonholes were full; the rooms were seldom vacant. Bycroft had never forgotten that Harrick had refused his generous offer of capital. Harrick's financial success and not having a share in it made the itch intolerable. The reception bell was too much of a temptation and it received the thumping Bycroft felt like giving Harrick. From behind the closed door of his private residence, the proprietor shouted. "I'm coming, I'm coming. Hold your horses." Harrick appeared in a state of upheaval.

"The service around here is pretty lousy," suggested Bycroft.

"It all depends on who's doing the servicing," Harrick jested lewdly. "So you're back." Bycroft went to stroll through the half-open door. "Hang on, wait a minute." Harrick closed the door behind him, preventing him from entering. The wait intensified the itch. "How was the trip?" The door opened and the housekeeper left bashfully. "All right, now you can come through." He tried to sound innocent.

"Getting a bit on the side, are we? She's a married woman." He scanned the tidy lounge room; all seemed in order. "That kind of publicity wouldn't look too good for a mayoral candidate if it got out, would it?"

Harrick laughed. "You've seen the paper. Good photograph, eh?" He began rearranging the cushions on the sofa. "It's surprising what a bit of publicity can do for one's image. Bastock was right."

Bycroft was abrupt. "What's he got to do with it?"

"He came up with the idea."

"You haven't got a chance in hell of winning." There was only room for one ideas man and Bycroft believed it was he. He was more incensed at Bastock than at Harrick.

"Who cares, I'm having a lot of fun being a candidate." He thrust his hips at Bycroft. "Anyway, even if I did, and I know I won't, we're all in this together, aren't we? So there's no disparity of agenda. How's that for a mouthful, disparity of agenda." He stood holding his coat lapel with one hand, the stance Bycroft believed he had the rights on. "Dis-pa-ri-ty of ag-en-da," he articulated again. "Don't you just love it?"

"Was that one of Bastock's?"

"Yeah, he wrote down a few for me. He said…" Harrick quickly stopped himself from continuing. Regrettably, he'd already lit Bycroft's fuse.

"Go on Sunshine," Bycroft encouraged quietly, unconsciously clenching his fist. "What did Mr. Bastock have to say?"

"No. He didn't say anything…it was nothing."

323

"Come now. If you're going to make speeches, you have to be prepared to answer all the questions that'll be asked of you. Where's this miracle document? Let me have a look at it. Come on." Bycroft discovered the housekeeper's bra when lifting cushions from the couch. "Evidence but not what we're looking for." He threw the undergarment in Harrick's face. "Let's see if Bastock knows what he's talking about. Where is it?" He walked to the bedroom door and opened it. "Is it in here?" He scanned the room quickly. "Nope, not here either. I give up."

"He didn't actually write anything down, just told me..." Harrick's voice dropped, "...what to say."

Bycroft ambled towards him. "Told you what to say – when?"

"A couple of days ago." Harrick could smell the whiskey breath in his face.

"No, not when he gave you the...what was it again?" he asked menacingly.

Harrick replied compliantly, "Disparity of agenda."

"Ah yes, I meant, when were you to use this...disparity of agenda?"

"Anytime I could."

"No, that's not what I meant." Bycroft liked seeing fear in a person's eyes. "All right, all right," he stepped back a pace, "let's try this – what conclusion can one assume from making such a statement?"

Harrick was feeling nauseous. Caught between Bastock's brainwashing and Bycroft's interrogation, he couldn't stop himself. "Defusion of angst," he replied.

"And when did Bastock tell you to drop that one into our conversation?"

"When I saw you getting pissed off," he blundered.

"What was it again?"

"Disparity of…" Harrick didn't finish. Bycroft belted him in the eye and sat him on his arse.

"What was that for?" he wailed.

"To prove a point," said Bycroft, holding out his hand, "let me help you up."

"What point?"

"One, it didn't work and two, you shouldn't always believe what you're told."

Harrick shied away from the outstretched hand.

"I'm not pissed off any more. Come on, up you get Sunshine." He got to his feet and Bycroft asked again, "What was it?"

Harrick was about to say it again then thought better of it. "I don't remember."

"Well, maybe you *should* write it down so it's not forgotten."

With a hand over his injured eye, he responded quickly, "Best it is."

"And so too this conversation I think. I look forward to your candidacy speech. You have three weeks to practise up. Here's a tip Sunshine – keep it short."

* * *

Life became complicated for Catherine as she waited for the Yakka Dakka partnership to be resolved. Fortunately, Bycroft had too many other distractions to contend with and his visits ceased for the present, but containing Wally's enthusiasm was

325

becoming difficult. He wanted to let the world know of their relationship.

Over the previous three weeks in the lead-up to the celebratory weekend, Bycroft's ego had grown, as had his animosity towards Bastock. They each avoided the other. Bycroft had cancelled the Wednesday evening get-togethers until further notice and the cronies' unity was in a state of confusion.

The community gathered in front of the hall at two o'clock on Saturday to watch the official proceedings. Pastor O'Dae blessed the completed building and then Bycroft positioned himself on the front steps with scissors in hand, orating for the occasion. "And so, ladies and gentlemen, boys and girls, it gives me great pleasure to declare the Gunnadoo Community Hall – open."

As the ribbon was about to be cut, Tom made his request. "Hold that pose, Mr. Bycroft. Mr. Harrick, could you please join your running opponent." Bastock egged him on and Harrick took his place. "Could I have both men with hands on the scissors please," Tom directed, "and shake hands with each other. Smile please."

Bycroft's thin lips pursed together; he grimaced at having to share the photograph. In the crowd, Catherine and her girls began flirting. They caught Harrick's good eye and he smiled broadly.

Like unruly schoolboys at assembly, Bastock and White giggled, digging each other in the ribs. Stoddard shook his head, "No good will come of this if you push him too far."

The doors opened for the public inspection. Either side of the large hall four windows let daylight in and stale air out. Six industrial lamps hung from exposed rafters. At the rear of the hall was an exit door either side of a stage. Two steps on each side and at the front gave access to the raised area. Red ensigns crossed diagonally above the portrait of King George hung on the rear wall.

Registration of residents began. Meg and Ruby had organised a small group of women who sat to one side taking names. Those who were illiterate could put a cross next to the candidate of their choice when the time came.

Clarrie officiated the calling for the council elections. He concluded, "…and so the voting will take place here in five weeks. That is the first week of October. Those who are undecided whether to run for office have two weeks to register. We'll now hear from the two candidates we have. Mr. John Bycroft will speak first." Polite applause and the standard amount of wisecracks encouraged him forth.

"Thank you, thank you. Today I'm not going to talk about me…I'm going to talk about what's important – you." He enjoyed the sound of his voice amplifying off the walls. Bycroft recounted his recent trip to Sydney in pursuit of Browning. The masterful storyteller weaved fact and fiction together with the threads of ambiguity. "…and I told the commissioner of Browning's disparity of agenda."

His audience gasped, suitably impressed, although many were left in the dark as to what it meant. Harrick's good eye immediately began twitching nervously.

"I informed him there was many an unhappy resident in Gunnadoo. I didn't pull any punches."

327

Bycroft worked the crowd. "Do you know what the commissioner suggested, do you know?" He gave them no time to ask. "A defusion of angst is required; that's what he said, a defusion of angst." Bycroft began laughing manically then stopped abruptly. "Have you ever heard such a mouthful of rubbish? What conclusion can one assume from such a statement, I ask you?" Many residents shook their heads and tut-tutted in agreement. Those who didn't soon did for fear of looking stupid. "I told the commissioner of police we want action. There's to be no atheists or anarchists in Gunnadoo."

Clarrie and Meg stood off to the side. "He's good," said Clarrie, I'm just about ready to vote for him myself and I haven't understood a single word he's said."

Meg was astounded. "He hasn't said anything yet."

"Yep, it's all about what they don't say – a bloke could be tempted to lay down a bob or two if the odds were right." He tapped his wallet. "Ah...Harrick's a dark horse though; it'll be interesting to hear what he hasn't got to say. What odds will you give me on him?" he asked Meg.

"That performance will take some beating. Let me get the rules of this wager correct. You're betting the winner of today's charade is the candidate who says the least?" Meg confirmed.

Clarrie nodded.

"I'll give you three to one on Harrick." She spat on the palm of her hand.

Clarrie did likewise. "You're on for two bob."

They shook on the bet.

Pastor O'Dae was now receiving lessons from Bycroft. He'd whipped up the constituents' enthusiasm to where they were hypnotised by hype. "...and so, in finishing I say to you, if you give me your vote, I'll give you a mayor who'll get things done. Thank you."

Stoddard was first to his feet applauding; the cronies and many other locals soon followed. Harrick went to stand but Bastock restrained him in his seat. "Don't stand, you're running against him."

Harrick felt his eye and mumbled, "More likely from him." Then, to his amazement and apprehension, Bastock stood, applauding, only stopping to place a hand on his shoulder to stop him from standing. He felt Bycroft's evil eye upon him and dragged Bastock down. "What do I do now?" he asked.

"Whatever you do, don't think about Bycroft's stupid look."

"You mean the one just before he gets pissed off?"

"Yeah," Bastock smiled, "that's the one...don't think about it."

"And now we'll hear from Mr. Noel Harrick," Clarrie informed the audience.

"Listen to your gut feeling," Bastock encouraged.

Harrick stood on the stage, nerves evident only to him. He looked to Bastock for support and received only a stupid face being pulled. He immediately thought of what he shouldn't. The dreaded consequence began in the pit of his stomach. He could feel the belly laugh slowly rising; the more he resisted the stronger it got. The audience waited in silence, watching Harrick's slight tremble escalating.

"He's having a fit," yelled a prankster.

"Hmm, hmm," Harrick cleared his throat and then smiled. Clasping his coat lapel, the larrikin grin began quivering until control was longer achievable. Harrick slapped his sides, gasping for breath. Each time he tried to speak, Bycroft's image, the one he'd been told not to think of, loomed large and he laughed even more. His laughing became contagious; the sight of Harrick with blackened eye shut and tears rolling from the good one had the crowd mesmerized. Harrick finally gave up and left the stage to thunderous applause. Bycroft's final humiliation occurred when they looked each other in the eye; he was pulling the stupid face that had instigated his outrageous performance. Harrick's brazen attitude of laughing in his face rubbed salt into the wound.

Meg looked at Clarrie, rubbing his fingers together. She shrugged her shoulders in disbelief. "Now I've seen everything."

"Learn from the master," he jested. "Boy, can I pick a *dark* horse."

"It's a pity you didn't pick Mr. Browning."

Clarrie waited until the crowd stopped with their one-liners and there was silence. "Thank you, Mr. Harrick," he responded. The women applauded loudly again and he was forced to wait. He stood composing a response to the performances witnessed. "Thank you ladies – settle down." Resembling a ringside announcer at a prizefight, Clarrie then shouted to everyone's surprise, "If that's what Mr. Harrick thinks of Mr. Bycroft's platform, we're in for one hell of an election. What do you reckon folks?" A cheer went up and to the crowd's delight, the musicians entered.

Ruby's face turned bright red as she coached 'Knees up Mother Brown' from the saxophone. Houten followed, squeezing the bellows of a squawking piano accordion and Jock, having had his town crier's bell confiscated, now achieved the desired effect of much noise by thumping on a bass drum. The crowd shouted their approval, men and women began dancing and when the musicians stopped, the dancers threatened them with a lynching. Ruby played the same tune until she was out of breath and could no longer continue.

"Gunnadoo is definitely in need of a social get-together," Meg informed Clarrie and Tom.

"The band is definitely in need of rehearsals," Tom suggested.

"I'll speak to our social liaison officer."

Clarrie looked at where Ruby was sitting. Jock was fanning her and Dr. Tubber was taking her pulse. "I think we've just about got all we're going to get out Ruby for the moment."

* * *

To resolve the escalating antagonism between himself and Bastock, Bycroft had Billings inform the cronies that the Wednesday night get-togethers would resume. The men took their habitual positions in the parlour. Harrick and Bastock, sitting on the leather lounge, immediately began their ritual pillow fighting. A vacant chair in the dimmest corner of the room made Browning's absence conspicuous. White kicked off his shoes and stretched out on another settee while Stoddard lounged back in the supposedly Chippendale antique; the winged chair was now under suspicion. Bycroft poured the sherry, handed out cigars and then took his position leaning on the mantelpiece. General conversation took place with discord simmering below the surface.

"Gentlemen," he announced, "we have quite a few lost weeks to catch up on." Each man waited anxiously as to where the statement would lead. Bycroft swirled the liquid in his sherry glass while drawing hard on the cigar, billowing smoke rings . "But…"

"Here we go," Bastock whispered to Harrick.

"…before we do, we seem to have had…" he gestured to Harrick and silently coached him.

"I'm not going near it," Harrick countered nervously, clutching a cushion, "I had a sore eye for weeks and now I got strained stomach muscles."

"A disparity of agenda," Bastock put forth. He received a king hit from Harrick's cushion.

Bycroft sneered. "And here's another couple of words to increase your vocabulary – displacement of loyalty."

White lay staring at the ceiling. "Displacement of loyalty – that's three." He still carried muscle from tree felling and could back up his mouth should the need arise. "If we're not gonna mince words ... let's all play by the rules."

Stoddard took on the role of peacemaker. "Come on fellas, we're all on the same bloody side. If you want to lose teeth, see me and pay for it." It didn't raise a laugh; he leapt onto White as though extracting a tooth.

"Get off, ya bastard." He threw Stoddard aside and sat up. "Only trying to – defuse the angst." Nervous laughter, from Bycroft included, lightened the atmosphere.

"This mess was instigated by you asking me to become pals with Radcliff," Bastock told Bycroft. "I did, and my so-called pal turned on me and asked me to run." Harrick received a covert blow.

"Not the face, not the face," he hollered, to everyone's amusement.

"I dunno – that u-beaut shiner got ya a root or two," White drolly suggested. "Now who's for another drink? Let's put this bullshit…"

"Semantics," Bastock interjected, to Bycroft's ire.

"…behind us and get down to the business of making money." Stoddard held his glass out and all men spoke at once until Bycroft gestured for silence.

"Have a listen to yourselves…you sound like rabble, not the community leaders we are." Silence prevailed. "Without direction, the boat – ship," he corrected himself, "goes up on the rocks, gentlemen. To steer a ship under full steam requires a crew, does it not Mr. White? You know about steam engines. Power, gentlemen, it's your choice; will it be sail or steam?" Again, they all spoke at once. "Mr. White, with your knowledge of steam engines, you will be the engineer – stoking the boilers." White returned to his horizontal position. "Mr. Harrick, our gigolo, will ply the ladies for their husbands' business information; this he passes to Mr. White.

333

Information," he eyeballed Bastock, "is the fuel that drives this ship...*right* Mr. White?"

Bastock found the temptation irresistible. He stood, cuffed his mouth for a megaphone effect and gave directions. "I believe that's port, Mr. White."

"Starboard," corrected Bycroft. A verbal altercation on nautical terminology began.

Stoddard braced himself, holding the armrests, and began shouting, "Rocks ahead." He then lifted his feet and began paddling, "Fuck you lot. I can't swim." The visual analogy of saving oneself took the heat out of the discussion.

White sat up again. He missed the ashtray on the smoker's stand, dumping the deposit on the floor rug. "For Christ sake, who's steering this so-called ship? I gotta complaint for the captain."

Bycroft moved to the centre of the room and calmly answered him. "I have no problem with Mr. Bastock being the captain if wishes to be. Mr. Stoddard, you can even be his lieutenant – together on the bridge, searching for new conquests." Stoddard refilled Bycroft's glass. "How's that sound, First Lieutenant Stoddard?"

"Anywhere but the boiler room," he replied compliantly.

"Mr. Bastock," Harrick threw the cushion, hitting him in the back. "I believe Mr. White wishes to register a complaint with you."

"Yeah, I'm not too happy 'bout being stuck in the boiler room when the party is on the bridge," he griped.

"Hang on," Harrick now protested, "if I'm passing him the fuel that means…no way. I gotta complaint too; I wanna be on the bridge."

Bycroft returned to his position of authority listening to the inebriated folly. He rested his arm upon the mantelpiece as Bastock stared daggers him.

"Logistics, Mr. Bastock," Bycroft saluted, "that's your expertise – is it not?"

"And what's your expertise?"

"I'm the strategist, the navigator and also – the admiral."

"Admiral? You're a bloody dictator more like it."

Bycroft raised the glass and clicked his heels together. "Benevolent dictator if you don't mind."

That statement silenced the shipmates. Stoddard began his paddling routine, Harrick clutched another pillow and White began putting on his shoes. Bastock stood like a shag on a rock trying to defend his stance. "There's not enough room on the bridge for me and your ego." He placed his glass on the sideboard, defiantly dropped the burning cigar in it and left without saying another word.

"Well, that certainly put a damper on the cruise," said White, "I'm calling it a night too…I got a big job on tomorrow."

Bycroft turned to Harrick. "What about you, do you want another drink?"

Harrick was relieved to hear him say drink and not black eye. He held out his glass in a state of confusion, not knowing where his loyalty lay. Stoddard sat quietly contemplating the Titanic situation.

Later that evening, Bycroft looked closely at the Bycroft Holdings relationship with Bastock Transport. Business earnings over the past year and projected profit showed a good investment. Financial returns were steadily rising and would continue that way unless competition arrived. The thought of destroying Bastock Transport was appealing. Bycroft whetted his appetite with the thought that council contracts would be on offer, transport one of them. He contemplated how to offload his twenty-five percent share in Bastock Transport, as it would eventually be worthless when he became mayor and the contracts went elsewhere. The thought of having to negotiate with Bastock was unpalatable; to make a profit on the deal would be difficult. He poured another drink, staring absentmindedly at the doorway, remembering Wally tripping over the luggage. He laughed, and then shouted loudly, "Wally."

By talking his partner into swapping his share of Yakka Dakka for the share of the soon-too-be-crushed transport business, one hundred percent of Yakka Dakka was obtainable. He would not have to deal with Wong Foo's counter offers either and Bastock would be taken out of the negotiation equation. The contents of the bottle diminished while waiting for Wally, but his frustration didn't. He thought about throwing something in the doorway for Wally to trip over but changed his mind and finally staggered off to bed.

The housekeeper had Sundays off and Bycroft took the opportunity of privacy to corner Wally at the breakfast table. "You were late getting in last night; I was waiting up for you. Have you got some woman you're not telling me about?"

Wally had been primed by Catherine should this question be asked. Two-up was a great excuse and he was ready. "Jeez'us, I nearly lost the shirt off my back. I hung in until breaking even and then got the hell out of there."

"You know, you have quite a gambling habit," Bycroft lectured him. "To tell you the truth, I've been worried about buying out the partnership with cash. I don't want to see you lose it in a game." He rose to pour a mug of coffee for Wally and refresh his own. "You're a mate, Wally. What I'm about to propose I wouldn't do for anyone else. I've been giving some thought to the situation and what's in your best interest."

Wally accepted the coffee placed before him. "And?"

"Have you ever thought about the transport business?"

"Can't say I have…what about it?"

Bycroft sat down and began pitching his idea.

Knowing of Bycroft's liquidity problem and the goldmine being worthless, Wally saw the offer proposed as a deal that couldn't be refused. It would also put an end to the secret relationship with Catherine; that made the offer all the more attractive.

"Jeez'us, one minute I'm a prospector then a potential transport tycoon."

"Well, that's about it. What do you reckon?" Bycroft asked.

Wally had the answer written all over his face but he tried keeping up the pretence. "It's a lot to think about."

"That's the way business works, Sunshine. It's not for the faint of heart." Bycroft was now seeing his bigger picture with clarity. "Get in there and learn what makes it work. You never know what could happen from there." His new transport business would need an up-front stooge so Bycroft could be a silent partner. Having Wally with inside knowledge of Bastock's business would be a bonus. Bycroft believed he had the upper hand and wanted the deal closed. "Say the word and we'll sign the papers tomorrow."

Wally shrugged, "Why not? You've got a deal." Both men shook hands. "That's not another new outfit, is it?"

"These are my church-going threads, not bad eh?" Bycroft boasted.

"Do they come with padded knees?"

Bycroft waved the finger. "It wouldn't hurt for you to get on the right side of you-know-who."

"I used up all me prayers at Bathsheba."

* * *

Uncomfortable as it was, through habit or stubbornness the cronies took their regular positions together in the front row. The assortment of chairs

338

clattered like tap dancers on the wooden floor as the congregation made ready for the service. Mrs. Chang chaperoned the girls instead of Catherine doing so. They hurriedly took their places as the low notes of the organ resonated and the worshippers stood, their voices pitching to the heavens. Pastor O'Dea held his bible in both hands and looked down on his flock from centre stage. He mentally counted the sheep, and his blessings; it was now time to proceed with his plans.

"Lord," he drawled quietly, "I ask you to bless this hall and all those who pray here today."

"Now aren't you glad I dragged you along?" Bycroft whispered to Billings.

"Lord – praise be to those who give of their time …"

Bastock nudged Harrick. "Guess who don't get any points in that department."

"… and of their wealth to build this great house of worship." The pastor took a step forward, raised his head and stood in silence.

"I hope he don't get the accumulated interest on our donation," Harrick replied.

Hell and brimstone then rained down. The pastor lashed out, his forefinger scanning the congregation. "Cursed the unbeliever, may their eyes shrivel up…" Harrick rubbed his eye. "…and they choke on their own bile." Bastock felt a rumble in his stomach. "He who points the accusing finger, beware …" Bycroft checked his cuticles. "Let the hair of the deceitful shrivel up and fall out." Billings covertly brushed dandruff from his sleeve. "Lord." I beseech you to consign their souls to purgatory."

"Bastock can have *that* contract," Bycroft told Billings.

The congregation sung hymns between the pastor's religious theatrics and at the end of the service, he watched the poor at the rear give copper contributions. As the collection plate moved forward, offerings rose to that of the lowest denomination in silver to a respectable shilling when the traders made their donation. He was pleased to see a handwritten note dropped into the plate by Bastock. Bycroft wasn't; he was tempted to take it out and read it. All he could do was double his original contribution, which he made sure everyone saw before handing the plate to the pastor. The organ stopped and O'Dae made the announcement.

"On behalf of mayoral candidate Mr. Noel Harrick…" Bycroft listened while staring daggers at Harrick, "…White's Timber Mill will supply timber for church pews." Harrick received much kudos with the appreciative response. Standing at the back, Robinson, who had the job of returning the borrowed seating, couldn't contain himself and gave a covert whistle of approval.

Selective clearing of scrub at the front of the hall left enough tree coverage where the congregation could exchange pleasantries in the shade of tall gums. The cronies didn't form in their usual huddle. Their unity had been split and they individually lobbied the congregation, always aware of where the opposition was and to whom they were talking.

Bycroft fronted Stoddard. "I know where those other three stand. Where do you?" Stoddard gestured his paddling routine and rowed back into the mingling crowd. Bycroft then spent his time talking with those he normally ignored. He even sought Robinson's alliance and by doing so learned of the pastor's desire to relocate permanently to Gunnadoo. His immediate thought was of renting the vacant assayer's office and residence; having the congregation's vote would be a bonus. Robinson reaped his reward of promotion into the new crony group being formed. He and Bycroft then sought out Pastor O'Dea for manipulation.

"There he is."

"Watch the master…listen and learn," Bycroft told him.

"Mr. Bycroft, your donation today was more than generous," O'Dae praised.

"Only doing my part – set an example, I say. Mr. Robinson tells me you're thinking of putting down roots?"

"Ah, Keith Robinson." The pastor laid his hand on Robinson's shoulder. "A God-fearing man and a good man." Robinson soaked up the admiration as though butter wouldn't melt in his mouth. "Always willing to lend a hand, bend a back – and donate…threepence wasn't it, Mr. Robinson?"

"Sixpence when I get a raise," he confirmed.

"Ah, yes, putting down roots," said O'Dae, returning to Bycroft's question. "We believe it may be nearing the time …"

"To look for a low-cost residence?" Bycroft interrupted. He gave a sly wink to Robinson.

"Yes and Mr. Harrick kindly offered us a room at his lodgings."

Bycroft wasn't impressed that Harrick's camp had received the pastor's news first. He believed the underhand approach of using religion for political gain confirmed his righteous quest to destroy Bastock, and made the counter-offer.

"Well, what if I was to tell you about ..." He informed the pastor of the vacant accommodation at the rear of the assayer's office, concluding with, "and the front office can be utilised for mid-week bible studies, counselling and such. Mr. Robinson will see to any requirements you may have. Well, what do you reckon?"

"It sounds ideal but Mr. Harrick's price ..."

"Whatever it is, I'll beat it."

"You too are a good man, John Bycroft." He held out his hand. "On behalf of my sister ..."

"Your sister?" Bycroft and Robinson declared in unison.

O'Dea quickly rectified the slip-up and placed his hand on Bycroft's shoulder. "Brother John, Sister Beth and I will gladly take you up on your most generous offer. You have an agreement."

"Of course, Sister Beth," Bycroft mumbled, embarrassed at the furphy. Robinson, as if looking for gold, kicked at the dirt underfoot.

O'Dea and Bycroft shook hands. Tom candidly snapped the photograph. Meg followed up with notepad and pencil. "Good morning, gentlemen, any news for the Advocate?" The pastor, wanting their agreement in print, made known Bycroft's offer. Robinson cagily made his presence known with supportive statements.

Harrick encouraged Bastock to make formal representation to Catherine's girls and awaited his introduction. "Good morning ladies…and what about you, can Mr. Harrick depend on your vote?" Bastock asked.

Mrs. Chang interrupted her conversation with Ying Lee to reply, "Do not desecrate the Sabbath with your politics, Mr. Bastock." The look he received wasn't as favourable as Harrick had received from the girls. Mrs. Chang returned her attention to Ying Lee, "Excuse me. Please continue."

"Missy should rest. It very difficult to make prognosis without seeing patient, if illness reoccurring, maybe best Missy see her doctor," he suggested.

"Thank you, Ying Lee."

"Next week if she no better, I shall be most happy to stop by."

20 – Rebalancing the Shift

Incubator or womb?
the Cuckoo choses not;
the chooks come home to roost

Billings' Monday morning started with a surprise from Bycroft – he had said, "Good morning." He then learned of the asset swapping between Bycroft and Wally when Bycroft asked him to witness the signing of documentation. With this information, Wong Foo would supply his night's entertainment. Hearing that Harrick had offered the pastor free accommodation and Bycroft had had no choice but to do the same, Billings believed his day couldn't get any better. It did – Bycroft told him he was going out to the property for a couple of days.

Catherine's morning began as it had for the last week, with nausea and vomiting. Looking pale, she sat up in bed as Mrs. Chang showed Ying Lee to her room. "Bonjour Ying Lee. I think, I …"

"Then why you ask for me," he enquired, ushering Mrs. Chang out of the room and closing the door, "you wish to play Chinese checkers maybe?"

"I think, I…"

"Patient always thinks they know reason for illness."

He sat on the side of the bed. Unfortunately, by sitting on the covers, Catherine was pinned. She rolled to her side, missing the bucket, making the deposit on his dress-up slippers. "Holy Mother." she gasped.

He didn't move his feet. He handed her the wet towel, and she wiped her face and then sat up, reeling. Ying Lee placed his thumb on the inside of Catherine's wrist. "Ah chow wee coo, ah chow wee coo," he mumbled quietly while taking her pulse. He then tapped her back and listened when requesting her to cough. He placed his ear to Catherine's chest, listening to her heart. "Mr. Wally lucky man," he told her.

Catherine misinterpreted the prognosis and jumped to conclusions. "What's that he be telling you?"

"Not what he tell me." Ying Lee calmly looked at his feet. "What Mrs. Lee tell me."

"To be sure I've not said a word to nobody…except Madame Chang."

"Not Mrs. Chang either…Mrs. Lee and you."

"Impossible. I've not spoken with …"

"Not speaking of talk." His nose lifted in the air and he sniffed, and then smiled. "I recognise smell. Catherine looked at him, puzzled. "Mrs. Lee reminded me each time she have baby." Ying Lee watched Catherine's face display an array of emotions as realisation of what he was talking about dawned.

"Now you've gone and done it." she chastised herself aloud.

"Excuse please, not me." His humour went unappreciated.

"Are you sure?"

Ying Lee breathed deeply again and said, "Very early. I get Wong Foo's authority to purchase *special* herbs from Sydney Chinatown. Healthy diet most important for healthy baby." I give you medical advice free; herbs cost. I make out list.

* * *

Wally had met with Benjamin Peck the lawyer, who now handled the affairs of James 'Wally' Beaumont. The original document between Bycroft and Bastock, now signed over to Wally, was legal, but Peck advised him in future to consult with him before signing anything else. In the afternoon, Wally paid a courtesy visit to the transport depot. Bastock was irate when he received the news, not at Wally but at Bycroft for not giving him the chance to buy back the share himself. He was now under obligation to be on good terms with Wally.

Catherine, under the disguise of black pyjamas and coolie hat, had become adept at moving through Chinatown unnoticed. Once at Wong Foo's love-nest, she would change and greet Wally. Until the early dawn, the night was a world with no contradictions or complexities, without apprehension about a past life or Bycroft always lurking like a nightmare to invade her inner sanctum. In this world, there was no one but she and Wally; in the reality of a new day, each would return to their unpleasant charade.

The previous evening was one of the few they had not spent together in the past seven weeks and, undecided whether now was the right time to tell Wally of the pregnancy, Catherine felt as though something special was required. This resulted in her cooking the evening meal and not having Wong Foo's daughters wait on them. She had laid the table with the cutlery and glasses obsessively polished and positioned until she was satisfied. The decision as to one or two candles had finally been resolved and one candle stood representing one shared life together. The scratching of the dog at the rear door informed her of Wally's arrival. She removed the pinafore, let him in and stood before him. The words tumbled from her mouth.

"Would ya be noticing anything different about me?"

With a woefully bad accent he teased, "And who be it I be meeting with tonight? My Irish lass or …"

She placed her fingers on his lips, and then felt a rush of blood to her toes as his arms enveloped her. Wally pirouetted with Catherine in his arms, her reality again lost in another world.

"Put me down, I'll be getting all giddy I will."

"I've been giddy since the first time I laid my eyes on you…marry me."

The dragon bed cushioned their fall.

* * *

Wally lifted his head from the pillow. Catherine felt his movement and heard him sniffing. Her eyes opened quickly, "Holy Mother, me rabbit casserole."

In the subdued light of the candle, which Wally had insisted on lighting, Catherine sat at the table watching him bravely finish eating the burnt offering. She apologised profusely, "You don't need to be eatin'…"

"Nonsense, noth'n wrong with it, eh Dog?" After salvaging what could be, Wally had given the remains to the dog and the mongrel gnawed on the charcoal remnants baked to the bottom of the pot. Catherine was just as surprised as Wally was when she found herself sobbing uncontrollably. He squatted before her drying her eyes with a shirt cuff. "Jeez'us, it's not worth crying over." The naïve statement didn't help. She flung her arms around his neck to bury his face between her heaving breasts. Comforting arms enticed more sobs. "Stop with the sobs," he gasped, when catching breath, "and I'll give you the good news." Catherine took a couple of deep breaths and sniffed. "I've been busting to tell you but waiting for the right time."

"Then now be a right time," she revealed, "I could do with some cheering up."

"Then let me head go." Wally pulled back to arm's length, resting both hands on her shoulders. "When did I last tell ya how beautiful you are?"

"Stop with the sweet talk … is that it?"

"I've solved all our problems – I swapped Yakka Dakka; I'm now a partner in Bastock Transport."

Her look of curiosity didn't change as the words registered. Catherine tried to compensate for the shock when replying, but only managed a wail. Whether through shock at the noise or her sudden jumping to feet, Wally found himself sprawling backward. Catherine sprawled on the bed, again weeping uncontrollably. The dog lifted its head from inside the pot but its howl of empathy abruptly stopped.

"Shut up."

Catherine immediately stopped and raised her head. "Not you." Muffled by the pillow her wailing resumed. The perplexed man sat on the bed. "Jeez'us, I thought you'd be happy." The wailing intensified. "Now we don't have to keep up with the charade." The wailing immediately ceased. She lay silent and still. Wally hesitantly touched her shoulder. "Catherine?"

She sprung up. "Hold me, don't let go." He complied.

He tried his hand at an accent again, "To be sure, I won't be letting go Lass."

"This be no time for kidding." She pulled back and looked straight into his soul. "I love you, Wally. I mean really love, so much that it pains the living daylights out of me." Her mind raced to keep ahead of the words tumbling out. "I now be asking of your trust." Her fingers sealed his lips. "If you love me...nobody can know yet Wally, no one. Promise me."

"I don't understand. Wong Foo's no longer in the picture, the deal's closed."

As the justification formed, words and sentences became easier for Catherine. "But Wong Foo hasn't exacted his revenge for the dishonourable business dealing Bycroft has perpetrated."

"What's it got to do with you?" Wally asked.

"Nothing, but if it should ever get back to your partner that Wong Foo and I were setting him up…"

"If I catch either of them so much as…"

Catherine lay back and pulled Wally's head onto her belly. "Shhh, just listen." She played with his ear. "In the past I've had to make decisions for me own welfare, but this one I make for both of us and then forever more after, decision-making will be your job. I've got something else in mind to occupy my time." He couldn't lift his head as she was holding him by the ear.

"And what would that be?"

"I be telling you that when I get back from Sydney."

Wally sat upright quickly. "Ouch. Sydney, when?"

"Tomorrow morning."

"Jeez'us … I'll come with you, we could have a holiday."

"No. We can't be seen together. Not even on the same coach."

"I could catch one in a couple of days and meet up with you."

She forcibly pulled him down by the ear and stated, "Monsieur Beaumont, listen to moi," she tugged his ear, "please agree; for doing this we will see the last of Mademoiselle Catherine, oui?"

Wally sulked. "Can I ask how long you are going for?"

"It'll be no longer than two shakes of a lamb's tail," she teased, "two weeks…and if you're a good boy I'll bring you back something."

"What?"

"It'll be a surprise."

Catherine lay wide awake but oblivious to the attention her fingers were paying to Wally's left ear and lobe. The scenario of leaving Gunnadoo with what money she'd managed to save and letting her partner have the establishment repulsed her. The thought of being in his arms repulsed her even more; Bycroft had made known he wanted her services to resume on Wednesday evenings. With no cash from the sale of the partnership to compensate for lost finances, Wally's involvement with Bastock Transport was like an anchor around his neck and a noose around hers. The plan to cut and run couldn't proceed but neither could the charade. She looked at Wally, peacefully sleeping, unaware of all the complications. There was no choice but to get away from Gunnadoo and try to solve the complications that would multiply each day. Catherine slid carefully from the bed.

As Wally slept, Catherine made several attempts at writing him a note of explanation. A pile of scrunched-up paper lay at her feet until, finally satisfied, she sealed the envelope, addressed it and threw the discarded papers into the potbelly stove.

"What are you doing? It's the middle of the night," mumbled Wally.

"My shopping list."

"Come back to bed."

Catherine let out a shaky sigh, hid the envelope and then snuggled up next to Wally, trying to put it out of her mind but not succeeding.

* * *

Wally and Catherine stood in each other's arms, neither wanting to be the first to break their embrace. In silence, they listened to the bush awakening.

Wally gingerly felt his ear, "I can't remember if it's the left or right...you know, when someone is talking about you," he complained, "just like when you're coming into money you get an itchy right palm. Well, I gotta sore left ear...I reckon somebody's having a go at me."

Questioningly, Catherine gazed up at him. She raised her arms around his neck, pulling him down. Her gentle kiss cooled the swollen ear lobe, then she whispered innocently, "It means somebody loves you very much...now leave it alone." She slapped his hand.

Each went their own way unrecognised in the swarm of workers leaving for the diggings. Catherine then double-backed to follow Wally unseen as he headed for Bycroft's residence to play out the morning charade, and she went to Bycroft Holdings to slip the envelope marked to Bycroft's attention under the door.

Later that morning, from a respectable distance, Wally observed Catherine board the coach. Catherine saw her fiancé raise his hand as if to wave and then stop short to rub his ear. She immediately thought, *it means somebody loves you very much.*

21 – An Unexpected Reunion

*Like old friends, words of wisdom if not lost
return when required most.*

After what seemed like many nightmares and only a
few hours' sleep, Catherine drank the last of Ying
Lee's medicine and then dozed again restlessly. The
train whistle and the conductor's shouting finally
woke her completely.

"Sydney Central, Sydney Central, last stop."

She had paid the price for her thrift in not
reserving a private sleeper. *Holy Mother,* Catherine
cursed under her breath when disembarking, *me back
feels like it's broken.* A woman's scream followed by
a constable's whistle echoed along the platform. She
held the suitcase tightly in both hands, the basket over
her arm.

"Excuse me, Miss."

The stranger's voice from behind startled her.
She turned to face a baggage porter in a scruffy
uniform. Granny Dunn's words reverberated in her
head. *Don't trust nobody not in uniform and them
that are, beware of.*

"Yes?"

"Let me give ya hand with that," he offered.
The frantic whistling grew louder. "Here we go

again…step back Miss." The jostling crowd parted as a villain rushed past with the pursuer on his heels. "Ya gotta be careful around 'ere. Just get in from the country, did we?" Catherine watched the chase, not answering. "Pickpockets; they're everywhere. Ya get used it…now how about it?" He stood with his hand out for the suitcase.

"I be recognising the likes of you," she shied away from him, "so don't ya be trying noth'n."

"Are ya gonna give it to me or not?"

"I can manage without your help, thank ya very much," she tersely advised him, "be off with ya. If my fiancé was here…"

Leaving the suitcase at the cloakroom, Catherine crossed George Street into the Haymarket district and Chinatown. The hustle and bustle was at first overpowering. Catching her breath in front of a jewellery shop, she stared in the window. The clock and watch faces stared back at her, mocking the pain she felt at losing Danny's watch to Wong Foo. Memories of a lifetime ago reawakened. Just as she had purchased a watch for Danny, she now had the urge to buy one for Wally. The fable of two lovers resurfaced and played upon her mind. Catherine couldn't remember if it had been told to her or she'd read it, but she did remember standing in front of another jeweller's reminiscing about the fable before purchasing Danny's timepiece.

In the fable, the fiancé traded his fob watch for a tiara to crown the long locks of his fiancée. Unfortunately, unbeknown to him, she had cut off her hair to trade for an Albert chain to adorn the fob watch. As providence would have it, he received the chain but had no watch to attach to the Albert, and she received the tiara but had little hair in which to wear it.

The heart-rending significance was seducing Catherine into another purchase. Her eyes immediately scanned the display for a tiara, but there was none. A range of gilded hair clips became a substitute so that her daydreaming could continue. The clang of a tram bell nearby sounded nothing like Clemet's anvil, but it produced the same result. As when she had first arrived in Gunnadoo and learned of Danny's death, Catherine now experienced the stabbing pain in her heart. She interpreted this as a need for more of Ying Lee's medicine, and it forestalled the temptation to make another purchase.

She studied the map Ying Lee had drawn for her and then followed one narrow lane after another. The appearance of residents in coolie pyjamas alleviated her growing apprehension at being lost. Catherine showed several passers-by the envelope addressed in Chinese, and amid much chatter, they pointed the direction in which to proceed. Surrounded by the chatter of Chinese and the familiar aromas of poultry, pigs and even the horse dung she sidestepped, Catherine felt more at ease than on George Street. The clatter of carts on cobblestone was alien, however; Gunnadoo's Chinatown was less progressive.

She would have missed the small sign above Chow Lung Importers had it not been for an elderly man who escorted her to the entrance of the shop. He bowed graciously, Catherine doing likewise before entering. The tiny bell danced above the opening door in welcoming. Behind the counter, a curtain of glass beads hung dormant until a young man entered.

"Good morning, how may I be of assistance?" The clinking of glass behind him enhanced the shop's mysticism as shafts of light reflected around the dimly lit interior.

"Bonjour. I wish to see Monsieur Lung."

"Monsieur Lung?"

"Merci."

"That is impossible, I am afraid, he is a very busy man."

"And I am a very busy woman." Catherine's insistence took him by surprise.

"He has been up all night."

"And so have I."

"He sees no one without an appointment."

"And neither do I…but I do believe I have one." She handed him the envelope. He looked suspiciously at the address and bowed his head in compliance. "Your name, please?"

"Catherine Dunn…Mademoiselle."

"Please wait." He gestured to a wicker chair shaped like a throne.

Catherine sat mesmerised, watching the shafts of light tire of their frantic stampede. The unruly lot gradually settled into a wallpaper of shimmering tranquillity. Muffled voices from above seeped through floorboard cracks. Incense wafted aimlessly as if searching for an exit. Catherine's angst eased in the meditative ambience and for the first time since waking that morning, a serene calm enveloped her. She opened her eyes to see the assistant bowing before her; that was unsettling, as there was no chink of glass beads and no shafts of light reflecting wildly.

"Please, this way," he requested softly.

Glass beads now chinked together as they entered the dank warehouse. From an opaque skylight, an insipid shaft of light lit what seemed the only remaining space not stacked high with merchandise. The lad beckoned Catherine towards it. The doorbell rang. "Excuse please." An overpowering smell of musk replaced the incense.

Mr. Houten would be impressed, she thought, moving through the towering canyons. The thought of Ruby not getting through the tight squeeze brought humour to the situation; a large rat scampering across her path removed the smile. "Monsieur Lung?" The thought of being deliberately shown to the wrong address crossed her mind. *Get a hold of yourself, girl,* she reprimanded herself. Uneasiness now replaced serenity; she too scampered through the labyrinth. "Monsieur Lung… Monsieur Lung?"

A table filled the semi-lit space, a semi-conscious man the solitary chair. Pillowed by his arms, his head rolled back and forth as he muttered words of redemption.

Catherine stopped in her tracks when she almost fell over the man. "Monsieur Lung, I have been told you can help me." She received no response. "Monsieur Lung. Sacré bleu, you must work very hard." She tugged his sleeve, "Excuse please." The whining noise of an electric motor and a rattling sound alerted her to the concertina grill door concealed in the shadows. A dull light descended to the floor. The empty lift stood waiting; a female voice echoed down the shaft, "Please enter, Miss Dunn."

The office above the warehouse was surprisingly opulent, red, gold and blacks being the preferred décor colour. Plush carpet covered creviced timbers. Cat statues of various shapes and sizes filled shelves, nooks and crannies. A Siamese cat sat on the deceptively large desk purring loudly as Chow Lung scratched behind its ear. He rose. "Welcome, Miss Dunn. Please sit." An air of influential confidence negated his dwarfism; he wore a resplendent black satin cheongsam with an embroidered dragon emblazoned across his chest. "Wong Foo has requested I extend my hospitality to you," Chow Lung informed her, perusing the letter. "I humbly do so should it be required." The letter of introduction did carry weight.

"That is most kind but it won't be necessary," Catherine replied sheepishly, trying to dismiss the penguin image of Chow Lung that her mind had created.

"May I then offer you refreshments?"

"Merci."

His extraordinarily large feet were a contradiction to his height, as were his hands, which clapped together thunderously to alert an assistant. The woman appeared with boiling water to begin the ritual preparation. "Please see to Miss Dunn's prescription." He replaced the telephone receiver and rolled up the document, placing it in a container and then inserting the container into a metal pipe. It rattled off through the tube to the apothecary. "You are dismissed," he abruptly told the assistant.

In silence, Catherine watched the dexterity of Chow Lung's bulbous fingers as he measured and blended a variety of herbs and mixtures from tea caddies. The boiling water when added to the mixture produced an enticing aroma. She instigated the conversation to stop herself from thinking about the arsenal Chow Lung must be dragging beneath the resplendent costume.

"I hope I am not keeping you up?"

"Keeping me up?" queried Chow Lung.

"Your business must be doing very good, oui?"

"And what draws you to that conclusion, Miss Dunn?"

"Your warehouse is full and your storeman is exhausted."

"You are most observant." He poured the brew from a small teapot and slid the teacup to Catherine. "This will help settle your nausea." He yawned, "We had long and difficult negotiations last night."

"We have a lot in common. I too have difficult negotiations underway at present. I hope to resolve them soon."

"I too wish for that outcome."

"Good Karma brings good outcomes."

"Encouragement is sometimes necessary also," he quickly added.

Catherine and Chow Lung exchanged pleasantries until the telephone rang. She fingered the intricate Ming pattern on her cup, eavesdropping to try and follow the story. "This is very good," he replaced the receiver. "Your order is also ready. I have enjoyed our meeting," he gestured her to the lift. "I shall see you out."

"That is not necessary; I've taken enough of your time."

"One must take time to smell the flowers, Miss Dunn."

The whine of the electric motor distracted her. The floor dropped away; Catherine felt her stomach lift as they descended. An upturned chair lay near the table, the pungent odour of urine filled the air. She said nothing but thought plenty while following the swaggering penguin through the labyrinth. He lashed out, kicking at a rodent. It squealed.

"I hate rats," Catherine confided.

"Rats cleaner than humans, sometimes preferable company also."

Glass beads chinked and shafts of light danced as they entered the shop. A package wrapped in brown paper waited on the counter.

"When you require more, it will be mailed to you," Chow Lung informed her politely, "and should there be anything else I may assist you with, please do not hesitate to ask…anything, Miss Dunn."

As much as her curiosity demanded it, she didn't dare ask what. Instead, returned the offer.

"If there is anything that I may do for you…"

"There is one thing," he requested. Catherine was startled at the immediacy with which Chow Lung took up her offer. He smiled, "Please give my regards to your gardener, Chung Dow. His workmanship is still held in high esteem; he worked for my grandfather and then my father."

She had dismissed the Chinese whispers about Chung Dow's infamous career and naively believed that there had been a previous connection with a florist. "The family business, oui?"

He tapped his nose with a forefinger, "Wong Foo is right…"

"Monsieur?" she queried, bemused.

"You would make an excellent chess opponent."

"Chung Dow is an excellent gardener."

"His pruning sheers are legendary."

"I could not manage without him."

"It is difficult to find good help."

Chow Lung kissed her hand, bowed and then left.

"What a charming man," she informed the assistant.

"Chow Lung is known for many things: charm is just one.

* * *

Catherine found lodgings at a boarding house in Glebe. The room was clean and close to transport. An appointment the following morning with a Pitt Street obstetrician confirmed Ying Lee's diagnosis. What the specialist couldn't confirm was Catherine's hidden dilemma – who the father was. She suppressed the unthinkable and wandered the city streets window-shopping. Then she went and watched 'The Sentimental Bloke' twice at a picture show.

Each day passed with no miracle solution forthcoming. Catherine visited museums, art galleries and libraries, where she could be distracted from the constant barrage of guilt and insecurity that her thoughts generated. In the evenings, she walked in solitude until exhausted and then collapsed into bed. Chow Lung's opiate medicine relieved the stress until the following morning when the ritual would begin again. After two weeks, the ritual was unknowingly becoming a habit and another visit to Chow Lung had been required to refill the prescription.

The boarding house where Catherine was residing was within walking distance of the unsavoury destination. She finally gave consideration to the unthinkable and made a decision. A chilly wind nipped at her ankles – the mortal sin about to be committed tore at her soul. She didn't recognise the woman's voice emanating from a darkened doorway, only the red tip of a burning cigarette.

"Mademoiselle Catherine, is that you?"

"Pardon?"

"It is you." The woman stepped into the circle of light beneath the streetlamp. "It's me, Lucky-Legs." She kicked up a leg like a Tivoli chorus girl.

"Lucy."

"I've still got it." She did another kick and nearly fell but for Catherine's support.

"It is you."

"I'm a little out of practice though," Lucy apologised. The exceptionally good-looking woman was but a shadow of her former self.

"You have not been dancing much of late, oui?"

"I'm not auditioning at present." The woman's malnourished appearance and hacking cough confirmed the obvious. "A new club is supposed to be opening soon."

Catherine studied the woman's face. "You stayed with us for so little time…why?"

"You know how it is when you're promised the world." A lucky prospector had promised her patronage. "I'm still with Norm; we're doing fine." The bruising on her cheek and wrist suggested otherwise; it couldn't be hidden and neither could her embarrassment. Her man was her pimp.

Catherine had found the woman's artistic talents wasted in her establishment and was of two minds when Lucy left. "I hope you have continued with your painting." Lucy had introduced Catherine to the Masters. "Sacré bleu, let us get out of the cold, I know a café."

"I can't." Lucy stubbed out her butt, immediately lighting another cigarette and looking around nervously. "I mean…I'm working."

"Then Mademoiselle Catherine shall pay for your time, oui?"

The ambience of the café was friendly, as was the welcome. Over the past week, Catherine had become a frequent customer. She removed the warm jacket and hung it over the back of her chair. Lucy sat opposite, shivering in a lightweight dress. A gust of cold air rushed through the opened door when a customer entered.

"Let's swap seats," suggested Catherine, "I'm wearing more clothing than you."

The hot meal and their company warmed the women's souls; it was like old times. Catherine did most of the listening, even though Lucy's disastrous story wasn't uplifting or unexpected. "… and the money was all gone. What was I to do? He threatened to leave me," she revealed.

"You should have left him. Why did you not leave the swine?" chastised Catherine. Lucy's silence and teary eyes confirmed why. "You could have returned to Gunnadoo."

"And do what? Raise a bastard to be ridiculed?"

"Pardon for my brusquerie, forgive me…I should not be so abrupt, I do not judge you," apologised Catherine. "What happened?"

"I had to make a choice. I made it."

"And?"

"It was the wrong one. There'll never be any chance of a bastard again."

Catherine felt as though the knitting needle had been plunged deep into her. The shock was stifling. Relief came by way of another customer leaving; she breathed in deeply the gush of air as though it was smelling salts. "I am so sorry."

Lucy stood, the pain etched on her face deeper than age-lines and exhaustion. "Under other circumstances I would have been a good mother."

"I am sure you would have." Catherine gestured to the back of the chair. "Don't forget your jacket."

The women's eyes met. Lucy affectionately remembered the Gunnadoo establishment and its Madam. She accepted the offer with humility. "One day I may be able to return the favour."

"You already have."

"Shut the bloody door." an irate patron yelled as Lucy opened the door to leave. Outside, she put on the jacket, pulled up the collar and crossed Glebe Point Road, returning to her world of bad decisions.

Au revoir, Lucy. Merci beaucoup, thought Catherine. The turbulence began to subside. She ordered a fresh pot of tea and reviewed her situation in a new light.

Catherine decided to make her pregnancy the reason to leave Gunnadoo and the complication with Bycroft. She would tell him it could be anyone's baby. If he made any threats of harassment or violence, she'd go public, dashing his mayoral aspirations. Hopefully, the partnership could be dissolved amicably with the inducement of her share in the brothel at a bargain price. She would inform Wally of the Pitt Street doctor's advice – for health reasons of mother and baby, the pregnancy should continue in the city. Hopefully, the men wouldn't discover her polygamous relationship. She and Wally could disappear into their own world and raise the baby.

"Thank you for coming, come back again." The proprietor placed the bill in front of Catherine. It was only then she realised the café was empty and so were her pockets. She had left her purse in the jacket pocket.

"Sacré bleu. I cannot pay, I have no money."

The man's polite mannerism changed immediately. "I'm calling the police."

"No, I mean, I do have the money …"

"You do or you don't, which is it?"

"My purse was in my jacket. The woman that dined with Catherine took it."

"You do-gooders are all the bloody same until you get ripped off. If you want to feed hookers, it's your business, not mine. The cops will soon pick the thief up."

"She did not steal it. I gave my jacket to her."

"Christ. Talk about giving the shirt off your back. That's going a bit far, isn't it? She's a bloody hooker. I've seen her soliciting customers."

Catherine leapt to her feet in terse defence of Lucy. "I will not hear such words. Mademoiselle Lucile was once a *great* dancer – gentlemen queued for her company."

The surly man stood his ground. "It doesn't look like her dance-card is too full these days. How come?"

"A puppet has no free spirit – and neither does an artiste when her strings are pulled. Especially by a pig gigolo. Does that answer your question?"

"One more if you please, Your Highness." His obnoxious attitude reminded her of Bycroft. "Who's gonna pay?"

"I shall return in the morning with your money, monsieur. I shall also give you extra. This will be for the weekly meal you are to provide Mademoiselle Lucile."

"Says who?" he challenged.

"Says…Chow Lung." Catherine watched the man's face turn pale.

Ultimo was the only suburb between Glebe and Haymarket where Chow Lung's influence ruled. The thought of drawing his attention into Glebe and upon himself registered and the obnoxious attitude quickly vanished.

"May I ask how long I am to provide this benevolent deed?"

"Until you are told otherwise. Bon soir."

The boarding house was a couple of minutes' walk from the café. Adrenaline stoked the fire within and Catherine didn't feel the chilly wind. The same as when she had first confronted and defeated Wong Foo's aggression, she felt her spirit rejuvenated.

Sleep came easily.

22 – Blarney. Mr. Booth

The customer pays
the Stonemason creates
the client lies oblivious…

Catherine paid her accommodation bill, had her suitcase forwarded to Central and proceeded to the café for the confrontation. A warm breeze replaced the previous evening's chilly wind. Walking through Jubilee Park, she observed the changing season with new clarity. Green buds were beginning to shoot on deciduous trees; it seemed that overnight, the weight of winter had lifted from both the park and Catherine. Unexpectedly, the café proprietor also offered hospitality. Along with apologies, he refused to accept the money owed and promised that Lucy would have his attention in return for him not having Chow Lung's.

The rattling of the steel rail beneath her seat was somehow comforting as Catherine observed her fellow passengers, the majority women, who sat solemn faced, dressed in black. Some men still wore the khaki, others suits, and most showed signs of fatigue. Children wriggled, uncomfortably confined by the formality of the occasion.

"Rookwood Cemetery." the conductor called.

Catherine moved along the main path with her fellow passengers as though still in the carriage. At their own individual stations, mourners stepped from the procession as though embarking from a moving tram. She automatically departed the formation at her stop and wandered the recognisable path. *Noth'n has changed,* she reassured herself.

Granny Dunn's plot was simple, no ornate fence or lavishly carved headstone marking her resting place.

"Excuse me, Miss."

The stranger's voice from behind startled her. She turned quickly, déjà vu driving her thumping heart. His face was familiar but not recognisable, the smile non-threatening. Her strangulation of the basket handle eased.

"Yes?"

"Don't tell me...it'll come," he glanced at the headstone inscription, "Edith Dunn...Dunn, paid cash...Miss Dunn...Catherine." He held out his hand. "Cedric Booth – stonemason."

"Mr. Booth." She crossed herself. "Holy Mother...to be sure I was just think'n about you."

"Nice piece of workmanship that." He gave the stonework a rub. "And how would you not think about me; you fair swindled me out of that piece of rock, you did." He gestured to a bench nearby. "I was most pleased to hear of your satisfaction with...don't tell me, it'll come..."

"Danny O'Shaunessy."

"Yes, yes," he scratched unkempt hair, "don't tell me..."

"The Celtic harp ..."

"Yes, a fine bit of work that."

"We'd be even then – it was a fine bill you sent to me too."

"Don't tell…"

"Gunnadoo." She gestured him to sit first and then sat with the basket on her lap. "And you, Mr. Booth, business or pleasure?"

"Business gives me pleasure, Miss Dunn." His gaze returned to the headstone. "Would you be interested in a Madonna and child for your Granny?" Catherine observed the splendid totems dominating the vicinity. Adjacent to Granny's plot, an angel hovered with her open wings providing protection for the occupant below. The shadow cast upon Granny's grave resembled a beach umbrella. "I'll even throw in a wrought-iron fence, noth'n too fancy mind you…tiff the plot up a bit – we don't want the neighbours looking down on her, do we? Catherine mulled over the idea. "Well…how about it?"

"It be a bargain too be sure but I like it just the way it is." Booth looked perplexed. "That is the first piece of land I bought, Mr. Booth. It will always remind me of my roots just the way it is – I be done with impressing the neighbours, thank you very much."

Booth smiled, "Thrice knock the Reaper." He fingered the sandstone scrollwork on the bench armrest awaiting her response.

Catherine sat with both hands on the basket handle, her posture that of an equestrian rider looking straight ahead. She didn't flinch. "That be an old wives' tale – to be sure you're a bullyrag, Mr. Booth."

He clasped his hands together, not in prayer but like a tax collector. "Apollyon told me."

Catherine looked at him bemused. "And who be Apollyon?"

"The Angel of the bottomless pit," he whispered.

"Get away with ya blarney, ya scoundrel." She looked around and then returned the whisper, "What will the neighbours think?"

He raised his eyebrows. "If ever I may be of service again, don't you hesitate – I always look after returning customers."

"I be in good health." Catherine paused, smiled and then continued, "And my fiancé is too."

"But I thought…go on, you've met a new fella?"

"And he be strong and fit." She waved a finger at Booth. "So don't ya be look'n to me to be a returning customer."

"Not for many a year at least – I hope you both have a long and happy life together."

"I'm sure we will."

He rose, hands still clasped together. "Death and taxes are the…"

"Go on, be off with ya."

He handed her a card. "We've recently moved to larger premises; a Government contract. Good day, Miss Dunn."

As quickly as he had appeared, he disappeared into the labyrinth.

Catherine sat deep in thought, casually tugging at innocuous weeds around Granny's headstone. *I guess ya was wonder'n when I'd be dropping by…I had a might lot of sort'n out to do first though.* The glare from the surrounding marble eased as the animated shadow shrouded her. *To be sure, I'd have Mr. Booth build ya a mausoleum if I thought that was what ya wanted.* A robin sang tunefully; an unseen but optimistic suitor returned it, making its intentions known. *Being where ya are you'd know about the harp...so I won't go on about it but Mr. Booth did a beautiful job.* Catherine watched the birds taking turns at chasing each other. *I be guessing Danny told ya about Wally Beaumont.* She paused, collecting her thoughts. *But so ya be hear'n it from me own lips – he's a good man and we're betrothed we are.* The courting robins landed, adding weight to the nearby crucifix that Jesus hung from. *We could visit Belfast for our honeymoon...sacré bleu. I didn't tell you, we're going to France.* The birds took flight, repeating their skilful sacrament. *When I next visit, I'll be introducing ya to my fiancé before tying the knot...it being the right thing to do and all.*

In the distance, a constable's whistle blew alarmingly. Her pounding heart thumped loudly, amplified by the silence. Armed with a pair of scissors from her basket, Catherine stood ready to defend herself. Wind whistling through memorial effigies replaced the tuneful robins. The banshee wailing of mourners carried on the wind was disconcerting, as was the figure of a young lad as he dashed past frantically trying to elude pursuers.

Formalities completed, the bereft mourners navigated the return route back to the main gates at a brisk pace. Catherine quickly rejoined the procession; it was somehow comforting. *Cum Agen...I must look,*

373

she told herself, approaching the sandstone archway. Mourners from other segregated areas within Rookwood converged into the bottleneck at the closed gates.

"Hang on, hang on," the gatekeeper called, "it's for your own safety."

Catherine searched the archway for graffiti; there was none. She observed the gatekeeper's oversized dust-cloak flapping as he leant with one arm pressed against the closed gates. *He be the Grim Reaper himself,* she thought. Her eyes lifted to the arch, *Stop with ya look'n, it's not there.*

"Awright gatekeeper, you can let them out." The boy's assailant shook him by the hair. "I've caught the culprit." He held up the slingshot and the dead robin as evidence. Catherine recognised the man as her horny antagonist from years past; he wore no constable's uniform yet the authoritarian persona remained. "Now get in there," he threw the boy toward the gatehouse, "and we'll get some details from ya."

"Move back or ya won't get out," the gatekeeper shouted callously at the mourners while slowly dragging the wrought-iron masterpiece open.

He's begrudging let'n us out, thought Catherine.

* * *

Catherine purchased a ticket at Central for the return trip to Gunnadoo. She left the suitcase in the cloakroom to make a courtesy call on Chow Lung before leaving.

374

"…he makes her life a misery," Catherine confided. She drank from the empty cup, defiantly swallowing the dregs. "Mademoiselle Lucile is an artiste – he is a pig of a man."

Chow Lung smiled. "Pork can be both sweet…and sour. More tea?" Catherine refused while politely acknowledging his witticism with a smile. "It would seem Miss Lucile's pig requires tenderising process." The smile disappeared. "It will be seen to by…master chef." He finished his tea. "Is there anything else?"

Catherine fingered the intricate Ming pattern on a porcelain plate. "There *is* one thing…Mademoiselle Lucile," she cajoled, "is a très bon dancer, oui." She winked at Chow Lung and then returned to fingering the embossed hallmark beneath the plate.

"Traditional dancing at Chinese establishments takes many years of training."

"Erotic dancing is most traditional, Monsieur Lung; it too takes many years of training. Mademoiselle Lucile is…" the plate flipped right side up in her fingers, "how you say, prime now. She is in no need of training." Chow Lung silently watched Catherine's absent-minded plate twirling. "A little rest maybe, some healthy food and she will repay your kindness ten-fold."

"It sounds as though Miss Lucile…" he casually retrieved the plate from Catherine, "is no longer lamb. Unlike I who appreciate old," he gently placed the porcelain on the table, "mutton is not appreciated by customers."

"Mademoiselle Lucile has many a trick in her yet." Catherine began stroking a ceramic cat, its streamline stature imposing, its fragility unstable. "She did not receive her 'Lucky-Legs' title for dancing only, oui? She is a fine contortionist also; I have seen many amazing positions with my own eyes."

"Female like feline, must be agile to survive," he advised, rescuing the artefact from Catherine. "Fragility most at risk when doctrine inflexible...I will make enquiries. Mademoiselle Lucile is most fortunate to have such a good friend."

"As I in you, Monsieur Lung – your friendship is most valued."

He removed an elaborate fob watch from his vest pocket, checked the timepiece and then wound it up. "Time requires maintenance, Miss Dunn, as does friendship." Chow Lung rose, "The value of friendship is revealed in time."

Leaving Chinatown, Catherine found herself in the jewellery shop perusing the fob watch display.

"A nice choice, this is rolled gold," informed the shop assistant as he handed Catherine the timepiece to study.

"Oui, it is lovely," she replied, flipping the protection cover open. Her face ambiguously reflected in the polished metal. "Time requires maintenance, does it not?"

"Rolex is most reliable...is it for a loved one maybe?"

Catherine imagined Wally's surprise at being given the watch and then at the news of becoming a father. She smiled. "Maybe."

The salesman jumped at the potential sale. "Our master engraver isn't busy at present; we could have something inscribed on the inside. I could have it done immediately." He licked his lips and then the pencil point. "And what would you like inscribed?"

Catherine contemplated, *Let's see, something simple.* "To Wally..." *What are think'n, girl, that's too informal.* "No." He rubbed it out. "To James Beaumont..."

"Beaumont." He showed her the spelling. She never called him James; that didn't look right either. "What else would Madam like?"

"Mademoiselle...and I've changed my mind." The assistant rubbed out that one also and waited. *Something simple...we're not trying to impress the neighbours.* "I think, 'To JB – love Catherine, 1921'. Yes, that will do." He scurried off to get the work done before she changed her mind again.

* * *

Two weeks had passed with torturing slowness while Wally awaited Catherine's return. Being stuck in limbo was bad enough, but being stuck under the same roof as Bycroft and having to put up with his mood swings was worse. His ongoing brawls with the issues of day-to-day business added to the tension. With the partnership settled, the welcome mat under Wally's feet was wearing thin.

Bycroft looked up from reading the Advocate. "How 'bout that," he remarked snidely to Billings as Wally passed by the window. "Mr. Beaumont has got up for lunch." He checked his watch as Wally entered. "Good afternoon, Sunshine."

"It looks to me like it might rain later."

"That's not what I meant. The transport business must be doing good?" Bycroft peered in the direction of Bastock's and then returned to reading.

"Yep. Being a transport tycoon sure takes it out of you. That chair looks inviting." Wally flopped onto it. "I'm going out to Yakka Dakka today…thought I might pick up the last of my personal belongings and see what Blackfella Jimmy and family have been up to."

Bycroft looked up. "Are they still out there?" He swung around in the swivel chair, stealthily placing the Advocate over personal papers on the desk as he called to Billings. "Cuppa time." He sneered at Wally. "I should be charging them rent."

"And they should be charging you for caretaking duties."

"What, for keeping down the snake population? Bloody freeloaders, I should be charging them for the tucker."

"Cancel the tea, Billings," Wally rubbed his belly, "that stuff would kill a brown dog – I got me Cure-All." He took a swig.

"Yeah, so have I." Bycroft opened the liquor cabinet. "Seeing as how we're talking accommodation, I've got a bone to pick with you…well not actually you – your dog." Wally gave Dog a belly rub with his boot. Bycroft eyed the culprit. "He's taken a liking to the Chippendale chair, the mongrel wouldn't get out of it and he snapped at me."

"Jeez'us, ya bloody lucky he didn't take ya head off – he must like ya." Wally put an extra effort in to his boot work. Bycroft shuddered at the sight of the dog lying squarely on its back with a rear leg kicking widely. His pink tongue was hanging out of his mouth and saliva flowed freely onto the floorboards. "Ya can't teach old dogs new tricks, can ya fella?" Dog received a mate's kick in the arse from his master.

Bycroft began pleading. "I wouldn't try and teach the bugger noth'n but I was hoping…"

"No way." Wally cried, "I'm not even gonna try." With his jacket sleeve pulled over his hand, he held up his arm in jest showing his hand missing. "You think I like having to share me swag with him and his bad habits? I learnt the hard way, I'm glad to be rid of him." Dog now gave himself a noisy licking. Bycroft wasn't amused. "Naw, he can keep the Chippendale."

Billings kept his nose to the account books listening to Bycroft's frustration heighten. When it peaked, he spoke up. "Excuse me, Mr. Bycroft. I'm doing your residential accounts for this month; they seem to have increased two-fold." He returned to the books. Bycroft cracked.

"When's the trucking tycoon gett'n his own premises?"

"Jeez'us, I thought you'd never get around to it." Wally stood up and stretched. "We'll be stay'n overnight with Blackfella Jimmy. Tomorrow I'll be meeting with me advisor," he gave Bycroft a wink. "I'll let you know Monday. Come on Dog."

The team of six, hitched to a wagon loaded with hay bales, waited patiently in the holding yard of Clemet's for the unloading to begin. As Wally waited for Buttercup and his rig, which were in the agistment and stables area on the lower paddock behind the blacksmith's, he watched the smithy's boy stoking the furnace. The lad's red face indicated the amount of work he was doing rather than the heat generated by the forge. "I'll be with you in a minute." he yelled, "I just gotta get rid of this rubbish."

"Under the spreading chestnut tree," Wally recited to the dog, stopping to take a swig of the Cure-All, "…I don't remember what comes after that, I think it…"

The loud explosion alerted everyone to the disaster, the thick smoke rising above Gunnadoo confirming the enormity of the situation. For the smithy's boy there had been no forewarning.

For Wally, there was no bugler's call to arms. The flash of white light was immediately recognisable to him, as was the gut-wrenching pain. What wasn't was the confusion of distorted noise that followed and the abstract sense of time. The force of the furnace explosion had flung him across the holding yard. Propped askew a split fence post, its back shattered also, the gut pain diminished and Wally watched flaming debris fall from the sky in slow motion. Terrified horses hurtled pass, blindly pulling what he believed to be a flaming hospital wagon.

He experienced no pain, albeit splintered bone was evident where a wagon wheel had crushed both his legs. His own blood extinguished his burning clothes. He descended a black void and listened to what now sounded like distant screaming. He waited for the return volley of gunfire. As if searching for a lost weapon, his fingers clawed the dirt until he felt the dog's head and wet mouth. Dog then ceased his crawling. The remaining Cure-All seeped from the bottle still clenched in his hand…some distance away.

* * *

Blinded by panic, the team of four pulling the flaming hay wagon careered along High Street and then veered into one of the laneways leading into Chinatown. Horse and wagon flattened shanties and bodies, and then bales of burning hay ignited the demolished material left in the trail of destruction. Where the wagon rolled over, a ring of fire extended outward, burning all before it. The Plough's roof caught alight and spread, the pub soon burning fiercely. Dadswell's Saddlery across the laneway began heating up ready to combust.

"Forget the pub, keep the water up on the saddlery." Clarrie yelled to Robinson. "We don't want a firestorm heading back into town." The bucket brigade received orders to start dousing the saddlery.

The blaze, temporarily held back at the bathhouse where there was plenty of water on hand, diverted around the rear of the building into the bush and headed southward. Creeping flames edged toward the house of ill repute; both sides of High Street were now alight. Frantic demolition and clearing of shanties continued as flimsy structures crashed under the weight of a timber-jigger used as a battering ram. Wong Foo shouted directions to clear an outer perimeter as a firebreak, hoping the inferno could be contained within. Unorganised and unprepared as the townsfolk were, they were managing to hold the containment line, but attrition would be the demise of Gunnadoo as there was more fuel to burn than able bodies to fight it.

Maniacal flames whipped up the wind and the intense heat became too much for the fire fighters, who pulled back. The saddlery caught alight; exploding tanning agents and solvents enhanced the potency of the fire. "We'll need a miracle if we're to survive this hellhole." Clarrie yelled to Dadswell.

Under the direction of Dr. Tubber, Mrs. Chang and the girls applied first aid to the many victims laid out on the lawns. Bycroft organised patrons from The Arms. The line of men and women passed buckets from the stream at the rear of the property to the bucket brigade inside the box hedge perimeter, which became the line to hold. A couple of men clambered onto the roof and put out embers that were rolling into the guttering. Choking smoke blinded all as the catastrophe intensified.

* * *

Wally lay silently as subconscious memories scripted by his short life passed quickly in a succession of images. The desert and heat mirages became Hades, tormented souls screaming for mercy as limbs torn apart by explosive white flashes rained down. Water then fell from the sky, quenching parched lips. The noise of battle dissipated as a sandstorm abrasively washed across the horizon and memory. Dates palms began swinging lazily in the breeze as he and army mates frolicked like children in an oasis of cool water.

Wally heard his name called; it was Ying Lee on top of a sand dune in the distance. "Mr. Wally, Mr. Wally." He couldn't understand how the Chinaman had found him in the middle of Palestine but was glad he had.

Ashen-faced, Ying Lee sat amongst burning debris, the man's head in his lap.

"I'm cold, Ying Lee, make sure water hot."

"Plenty hot, Mr. Wally, enough for fat lazy dog too."

He lifted Wally's hand from its frantic clawing in the dirt and gently placed it on the dog's head again. The clawing motion immediately became that of caressing, serenity veiling them both. Wally took his last breath through flaring nostrils. "Christine?" he murmured.

The portal closed and his fingers ceased moving. James Walter Beaumont was no more.

Ying Lee raised his head and rocked back and forth. "Ah chow wee coo, ah chow wee coo," he chanted loudly. Tears and then gradually rain diluted the patch of red earth where he sat.

* * *

The heavens opened up, helping extinguish the flames. Charred ground soon became mud with pools of water collecting in hollows. South Gunnadoo resembled the battle landscape of Flanders. Burnt-out structures hissed as steam rose from smouldering embers buried beneath. Acrid smoke hung heavy and exhausted townsfolk collapsed where they stood. Deceased animals and residents unable to flee the onslaught lay silently interned under blackened rubble, evident only by bloodstained watercourses.

At the time of the disaster, most of the town's school-age children were watching a puppet show. The ploy to gain their interest in education had saved many and they were now herded to the north of Gunnadoo. Residents assembled at the community hall, which became a makeshift hospital. Medicines, burn creams and balms were urgently required. The injured received Dr. Tubber's or Pastor O'Dea's services. The doctor's office was for major surgery only.

A hastily convened meeting took place at the Advocate; it became headquarters for the disaster coordination team. The extent of the damage was becoming apparent.

"One third of Chinatown destroyed," Wong Foo informed Clarrie. "I estimate two hundred people without shelter." He awkwardly raised his cup with a bandaged hand.

"That many."

"How many deceased?" he enquired.

"There's a body count of twenty-five at the moment with more not expected to survive the night."

"More bodies will be recovered in carnage," Wong Foo added.

"Not too many I hope," interrupted Bycroft, "we're out of morgue space already. The doc can't keep up." He raised his mug to Meg, "Good tea."

"How long before we can get another doctor here?" she asked him.

"At least three days…we need a dentist also, Stoddard's time was up."

"Three days, that's too long, we need another doctor now," Clarrie stipulated.

Wong Foo spoke hesitantly. "I know a physician ... "

"Who?" Everyone asked in unison.

"… unfortunately he longer wishes to practise."

"It's an emergency," replied Clarrie, "there's such a thing as a Hippocratic Oath."

"I will make the enquiry."

"Food and shelter are the next priority," Meg stated. "This rain was a God-send but if it doesn't stop…" she shook her head, "Gunnadoo will be in more strife than what we are now."

Bycroft threw in his support. "We can set up temporary accommodation in The Arms and I'll get Robinson to pitch the church tent, that'll house quite a few."

Wong Foo added his assistance. "My facilities are functioning; they can be expanded for food preparation and cooking."

"All right, let's get that happening." Clarrie checked the time. "We'll meet back here at four o'clock for a progress report. I suggest someone ride like hell to Dundee and wire Sydney for the support that will be required." He looked to Bycroft.

"I'll look after it."

"What about sending out a coach with the injured?" Meg suggested. "They could be on the train in the morning."

"Find out from the doc if that's what he wants and organise it," Clarrie instructed her. "Is there anything else? Right let's get moving."

Displaced families relocated at The Arms and the tent was pitched at the rear of the community hall. Volunteers under Mrs. Foo's direction staffed the kitchen. Food became communal and was deposited in extra drums prepared for the cooking of meals. Wong Foo's tent began serving non-stop; it too was to be procured for accommodation. At four o'clock, the meeting reconvened.

Meg finished giving her report. "Dr. Tubber says there are nineteen people who can be moved, many more will require hospital treatment. Another eight have died. He's given me a list of medical supplies."

Clarrie turned to Bastock. "Can you handle that?"

"The rain's easing, I don't reckon the crossing will be flooded. We'll convert three wagons and put a couple of riders out front of each with lanterns...it'll be slow but they'll get there. I'll send another bloke ahead to warn Dundee of their arrival."

"Is there enough accommodation?" Clarrie asked Bycroft.

"It's tight but everyone will have cover."

He turned to Wong Foo. "And what about the food situation?"

"No one will go hungry. Supplies from Chinese gardens still available."

"I'll organise a shooting party to stay in the bush," offered Sgt. Doyle. "This is a list of victims identified so far."

Clarrie quickly perused it, stopping at Wally's name. He sighed heavily and then continued reading. He passed the list to Tom. "Sorry, mate."

At the front of the hall later that evening, the community assembled silently. Citizens carried the injured on stretchers to tarpaulin-covered wagons, others assisted the walking wounded to the coach. Light rain fell on the sombre atmosphere as a morbid procession began its journey.

* * *

Catherine boarded the train and sat waiting impatiently for its departure. It had been a long day. She had revisited the museum, seeing exhibits in a new light as she now saw her future. With apprehension and guilt abated, and a new clarity, she eagerly wanted to get back to Wally and put her plans into action. Once underway, the monotonous lullaby of the rocking carriages encouraged peaceful sleep.

As the train pulled into the Dundee siding, Catherine could see that all was not normal. Victims lay on the platform ready for transfer aboard. At first, she thought a mining accident had occurred. When told of the tragedy, anxiety consumed her. A list of the deaths wasn't available. It would be another five hours before she would have those details, however she was informed her premises had not burnt down.

The rain had cleared overnight and the sun shone brightly, although it gave little warmth during the journey. As the wagons approached from the clearing, she could see north Gunnadoo. It didn't look as bad as what she had imagined; smoke had cleared but a stench lingered. The other wagons stopped at the depot. Catherine's coach kept moving down High Street and as it did, the disaster became evident. Mrs. Lee saw her pale face staring from the coach as it passed slowly and she immediately went to tell Ying Lee.

Catherine was reliving the nightmare of when she had first entered Gunnadoo…sapling poles spearing earthen walls conjuring images of voodoo; black shapes void of front doors and windows morphing into charcoal faces screaming in terror…the conjured images all now screamed in terror again. Dropped off in front of her establishment, she stood gazing at the desolate scene opposite. Individuals combed the ruins searching for lost relatives and retrievable possessions. Cast iron pots and such implements were the only things not melted in the firestorm. The wailing of lost souls drifted across patches of still smouldering earth, pockets of smoke clinging like small fog banks. Running up the street towards her, Ying Lee diverted Catherine's attention.

"Missy. Missy."

"How did this happen, Ying Lee?"

"Nobody know, large explosion at blacksmith's." He picked up her suitcase and quickly moved inside before she could ask the question he most dreaded.

Mrs. Chang met them at the front door; it had a 'closed until further notice' sign upon it. The brave face she put on concealed her pain. Chung Dow had also died, of a heart attack. None of the girls greeted Catherine, having chosen to stay in their rooms. She stood looking up at the empty balcony listening to the ominous silence. The sound of a spoon dropping onto the tiled floor in the kitchen resembled Clemet's hammer upon anvil, echoing up the passage to toll in the stillness of the foyer. Unable to speak, Catherine gasped for breath and shook her head as the foyer spun on the chandelier axis. Words disseminated into letters; she tumbled into the black abyss together with the broken alphabet.

Through the eucalypts, stars distanced themselves. Listening to the silence reinforced the remoteness; the rustle of leaves averted her panic. "Wally?"

"Shhh." he appeared next to her. "There's not much further to go."

"Exactly how much further is your not further?"

"There's our getaway. You can see the outline of the wagon if you look hard enough. I found a possie to hide Lightning just in case there was a raid."

Catherine sat up, "Where?" she asked.

Ying Lee placed his hand behind Catherine's neck, returning her head to the pillow.

"Missy in much shock," he told Mrs. Chang, "You keep her in bed … I get strong medicine."

The girls immediately asked a multitude of questions as they followed Ying Lee down the passage. He stopped at the top of the stairs. "Shhhh. You must be very quiet, Missy, very ill. Mrs. Chang boss-lady for present time, she tell you what you need know."

When he returned, the girls were still congregated where he'd left them and they pursued him back along the passage, stopped only by the closed door. Mrs. Chang sat on the bed dabbing Catherine's forehead with a wet towel.

"She is delirious."

"Some hallucination comforting, some not." He looked to the door. "Girls wish answers."

"So do I. What do I tell them?"

"You now boss-lady of girls, me now physician of patient." He raised the medical bag he carried. "We try best to make right decisions."

Mrs. Chang moved to the door.

"I will require towels and water be boiling all time."

The girls followed Mrs. Chang along the passage all questioning her together. Ying Lee's chanting filled the boudoir as Catherine's delusions continued.

"Ah, chow wee coo…ah, chow wee coo."

"How is he?" Catherine asked.

Ying Lee leant on the sulky and stared into the tray, then exploded.

"He like fat lazy dog – eat too much. Get up fat lazy dog."

What her vacant eyes saw, he could only imagine. Ying Lee closed Catherine's eyelids, spoon-fed her Chow Lung's opiate elixir and then commenced laying out various instruments and paraphernalia. "Ah chow wee coo…ah chow wee coo."

Catherine gasped.

He replaced the wet towel, brushed back her hair and then whispered in her ear. "If you Christine find Mr. Wally, he cannot find you – questions asked may now be answered."

Mrs. Chang entered with the requested items. "How is she?"

"She has courageous soul…but Ying Lee has two other souls he must consider also."

"Two?"

"Baby … and Mr. Wally, he still wanders."

"It may be a long night," said Mrs. Chang, lighting a lamp.

"Long night determined by journey travelled." He removed the brown parcel from Catherine's wicker basket. "You watch Missy. I have much work to do…make stronger medicine."

"Use the back stairs," Mrs. Chang suggested, "the kitchen is closer that way." She opened the balcony door for him.

As the practitioner left, the lingering odour of yesterday's tragedy wafted past; the smell of death followed closely. He shuddered.

Mrs. Chang stood holding the balcony rail with one hand, the other twisting her pearl necklace. She stared ahead, oblivious to the red sunset lazily stretching out upon a black horizon. Catherine's occasional incoherent outbursts brought Mrs. Chang back to reality, only to drift back into her memory of the cherry blossoms lying beneath the white mist. She too muttered her inner thoughts.

"Yes, I agree." Ying Lee's words startled Mrs Chang. "Sometimes fate play cruel tricks. Please…" he handed her two steaming pots, "cover with towels and then remove Missy clothing." He followed her inside, leaving the door open. "Please keep door shut."

Mrs. Chang placed the pots on the side dresser and moved to close the door.

"Not yet." he requested.

Ying Lee selectively chose an incense stick. Opposite the open door, he lit it, and then with outstretched arms, began chanting. "Ah chow wee coo." He took a step forward. "Ah chow wee coo."

He took another. The sacrament continued until he reached the open door. "Now door may be closed; I not be long." He returned to the kitchen.

Catherine showed no sign of being aware that her clothing had been removed from her limp body. Mrs. Chang prepared the sofa for a long night. She fluffed the pillow and sat awaiting Ying Lee's return; his chanting woke her.

"I must have dozed off."

"Good you sleep now…we take shifts."

"I will prepare refreshment."

"Hot brew in teapot," he told her.

Ying Lee waved acupuncture needles through the flickering flame. She lay watching until she drifted off again. The master practitioner continually inserted and removed the silver slithers, each attaining its precise destination.

"I must have dozed off for a few minutes."

"Ying Lee will have cup too," he requested.

Mrs. Chang rose and poured the tea. "It is cold."

"Few minutes," he paused, pondering, "maybe three hours. Your shift about to begin. You make fresh pot first." He lit an incense stick as she left.

When Mrs. Chang returned from the kitchen, Ying Lee thirstily drank the hot tea as he removed the acupuncture needles. The past thirty-six hours had been exhausting for him also; he'd assisted Dr. Tubber with many surgical procedures.

The contents of the towel-covered bowls when uncovered overpowered the aroma of the meal Mrs. Chang placed upon the table. When Ying Lee combined the pungent-smelling mush, the odour immediately vanished and a green mixture crystallised. He crushed the crystals to a fine powder and added a minute amount of red solution to produce a translucent balm.

"You cover Missy all over in this except for nose and toes and then wrap like Egyptian mummy."

"Leave face and toes uncovered," Mrs. Chang repeated, in a trance-like state.

"Leave nose and toes uncovered; Pharaohs believed soul breathe through nose. Balm to reduce body heat," Ying Lee explained.

While eating he studied text from a parchment scroll. "Not too tight or circulation stop completely," he warned Mrs. Chang. When she had finished he checked the bandaging and then collapsed onto the sofa. "Four hours only…wake me at…"

"One-thirty," she confirmed.

"Yes. Most important you do *not* fall asleep – Missy not return if you do."

Mrs. Chang stayed on her feet for fear of falling asleep; she stood by the bed studying Catherine's face for any sign of movement.

"Ying Lee," she shook his arm, "it is one-thirty."

He rose from a slumber.

Catherine lay like a mummified Cleopatra with Mrs. Chang's necklace adorning her. Ying Lee said nothing, listening to Catherine's erratic and shallow breathing. "Please fill bathtub with cold water," he removed the jewellery, "amulet will not be required."

"Mademoiselle will be well again?"

"Missy returning from journey."

"And the baby?"

"We will soon know. We learn of other…only if Missy wishes."

They carried Catherine's rigid body to the bathroom and submerged her in the bathtub. Ying Lee held her head above the waterline while Mrs. Chang removed the bandaging. Catherine's blue body floated like an iceberg until her body temperature began rising slowly. Then the water temperature was increased, her limbs became supple and her breathing stabilised.

"Thank you, Ying Lee…you saved her."

He acknowledged Mrs. Chang with a humble gesture and then added, "Baby too, I hope." There were no telltale signs in the water to say otherwise.

Catherine received more acupuncture when returned to the warmth of her bed. Ying Lee continually opened her eyelids checking on dilating pupils with a candle. Mrs. Chang paced the room.

"Patience, journey may be long – I administer strong medicine when she wakes."

"Now be a good time," Catherine mumbled. She coughed weakly. "I could do with some cheering up."

Hearing Catherine's words was a paradox for Ying Lee and Mrs. Chang received the miracle she had prayed for. Tears streamed down her face. "You *have* returned – you are back."

"But with unanswered questions, I fear." Ying Lee noted the time and injected the opiate. "Missy will now sleep twelve hours," he rubbed her arm, "Ying Lee get four if lucky; kid's drive me stupid."

* * *

The pious and those hedging their bets gathered for the Sunday church service held in the open air at the front of the hall. It was the largest congregation Pastor O'Dea had witnessed in Gunnadoo. Many people had left their sickbeds to attend, Catherine included.

"We had a terrible argument," Mrs. Chang told Ying Lee, "she has never spoken to me that way before."

"Missy is not same person – part of her missing."

"Blessed are the meek," the Pastor began, "for they shall inherit the earth."

Robinson nudged Bycroft. "The burnt crust more like it."

"I shall provide all with bread loaves and wine," he assured him.

Robinson looked at Bycroft. "It's a miracle."

"It's only a metaphor, you idiot."

"A what for?"

Bycroft ignored him.

"Lord, take into thy house those souls of the departed…"

"How many did you lose?" Bastock asked Harrick.

"Six…but I didn't get a chance to hang out the 'No Vacancy' sign."

"Yeah, business is gonna boom…Stoddard certainly got screwed."

"…and Lord, we give thanks that it was only Chinatown and not Gunnadoo that burnt down."

"Not quite the words I would have used," Clarrie whispered to Meg.

"Fatigue, I'm sure." She took hold of his arm.

It was a short service and at the end of it, Clarrie took the opportunity to address the gathering.

"Ladies and Gentlemen, Rome burnt while its Emperor, Nero, fiddled …"

"Should I be burning me fiddle then?" an Irish satirist called.

"It's the Devil's instrument," the Pastor shouted and returned to the steps.

"Where was your God on Friday?" an atheist yelled.

The question was lost in the verbal eruption between pious and atheists. The Pastor gave as good as he got until Clarrie requested he remove himself from the steps. "What I'm saying is…"

"What are you saying?" a bereft woman screeched, then collapsed. Antagonists took her place, turning on him until Sgt. Doyle and his constables restored the peace.

"What I'm saying is, we can't afford to be complacent. We need a stable council now more than ever. I suggest the election take place two weeks earlier than proposed."

There were no objections.

"Did you see that?" Clarrie asked when rejoining Meg.

"Fatigue." She took hold of his arm.

Sister Beth moved through the crowd handing out a schedule for the first of the funerals later that day. Bastock handed out political propaganda with Harrick following. Bycroft worked the congregation for votes also. Both men made all the grandiose promises of campaigning politicians, and then some. Bycroft preached bread and wine to the pious and then talked footy and beer with atheists. On a couple of occasions, he covertly caught Catherine's attention. Each time, all he received was a glazed stare. Disconcerting as it was he continued trying to communicate with her. Confusion and pain cloaked by the opiate, she went through the motions of conversing with Ruby and Meg and then left with the entourage of girls.

23 – In the Name of Progress

An elixir is a bitter pill to swallow
…even harder to digest is its consequence.

In the morgue, the next consignment of coffins was stacked ready for use. The rigor mortis remains of Stoddard now received the undignified attention of Dr. Portious. "Oh. The irony, the irony," he repeated drunkenly as he pried open the dentist's jaw – crack. "Like you said, Mr. Stoddard, it's bad luck for gold …" he belched loudly, "… to go back in the ground once discovered." The undertaker's sluice jar received Stoddard's contribution; ultimately, Bycroft would receive the sluice jar contents.

Clearing of burnt-out rubble from the northern side of Chinatown had commenced at daybreak. The disaster coordination team made the decision to peg out a grid and have the residents stay within boundary lines, thus averting highly combustible ghettos with impassable narrow streets and laneways. They also came up with the idea of a ballot offering quarter-acre blocks to uprooted residents; volunteers who helped clear the carnage could enter in the first draw.

"This area will be cleared by evening," Robinson told Bycroft. "As soon as I get the allotment plan it can be pegged out."

"Thursday is the release date, as long as it's laid out by then." Bycroft lit a cigar and threw the burning match on the blackened soil. "What about those teamsters we were discussing? Is anything happening on that front?"

"Yeah, I've checked. We got three men that can handle a full rig and another couple who can soon be brought up to scratch if needed." Robinson wiped his brow. "I know ya don't like the Chinks but we could hire them to do all the manual work, it'd be cheaper."

"Nonsense. I'm all for it," Bycroft shrugged. "Besides, it'll create goodwill with the Chinese voters. What about the rebuilding of the Plough, how's that progressing?"

"The timber's being delivered today. It'll be up and ready in a couple of weeks."

"By that time, I'll have the wagons here from Sydney and we'll swing the men onto them then."

Bycroft had no qualms about making a profit from others' misfortune and the opportunity now presented itself for another transport business. "Billings." he shouted upon return to the office. "We're going into the transport and building supplies business."

Catherine, Mrs. Chang and the girls attended the Tuesday service for Chung Dow. Yip Tung had been a casualty also and out of respect for Wong Foo, they attended his nephew's burial. Eight other patrons of Master Ho's opium den had lost their lives when caught unaware; they were designated plots in the pauper section.

The following day, dressed in the coolie disguise, Catherine attended Wally's funeral incognito. A Chinese dragon carved inside the casket lid signified the warrior's status; only the artisan who had carved it knew of its existence. The meticulously built coffin lay closed, supported above the open plot on its bier. Tom's Australian flag shrouded the casket; Ruby's wreath of daffodils and willow lay atop the flag, the willow manes flowing into the open pit below. At the rear of the mourners, Mrs. Chang and Ying Lee stood either side of Catherine supporting her, surrounded by many Chinese. Unseen, Blackfella Jimmy and the tribe paid their respects. The shovelling of two gravediggers preparing another site rhythmically fell in time with Gemma's and Jeddah's wailing emanating from the bush.

Pastor O'Dea delivered words over the man he didn't know.

"... and so Lord, we commend Wally Beauford's ..."

"Beaumont," whispered Bycroft.

"... Beaumont's body to the deep..." He shut the bible and stood with eyes closed.

"Not the words I would have chosen," Clarrie whispered to Meg.

"Fatigue." she snapped.

Tom wasn't impressed either. O'Dae had repeatedly referred to Wally as having been in naval service.

Bycroft stood with his eyes closed reflecting on Bryant's penchant for pirate talk.

The Pastor nudged him. "Mr. Bycroft. We're waiting for your eulogy."

"Aye." He collected his thoughts and proceeded with the rehearsed lines. "Ladies and gentlemen, friends…" he paused, breathing deeply, "…friends of Wally. Wally was not only my business partner but he was a mate, a good mate who I'll miss … "

"He wouldn't miss his own mother," Tom whispered to Meg and Clarrie.

"…Wally was the younger brother I never had; we enjoyed each other's company. We shared everything like brothers – our dreams, wealth…even accommodation. It was only *that* morning we joked about ending up as hermits living under the same roof."

Bycroft's hypocritical tribute fuelled Catherine's contempt for him. Every muscle and sinew in her body became enraged. She straightened her slumped posture; had it not been for the opium elixir, her Irish temperament would have betrayed the disguise. *You'll pay…I swear you'll pay,* she thought. The pounding of pumping blood through aching temples drowned out the folly. Catherine left the service and walked to Danny's grave.

She stared at the weeds growing around the headstone, recalling Cedric Booth's words – 'Thrice knock the Reaper.' An errant cloud in an azure sky cast a shadow; it conjured the angel's umbrella shading Granny Dunn's grave. From the abyss, Apollyon whispered Mrs. Chang's prose.

'Fate sometimes plays cruel tricks.'

Once again, there were no arms to fall into and be comforted by, or to stop the falling. Catherine struggled to gather her own thoughts. Threading its way through leafy foliage, the wind offered solace as she felt it cooling her face and rage. She thought of Buttercup and the sulky ride. *You still like the wind in your face, I see.*

"Wally?"

Startled, Catherine opened her eyes – she was alone; the shadow had moved on. She listened to a bird calling for its mate but there was no chirp of recognition – they both were alone.

"I don't have to be telling you a lot has happened in the past couple of months," she told Danny. "I'm sure Granny would've let ya know. I'm not sure what is to happen now, I'm betwixt and between. I know you'll be looking after Wally..." she paused, wiping tears on her sleeve. "Don't you be getting him drunk, he hasn't a cast iron belly like you."

"... mateship, that's what it's all about. In closing, I say this – those of us who knew Wally are better off for doing so. Rest in peace, my friend...rest in peace." Bycroft bowed his head and the pallbearers lowered the casket.

Pastor O'Dae delivered the last words. "Our Father which art in Heaven ..."

On departing, the mourners threw wildflowers into the grave. Wally's gambling mates threw pennies.

Catherine knelt at Wally's grave. She lifted her face to the sun to feel the warm rays but felt nothing. "The first thing I be telling you, Wally, is, where I kneel, I'll be placing you a grand headstone." She clasped the gold fob watch tightly in her hand, then held it to her chest and slowly looked upon the offerings below. "I bought you a surprise in Sydney, the man said it's a fine watch, I'm sure you'll love it, I put my picture in it for you, I'm gabbling on, aren't I?" She paused, lifted her head again and confessed, "I'm exhausted...I got no tears left in me." Immediately, unknown reserves signalled otherwise. "Mother of Mercy, I don't have the strength."

Catherine fought the dizziness and managed to sit without toppling over. Her consciousness began floating on the dreamtime chant as it grew louder. Surreal in a blue haze of burning eucalypt, Blackfella Jimmy and family appeared, their painted bodies glistening. The women bore offerings of indigenous tucker, the men trinkets from woven reed bags.

"Bossman, Mr. Wally – good man."

"Yes...a good man," Catherine sobbed.

She looked up at Blackfella Jimmy. His pearly white smile and blood red eyes set in an opal black face taunted her and she recalled Roebuck's Misery and Browning's words:

'Woe befalls he who commissions the black opal.'

Catherine's wailing then united with Gemma's and Jeddah's and continued until she realised hers dominated. The family was gone and so was the azure sky, the blue expanse drained, replaced by a brown hue. Tears wet the cupped soil she held in her hand; in the other, she clasped the fob watch to her heart uniting it with her own life-rhythm.

"... I'll be giving it to the child I carry, which was my other surprise, I should've told you but I wanted to be sure I was carrying, I'm sorry. But I be promising, James Beaumont, this baby will not want for noth'n," she paused, "that is my solemn promise to you."

Ying Lee returned to make his presence known. He felt the blister in his palm, a consequence of the carving chisel. "Mr. Wally look fine in suit and new shoes."

Catherine didn't look up. "They give him blisters."

"Slow him down – that way Mr. Wally not travel too far ahead."

She looked up at his smiling face.

"Mr. Wally not alone," he shook his head, "fat lazy dog travel with him like always."

"You mean?"

He nodded. "Ying Lee always tend Mr. Wally … and fat lazy dog."

After bathing Wally, Ying Lee had also bathed the faithful mongrel and placed him in the coffin across the shattered body of his warrior master.

"He was a fine-looking dog – and smart too," asserted Catherine.

"Fat lazy dog most smart."

His agreement didn't help ease the pain. Catherine held her hand over the casket and let the soil filter slowly through her fingers until all that remained was a small lump of wet soil in her palm. She stared at it, deep in thought.

I'm not angry with you for leaving me, Wally.

She was lying.

* * *

The disaster coordination committee met at the Advocate. Tom lit the lamps as Dr. Tubber finished his report.

"The risk of disease was too great. I had no choice but to do a mass burial. Dr. Portious couldn't get identification on eighteen; there are thirty-three confirmed dead." He rubbed his tired eyes. "The medical supplies arrived this afternoon...there shouldn't be any more deaths."

"Thank God for that." Meg placed a mug of tea before him. "I don't know what we'd have done without you."

"Or I Ying Lee," he replied. "There would have been many more lives lost if he'd not assisted me. Why isn't he practising?" All faces looked to Wong Foo.

"Why is for Ying Lee to know."

The doctor stirred his tea slowly. "Well he certainly knows his biology...he showed me a couple of procedures I'd never seen."

"Excuse me," Bycroft interrupted, "can we get on with this. I have another appointment to attend this evening."

"Did the tents and blankets arrive?" Clarrie asked.

"Yeah – there's forty tents I believe."

"Good. They can be handed out tomorrow with the residential blocks then. Tom, you've got the plan finished, haven't you?"

The group huddled over the rough layout Tom had drawn up.

"You know, this doesn't look half bad," stated Bycroft. If we were to run another three parallel streets crossing High Street with an access lane at the rear of the traders, there's room for another three blocks of twenty once this bush area is cleared."

"It would be a grid pattern for future development," agreed Meg. "What about naming the streets?"

"I suggest we leave that for the present," interrupted Clarrie. "If there's nothing else that needs to be discussed urgently, we've got a paper to get out tomorrow."

Picking up the pieces and resuming normality was easier for some than others. Opportunists took full advantage of the situation and Bycroft led the charge. The only negatives he'd experienced recently were the collapse of the cronies' brotherhood and not having a Wednesday night rendezvous with Catherine; and that was about to be remedied.

Catherine had tried to put the evening's unpleasant liaison from her mind; negative thoughts now pierced her soul like hot shrapnel. She was struggling to stay afloat; but for the elixir, Ying Lee feared she'd drown in her own sorrow. Her pacing increased as the dreaded moment closed in upon her. She could hear Bycroft's footsteps climbing the private stairs. The door opened.

"Hello stranger, long time," he slurred. She turned to see him swaying in the doorway. "Well, aren't you going to invite me in?"

"Did you get my note?"

"Yes, I got your note." He closed the door. "It didn't say much." He leant against the glass panel.

Apollyon whispered from the abyss, *Push him through the glass.*

Catherine collected her thoughts and exclaimed, "I did not know much at the time and I did not know if your Mr. Billings could be trusted to give it to you without reading it first."

"That was over three weeks ago."

"And a lot has happened in three weeks, oui?" She changed the subject. "I believe congratulations may be in order – you will make a fine mayor."

"Better than Harrick. Come here." Bycroft lunged forward, taking her in his arms. She broke free.

"I will get you a drink." She had purposely left the whiskey bottle almost empty; it would make for a plausible escape if required.

The rejection irritated him. He grabbed at her again; she pushed him away only to struggle helplessly when secured by the wrists. "What's going on?" He applied pressure, coercing her. "Something's not being said."

"Nothing is going on," she retorted. "I am not well."

"And neither am I. I don't like being stabbed in the back and that's all I've been getting in the last month." He squeezed her wrists harder, feeling the satisfaction of seeing her pain.

"Stop it. You're hurting me." Catherine's left hand opened in submission; her right stayed tightly clenched. Half submission wasn't good enough and he twisted the right wrist maliciously. Her hand opened, revealing the fob watch.

"And what do we have here?" he enquired sarcastically. "I told you, I don't like secrets." Bycroft confiscated it. Letting her go, he flopped onto the bed. "Make it a large one."

Cut him up. Catherine fantasised smashing the bottle and ramming its jagged edge into his jugular vein. She imagined the startled look of horror in his eyes and the gushing blood.

He read aloud, "'To JB – love Catherine, 1921'. When were you going to give me this?"

Catherine couldn't believe what she'd heard but especially what she'd missed. For the first time she realised that Bycroft's and Wally's initials were the same. The oversight may have just saved her hide. She poured the whiskey and then handed him the glass and with it, unpalatable as it was, a rushed explanation. "It was to be a present for when you became Mayor Bycroft."

Bycroft's aggression immediately changed to cordiality. The black circles around his eyes disappeared, as did the tension in the boudoir.

Catherine took what seemed like her first breath since he had walked through the door. "Now you have spoilt the surprise."

"I told you, I don't like secrets…or surprises; but I do like the watch." He emptied the glass in a couple of gulps. "Come here, I've got something for you too."

"No. I cannot make love with you." She saw the mood swinging as the dark circles began forming around his eyes again. "I am pregnant," she divulged.

He sat up. "You're what."

"There will be no claim against you. I want my child," Catherine pleaded. "You can buy me out. I will sell my share cheap and I will go away. Nobody will ever know." Her heart was pounding. She didn't bother with a spoon and swallowed straight from the elixir bottle.

"Hold on a minute, Sunshine, you're moving a little too quick." Bycroft slipped the watch into his waistcoat pocket and rose from the bed. "I'll know – what about me? It's mine too."

"Pardon, I do not understand?"

"What's there to understand?" He casually poured another drink; his thirst, as his greed, was unquenchable. "We're partners, fifty-fifty, equal shares in it."

Catherine believed Bycroft could sink no lower than he had with the eulogy delivered at Wally's funeral. This latest statement informed her otherwise, and she tried to tell him the father was unknown but the words wouldn't form. She heard Ruby's words.

There are some things a man shouldn't know.

Do it, do it, emanated from the abyss.

Catherine watched him flop back on the bed.

"Now come here, there are other ways pleasure can be given." He lay back smiling, "I didn't come here to discuss business." He grabbed her wrist as she reached for the bottle, drawing her down upon him. "I've had enough booze…"

"It was for me."

"Drink this."

The abyss was silent, cold, a nothingness of black – she welcomed it.

Catherine woke in an opiate haze to find Bycroft gone. She lay staring at the blue bracelet on her wrist – like Lucy's, inflicted by her pig gigolo. She reached for the bottle and cleansed her throat.

The whiskey tasted bittersweet, as did the thought of revenge. Various images repeated but all ended the same – in blood. Having drunk the remaining whiskey, she sought Chow Lung's elixir in the wicker basket. Returning to the bed, she collapsed onto it with the contents of her basket.

Forfeiting the fob watch to Bycroft's ignorance was again fate, unavoidable, but tainted fingers had reached into his victim's very soul, desecrating the cherished fable. Next morning Mrs. Chang found Catherine asleep fully clothed beneath a blanket of shorn locks, her hair and scalp bloodied from self-flagellation. Clasped to her heart, scissors replaced the fob watch.

* * *   .

The Advocate's staff met the hectic rush of the Thursday deadline. Meg and Tom, depleted of sleep and of the adrenaline that had enabled them to work through the night, sat browsing the edition devoted mainly to the destruction and its aftermath.

"Tom."

"What?" He spilt his remaining coffee.

"You were dozing off."

"No I wasn't… I was resting my eyes."

Dark rings were forming around Tom's eyes and Meg recognised the telltale signs of stress. "I'm worried about you…you've got to rest. That's not a request: it's an order."

Tom rubbed his eyes. *Yes, Sir. Right away, Sir,* replied the voice in his head.

"Are you listening to me?" she questioned, seeing the vacant stare.

"I'm just about to get a few hours now," he replied.

Tom had photographed all of the funerals. His investigative report quoted Sgt. Doyle: "The explosion is a mystery and its cause may never be known for sure." Accounts taken as evidence stated that eyewitnesses had seen the smithy's boy stoking up the furnace prior to the blast, the force of which they described as that of a 200-pound bomb. Theory was the kid had unknowingly thrown a dynamite charge in the furnace along with the other bits and pieces being disposed of at the time. Very little of his remains were found, let alone identified. Clemet was well away from the blast area and had survived, but he couldn't shed light on what had happened. There could be no good spin put on the edition, aside from stories of miraculous escapes and near misses. Wally made the front page again; the rag read like an obituary column from front page to back.

"Buck up, the Advocate won't always be full of bad news," Clarrie told them.

"Yep, we don't make it," Tom replied lethargically, "we just report it."

"The land giveaway this afternoon should boost the community's morale," Clarrie offered as stimulus.

"Some shut-eye will boost mine," said Meg, "call me when it's time. Tom?"

"Yes, all right, I'll get some too."

The community gathered at the hall. To quell the rumour of bias, Wong Foo drew names from a barrel. Bycroft drew lot numbers from another. Those fortunate in the first draw received their quarter-acre land grant and a tent. Those who weren't lucky received the proposition of clearing a second parcel of land for residency on those blocks. White would oversee the felling of the larger trees before the scrub clearing commenced. Temporary facilities opposite this land would also be set up for tents.

The exodus of displaced persons from the community hall to the new suburb began early Friday morning – a week to the day after the tragedy. Bycroft leant with his back to the bar watching the exodus begin from The Arms. He smiled contentedly. Having consigned the refugees to replenish the dwindling occupancy of the community hall, he was glad to be rid of the freeloaders and the cluttering up of his premises.

"Hey, Sunshine, is that all I pay you to do around here?" Bycroft complained to McSloy, the barman. He did not move while he watched a woman packing up her family's possessions.

Bleary eyed, McSloy continued wiping glasses. "Crikey, I puts more 'ours in 'ere than when I wuz shovl'n dirt."

"Shovelling dirt is shovelling shit. Think of the rewards you'll get from a stable job."

"Twenty-four-'our days I've been putt'n in since this lot arrived; I'll be glad to see the last of 'em."

"Profits should be above average then." Bycroft raised his hat as a large group left the premises. "Vote for Bycroft." he spruiked.

McSloy continued, "Not likely, I 'ad one of the sergeant's men sleeping 'ere."

Bycroft turned and eyeballed him. "Are you telling me he drank the profits?"

"No, 'e … I mean … me, I closed the bar at six – I 'ad no choice."

"I'm not stupid … just because I haven't been showing my face around here doesn't mean I don't know what going on." McSloy struggled to find the right answer. Bycroft stretched, resumed his original position and then continued watching the woman struggle with possessions under her arms. "Hey, McSloy," he called over his shoulder, "it was to be expected…we can't have the mayor breaking the law, can we? Excuse me…lady." He stopped the exhausted woman from exiting. "Do you have children?"

"Yes…three."

Bycroft eyeballed her. "Then don't forget to take them with you – unless they're of voting age." Her jaw dropped. "Only joking…McSloy, jump to it man, help this lady to her cabin."

"Cabin?" he queried.

"The hall, you idiot…learn the jargon, shape up man."

The straight lines of the street boundaries were evident by the parallel conformity of tents and add-on structures. By mid-morning, the new suburb was rising from the barren soil. Tom had taken photographs from all directions and now stood on the balcony of Catherine's establishment. She overlooked the rising phoenix as he began fitting a wide-angle lens to the camera.

"I appreciate you letting me get a couple of shots from up here." Covertly studying her profile, he saw little but chin, nose and forehead. A beret concealed her welts and the large, upturned collar enhanced her French mystique. "I've always been interested in portrait photography."

Only her mouth moved. "And now you wish to photograph the disfigured face of Gunnadoo?"

The words took him by surprise and he floundered for something positive to say. "Chinatown will always live on…it can be rebuilt," he assured her.

"Unfortunately for lost souls and memories, Monsieur, they cannot be…and neither can Chinatown; Chinatowns are an evolutionary process."

Tom looked through the viewer, covertly turning the camera slowly towards Catherine. He stopped when her image appeared at the very edge of the frame. "I took photographs before…"

"Before fate played a cruel trick, Monsieur?"

He cunningly stretched his back. "I'd rather think destiny than fate." The aperture jammed as he tried to get the shot with Catherine in the foreground. "Yes, I suppose progress does have its drawbacks." He changed the topic and fiddled with the trigger lead. "I'm not one to brag, but my…" The aperture released; his heart was racing, "…boss reckons that one day …"

She interrupted him. "I have seen your work; it is excellent."

Tom ducked behind the viewfinder; it was as though he was photographing a statue. She hadn't moved from the first instant he had imaged the potentially award-winning shot. Again, he stretched his back, this time stealthily picking up the flexible trigger lead. Not looking at his subject, he squeezed the trigger: nothing happened – *I don't believe it,* he thought, *I've taken photographs in hell and never forgotten the powder cap. Say something.* "My sister Meg speaks highly of you." He looked at the bag containing the caps. *She's sure to look at the idiot fossicking in there…bugger.*

"She is an excellent journalist, oui?" Catherine responded.

Get a move on there, son, find the cap, don't panic, the voice commanded, *remember to breathe.* His fingers searched the bag and then fumbled to load the cap in the camera cartridge. Tom didn't dare look in her direction. *Say something, idiot.* "Do you read Ruby Houten's column?"

"Are you taking a photograph or a survey?" Catherine enquired.

She knows…no she doesn't. His mind raced; he took a quick peek. *She has to – she hasn't moved. Say something.* "I won't be long." *Damn. Now she knows I know. Just take the shot.* He moved to the rear of the tripod, picked up the trigger and looked through the viewer. *She does know.*

"Monsieur Lennard, answer me…and you must promise you will be truthful." She paused, waiting for an answer.

He hesitatingly gave it.

"What is more important, the subject or the content?"

"It depends on what the photographer sees." *Where's this going?*

"Then close your eyes, tell me what you see."

415

Tom did as requested. "I see progress, lives being rebuilt." He peeked out of the corner of his eye to see if she was looking at him: Catherine hadn't moved.

"I see promises not being kept, Monsieur."

He tightly shut both eyes as though trying to block out the voice. *Guilty as charged, Sir. Say something.* "I believe it to be the truth."

"Truth is precious." She paused and smelt the burnt earth. "It should be used sparingly."

Right…for King and country, no shirking lads, shoot straight. He squeezed the camera trigger, *Gotcha.* "It's all about capturing the moment," Tom stated proudly. There was no reply and he squinted in Catherine's direction. The subject of the picture hadn't been captured, only the background. "Damn."

24 – The Stakes are Raised

Better to gamble with money,
not the soul –
it cannot be replaced.

Over the past month, Gunnadoo had begun to regain its composure, although the bitterness of the upcoming election had divided the community as the the two candidates went head-to-head. Hecklers from both parties became antagonists for any impromptu lobbying on the street. Moustaches, spectacles and devil horns immediately appeared on any advertising material; graffiti became a popular pastime. Sgt. Doyle and his men broke up skirmishes on various occasions. The constabulary now showed their presence at the polling booths so no more shenanigans would take place. On the front steps of the community hall, the candidates and their minders stood either side of Clarrie having photographs taken.

Clarrie informed the swelling crowd, "The polling will close at five o'clock and the result will be announced at six. Mr. Charles Roister, our bank manager, and Mr. Benjamin Peck, attorney at law, will oversee the counting process. Ladies and gentlemen, it gives me pleasure to announce

Gunnadoo's first election now open. Please cast your votes inside."

"Let's hope they haven't been bought off," Bastock whispered to Harrick.

"And while the counting takes place," Clarrie added, "entertainment will be supplied on the piano donated to the community hall by Mr. Bycroft. May the best man win."

Bycroft raised his hat to the crowd and under his breath he informed Robinson, "I already have; this is money in the bank." He puffed on a huge cigar, savouring the moment.

Robinson took the opportunity to exploit Bycroft's good mood. "I should think there would be something in all of this for me?"

Bycroft watched Bastock still handing out Harrick's publicity leaflets. "Yes, you would think so wouldn't you?" He thought for a moment longer. "What about managing the new transport business, and a third share in it…how's that?"

As stated, at five o'clock the polling finished and the counting began. Men gathered around bonfires at the front of the hall to talk politics and sport. Inside, the women congregated with their knitting entertained by various musicians taking turns on the piano. Ruby had organised women to serve tea with scones and damper; this was her call for participants to join the Gunnadoo Ladies Guild. Children ran throughout the hall playing games of tag and hide-and-seek. The event was turning out to be a social occasion for all to let off steam.

Clarrie collected the results and moved to centre stage. "Ladies and gentlemen, the results are in. I won't keep you in suspense. By an overwhelming majority…John Bycroft is Gunnadoo's first Mayor."

Bycroft received both applause and disgruntled jeers on his way up to the stage. He shook hands, receiving well-wishers' acknowledgements, and then launched into his acceptance speech. "Thank you, thank you …"

Catherine, incognito again, stood with Ying Lee and Wong Foo at the rear of the hall. Under the rim of the coolie hat, Ying Lee saw her white teeth flash when she heard the decision.

"I do not understand why you are smiling?" he enquired. "I thought you would have wished he lose."

"On the contrary," she replied. Ying Lee threw her a questioning look. She wasn't smiling now, her eyes coldly fixed on her prey. "The more he has, the more he will lose."

Wong Foo smiled, saying nothing.

The following day, having received a message from Benjamin Peck requesting they meet, Catherine sat in the pagoda awaiting his arrival. She observed Mrs. Chan and the punctual lawyer approaching across the lawn. The tall man in a crumpled suit walked with an air of authority, carrying a bulging satchel. She was mystified as to why he wanted the meeting. "Good morning Miss Dunn."

"Bonjour, Monsieur Peck, please be seated."

When the social niceties were out of the way, he opened the satchel and removed various documents. "I'm here representing the estate of the late James Wally Beaumont." Catherine closed her eyes, taking time to compose herself. "Mr. Beaumont designated you as his sole beneficiary."

Like Danny's, Wally's possessions for the time he had spent toiling didn't amount to much. The share in the transport business was his only wealth. After discussing details of the bequest, Catherine gave Peck his instructions.

"Monsieur Beaumont's horse and sulky I wish Ying Lee to have. My being a beneficiary I wish kept confidential. You will see to this, oui?"

"Of course, as you wish." He lifted the fob watch by its chain from his vest pocket and checked the time. "Well I must be off, if there is anything else I can do," he handed her a card, "please don't hesitate to get in touch – my condolences to you, Miss Dunn."

"That is a lovely watch and chain, Mr. Peck."

"Thank you. My fiancée gave it to me. Good day."

She watched him depart, her vision blurring. The smallest of incidents brought on painful memories; the thought of living with twice the trauma was overwhelming. Catherine removed the elixir from her wicker basket and gulped its contents. She required a refill. Ying Lee had warned her of the dire consequences of addiction but she believed her shattered heart would kill her before the addictive compulsion would.

* * *

The council steering committee and Bycroft had spent the last two weeks of September writing up funding applications to all levels of State and Federal

Government. Bycroft then followed up the documentation with a trip to Sydney and there he reacquainted himself with Lockett and Bryant.

Robinson took charge of the work party clearing the land at the rear of Bycroft Holdings and the pastor's residence. This was where construction materials and supplies could be stored safely; the extension of a laneway behind the community hall allowed access for delivery wagons. The formation of a new transport business had successfully been kept quiet. Bycroft had been wary of Bastock finding out and having his weekly beer delivery put in jeopardy. With his own wagons, that would be the first contract Bastock would lose.

Robinson and his drivers caught Bastock's coach to Dundee and they were waiting at the rail siding when Bycroft and his delivery arrived. A dray laden with beer barrels and two large wagons laden with corrugated roofing iron were unloaded from the flatbed-carriage. Under Robinson's supervision, the teams of horses were released from the livestock carriages, exercised and watered and Bycroft Transport signs attached to the vehicles.

Bastock's coach driver and his offsider took particular notice of the new opposition as they too received freight consignments and passengers. Bycroft chose to buy a ticket and ride in the coach; it was more comfortable than the wagons and the brazen act would put Bastock's nose more out of joint. The coach pulled out of Dundee ahead of Robinson and his crew without a word spoken between the drivers. The extra workforce brought back by Bycroft clambered aboard the wagons.

When the coach arrived in Gunnadoo, Bycroft disembarked and watched the driver immediately go into the depot office. Bastock appeared at the window and stood with his hands on his hips. Bycroft ignored him, told Dempsey to deliver his luggage to the residence and strolled off, pleased with the desired outcome.

Word of the pending arrival of the roofing iron had spread and when the wagons stopped in front of Bycroft Holdings, the public relations exercise for the launch of the transport business began. The promotion proved most successful. Residents surged forward trying to place orders for the scarce commodity. "Ladies and gentlemen," Robinson spruiked from atop a wagon, "in the spirit of competition, Bycroft Transport offers six sheets of corrugated galvanised roofing iron for the price of four. Sales commence tomorrow morning. Due to limited stock – six sheets per customer only."

Bycroft stood in the doorway with Billings behind him. "That's very decent of you."

"There's one hell of a delivery cost though," he gloated over his shoulder.

Bastock stood with Harrick at the rear of the crowd listening. "He doesn't want competition," Bastock snarled, "he wants my hide, that's what he's after."

Harrick enquired uneasily, "What are you going to do?"

"I'll give him bloody competition; I'll play the bastard at his own game, that's what I can do." He stormed off to inform all employees and cohorts to be on Bycroft's doorstep at daybreak, amongst the first in line for the roofing material.

Safety was the community's priority and any business that utilised fire or explosives was required to move from the town centre. High Street was extended and Bastock Transport rose to the call, relocating the farriers feed sheds and blacksmith equipment that hadn't been destroyed further south. The IOU Clement had given was now being called in.

"Competition, he reckons. The bastard's out to get me," Bastock told Clement, "and my sources have told me he's considering the idea of starting another business to give you competition." This was untrue but a great inducement to rally Clement to his quest.

"He is, is he…we'll see about that." exploded Clement. "I'll punch the bastard's face in."

"Let's not be too hasty, my friend, that's not gonna hurt him," Bastock shrugged, "he's already an ugly prick anyway."

"He'll be gett'n no feed or agistment from me."

"No, we've got to play him at his own game. Don't let on you know anything for the moment and when the time's right we'll come down on him like a ton of bricks."

"I'm in – what can I do?"

"There's sixty sheets of roofing iron I want you to take delivery of for me. Have a wagon at his yard tomorrow morning offering free deliveries to everyone. You'll be given the names of my people and…"

"I deliver their sheets to you."

"No…you bring them back here and store them. Keep it quiet."

423

"That's it." yelled Clement, "I'd rather punch..."

"When he climbs out from under the bricks then you can."

"And when will that be?"

"Here's the plan ..."

The conspiracy began.

The following morning when Clemet arrived with his wagon, Bastock Transport couldn't make a delivery charge and consequently made no profit on the sheets of roofing material. Bycroft had been caught out. The matter couldn't be pursued further with Clemet as agistment for the horses was at the farrier's and Bycroft didn't want to alienate him. Bastock's scheming had won round one.

"Bugger. We won't be offering a deal like that again," Bycroft told Robinson as they watched Clemet's wagon leave with the goods.

"Are we still..."

"Of course we are. We'll make it up on the next lot – the price just went up."

* * *

Houten entered the shop and pulled the latest edition of the Herald from the paper rack. He could feel Clarrie's eyes on him, although Clarrie pretended to be otherwise occupied. Houten casually thumbed through the pages to the sports section and then onto the racing guide. He then ambled up to the counter, "Good evening, Clarrie, how was your Monday?" He continued reading the unpurchased paper knowing how it irked Clarrie Radcliff, the proprietor of the

Gunnadoo Advocate. The two men were playing a game of their own.

Clarrie ignored the pleasantry and instead asked, "Why bother? The latest edition is due in…" he looked at his watch, "why, if you were to walk up to the depot you could get one hot off the press."

"Naw, I'm lazy. Besides, here you get the pleasure of my company and the chance to gain from my equine knowledge."

"I find humans a safer bet." Clarrie studied Houten knowing that Houten studied the form guide anywhere he could without Ruby catching him. *One day, my friend,* he thought*, it will cost you more than a few unpaid papers.*

"Now, picking a Cup winner takes time. It's not what's in the head, it's what's in the guide," he waved it in Clarrie's face. "The form guide is not simply read, it is consumed like fine wine, it's in the breeding, Mr. Radcliff, bloodlines. That's what makes a champion a winner."

"Gee, and I always thought," Clarrie lifted his spectacles to his forehead, "the jockey had something to do with it."

"Well that helps," Houten agreed. "Uh ha. Here we are, 'the Rover' has gotta be a sure thing."

"Naw, that nag couldn't win a chook raffle." Clarrie readjusted his spectacles.

"You're talking to a man that knows horseflesh. I do my research and I say…"

"It hasn't got a hope in hell," Clarrie interjected, "now give me a look at that guide." He ran his finger down the list of horses and read aloud, "Sister Olive, a chestnut filly ridden by E.

425

O'Sullivan." He thrust the guide back at the non-paying customer. "There's your Cup winner – E. O'Sullivan."

"You gotta be kidding?" Houten jibed. He performed a blind man's routine, staggering around feeling for obstacles to knock into. "You're blind. You couldn't tell a thoroughbred from a bloody greyhound."

Clarrie refused to encourage him and looked out the doorway. "Eh, look who's coming. Now behave yourself and don't go buggerising around," he warned Houten. O'Dae entered; Clarrie smiled. "Good evening, Pastor O'Dae, what can I do for you?"

"Mr. Radcliff – a postage stamp if you please. Good evening Mr. Houten."

"Pastor O'Dae." Houten scratched his head, "Pastor, I know there are a lot of religious orders but is there a chance you may have come across or know about Sister Olive?" he enquired.

"Sister Olive?" The Pastor contemplated. "No, I don't think so…I'm not familiar with her."

"That was an excellent service you gave yesterday." Clarrie handed O'Dae the stamp. "Do you require an envelope?"

"No, thank you." O'Dae turned to Houten. Clarrie frowned at him from behind the Pastor's back as he asked, "What order is she with?"

Houten immediately delivered his punchline with a deadpan face, "The 'Outta', I believe."

Clarrie cursed at Houten under his breath as 'out of order' registered. Houten's satire fortunately went over O'Dae's head and the preacher shut his eyes, searching for the answer. "No, sorry, I can't help you. I have no recollection of a Sister Olive. May I be of service in some other way?" he enquired.

"I'm good...how 'bout you?" Houten asked Clarrie.

"Nope...I'm fine."

"Then good evening, Mr. Houten...Mr. Radcliff." He left the shop, unaware of Houten's lampooning.

"See, the Pastor doesn't even recognise Sister Olive," Houten teased.

Clarrie shook his head, "I give up." He eyeballed Houten. "Eh, what horse did you pull in the sweep?"

"I didn't bloody get one, did I?"

The Advocate had run a sweepstake on the Melbourne Cup. Many of the locals originated from the Victorian goldfields and interest in the event warranted the newspaper promotion. "That's a bit of bad luck," Clarrie mocked. "Then again, there are only so many nags in the race, eh?"

Not letting Clarrie get the better of him, Houten enquired irritatingly, "How many entries did you finally get...fill up the barrel, did we?"

"Not as many as I thought we would have." Clarrie's grin disappeared. "Maybe it's the prizes on offer."

It was Houten's turn to grin. "A box of nougats and a month's subscription ain't much of an inducement to gamble. No, I'm afraid you'll have to do better than that."

"Hey. The Advocate's doing nothing illegal – no money changed hands. What are you insinuating?"

"I'm not insinuating anything. The principle of gambling is what we're talking 'bout here," Houten stated proudly. "It's character building for the punters when losing their dough to the SP bookie." He stood to attention and saluted. "This is what our boys fought for – freedom to express ourselves the way we choose."

Clarrie looked confounded and made ready to do some debating, but then thought better of it. "Well, the Advocate doesn't encourage gambling, not like some people I know." He leant forward on the counter and asked quietly, "Are you still running a book?"

"How much do you want on Sister Olive? If you're silly enough, I'll take your bet." He placed the form guide in front of Clarrie. Have a look, go on...I'll better the odds."

"Naw ... I don't like 'em."

"Blimey ... I haven't told you what they are."

"If Ruby finds out she'll skin you alive."

"If who finds out what?" Ruby entered the shop from the residence with Meg. Both women were dressed as if heading off to church. Houten quickly eluded her questioning.

"I hope today is Monday, otherwise I've lost a week." He smiled innocently. "I didn't know you were over here..."

"Precisely – I'm no longer chained to your counter. Have you closed up already?"

He looked at his watch, "Fifteen minutes ago."

"We won't be long, Clarrie; Ruby and I are going to the depot to meet Mr. Bond."

Ruby poked Houten in the chest, "You're not running an SP book, are you?"

"No dear, it's not me with a racing form in my hand." He threw a glance in Clarrie's direction.

"Come on, Ruby." Meg checked her watch. "We're running late."

Clarrie threw her a kiss, "Let him know I'll catch up when he and the missus settle in."

"I'll catch up with you later, Mister." Ruby threw Houten the evil eye. "Alrighty, I'm coming, wait up, Luv."

"Give that back to me." Houten retrieved the form guide from Clarrie and returned to reading. "I'm the racing expert around here. Who is this Bond fellow anyway?"

"Randolph Bond, an upstanding gentleman from Sydney, originally Melbourne I believe."

"Amazonia is an inside chance for a place, I reckon…and what does Mr. Bond do for a crust?"

Using the racing vernacular, Clarrie responded, "His form, you mean?" Houten acknowledged with a patronising smile. "If you would stay awake at council meetings you wouldn't be asking me – he's the new dentist." *And that's all you're going to get out of me,* he thought deviously.

Houten's grinned. "I'm glad all my teeth are good…not keen on pain. He won't be getting a tooth or penny out of me."

Houten's nonchalant attitude to life mystified Clarrie. Nothing seemed to faze the man. Ruby wouldn't be the easiest of people to live with and the associated problems of running a business must weigh heavily, but as far as he could see, Houten breezed through life without a care in the world. This Clarrie sometimes found annoying.

Houten returned to his racing agenda and continued, "Bloodlines, it's all in the bloodlines," he said, tapping his front teeth and whinnying.

"Don't be so cocksure of yourself and make room for a paying customer. Good evening, Mrs. Chang, I have your newspapers and mail. The coach is due…"

"It's probably already in," Houten irritatingly informed him.

"Thank you, Mr. Houten," Clarrie noted with a touch of sarcasm.

"Mr. Radcliff." Houten nodded to him politely. "Mrs. Chang … good evening."

"Mr. Houten," she returned the gesture, "Mr. Radcliff."

Clarrie handed her the newspapers. "Did you get a horse in the Advocate's sweep?" With a glance, he warned his antagonist not to interrupt.

"No, to be truthful we never entered; we are running our own sweep."

"And the response you got?" Houten enquired annoyingly.

"We were overwhelmed by the response, Mr. Houten. Now, good evening Mr. Radcliff, Mr. Houten."

"Mrs. Chang," Houten nodded. She waited for Clarrie.

"Mrs. Chang." They nodded to each other and she left the shop.

"Good grief. I wish you would stop doing that."

"What?"

"You know very well. I feel like I'm caught in a comedy sketch at the Tiv' when you pull that farewell routine."

"The Tiv', you reckon?" Houten puffed out his chest. "I always did believe my talent belonged on the stage."

Clarrie egged him on. "It's certainly wasted behind a hardware counter."

"Ruby could mind the store while I'm on tour," he stated as the fantasy took shape. "I could tell a few jokes, play a tune or two on the accordion and perform magic." Houten stood with arms outstretched. His stance almost coaxed applause from Clarrie, but instead he retorted, "You don't know any magic."

"Da dah." Houten exclaimed with gusto. "Disappearing from Ruby's sight would be a bloody good trick."

"You're a clown," Clarrie chastised.

"Then I could run away and join a circus."

"Before you do…back to the tooth fairy – Mr. Bond." Clarrie leant forward on the counter and eyed Houten. "I'll lay a wager Mr. Bond will get you in his chair. Let's see if you'll gamble on providence other than the four-legged kind."

"What's the timeframe?" Houten enquired.

"Let's say…how about within a month."

"And how much?"

"A quid."

They shook hands.

"I know what's going on inside my head better than you," Houten confided.

"But you said it's all in the form guide."

Houten held out his hand, "Name your price on Sister Olive. If you're dumb enough to bet on the tooth fairy, I'll take your money."

Clarrie shrugged. "It's character building, right?"

Houten nodded and gave him a wink. "Correct."

At the depot, passengers alighted from the coach and then waited for their luggage to be unloaded from atop. The town's new dentist, Mr Bond, tugged his large, bushy muttonchops. Immaculately dressed and in his late fifties, he stood head and shoulders above Mrs. Bond. The small woman made her presence known by her concealed orthopaedic boot. The timber sidewalk magnified the clunk from beneath her long, dowdy dress as she polio-waddled inside to the clerk's desk.

* * *

November was a big month. The schoolteacher arrived and began classes in the community hall. An extension to the savings bank facilitated the opening of a post-master general's branch, and a telephone exchange behind the post office was under construction. The telephone cables from Dundee would soon arrive.

Opposite the rebuilt Plough Inn, a new two-storey structure had begun to rise on the blacksmith's former land. Rumours abounded. The 'BCH&W Enterprise' sign displayed on the property added to the intrigue. New infrastructure propelled Gunnadoo ahead; the housing boom continued and the reef mining expanded. The tonnage of freight hauled to Gunnadoo continued to climb and the transport companies went head to head. Bastock's bank overdraft rose as Bycroft raised the ante. Within two weeks of Bycroft starting another passenger coach service, Bastock countered the attack. The motorised Ford was immediately successful, putting Bycroft's coach out of business, although the cost of repairs and upkeep of the mechanised vehicle balanced any financial gains made.

Bastock finally gave the story of the new venture to the Advocate after receiving a liquor licence. The two-storey hotel with accommodation would be completed and ready to open for trading in March. Bycroft wasn't impressed when he read the headline, 'Spirit of competition'. There was no way he could officially stop his opposition from opening; however, there was always the possibility of personally kyboshing the venture by other means. The partnership between Bastock, Clemet, Harrick and White denoted that the ante had risen yet again. Bycroft quickly opened a dialogue with Lockett in Sydney.

Ruby achieved the presidency and Charlie Roister's wife, Carol, was the obvious choice after Meg to be the secretary/treasurer of the newly formed women's guild. At the inaugural meeting, Meg had politely refused the position; her commitments to the Advocate and the steering committee for council activities kept her busy. When discussing what their charter would be, all the women present agreed the health and welfare of the community was priority. When discussing how they'd go about it, Meg had suggested that the simplest way was the best way – keep the men of Gunnadoo on the straight and narrow.

At the mere mention of the words straight and narrow, tensions had risen and a distinct faction formed around the opinion of Sister Beth. The pastor's wife believed the straight and narrow should also apply to other sections of the community. Catherine's establishment was at the top of the list. After a somewhat turbulent meeting, the guild had decided it would convene at the hall on the first Tuesday evening of each month.

Ruby and Carol sat behind the trestle table set up on the stage. "How many do we have in attendance?" Ruby asked.

"Twenty-seven," replied Carol.

Ruby was astonished. "That's twelve more than last time. I thought after the last debacle we'd be down on numbers."

While waiting for the meeting to start the women sat chatting, it sounded double the number. After numerous requests from Ruby, Catherine capitulated and attended the meeting. She was there to act as an interpreter and sat with Mrs. Lee, Mrs. Foo and the oriental contingent to one side of the hall. Beth O'Dea and her pious delegation, the snobs as Ruby called them, sat opposite.

"Silence please, ladies, could I have your attention." The meeting commenced. "Would you please welcome Gunnadoo's first school teacher, Mrs. Jean Tompkins."

The middle-aged woman was of thin build, her hair tightly pulled back and rolled into a bun. She rose, acknowledged the applause and demurely returned to her seat next to Sister Beth. The applause had no sooner finished than the Chinese women stood and began vilifying her loudly. In the verbal assault, very little but the gist of displeasure could be understood. Ruby and Carol looked at each other in amazement. The pious delegation immediately entered the fray and laid the condescension benchmark.

"Order, order." Ruby pleaded with little effect. She removed a shoe and slammed the table with the heel, getting the desired result. "Quiet." she yelled. Barking dogs in the near vicinity obeyed. "Now settle down the lot of you…let's talk this though like ladies."

Apparently, the attention shown to the oriental students during the previous week's lessons had been non-existent. They had sat at the back of the class and been ignored. "You teach good or we strike." Mrs. Foo warned. The irate mothers had nominated her to speak on their behalf. The pious delegation's oral defence ceased; many of the oriental women worked as their housekeepers. Carol placated the mêlée by hurriedly bringing forth the next item on the agenda.

"'The need for a higher standard of health services and more doctors'," Ruby read. "The floor is open for discussion."

"What's there to discuss?" said Sister Beth, "We saw the lack of organisation and the results. One doctor isn't enough." Her side of the hall agreed.

Catherine stood up. "May I suggest the services of Monsieur Lee be utilised." A chorus of verbal abuse howled her down.

Sister Beth stood up. "When I visit a doctor, I want a diagnosis, not my back washed."

Mrs. Lee sprang to her husband's defence with a Gatling-gun-like spray of oriental expletives.

Catherine was outraged. "You silly, silly, woman; you do not know what you are talking about."

"And neither do you – *you* weren't here."

Her words struck deep and Catherine sat.

Aspersions flew in the fierce debate that followed regarding the merits or otherwise of oriental medicine. Ultimately, the feuding factions reached a stalemate and then tea and scones were partaken of. The discord lay simmering below the surface, although when Tom arrived the women were all smiles and they posed for a group photograph. Recommencing the meeting, Ruby immediately moved Carol to the next item on the agenda, hoping for a more harmonious reaction.

"I thought we should have a social on New Year's Eve," Carol informed the women.

"This could be a fundraiser also," Ruby added, "but we need some kind of entertainment. Carol and I thought a talent quest … ideas please, ladies?"

"Ruby's trio … and guest musicians," Carol declared.

"But no Sister Beth," Ruby quickly whispered to her.

"The children could present a special program," proposed Mrs. Tompkins.

"That's an excellent idea … any more, ladies?" The women chattered among themselves. "There we are," Ruby enlightened Carol, "we just need a common focus."

Mrs. Lee rose to her feet, struggling with her English. "Children learn good." Catherine stood up beside her.

"The ladies wish Madame Tompkins is given the chance to prove her worth with the talent quest."

The pious delegation received the intelligent statement like a slap in the face.

Sister Beth stood up and retorted. "Prove?"

"Yes. They will then see how their children are progressing, oui?"

"Progressing."

"Oui … and then they will decide whether to strike."

The meeting once again became chaotic. "Gee, they're a touchy bunch," said Ruby, removing her shoe.

Carol agreed and closed the minutes book. Ruby slammed the table with her shoe and closed the meeting.

The following evening the first sitting of the Gunnadoo Magistrates Court took place. Offenders could now have their 'day in court' rather than paying a bribe to the sergeant or travelling to Sydney to contest the charges. The crossed ensigns loomed behind the magistrate's bench standing centre stage. Constable Jones had placed the witness chair to its right and the clerk's desk to the left. The prosecution and defence tables stood side by side before the bench. The enthusiastic constable, a recent addition sent from Sydney to boost police numbers, had positioned the pews for spectators and families of the defendants to view the proceedings.

"It's a full house," said Bycroft, noting the attendance, "a bloke should sell tickets."

Robinson turned to look behind, "I'll take the rights to the hangings."

"You'll get them only if I give them to you," stated Bycroft. He acknowledged Clarrie and Meg with a smile. "I bet this is the first time you've been in a court and haven't been part of the proceedings." He received no answer.

Sgt. Doyle entered from a rear door and then sat at the prosecutor's table, removing paperwork from his satchel. Constable Jones entered with a jug of water for the magistrate. He then traversed the stage performing superfluous duties for the audience to watch.

Meg acknowledged Ruby and then whispered to Clarrie, "Well, it certainly looks like a court of law." She noted Jones leaving through the rear door. "He looks quite efficient."

Clarrie sat with notepad in hand. "Efficient doesn't necessarily mean competent." He egged her on with a meaningful look.

"All right, how much and for how long?" she queried.

"How about five bob and let's say...five minutes." They shook on it. Clarrie observed the red ensigns. "Tom wouldn't be impressed by the colour of those flags." Meg didn't answer and sat quietly controlling her angst; just the thought of Tom and the law made her heartbeat rise. "Here we go, let's see how well our taxes are spent."

Constable Jones entered, followed by the Clerk of the Court, Mrs. Bond. Jones came to attention, raising the document in both hands, and then cleared his throat to make the formal announcement.

"P-p ... please st-st stand f ... "

"F-f ... Christ sakes." echoed the Irish satirist sitting in a pew at the rear.

Howls of laughter and mimicking followed. Harrick empathised with the officer's situation. Bastock laughed hysterically and slapped him on the back, remembering Harrick's stage fright when delivering his mayoral candidacy speech. Bycroft laughed until he noticed Bastock's enjoyment and then composed himself, telling Robinson to do likewise.

Clarrie held out his palm to Meg and shouted above the mocking voices and laughter. "Five bob you owe me. Boy. Can I pick 'em; I'm in the wrong business."

The frivolity ceased abruptly as the black cape caught everyone's attention; it flapped behind an irate magistrate making his entrance. He smashed the gavel down repeatedly before sitting, although silence already prevailed. "I'll have no unruly behaviour in my court, do – you – understand." He then sat. "Proceed if you will, Constable."

"P-p...please st-st stand f-f for ... "

All stood, all thinking the same thing – this is gonna be a long night.

"M – m – Magistrate Bond."

Randolph Bond tugged at his mutton chop whiskers. "Thank you, Constable."

"S – sit." The red-faced officer moved less assuredly to the rear door and stood at ease. Bond perused the court agenda.

"I'm leaving first chance I get," whispered Meg."

"Don't go. Double or nothing…your choice," said Clarrie.

Ruby gave Meg a nervous smile as Meg conceded to the wager. "All right…Mr. Peck versus Sgt. Doyle."

"Clarify…"

"I bet you'll be the loser at the end of this sitting, Mr. Smartypants."

They shook on it.

Doyle rose to his feet. "The Crown versus Mackellar, your Honour."

Constable Jones opened the door. "M – m – Mackellar." He then marched the accused directly to one of two chairs behind the defence table. With no legal representation, Jock sat by himself with his head down. Much to everyone's relief, Doyle, not the constable, read the drunk and disorderly charges.

"Well, what have you got to say for yourself," Bond demanded. "Stand up straight and look at me when I address you."

Jock looked up and saw red: literally. His Scottish temper erupted. "I'll not be judged under a British flag – to hell with ya."

The gavel came down like an ore crusher. "Contempt of court as well; that's another two days – that'll be four days. Constable." Jock's tirade of abuse continued as Jones marched him outside to the custody of Constable Clarke. "Next case, Sergeant."

Wong Foo noted a lack of leniency in Bond's persona.

A stream of lawbreakers with miscellaneous offences faced the Magistrate's sentencing; some received rock-breaking duties but most received fines. Those choosing to defend themselves, and waste the court's time with fanciful tales, received hefty fines. The inexperienced prosecutor's conviction rate was one hundred percent, and Doyle's bravado grew with each conquest.

Bycroft tallied the fines. "Not bad for an hour's work," he told Robinson, "I wouldn't mind giving it a go myself."

"The Crown versus Houten," Doyle announced.

Clarrie rubbed his hands together. "Here we go – the main event."

"H – h – Houten," called Jones.

Meg threw Ruby an encouraging wink as Abe entered from the rear door. Mr. Peck made his grand entrance through the front doors. A roar of approval from the spectators greeted the defence barrister as he strode the length of the hall. With his black cape flying he also wore a barrister's wig, adding to the visual display. Bond sized up Peck as he laid out the paperwork and prepared to take on the prosecutor. He gestured for Doyle to begin.

Doyle rose to his feet. "Mr. Houten is running an SP book, your Honour."

Bond sized Houten up. "How does the defendant plead?"

"Not guilty," Peck answered.

"And how do you intend to prove the Crown's case, Sergeant?"

Doyle hadn't prepared, naively believing all villains would fess up and pay up like they always had done. He now flicked through the paperwork searching for the witness list Clarke had given him. "I have credible witnesses, your Honour."

"Proceed…call your first witness, Sergeant." Doyle stood red-faced staring at the list. "Call your first witness Sergeant."

"Jock Mackellar."

Doyle received the same treatment as had Jones. Meg smiled; her bet was looking good. Houten grinned confidently to Ruby. Laughter and mimicking continued until Bond rose to his feet and then brought down the gavel with the force of Thor's hammer.

"Those of you who wish to bed down with Mr. Mackellar this evening – keep it up." He sat. "Sgt. Doyle, may I see your list please." He perused the names, crossing off those he'd just convicted. "Call your *only* witness, Sergeant."

"Yes." Meg jabbed Clarrie in the ribs and gave the thumbs up to Ruby.

"Don't be too sure," he told her, "it's not over until Bond delivers his verdict."

"Come on Clarrie, Sgt. Doyle has no idea what he's doing."

"Ineptitude doesn't necessarily mean he'll lose the case."

"It will be a miscarriage of justice if the prosecution wins. Double or nothing Mr. Smartypants – make it a pound."

They shook on it.

"Pastor O'Dae," called Doyle.

The lean figure of the pastor, also dressed in black, strode to the witness chair followed by the clerk.

"Raise your right hand and…"

"I have my own bible," he told her, and held it aloft pompously as though about to deliver a sermon.

"So does this court, Pastor O'Dae." Bond gestured to the bible the clerk held out. "And that's it." O'Dae's bravado diminished.

"Oooo…" The satirist's mirth echoed beneath the pews leaving the gallery giggling covertly.

The clerk swore him in. "Repeat after me – do you swear to tell the truth…"

Bycroft lit a cigar. The majority of eyes in the gallery followed the smoke rings rising upon the humidity in the hall. "I don't like what I see here," he whispered to Robinson. "The man's too honest."

When sworn in, Bond directed the pastor to sit and then gestured to the Sergeant to begin. Looking O'Dae straight in the eye, Doyle strode to the witness chair and asked, "Who told you Mr. Houten was running a book?"

"My parishioners, they confessed to me."

Doyle turned to the gallery and announced to the crowd. "There you are – would you not believe a man of the cloth?"

"Excuse me, Sergeant…" Doyle turned to face him, "the gallery is not a jury. I make the verdict, not them…is that your case?"

"A man of the cloth, Your Honour – the truth revealed in confession. What more can I say…I rest my case." He returned to the prosecutor's table and sat there planning to give Constable Clarke stable duties for the next month.

"Your witness, Mr. Peck."

O'Dae wriggled uncomfortably as he watched Peck rise and slowly amble toward him. Peck's poker face revealed nothing of what he might ask and, most alarmingly, what might have already been probed.

"Pastor O'Dae, figuratively speaking you being the shepherd of your flock would recognise a lame lamb, someone down on their luck, would you not?"

The Pastor rose to his feet, "The meek shall inherit the earth…"

Bond interrupted. "Just answer the question…yes or no, thank you…and remain seated."

O'Dae sat. "Yes, I would."

"Yes, of course you would." Peck turned his back on the witness and announced to the court, "I've done some background research on Pastor O'Dae…" O'Dae's angst multiplied as Peck continued, "it is all commendable. Working with the destitute, bringing the word of God to them – Gunnadoo is *most* fortunate to have a man of his character here in our community." O'Dae composed himself and his angst levels subsided but they rose quickly when Peck asked, "And what about Sister Beth?" O'Dae felt queasiness in his belly. "Sister Beth…what do we have on Sister Beth?" Peck shuffled through his papers on the defence table, "Who would have known?" He returned to the witness, page in hand. The Pastor sat pale-faced with the contents of his stomach fermenting. "The woman is…" Peck held the page up in front of O'Dae's face, "…a saint."

The pious applauded.

"May I have some water?" O'Dae requested. "I don't feel well."

Jones responded with glass and pitcher. The Pastor's hand trembled as he drank.

"I won't keep you long if you're not feeling well," Peck empathised. "One last question, Pastor. How do you recognise the lame?"

"The collection…" he stopped abruptly.

"Yes, the collection plate; it was down the Sunday after the Cup was run. Wasn't that how you knew your congregation was gambling? Your takings were down…you too gamble – on the generosity of others."

The pious erupted, vilifying Peck; the atheists applauded him. Peck returned to the defence table and sat down. Doyle was impressed and noted Peck's aggressive tactics.

"Where's ya God now." the satirist hollered.

"Order. Order." Bond shouted, repeatedly slamming the gavel down to no avail. He gestured for Jones to remove Houten from the court and sat waiting for silence; it worked. "Mr. Peck, you are out of order, next time I'll hold you in contempt. I will not tolerate chicanery or theatrics, do – you – understand. And if there are any more outbursts from the gallery, I'll have the court cleared." He gestured to Jones for Houten to return. "Continue, Mr. Peck."

"Yes." Clarrie nudged Meg. "Now, that's what I call taking charge."

Peck rose, "No further questions, your Honour."

The Pastor and his deflated ego exited the hall through the rear door as Houten entered.

445

"Should I check your list of witnesses before they're called, Mr. Peck?"

"I have only one Your Honour – Mr. Abe Houten."

"Proceed. Swear him in."

"Yes." Meg elbowed Clarrie.

Houten sat in the chair before Mr. Bond. Ruby gave the magistrate a nod and smiled. Her gesture ignored, she turned to receive encouragement from Meg.

Peck stood up and moved slowly toward his client, quietly enquiring, "You are not a religious man, are you Mr. Houten? No, you're not..." his intensity increased, "... but not having religious persuasions doesn't mean you're not a generous man, isn't that so ... yes." He looked to the rafters. "Isn't it true that you have never attended any of the Pastor's services?" Peck eyeballed his own client accusingly. "Yes it *is* true, Mr. Houten...and would I not be right in presuming you don't even *know* Pastor O'Dae?"

Doyle jumped to his feet and naively yelled, "I object."

Peck was derailed. The gallery shrieked with laughter. Bond raised the gavel; silence prevailed before it fell.

"And what is it exactly that you're objecting to, Sergeant."

"He's talk'n too fast," the satirist covertly replied.

Frivolity broke out again. This time Bond sat waiting patiently for silence without raising the gavel. He then acknowledged the satirist. "Our humorist is quite a wit. Overruled ... sit down, Sergeant.

446

Continue Mr. Peck …and make it brief, my patience is running short."

"Your Honour, my client is a respected citizen, and an honourable merchant filling out orders, ordering supplies, servicing the community; he's too busy to be a bookie. I request this case be dismissed now."

"Are you telling me he can't be a bookie as well, Mr. Peck?" Bond tugged his muttonchop whiskers, "There is such a thing as subsidising a career – as well you know and are about to find out when you've finished with your theatrics. Proceed."

"No more questions, Your Honour."

"Sergeant …your witness."

Doyle knew when to leave well alone. "No questions."

"The defendant will stand." The clerk handed Bond the hearings notes for signing.

"Mr. Houten," Bond tweaked his whiskers, "I commend you for not representing yourself albeit your counsel's defence is weak to say the least…"

"Yes." Clarrie shouldered Meg.

"…unfortunately the prosecution is weaker."

"Yes." Meg shouldered Clarrie.

"Mr. Houten, I am a magistrate but I also have another profession, do you know what it is?"

"A dentist."

"Ah, you can talk. A little louder so everyone can hear … again."

"A dentist."

"Thank you … and where is my practice? Speak up, nice and loud."

"Across the street from Dr. Tubber's practice."

"And what are my hours?"

"Business hours?" Houten wriggled uncomfortably.

"I hope t'at your other chair be more comfortable," the recognisable voice called.

This time Bond chuckled along with the gallery.

"Very good...and yes it is," Bond announced, "and I give nitrous oxide to those who like a good laugh...and I see we have many here tonight that do. He returned his attention to Houten. "Not guilty." Bond sat waiting patiently while the gallery enjoyed the win.

"Yes. Gotcha." Meg placed the pound note she received from Clarrie down her brassiere.

"Order please," the gavel tapped quietly, "order, thank you."

The noise of celebration ceased to a murmuring, all eyes on Bond. "Under these exceptional circumstances I too wish to give a performance, Mr. Houten, and as you're in *my chair,* I'm going to extract from you one pound for the community poor-box, you being the generous man you are." The bet with Clarrie rang true; he was in the chair for an extraction. The gallery appreciated Bond's humour. "Pay the clerk later – stand down." Houten returned to the defence table and shook hands with Peck. "Before closing proceedings I'd like to thank Mr. Peck for his performance." He gestured for Peck to stand and then instigated the applause. The gallery followed suit until the gavel fell. "Sgt. Doyle, our prosecutor." He stood to receive boos and sat quickly. "Our court constable." Jones received cheers and stepped forward, lifting his cap.

"This is like having a front row seat at the Tiv'," Bycroft told Robinson. Robinson was applauding too loudly to hear.

"I'm rooting for the Constable," Harrick told Bastock.

The gavel lifted but did not fall: silence did. Bond addressed the gallery. "And for making proceedings most enjoyable, our humorous bard." Paddy stood to receive his kudos. "Contempt of court: two days. Lock him up, Constable."

The gallery erupted in laughter. Bond sat back, twirling the Merino-like growth. It was his court and he'd let it be known. Now he savoured the moment.

Paddy accepted his incarceration without aggression or humility. "Trickery. Noth'n has changed," he yelled at Bond. The rear door slammed. A muffled voice pleaded, "I'm innocent."

"And thank you to our community-minded citizens who came to see justice done. This first sitting of Gunnadoo's Magistrate Court is now closed." The gavel fell. Crack.

Clarrie, Meg and Ruby waited out the front of the hall for Houten when he exited. "I told you I was innocent, Ruby."

"You weren't innocent – you were bloody lucky."

"And so was I." Meg waved the pound note.

"And so was I." Clarrie waved his open palm in front of Houten. "That's one pound I believe you owe me."

Houten exploded, "I reckon that was a low-down act you pulled."

449

"You were the one that took the bet without doing the research…you're lucky I didn't put ten quid on Sister Olive, aren't you." The Melbourne Cup winner had taken many a bookie to the cleaners. "It's all in the precise wording – not just the form guide." Houten paid up. "Meg?" Clarrie held his hand out to her. "I believe that's my one pound and you still owe me one."

"What?"

"I'm not down a quid; I've just broken even – which means…

* * *

Summer had begun with its azure skies, insignificant breezes and relentless sun. The heat was barely tolerable by mid morning. Across the Spinifex plain at the northern side of Gunnadoo, linesmen strung cables between telephone poles. Except for the final stage, they had strung the majority of the cable between trees. It was rumoured bribes had been taken from individuals in the business community to jump the queue for early connection. When it was brought to Bycroft's attention, he had smartly brushed it off. It was he who'd instigated the inducement system and his was the first business to be hooked up after the post office itself. His residence and the line out to the property soon followed, after which came the rest of the community.

Meg immediately felt their cloak of isolation lift when the new Advocate telephone rang for the first time. "The Advocate, Clarrie Radcliff speaking … " She stood watching. He gave her a wink. "Thank you for the notification and Merry Christmas to you." He hung up.

"Progress has arrived," she declared.

Throughout Gunnadoo, telephones began ringing and callers flooded the manually operated switchboard. Many were practical jokes carried out on unsuspecting victims. Bastock fell for many of Bycroft's hoax calls and despatched wagons to various locations on a wild-goose chase. Billings had to be content to sit in the office listening to Bycroft's one-sided conversations. Creative thinking would be required if he was to keep Wong Foo up to date with information so that his supplies would continue unhindered.

"Bycroft Holdings, John Bycroft speaking."

"Mr. Bycroft, I have your trunk call to a Mr. Lockett of Cowper's Brewery, Sydney. Putting you through," the operator informed him cheerfully.

A position on the board of directors had become available by the fortuitous death of Mr. Sloan, the elderly Vice President of Cowper's Brewery. Lockett had replaced him – he was now VP. "Good news, John," Lockett informed him, "your nomination has been accepted by the Admiral. You and another candidate called Whittington are on the short list. If I was a betting man," he wisecracked, "I'd bet the wife and kids on you."

"You think it looks that good?"

"If O'Keefe accepts your wife as the pious woman you've described her to be, it's a sure thing."

"Excellent," replied Bycroft, "she'll be over the moon."

"When will we catch up then?"

451

"I'll get back to you...most probably in January."

"Jean and I look forward to meeting Catherine."

Billings wasn't sure what to make of the conversation. He didn't know of Bycroft's plans to sabotage Bastock's beer supply or make Lockett a new partner in the Yakka Dakka goldmine.

* * *

Catherine sat at the outdoor table on the balcony of her boudoir. She detested Wednesday mornings; ahead would be a stressful day envisaging the evening. Looking at her refection in the window, she listened unresponsively to Mrs. Chang reading Christmas messages, the accounts book in front of her. "It's from Lucky-Legs – marked personal." Mrs. Chang handed her the envelope.

Catherine read the note without smiling. "This is unexpectedly good news." She returned to staring in the window, perceiving a slight smile in her own reflection.

"There is one thing I feel should be brought to your attention ... "

"Oui, go on?"

"A new client requests...special attention."

"Is he a gentleman?" asked Catherine. Mrs. Chang nodded. "And a girl?"

"Jennifer…"

Catherine pondered. She sipped the cold coffee. "Jennifer…yes, she has a nasty streak. Is he capable of paying for this particular service?"

"I believe Mr. Bond has the funds."

25 – Joy to the World

*The Judas Goat is but the 'black dog' in sheep's
clothing
...into the abyss the impaired are escorted.*

Catherine's pregnancy was yet to show. The morning
sickness had ceased on the black Friday, but her
mental condition was of concern to Ying Lee. If not
for her depression, he would have discontinued the
medication and stopped her growing dependence.
Catherine had abandoned her usually impeccable
appearance, her affinity for coolie pyjamas was
becoming unhealthy and she rarely ventured onto
High Street not dressed in the disguise.

"You should try harder," Ying Lee lectured her,
"not good for baby if you continue this way."

"It be my baby." she retorted. Her mood swings
were starting to become uncontrollable. "Sure'n be
God I know what's good and what's not good for…"
The tirade abruptly stopped. She bowed her head.
"Holy Mother. I'm sorry."

Ying Lee said nothing; his silence did the
talking, roaring in Catherine's ears, as the habit
gnawed at her insides. She raised her head and looked
him in the eye. "This be my third Christmas I have
spent alone in Gunnadoo."

"You now have Mr. Wally's baby for company."

"We'll see." The ambiguous reply was disturbing.

"You know you are always welcome at table of Ying Lee." He handed her the elixir bottles.

"You're a good friend."

Catherine shuffled along High Street lethargically with the Hessian bag over her shoulder. Ying Lee observed what he recognised as another torment Catherine would have to deal with.

She spent the rest of the day reading in the pagoda. That evening she did not bathe, change attire or bother to add blusher to her gaunt face. She lit the lamp and waited, listening for the dreaded footsteps on the outside stairs. The boudoir finally became suffocating and she went out onto the balcony. Seeing the red glow approaching, her intuition told her not to underestimate Bycroft's mean streak. She returned inside to sit at the Davenport.

"Good evening, Catherine." Bycroft stood at the door with a gift-wrapped box of nougat. He wasn't drunk or out of breath. His shirt bore no signs of sweat and was neatly tucked into his trousers. "I hope all is well with you and our child."

Catherine felt nauseated at the statement and confused at what she saw. "Does it look like I am well?" She partook of the elixir straight from the bottle.

"These are for you; Merry Christmas." He did not make the usual aggressive grope. He placed the gift in front of her and she received a kiss on the cheek as she turned her head away from him. Bycroft sat in an easy chair. "You've cut your hair, it's very becoming."

"It is falling out," she lied, "I had no choice."

"I've heard that worry can do that, look at me. I once had..." he stopped and smiled. Catherine didn't. "But it's not about me, is it? I'm worried about you."

"Or is it that you are worried about who will run this place should anything happen to me?"

"Since the fire I've come to realise life is precious, it's not just about making a quid...*and* I do have other responsibilities besides mayoral duties." He stood up; Catherine flinched as Bycroft stepped toward her. He stopped. "I've not always lived by the Good Book, to be honest I've never read it but I know what I now feel." He walked to the door and stood looking out. "Truly magnificent." He paused, removing the fob watch to check the time, "and I do appreciate this." He wound it up. "I'll get the cash together – it may take a month or two. Goodnight Catherine."

When she heard his departing footsteps after each visit, Catherine's anxiety always lessened. She now sat bewildered, listening to them earlier than expected – there had been no humiliation. A multitude of reasons now crashed down upon her. Anxiety increased: elixir decreased.

The morning sun baked the once-lush lawns; a replacement for Chung Dow hadn't been found. Shaded in the pagoda Catherine sat daydreaming. Overnight her anxiety had decreased, the void replenished by a morose ache. She reflected on the return trip from Yakka Dakka when Wally had revealed his service record. She yearned to feel the

455

welts on his body and lie in his arms. The Advocate's first Christmas edition lay open on her lap. 'Peace unto Mankind: A Christmas Story'.

Under a pseudonym, Tom recounted a scene he'd witnessed on the Western Front; an unauthorised Christmas Eve armistice. At midnight in bleak winter conditions, opposing sides put conflict and weapons aside, the religious significance apparent to the man in the trench if not to the generals at HQ. Enemies fraternised on neutral ground swapping cigarettes, playing football and exchanging photographs of loved ones. Many carols sung were recognisable even if the words weren't. Tom had photographed farmers, tradesmen, schoolteachers; boys and men with faces ravaged by atrocities in the simple act of shaking hands. Unfortunately, there was no photograph accompanying the story; the high command hadn't seen eye to eye with Tom when the plates were developed.

The story didn't say that military order was finally restored when the white flag was felled by a single shot from an Enfield. The alleged officer who fired the shot died in suspicious circumstances in the following battle, before he could lay court-marshal charges against the enlisted man who had refused to carry out the original order. The military provost immediately confiscated the prints and plates, destroying all evidence. Tom's memory couldn't be erased; it confirmed the futility of war. Christmas was not a time of joy for him either.

Mrs. Chang joined Catherine. "The girls are beginning to talk."

"About what?"

"You…they are worried."

"They do not suspect anything?"

"No, but speculation is rife."

"They need not worry. I am fine."

"Then tell them."

"At present there is nothing to tell. As soon as there is, you will know."

Over the festive season, Catherine was rarely seen, although the girls would hear her pacing the establishment in the dark after they'd all retired. Catherine took refuge in her boudoir, the pagoda and her reclusive existence. The routine of the establishment wasn't to change. Mrs. Chang ran the show in Catherine's absence, delivering the girls to the pastor for weekly cleansing of the soul. They also attended the early service on Christmas Eve.

The establishment celebrated New Year's Eve as it had in previous years. Good cheer and testosterone overflowed; however, Catherine wasn't at the imposing entrance to welcome revellers. Attendances at the annual two-up regatta on the banks of the Yapsly exceeded the promoter's expectations; many vendors now made the event a pilgrimage. At the community hall, the inaugural Women's Guild social took place.

Mrs. Tompkins had kept the oriental students busy for weeks. They had excelled at cutting up past issues of the Advocate to make streamers. Strung from the central rafter, the dyed strips of paper glued together with a mixture of flour and water created a paper canopy. To placate the Irish and Scottish guest musicians, a banner wishing all a Happy New Year covered the red ensigns. Ruby's trio plus pianists and fiddle players provided the music.

"Ladies and gentlemen," Houten announced, "please take your partners for the beer barrel polka. And you kids dance properly or get off the floor," he told them.

Jock thumped the bass drum: Boom. Boom.

"I got to sit down, Meg, my feet are killing me," Clarrie complained.

"Not now...take your shoes off. Where's Tom?"

"Stop worrying...he's over there with his camera."

"I'm not worrying...well, maybe a little. I want him to have a good time. He's been..."

"Here we go." The introduction began and Clarrie swung her around; it was better to have blisters than to have Meg worrying about Tom for the rest of the evening. "Come on, Meg, join in, sing up."

New shoes were the hot item for Christmas; recipients were recognisable as those with blistered heels and dancing in bare feet. The floor pulsed under the dancers as they skipped to the polka beat. Bycroft steadied his glass on the trestle table.

"I'm glad we didn't shirk on the bearers and joists," he yelled to Robinson. He received no reply, just a blank look. "Tell me you didn't...shit."

Irish lads of Ulster County wore their Donegal tweed proudly. Those who wanted to impress the opposite sex and maybe get-a-bit without having to pay for it at Catherine's establishment, tried their luck and sang their lungs out with the band providing entertainment also. During the breaks, while

458

musicians caught a breath and wet their thirst, the schoolkids presented the program Mrs. Tompkins had suggested. The men retreated to the wet bar set up in a tent at the rear of the hall.

Bastock and his coalition eyed Bycroft's newly formed alliance with contempt. "Say the word and we'll sort 'em out," Dempsey informed his boss.

"Let me pay Bastock a visit," Robinson drunkenly pleaded, "I'll give 'im a belated Christmas gift."

Bycroft imagined Robinson slipping down Bastock's chimney with his bag of tricks. "It's a nice thought."

"Tis the season for giving," he confided.

"Aye it is, matey." Bycroft wished Lockett and Bryant were beside him. "But hold that thought, Easter will soon be upon us...we may just nail the bastard to the cross then."

It was soon evident that the oriental kids weren't getting their share of stage time. The singing of God Save the Queen, when they did, impressed only the pious coalition. An eruption was imminent. The Chinese mothers huddled together, all speaking at the same time.

"Not good, not good," Mrs. Lee shook her head.

Mrs. Foo shook her fist, "Insult to Chinese."

Ying Lee tried in vain to pacify the women. Adding fuel to the impending disaster, Mrs. Foo's daughters were trying her patience; many of the young Chinese labourers from the mines were paying them attention and they were reciprocating. Mother was cranky and patrolled the perimeter of the table at which the disobedient daughters sat. Wong Foo was unavailable to do the chaperoning. "I give him plenty fireworks," she screamed at her daughters.

Women not involved with the Guild were oblivious to the simmering situation, as were all the men. On the surface, the night was preceding without drama. Ruby could feel the animosity increasing between the two opposing groups but there was little she could do from the stage; it was Carol's job to quell any disturbance. Carol joined Ruby at the musicians table.

"Hello, Luv…enjoying yourself?"

"It's becoming quite heated…I feel like the meat in the sandwich," she grumbled.

"What time is it?"

"Eleven thirty."

"Alrighty. If we can keep them apart for the next thirty minutes…we're home."

"What should I do?" asked Carol.

"Well, whatever you do, don't take sides. Come on," Ruby told her musicians, "let's get them on their feet and dancing."

"We're out of songs," Houten informed her.

Jock waved a drink in one hand, his drumstick in the other, and slurred, "I can do a wee solo if ya want, Lassie?"

"If we keep up this pace I won't see midnight," Houten complained.

"If we don't neither will they. Bring your glasses with you, gentlemen."

Jock rose unsteadily on his feet. "Point me in the right direction, Lassie."

Having sprinkled a fresh layer of sawdust on the dance floor, Robinson returned to the table with two beers for himself. Bycroft drank from his hip flask.

"What was that all about, Sunshine?"

"What?" he slurred.

"You and the paddies."

"You saw?"

"Enough to know something is going on."

"An Irish prank." Robinson skulled a beer and then burped long and loud. "A couple of the lads gave me a handful of horse hair."

"And so?"

"They reckon a woman's swirl'n skirt causes an updraft."

Bycroft looked puzzled. Robinson began laughing and then demonstrated by scratching his crutch. "It's supposed to send 'em silly." He eyes constantly moved from Ruby to the dance floor. "I gotta see this."

"I gotta take a leak."

"Yeah, I need another one too, hang on and I'll come with you."

"I don't need you to hold my dick. Watch the entertainment, idiot – you provided it." Bycroft sized up the best option to exit inconspicuously.

"Ladies and gentlemen, your attention please," Ruby shouted. The crowd chatter silenced except for the guild women who were oblivious to the proceedings. A screeching note from the saxophone caught their attention, achieving the desired result. "Have you had a good time?"

The response was overwhelming. "Yes." the crowd yelled.

"You're not too tired to dance some more, are you?"

"No." the crowd shouted.

"That nearly lifted the roof off," Robinson laughed.

"It's not the roof we gotta worry about, idiot." Bycroft checked his watch. "Where's the bag of tricks?"

"Out at the property…why?"

"We need a diversion."

"What for?"

"Forget it." He rubbed his jaw, thinking.

Ruby puckered her freshly painted lips, "If you ain't got blisters, you soon will have, because we're just warming up…boys." She turned to the musicians, lifting her hands. They rose. "Alrighty. Mr. Houten, if you please."

"It's ladies' choice," he announced. "The band has requested the beer barrel polka, and the ladies," he cunningly added, "have requested a quickstep arrangement. Ladies, choose your partners."

"No, my feet won't take it, Meg…and no I won't take my shoes off. I'm the…"

"You're the one missing out."

"Where's Tom?"

"Over there. Where's the children?"

"They're fine." Meg spotted Bycroft.

"You wouldn't."

"I would too."

"How much?"

"Five bob."

"You have to keep him on the floor for two full dances."

462

"You're on."

They shook hands.

Through the viewfinder, Tom focused the camera on Mrs. Foo and her daughters. *Up a little,* he told himself. *Get that rifle butt in the shoulder, son,* stipulated the internal voice.

Meg joined the rush of women moving in on their targets. They crisscrossed the dance floor, heading in all directions. Men not sitting at tables mingled uneasily on the right side of the hall, many holding up the walls and vice-versa. Camouflaged in the jostle, Bycroft stealthily dropped his cigar into a dune of sawdust as he made his getaway. The Irish boys casually waited for their sweethearts to approach and Robinson waited with bated breath for the outcome.

"Mr. Bycroft."

He raised his derby. "Marge…" His cheesy grin camouflaged his 'caught with your finger in the cookie jar' look.

"You're not leaving, are you?"

"No," he cleared his throat, "…just stepping outside for some air."

She held out her hand, "Ladies' choice."

"I haven't danced in years. No, I really think…"

"And I have looked after your account at the Advocate so well."

"Well…when you put it like that, how could I refuse?"

As soon as the music began, Bycroft displayed his angst by doing bouncing dance movements.

"Relax, you're too tense," Meg coached. "This is a quickstep, stop bouncing – slide."

463

The only bouncing was in his head; the unstable floor wasn't moving under the skating-like motion of the quickstep.

"That's it, slide. Now sing up," Meg encouraged.

"… of fun." Bycroft chirped.

They synchronised with the music and his movements became fluid.

"You're a very good dancer," Meg complimented, "so light on your feet."

Through a fixed grin, Bycroft sang along with the crowd. He gained confidence and twirled, once, twice, three times, and then his fixed grin ceased as a feeling of nausea invaded the pit of his stomach. The room kept twirling after he'd stopped. He lost his sense of direction and they collided with Mr. and Mrs. Tompkins.

"Hallelujah." she sang at the top of her voice in Meg's face.

Meg and Bycroft's fixed grins were identical.

"Come on." Ruby shouted, "Big finish, everybody sing up."

Bycroft sighed with relief when the music stopped. Houten stepped forward and shouted, "Same verse, same as the first."

"Come on." Meg grabbed Bycroft and they continued dancing.

Bycroft squirmed, "I feel like I'm … "

"I feel like I'm floating on air … you should teach," she shouted.

The compliment distracted his penchant for self-preservation and awakened his ego. "I should, shouldn't I?" They pirouetted then glided as though on ice, attracting the attention of many dancers. Bycroft acknowledged the applause by nodding and gesturing, all the time covertly craning his neck to look in the direction of the burning cigar he'd dropped previously.

The crowd wailed for more at the conclusion the dance.

"Most enjoyable, Marge, we should do it again some time."

"You're not getting away that quickly, you're the best dancing partner I've had all night."

"Form a circle," Houten directed, "ladies on the outside." He turned to Ruby. "Why, I do declare, I see a robin."

She puffed out her chest, bobbing up and down, and pressed the sax to her lips.

"It's the red, red robin and she's bob, bob, bob'n." Houten shouted. The signature timing of the introduction prepared everyone for a progressive barn dance. The piano and bass accompanied by the accordion and a drunken Irishman playing the spoons came in on the downbeat, as did the dancers.

Ruby's antics added to the frivolity of the moment; the spontaneity of the dancers bouncing added to Bycroft's angst. Other participants and the inebriated onlookers at the sides of the hall didn't notice the pulsing movement, but each bounce terrified Bycroft. He danced on tiptoes, trying to lighten pressure on the unstable floor.

"Sing up." Meg shouted, as she twirled away from him, moving on to her next partner.

Industrial lanterns swung in synchronisation overhead; below, the combustible streamers hung, cloaked in cigarette smoke. The barn dance seemed like an eternity to Bycroft. As his body temperature rose in the stifling heat, he couldn't stop the sweat trickling into his eyes or escape the changing of partners. Mrs. Bond's clubfoot was lethal. The hall swelled as folk began to enter for the official countdown to the New Year.

Meg greeted Bycroft as the full circle was completed. "Ah, here's my favourite dancing partner."

The grin was now rigid upon Bycroft's face and his tongue was silenced by a dry mouth.

Her red face glowing with intensity as her bobbing climaxed, Ruby shouted, "Big finish."

The floor stopped heaving; Bycroft's stomach continued. His heart beat as wildly as Ruby's thumping. The dancers stood applauding rowdily and more people crowded onto the floor. Bycroft's panic rose as the floor sagged.

"Thank you, Marge, gotta go. Excuse me; thank you…injured man coming through."

Overcome by the moment, Ruby gestured for silence. Bycroft limped toward the exit; his ankle throbbed, having been the recipient of the clubfoot's attention. Sister Beth, the pastor and Mr. and Mrs. Tompkins now blocked his path.

"Good evening, Mr. Bycroft," Pastor O'Dae greeted him. "You know Mr. and…"

A loud boom interrupted the conversation.

Bycroft's heart shot into his mouth. "Fuck." he shouted in Sister Beth's face, throwing her to the floor with him on top in a blatant act of self-preservation. One of Wong Foo's skyrockets had

466

exploded prematurely, unfortunately on the hall roof. Observers of the incident stood aghast and then helped Sister Beth to her feet.

Bycroft dusted the sawdust from his trousers. "Guess I'm still a little gun shy," he admitted sheepishly.

Sister Beth rearranged her attire. "Thank you, Mr. Bycroft. I froze when you shouted, 'duck.' If the roof had fallen in on us, you'd have saved my life – thank you."

The pastor laid his hand on Bycroft's shoulder. "God bless you."

"Now, now, it was just a reflex action. Don't go making a big thing of it. As long as Sister Beth isn't hurt."

She took a deep breath, "Oh my." She then began squirming.

"Well, I must be going, excuse me…I've some business to attend to."

Sister Beth's face contorted, "I'm all right." She tried crossing her legs and prancing on the spot – it didn't help.

Houten held his watch in hand. "Form circles and join hands," he instructed. Ruby put an arm around him. The pianist put an arm around the spoon player and Jock lay slumped over the bass drum. Many circles formed within each other. Sister Beth had both her hands taken, the pastor one side, Mr. Tompkins the other. She began kicking up her legs and hopping about like many of the women. Robinson grinned from ear to ear when given the thumbs up from the Irish lads.

"Here we go." Houten called. The crowd joined him. "Ten – nine …" The hall roof nearly lifted off as each number was shouted.

Bycroft hurriedly exited. "Coming through, excuse me. Make way for the lady with the pram."

Meg thrashed about wildly between Tom and Clarrie, "Eight – seven." they yelled.

Between his wife and Mrs. Foo, Ying Lee nearly had his arms pulled from the sockets. "Six – five." he bellowed.

Mrs. Foo lashed out, kicking her legs high, also unable to scratch the compelling itch. Lotus-Flower, at the other end of the line of daughters, held Tom's hand. *This is it, lads,* the voice roared, *on the whistle – take no prisoners.*

Being at capacity, the hall could not hold any more revellers. Unable to enter, the masses had gathered on the front steps. "Four – three." they shouted.

"Get out of the way." Bycroft shouted. The thought of women and children first was never entertained. Now panic-stricken, he pushed his way through the wall of people, knocking down many. Their voices reached a crescendo.

"Two." a woman screamed in his face. He shoved his way between the couple.

"One." her partner bawled, in anticipation.

"Happy New Year."

The boom echoed throughout Gunnadoo and region.

* * *

Catherine raised her head, listening to the Beersheba barrage that Wally had spoken of, and then began running toward his unpretentious headstone. Her tears enhanced the incandescent beacon surrounded by silhouetted obelisks.

* * *

Thrust from the hall, Bycroft stumbled down the front steps and fell to his knees gasping for air. Another explosion rattled windows and the crowd lifted their heads to see a magnificent burst of sparkling colours.

"You right there, Mr. Bycroft?" McSloy asked.

"I dropped two bob." He stood, composing himself. "One of the kids can find it. Hey, you're supposed to be…"

"I'm on me break, fair go."

Another explosion overhead made Bycroft jump.

"A bit never nervous, ain't we, Boss?"

"Mind your own business and get back to work."

The sky lit up as Bycroft limped away from the chorusing voices. He sat across the road on a customer's bench watching both sky and structure. Under his breath, he joined in with the bits of the song he knew. "We'll lah lala lah lah lala for the days of Auld Lang Syne." His angst eased as many people flowed from the hall to watch Wong Foo's fireworks. Robinson drunkenly wandered through the crowd spotting women surreptitiously scratching the irrepressible itch. Inside the hall, fireworks erupted also; the slanging match began when the singing of Auld Lang Syne finished.

469

"Strike." yelled Mrs. Lee. Her alliance quickly took up the chant.

"I think me time to help Wong Foo," Ying Lee politely told his wife. He put a hand to his ear, "Ah. Fireworks ... yes, me think now good time."

The pious threw accusations and insults; the Chinese, expletives and a chair – all hell broke loose, fur and feathers also flying.

"Come on, boys...this will bring them to attention." Ruby began playing God Save the Queen. Houten joined in.

"I'll not be play'n tat shit," Paddy declared, and slammed down the piano lid. The spoon player threw his instruments in the air and staggered off the stage with Paddy. Ruby played on regardless.

Jock raised his body from over the bass drum to a sitting position in his chair. "Ouck now Lassie...nor I." He passed out again.

Houten collapsed onto a chair, his arms hanging limply at his side. A disjointed sound emanated as the accordion bellows unharmoniously expressed air and hung limply over his knees.

Meg sat opposite Clarrie, the table offering privacy to attend the itch. She was disgusted. "And I thought progress would bring civility, huh."

"It just shows Gunnadoo hasn't lost its pioneering spirit," replied Clarrie.

"Come on. Find the kids and *you* find your pioneering spirit – you have some work to do. Where's Tom?"

Bycroft strolled through the crowd with his hands in his pockets. He idled up to Robinson and stood beside him watching the display overhead. "About those bearers and…"

"Look at the women…look," he slurred, and elbowed Bycroft solidly in the ribs. "It works."

"So does the floor, Sunshine." Bycroft felt his right fist clenching; he removed his left hand from his pocket. "Now, about the bearers and joists?" he questioned.

"Naw … I'z only kidding."

All arms, including Bycroft's, rose in unison, fingers pointing at the flash above. Robinson looked up.

"Sieg Heil," Bycroft whispered.

A sharp right hook toppled Robinson. He lay sprawled on the ground wailing in consternation, "Me eye, me eye, I can't see."

"Watch out." Bycroft warned the crowd, "Protect your eyes from the falling debris."

Skittish spectators relayed the warning, resulting in the crowd stampeding for cover.

Bycroft offered his hand to Robinson. "Come on, I'll help you get home."

Bycroft slung Robinson's right arm over his shoulder, grabbed a handful of trouser at the rear and aggressively lifted. Robinson half trotted and half staggered on the balls of his feet as Bycroft led him off.

"A damn good mate you are." He held his hand over the swollen eye, his breath putrid. "I won't forget this."

Bycroft knew exactly the opposite to be true and at the first chance, when not observed, he swiftly jettisoned the baggage. Robinson conveniently

471

tumbled through a bush into the ditch on the other side. The dull thud and expressing of wind was satisfying.

"Sleep that off, idiot."

With both hands in his pockets scratching his nuts, Bycroft strolled up Main Street whistling, 'when the red, red robin comes …'

* * *

Mrs. Chang sat alone in the dark, resolutely trying her best to support Catherine and trying not to think the worst. Her tea long cold, she reminisced over the good humour and spirits of Catherine and the girls the previous New Year's morning. Celebrations at the establishment had been contained to the invited guests only and the evening had passed with no trouble – until now. Mrs. Chang hadn't seen Catherine since late afternoon, and after much searching still hadn't been able to find her. Her heavy eyelids struggled to stay open; she tried focusing on the first hint of the pending dawn. It would be a hot day; she waited to see what 1922 was about to drop in her lap.

Going out to check the pagoda one last time before retiring, she was alerted to what she had dreaded – bloodied footprints. Catherine had slipped past her. In the half-light, she followed the trail through the kitchen and passage to the foyer and up the stairs. She paused before entering the dark passageway, unsure whether to get Ying Lee first. Each hesitant step taken toward the boudoir door quickened her heartbeat. She stopped, took a deep breath and prepared herself before entering.

Still dressed in coolie pyjamas, Catherine lay asleep, her blackened and cut feet testimony to the many miles aimlessly walked. Her small baby bump, noticeable for the first time, was verification that she was still carrying. Relieved, Mrs. Chang stood at the end of the bed observing the woman sleep – she looked no more than a child herself.

* * *

Clarrie woke with Meg tugging his arm, "Clarrie wake up."

"No, not again Meg, I need to rest."

"Clarrie," she yelled, "Tom isn't in his room…his bed hasn't been slept in."

Clarrie's eyelids opened immediately and he sat up slowly. "Don't go jumping conclusions, there's probably a rational explanation."

Meg lay back down, staring at the ceiling, "He wouldn't listen, I've pleaded with him …"

"I've told him to slow down also, Meg." He paused. "We've talked about this …"

She sat up startled, "You don't think…"

"I don't think anything."

"Tom and I don't have secrets but lately…he goes off on his own and won't say anything …"

"He can't be watched twenty-four hours a day and then interrogated relentlessly."

Meg lay back on the pillow, evaluating Clarrie's statement.

"Stay there," he told her, "I'll make you a cuppa…you've certainly earned it."

She raised an eyebrow gesturing agreement.

* * *

Wong Foo woke with Mrs. Foo tugging his arm, "Wake up."

"No, not again, Wong Foo need to rest." He received a thump in the ribs.

"Wake up, Lotus-Flower missing."

He sat bolt upright, "What you mean missing?"

"She not with other daughters…her bed not slept in."

Wong Foo quickly put on a robe and checked. He then returned to abuse his wife. "You chaperone – you to blame."

Mrs. Foo let fly with a torrent of expletives.

He retreated. "Maybe Wong Foo too hasty, I make enquiries ... I make you cup of tea also."

Although it was a day off for most residents in Gunnadoo, the Golden Dragon restaurant never closed. The daughters, albeit one missing, attended their duties.

* * *

Pastor O'Dae woke with Sister Beth tugging his shoulder, "Brother, wake up."

"No, not again, Beth, I need to rest." He received a thump in the ribs.

"Come on. You can do it."

* * *

Robinson woke with Constable Clarke tugging his arm, "Wake up."

"No, I need rest."

"On ya feet, mate. Where you're going you'll get plenty of time to rest."

* * *

Ruby lay comatose with her mouth wide open, snoring loudly. Houten lay beside her, his arms twitching as though accompanying his wife's solo performance. Overlooked in the kafuffle of the previous evening, Jock lay sleeping it off still slumped over the bass drum. Ying Lee, like many men whose women had attended the social, made them cups of tea. Bycroft made himself a cup of tea and began whistling the *Red Red Robin* again, satisfied with his own previous night's performance. The telephone rang.

"John Bycroft … Sgt. Doyle? Business hours may be nine to five but today is a public holiday…uh ha, yes. Just hold on a moment." He casually whacked the bakelite mouthpiece with the receiver. "Sorry about that, go on…in a ditch you say, I'll be buggered." He opened and closed his right hand, observing his knuckles. "Was he mugged?" Bycroft listened unsympathetically, gnawing upon a cuticle. "A skyrocket in the eye…my knees are red raw…I reckon *I* should sue Wong Foo…What about his daughter?" Bycroft paid closer attention. "Keep me informed … Robinson? Naw keep him locked up for

475

the rest of the day." He thumped down the receiver and hung up. "Sorry."

At ten o'clock when The Arms opened, Bycroft received a call from the pub. "Stop your complaining, McSloy, that's all you ever do. Yes, Jock can chalk up his breakfast but you get the money from Ruby Houten when he *is* paid or it comes out of your pay-packet, Sunshine." He had no sooner put the receiver down than he was picking it up again and shouting into it. "McSloy. Sorry Sergeant, I've got a bad line here," he whacked the phone again, "Sergeant?" he waited for a reply. "That's better, I can hear you now. Uh ha, yes…it's beginning to sound a little more serious. Pacify the Crown and I'll be down in ten minutes."

* * *

"The Advocate, Meg Radcliff speaking. Ah, my favourite dancing partner, don't tell me, you wish to place an ad for dancing…well excuse me. Who got out of the wrong side of the bed this morning…Clarrie's not here, I can get him if it's important – it *is* a public holiday for some, hang on." Meg wandered to the rear door and shouted, "Clarrie, telephone."

"Bloody marvellous," Clarrie mumbled, "if it's not the flies, it's the telephone…a bloke can't get five minutes to himself. Who is it?" he shouted.

"Bycroft."

"Tell him it's a public holiday."

"I already have. He's got something up his nose."

476

"So have I, but you don't hear me complaining. Hang on."

The Advocate was for reading…and swatting flies.

"Come on, big fella, give it your best shot." Clarrie's eyes followed the monster as it ducked and weaved in and out of range, its loud drone taunting his raised arm. "Come on, come on," he whispered, "stop flapping them propellers and land." The buzzing stopped.

"Cla – rrie."

Bzzz – bzzz – bzzz.

"Damn," he threw the rolled up paper at his antagonist. "Hang on."

Meg sat at the kitchen table amused by the thought of Bycroft sitting at the end of the telephone line stewing. She watched Clarrie amble in to the kitchen. He leant on the back of a chair pondering and then confided to her, "I swear it's the same fly, Meg."

She gestured to the telephone.

"Clarrie Radcliff." His persona altered as he listened. "How long has Lotus-Flower been missing?" The words startled Meg. "That long…" His reflex action to look immediately at Meg struck fear in her. "I'll meet you there." He hung up.

"Don't say it's a coincidence," she warned him.

"I wasn't going to. What I was going to say is this – the court found Tom not guilty. You have to have faith in your brother." He put his arms around Meg.

"I do but …"

"But what?"

"No matter how much I try, how much I turn myself inside out to get rid of that tiny piece of remaining doubt, I can't." She pulled from his arms. "Does that make me a bad sister, am I a bad sister? I can't get rid of it."

"Other than Wong Foo's daughter staying out all night and disobeying his rules, nothing has happened. Christ. She must be all of twenty-five. The men are mounting a search of the bush." Meg gasped. "It's a wild goose chase," he assured her, "but I should put in an appearance."

"What will you say to the Sergeant?"

"I'll tell it like it is; no more and no less."

Word of the disappearance soon spread courtesy of Betty at the telephone exchange. Along with the Advocate, the telephonist was the prime source of the region's bush telegraph.

Clarrie watched Meg as she scurried about picking up dirty clothes from the children's room. She folded each article neatly before placing it in the washing basket.

"If I hear anything I'll give you a call," he told her. "I can be reached at the police station if you need to get hold of me." There was no answer. "Meg...did you hear me?"

She held up a sock with a hole in it. "I must remember to get some more darn from Ruby."

"Meg."

"What?" she snapped.

"Today's a holiday...take a break."

"Tell that to the housework." She rolled up two odd socks together. "There's a million things need doing."

As Clarrie walked to the police station, he mulled over the vexing murder trial two years previously. The unsolved case known as 'The Portrait Girl' – so called because of the positioning of the deceased girl's body – led police to believe the murderer was a photographer. The prosecution had put forth evidence of an association between the girl and Tom.

"Hey Clarrie," called Bycroft, "wait up." He limped across Main Street.

"What's wrong with you?"

"Bloody fireworks, I'll have Wong Foo's hide. Did you hear about Robinson?" Bycroft didn't wait for an answer. "He got hit in the eye with a skyrocket. How 'bout that."

"And now you're both going to sue Wong Foo, are you?"

"Slow down and no, I'm not going to sue him…yet…unless I've sustained permanent injury," he gave Clarrie a wink, "then he'll be hearing from my lawyers."

A crowd, mainly Chinese, had gathered at the front of the police station.

"Make way, coming through," Bycroft announced.

The late arrivals joined Wong Foo, Ying Lee and four bleary-eyed constables as the sergeant gave directives.

"Now take a look at this photograph," he gestured to Wong Foo to give him the family portrait, "this is the girl in question." He fingered the wrong face.

"That not Lotus-Flower, that Rose-Petal," Wong Foo protested, "that Lotus-Flower." He pointed to another girl in a sea of smiling daughters posing for the camera.

"How old is that photograph?" Clarrie enquired.

"Alas, I much younger five years ago," Wong Foo confessed.

"Cor. All Chinks look the same to me," Clarke announced, "here Bluey, you have a look."

"Naw, I can't tell 'em apart either."

The other constables agreed; Blake even said he had difficulty understanding them.

Doyle reprimanded Blake, "Pay attention, it's simple. Ya know the area I want covered. Keep ya eyes open and call her name." Blake looked baffled. "Lois-flower," he reiterated. "Right, you blokes ... any questions?"

Doyle's ineptness challenged Clarrie's faith in him. "What's she wearing?" he asked.

"I dunno…Wong Foo?"

"Lotus-Flower wear blue cheongsam with white dragon – blue slippers."

"Any more questions…anybody?" Doyle looked around.

Clarrie casually addressed the constables directly. "Keep an eye out for my brother-in-law, Tom. He's off somewhere with his camera – the silly bugger's probably fallen down a mineshaft somewhere." Doyle's lack of judgement and empathy became apparent.

"Well, we haven't got all day…let's find a body or a suspect," he ordered. "Hop to it."

Wong Foo and Ying Lee left amidst a torrent of chatter. The constables did likewise, grumbling at having to work on a public holiday. Robinson's voice erupted from the lockup at the rear of the station and Doyle walked to the open window. "Shut up out there or you'll go without lunch too." He turned to Bycroft. "What about Robinson?"

Bycroft cunningly threw him a curve ball. "Naw, Robinson hasn't got a mean bone in his body." He rose and joined the perplexed sergeant at the window looking in the direction of the lockup. "Besides, you said he got hit in the eye with a skyrocket and doesn't remember anything after that."

Doyle rubbed his chin. "That's what he reckons." He crossed his arms considering Bycroft's allegation.

Bycroft mirrored the suggestive action. "Yes, I now see what you're inferring…"

"The first rule of policing, Mr. Bycroft – everybody is a suspect."

"Good work, Sgt. Doyle," Bycroft slapped him on the shoulder. "When the suspect gets hungry enough he'll soon talk."

"You've read my mind, Mr. Bycroft."

Having witnessed Bycroft's manipulation of the naive sergeant and weighed up the situation, Clarrie was apprehensive about revealing the facts of the murder trial and Tom's alleged involvement. "I'll be on my way, gentlemen, there's nothing more that can be done. Please let me know the minute you hear any word."

"We'll find your brother-in-law," Doyle assured him.

"All in capable hands," added Bycroft. "Tell Marge not to worry."

Clarrie returned to the Advocate with Bycroft's words of assurance to Meg ringing in his ears. He entered through the rear yard. Bed sheets billowed in the warm wind; he stopped and hung the remaining washing from the clothesbasket. A bucket and mop at the rear door confirmed what he knew he was about to enter – the manic psychosis displayed by Meg during Tom's trial had resurfaced.

* * *

Houten woke with Ruby tugging his twitching arm, "Make us a cuppa, Luv," she croaked, "my throat is as dry as the Nullarbor."

He lay collecting his thoughts and the strength to rise. "I reckon we would have given Paul Whiteman and his orchestra a run for his money last night," he declared. He threw his legs over the side of the bed and sat. "Give me a hand." Ruby put a foot in his back and pushed. He stood up, swaying. "Blimey, the ol' head's a bit thick this morning."

He shredded a page from the Advocate and used it to restart the stove fire. The remaining pages he tucked under his arm and strolled up the back yard – his daily ritual. All newspapers went down the deep hole, except for the form guide; once read he stashed that away for future reference. The ten-minute ritual included lighting the stove and boiling the kettle. Under the afternoon sun, the thunderbox was like a sweatbox and he returned to the kitchen while the kettle boiled. He replaced the receiver on the telephone, having removed it the prior evening, and no sooner had he done so than it began ringing. It did little for his hangover.

"Houten's Hardware, hello Meg…no worries, four cakes of Velvet soap and some darning thread, come around to the back door. Are you still there? Well goodbye to you too."

"Would you like some damper?" Abe called to Ruby, placing it in the oven. He then answered another telephone call. "Houten's Hardware…hello Clarrie…Meg just called, what did she forget?" He listened as the kettle began spitting onto the stovetop. "Yep, yep, I understand. Cancel the poker game this evening and have the soap ready for Meg, bye." He hesitated as whether to hang up or not. *Naw, it's a public holiday,* he thought and hung up the receiver.

He stood in disbelief watching the kettle spitting as the annoying bell started again.

"Houten's Hardware … who? … McSloy. Yeah, yeah…all right, come around to the back door."

Three consecutive calls and Ruby was suspicious; she stood at the kitchen door. "What's going on … you're not running another book, are you?"

"No, honest I'm not. That was …"

Bang. Bang. Bang. The flywire screen received a hammering.

"Alrighty mister," she put her hands on her hips, "who's that then?"

"Blimey, McSloy was quick," he answered.

"Clarrie." Meg's penetrating shriek surprised them both.

483

The search continued throughout the region until evening. Clarke limped into the compound leading a lame horse. Doyle met him at the stable.

"What happened?" he enquired.

"A rabbit hole, Sarge. Nugget didn't see it." Clarke lifted the horse's foreleg and rubbed its fetlock. "Just bruised I think."

"And you?"

"Blisters."

"Did ya find anything?"

"A still up the back of the Chin gardens and a new two-up site," he reported.

"How 'bout the others," Clarke asked, "did they find anything?"

"Bluey got bitten by a Redbelly, he'll survive. Blake and Jones aren't back yet."

"Hey. Walloper," Robinson yelled, "I'm starving in here. How 'bout some tucker."

"Not until ya do some talk'n," Doyle shouted.

"I'm ready…it was me, I fess up."

"There ya are, Clarke, that's how policing work's done." Doyle ambled over to the lockup and peered through the small window. "Now wouldn't it have been a lot easier if you'd come clean this morning…I'm listening, Mr. Robinson."

"I did it but the Irish lads put me up to it."

The sergeant listened until he'd heard enough. "Are ya thirsty too?" he asked mockingly.

"You'd better believe it."

"We'll soon fix ya up." Doyle strode back to the stable. "All right, Clarke." He slapped Nugget's neck. "Water him down…and throw a bucket over Robinson too."

* * *

Clarrie stood at the twins' bedroom door listening to the drawn-out procedure.

"… and God bless Uncle Tom," Albert concluded.

Michael added, "And if he's fallen down a mineshaft …"

"I'm sure he hasn't," Clarrie interrupted, "come on, into bed."

"Where is he then?"

"Michael, your uncle knows many people … he's probably staying out at a property. You know what he's like when taking photographs in the bush …"

"He wouldn't know what time of the day it was," Albert suggested.

"Don't repeat what your elders say, young man." Clarrie snuffed out the lamp. "Good night, kids."

"When's Uncle Tom coming home?" Michael asked.

"I'm not sure."

It had been a long day for Clarrie. He'd followed Meg all day, finishing the jobs she started but didn't complete. She now balanced at the top of a stepladder with the curtains removed for washing.

"Clarrie, can you give me a hand with this?" she called.

"Coming…" He stepped over a rolled up hallway runner and called, "Do want a cuppa?" There was no reply. "Do you…"

"No I don't. – I want a hand."

Under the pale glow of a new moon, Clarrie hung out the washed curtains. He contemplated the repercussions of withholding information from Doyle. Lotus-Flower's disappearance now played on his mind and Meg's erratic behaviour was exhausting.

"Clarrie."

Meg was scrubbing the parlour floorboards, around her the furniture stacked precariously.

"No more Meg, I'm buggered; I've been going all day." His white singlet soaked in sweat matched the colour of his legs; he rarely wore shorts. "Let's get some sleep."

"Fine." she slammed the scrubbing brush into the bucket. "Live in a pigsty. I'll clean Tom's room."

Clarrie lay upon the bed listening to the banging and thumping from down the end of the hallway.

* * *

January's daytime heat was stifling. The nights brought relief yet Catherine dressed as though it was winter. She stood on the boudoir balcony staring at the crescent moon pitching in its perimeter haze. Bycroft's last visit, a month previously, had been courteous and brief; she was hoping for more of the same.

"Good evening, Catherine." His voice took her by surprise. "May I come up?"

He stood at the bottom of the stairs. A bunch of freshly picked wildflowers in his hand replaced the usual cigar.

"Oui," she stated without expression.

Bycroft struggled up the stairs; his bruised knees were painful but he didn't show it. "I have good news…by the way, happy new year for last night." He handed her the offering. "These are for you, I picked them myself."

"Merci." She immediately threw the flowers over the railing. "I have hay-fever."

His knees were throbbing. "May I sit down?"

"If you wish."

The chill in her voice was contradictory. Catherine limped behind Bycroft. Her cut feet were throbbing; she watched his every move. Instead of flopping into the easychair, he sat down carefully.

"The cash is available, a couple of weeks earlier than what I thought it would be." Her silence was unnerving. "That's a bit of good fortune, eh?"

"Oui." She sat at the Davenport, her anxiety lessening but not showing it.

"There's a pile of documentation to sign, legalities, and all those sorts of things." He pulled at his stiff collar, "All is going as planned, there's no problem."

"I hope not."

"There is one little thing though." He let go of the collar. "To pay you out, I require a personal loan; to get that we'll need to present a united front."

"I do not understand. Where is the personal loan coming from?"

He sat upright at her interest. "Business acquaintances in Sydney, I'm not going through a bank, I can get a better deal in the private sector."

"It is not illegal?"

"The organisation is most respectable…their philanthropic ventures are …"

"Philan what?" she cunningly asked.

"They give money to worthy causes."

"With your goldmine and your hotels, would they think you a worthy cause?"

"No, you don't understand, I'm joining the club." He moved to the edge of the easychair. Let me explain…" He revealed little more than the religious aspect of Admiral O'Keefe and the tottering Mr. Tanner, not the real agenda, that of hoodwinking the Admiral into believing he was married. "…and the old gentleman kept falling asleep between courses, God bless him," Bycroft concluded.

"Is not Gunnadoo a long way for old men to travel?"

"Ah…no, they aren't doing the travelling; the legalities have to be done in Sydney."

"What are you saying?"

I'm going to Sydney in a couple of weeks," he tugged at his collar again and paused. "Is it me or is it getting hot in here?" No answer was forthcoming and he continued nervously. "At my cost, of course, if you'd like to accompany me, we can conclude all the legalities required at the same time."

Catherine showed no signs of gratitude despite the offer being made at a favourable time; she had an appointment for a check-up in Sydney. "What is it that I must sign in Sydney that I cannot sign here?"

"Well … nothing. It would be time saving though. You just have to look your beautiful self and make me look half as good."

She observed her gaunt features in the dresser mirror and thought of Lucy.

"In two weeks," she mused, and then questioned, "and I will have my own room, oui?"

"Of course," Bycroft crossed his heart with his forefinger, "I promise."

"How do I know you can be trusted?"

"I may have," he paused, placing both hands on his knees and bowing his head, "no, *I have* been unjust in the past but that's what it is – the past." He looked her in the eye, "I'm not the man you knew, I've changed." He automatically reached for a cigar in his pocket but stopped himself. "I realise how distasteful this charade is for you …"

"It is pretend only, I can manage."

"Can you manage that of a man and his wife," he asked, "joyous with the expectation of their first child?" Catherine pondered his question. He then told her. "Actually, the thought of becoming a daddy *is* quite appealing to me." A cold shiver shot up his spine as though somebody was walking over his grave.

Catherine was now confused. "But the thought of legitimising your child is not?" she snapped.

"I was under the distinct impression you wanted as little as possible to do with me."

"I was under the distinct impression you thought of me as nothing more than your whore."

The undeniable swing in Catherine's attitude was in Bycroft's favour and he now felt comfortable for the first time, although he still tugged at his collar.

"Under different circumstances

"I do not understand," she interrupted, "what is it you are saying?"

"Another time, another place, I would consider making an honest woman of you," he looked away melodramatically. "There, I said it."

"You would?"

Bycroft moved toward Catherine; she flinched and he immediately sat back in the chair.

"It's not possible at present, I'd be crucified and we'd lose everything. What kind of a father would I be…what kind of a legacy would the child have?"

"My ears cannot believe what they are hearing." The extra clothing that Catherine had worn as protection was beginning to take its toll. She too felt like tugging at her high collar but resisted.

"I'm saying that for the time being our relationship must be kept quiet but who knows what the future holds. We were not just lovers, Catherine, you and I have been through a lot together. We each possess certain talents that the other doesn't; that's what makes this partnership work. We have to look after each other." He remembered pacifying Wally with similar words. "There are plenty of bastards out there who would soon bring all we've worked for down on our heads if we let them." Bycroft stood up and moved to the door. "If you don't wish to leave Gunnadoo, don't. I'll still buy you out and you'll have your financial independence…if that's what you want."

"Sacré bleu, so much to think about, my head is swimming. Please go. Bon soir."

Upon his exit, Catherine immediately began peeling off layers of clothing.

The next morning, while cutting Catherine's hair, Mrs. Chang noted the change in her attitude.

"Merci, I do not know what I would do without you. You have many talents." Catherine's cropped hair resembled the stylish flapper look; the *Womans Weekly* had provided the inspiration.

"And you have a lovely head of hair again," Mrs. Chang replied, removing the wrap from around Catherine's shoulders.

"This flapper style is all the rage, oui?"

"I don't know what has changed but I'm glad that it has," confided Mrs. Chang. "Is there anything you wish to tell me?"

Catherine stopped fussing with her hair and looked at Mrs. Chang's reflection in the mirror. "Do you believe that people can change for the better?"

"I would like to think so."

"I would like to think so too."

Mrs. Chang pursued Catherine's question no further but felt the time right to inform her of the missing Lotus-Flower.

"Sacré bleu. Why was I not informed, it is *me* who runs this establishment – you should have told me – I must see him straight away."

"I shall draw your bath."

"There is no time." Catherine didn't listen to Mrs Chang's explanation as she rummaged through her shoe closet to get her Coolie disguise, which she could slip on in no time. The soiled pyjamas that had never been washed stank to high heaven. "What will Wong Foo think of me?"

Catherine's empathy for the father took priority. The leather binding of her sandals cut into her feet again causing her agony but she didn't stop to take them off. Her appearance was not surprising to Wong Foo; he was well aware of her previous erratic behaviour and passed it off as another episode.

"Monsieur Foo, forgive me … I have just heard."

"Yes, very distressing." Wong Foo sat behind the abacus idly pushing the beads back and forth. "Lotus-Flower disgrace … brings much shame on honourable Wong Foo."

"You hypocrite." Catherine flicked the beads solidly. "It is me who you are talking to."

Her outburst didn't surprise him. "I do not understand my daughter, my Lotus-Flower." He appealed to Catherine, "Why has she done this?"

"Your daughter, your Lotus-Flower – is a woman. You treat her like a girl, no…a servant to wait on you hand and foot."

"This I find hard to believe," he clapped his hands, "Wong Foo always most considerate." Rose-Petal appeared in lieu of Lotus-Flower with the tea tray. He motioned Catherine to the table. "Please, you join me." Catherine removed her sandals as he continued with his theory. "Australian ways corrupt daughters…firm hand required."

"A firm hand yes but not a bamboo switch."

Wong Foo observed Rose-Petal's procrastination. He waved the fingernail at her and waited in silence until she poured the tea and left.

"Your observation most cutting, Miss Dunn."
He blew on the rising steam.

"Your treatment of women is shameful,
Monsieur Foo. If you do not change your ways all
your daughters will run away."

He sipped the brew and smiled, "Mrs. Foo very
happy with…"

She interrupted him, "Mrs. Foo will not give
you grandchildren."

"This is so." He contemplated the assertion and
then stated, "But what if Wong Foo not want miner
for son in-law?"

"You elitist – Wally was a miner," she
reminded him.

"Forgive me…point taken."

"And how do you know he is a miner? As a
matter of fact Monsieur Foo – he may not even be
Chinese."

The Chinaman's eyes bulged behind his thick
spectacles. He choked on his tea and clasped his
chest, coughing. Catherine immediately dismissed the
thought along with the astonished look on her own
face.

"Why do you say that, Miss Dunn? Is it true
what they say … are you clairvoyant?"

Neither confirming nor denying, Catherine blew
over the top of her tea to cool it.

"Mr. Foo." There was urgency in Meg's call on
entering the shop.

Catherine recognised the voice. She quickly
replaced the coolie hat, lowered her head and slid
both hands into her sleeves out of sight. Wong Foo

observed the covert action and then Meg's unkempt appearance. Her puffy face implied a sleepless night.

"Good morning, Mrs. Radcliff," he greeted her. "How may I be of service?"

"No, please don't get up. I won't take up much of your time."

Catherine sat with her back to Meg. She could feel the woman hovering over her until Meg caught a whiff of the pyjamas. She then moved opposite Catherine.

"Do you recognise this woman?" Meg asked Wong Foo.

She handed him a folder. From it fell two large photographs, one landing in front of him and the other, like a kite out of control, doing a loop, landing on the table and sliding to a stop in front of Catherine. A woman with her face painted white that of a Geisha lay naked in front of a mirror. Meg leant across the table and slipped the photograph to Wong Foo. He placed both before him and leered under the pretence of fulfilling the request.

"I cannot help you, Mrs. Radcliff." She went to pick up the photographs but he stopped her with the fingernail gesture. "Please leave with me, I will make enquiries and inform you."

"I would appreciate it if you could…soon as possible." Meg left as she had entered – agitated.

Catherine lifted her head and sipped on her cup of tea again. "Tell me, Wong Foo," she observed his studying of the Geisha, "what do you see?"

He twirled his wispy moustache pondering. This photograph I see female silhouette, most pleasant to look at.

494

"And the other?"

"I see Geisha, Japanese lady most pleasant to be with," he smiled. Then he quickly added, "More so than Japanese man," and scowled.

"You are a chauvinist."

"I am a man," he parried and slurped his tea uncharacteristically loud.

"You are a chauvinistic blind man."

He lifted his heavy lenses and squinted mockingly at her.

"Then tell me what you don't see?" she jousted.

"I prefer to tell you what I *do* see." Catherine let Wong Foo's lusting wax lyrical with his lewd remarks until he tired of his own game. "Tell me, what is it then that you see in photograph, Miss Dunn?"

"It is what I don't see," she paused, rubbing her temples, "that is most revealing."

"I am curious." Wong Foo picked up the ten by eight glossy, adjusted his spectacles and scrutinized it until finally giving up and looking at Catherine in bemusement.

"You are a chauvinistic blind man…"

"That you already tell me."

"You are a bigot too."

"As are many in Gunnadoo."

"You are also a father in denial. Take a good look…do you not recognise your own daughter?"

He turned pale, quickly placed the photographs in the folder and shut the cover. "Mr Tom Lennard." he announced loudly.

Not only did Catherine recognise the photographer's handiwork and his model but also where Tom had taken the shot. Easily overlooked, the insignificant background reflection behind Lotus-Flower's head wasn't what it appeared to be: a gilded hairclip. It was a portion of the dragon bed ornate bedstead. She didn't point this out to Wong Foo.

"I know where Lotus-Flower can be found."

"It is true – you do possess psychic power." Catherine sipped her tea, saying nothing. "Where is daughter?" Wong Foo demanded, "I shoot Mr Tom Lennard – he bring much shame on Wong Foo."

"You are a hypocrite, not a murderer."

"I am outraged father…"

"…who may have recognised his own daughter but for his lustful notions. Besides, did you not say you were opposed to a miner for a son in-law?" Catherine had him in checkmate. "Perhaps the knowledge of your perceived shame can be limited? All is not lost but will be if you do not listen to me."

Wong Foo bowed his head and conceded. "Your wisdom is…"

She interrupted shrewdly, "It has nothing to do with psychic powers."

* * *

Catherine was right about many things, one being Chinatown; the new subdivision was sterile. The labyrinth of alleyways that hadn't burnt down in what was now known as 'old Chinatown' hummed with activity. With the potato sack over her shoulder, she felt her spirits lift as she joined the ant-like procession and entered the hustle and bustle. She accessed Wong Foo's love nest through the rear, making lots of noise as she did. There was no sign of Lotus-Flower or Tom. All was how she remembered. Catherine lit the potbelly and prepared the bean stew and dumplings from the contents of the potato sack. She set the table for two and sat pondering the ramifications of Tom and Lotus-Flower's relationship.

At the cemetery, she'd experienced first hand the prejudice the Chinese had to deal with. Lotus-Flower had shown Catherine the most kindness out of all of Wong Foo's daughters; she had waited on Wally and her when they had resided at the shack.

26 – A United Front

A wall of adversity when toppled
...lays a solid foundation.

Bycroft sat looking out the window, telephone in one hand and a cigar in the other. "I'll be in Sydney in a week or so – we can talk about it then," he told Lockett. "Billings," he shouted, "tell the pastor to quieten it down; I can't hear a bloody thing." The counselling service Bycroft had originally suggested had blown out to bible classes and songs of praise.

Billings put down his pen, rose from his desk and apprehensively moved to the door. "What will I say?"

"You tell him it's a residential lease for starters, Sunshine...on ya bike." He watched Billings pass the window. "Are you still there? Naw, you never know who's listening...do you Betty?" The telephonist disconnected her headphone jack from the line. "The walls have ears, my friend. Two weeks...I look forward to seeing you. Good bye."

The telephone rang as soon as he had hung up.

"Bycroft Holdings, John Bycroft." He listened, displeasure producing furrows in his brow. "Bastock offered him a job, are you sure? Did you actually hear it being discussed?" He turned to look out the

498

window again. " Ah, yes, I see him coming. That's one I owe you." He hung up and pretended to be deep in concentration when McSloy entered. "Paul." I was just thinking about you, come in and sit down. Let's have a drink and discuss some of them rewards I've talked about, it's about time you saw a few."

* * *

Clarrie fumbled with Mrs. Bond's change after the altercation.

"Sorry about that."

Her right boot thumped on the bare floorboards as she left, sending shivers up his spine. Meg was still in a cleaning frenzy and he'd put up with plenty of noise over the past forty-eight hours.

Houten held the newspaper as if he was holding his piano accordion. He peered over the top of it. "That's the first time I've ever seen you short change anybody."

"It's been a rough couple of days." He gestured to the muffled bangs and thumps emanating from the rear residence. "I've got housewife knees, and it feels like I haven't slept in days." The thought of the sergeant charging him for withholding vital information had kept him awake, not Meg.

"Mr. Radcliff, Mr. Houten," Doyle greeted them.

Houten slipped his greeting in first, "Sgt. Doyle."

Clarrie fumed; he could feel Houten instigating the Tiv' routine and refused to be caught up in it. "Good morning and what a fine morning it is," he proclaimed uncharacteristically. Upon saying it and deeming the words to be those of a person trying to hide something, he became more nervous than what he had been originally. The sergeant's words 'find a suspect' echoed in his head. "What can I do for you?" he asked apprehensively.

"Some information, if you please." Doyle leant on the counter.

Clarrie felt his legs wobbling, "Information?" he asked.

"That's right, chum," Houten chipped in from behind the newspaper, "information. I 'eard 'im clear as day meself, I did. Right impressed too, I was." The Cockney accent impressed nobody.

"I'd like you to take a look at this." Doyle reached into his inside jacket pocket.

Clarrie imagined him pulling out a *Herald* clipping from the murder trial. A wave of remorse swept over him; he would have made a confession but his mouth had dried up and he was unable to speak.

"This new-fangled fountain pen won't work – it's bloody useless."

Clarrie's legs buckled as he listened to Houten prattle on. "I said to missus, I did, I did, giv'us a kiss."

Clarrie regained his composure to discover the problem with the fountain pen. "It won't work without ink...here you go. This is a fine ink for a fine fountain pen." The demonstration of how to fill the pen highlighted Clarrie's nervous condition; his hands trembled. "That'll be tuppence, thanks."

"Tuppence, I said to missus … tuppence for a kiss."

Clarrie took the coin from Doyle and put his finger to his temple, gesturing Houten's craziness.

"By the way," Doyle looked him straight in the eye, "some more details have come to light that are of interest." Clarrie's legs went to jelly again.

Houten shouted, "Everybody sing – 'By the light of the …'"

"Shut up. You idiot," Clarrie screamed, taking Doyle, Houten and himself by surprise. Houten peered over the top of the newspaper. "…'ear. 'ear. What's going on then?"

The performance was too much for the sergeant and he lost his train of thought. "I'll be on me way, gentlemen. Mr. Radcliff, Mr. Houten." Doyle tipped the rim of his cap and spun on his heel.

Clarrie threatened Houten with his fist as Doyle left; the sergeant caught the hostile gesture. He peered long and hard at Clarrie and moved to the counter.

"Is there is anything you've forgotten, Mr. Radcliff?"

Clarrie's heart rose in his throat.

"Me change, if ya don't mind." Doyle held out his hand for the penny.

"Sorry about that, Sgt. Doyle."

Houten sprang at the opportunity, "Sgt. Doyle."

The sergeant came in on cue. "Mr. Houten, Mr. Radcliff." He left, flipping the coin in his hand.

"So help me I'm gonna…"

"Clarrie." Meg called.

* * *

Catherine watched in amazement as the tapestry began moving. From a small room behind it Lotus-Flower emerged, followed by Tom. He was wearing the same robe as Wally had.

"Sacré bleu. I did not know of a secret room." Catherine peered into the entrance of the cubbyhole.

"My father has many secrets."

"You take after your father; apparently you have secrets too."

"And it appears so do you." Tom put his arm around Lotus-Flower. "I have just been informed about you and Wally – he was a good man."

Catherine nodded agreement and motioned them to the table. "Are you, Mr. Lennard?"

Lotus-Flower defended him. "My Tom good man, he like your Mr. Wally."

Catherine recognised the passionate look Lotus-Flower gave Tom. She found herself in a déjà vu situation but with the shoe on the other foot; it was she who now performed the domestic duties. "The sergeant and his men are searching for you," she told Lotus-Flower. "Tom, there are many people worried at Lotus-Flower's disappearance; you can't hide out here any longer."

"How did you know we were here?" he asked.

"As always, your photographs revealed a subject and content," she informed him, while stirring the stew. She lamented over the debacle of the burnt offering she had served to Wally. "Are you hungry?"

"For a hot meal, you betcha I am," Tom assured her, "we didn't dare light the stove."

"And how long were you planning to survive on love alone?"

"Things just got out of hand."

Lotus-Flower blushed. No explanations were required as three heads turned simultaneously to look at the dragon bed.

"Your sister discovered the photographs and asked who the woman was."

"Did Meg show them to you?"

"No, she showed them to Wong Foo. I was there when she did."

The woman's face turned pale. "Lotus-Flower shame father." she gasped, and then began sobbing.

"Well that's it then, the cat's out of the bag."

"Do not worry, he did not recognise the Geisha in your artwork," Catherine lied. She saw the angst remaining on Tom's face. "There is more, oui?"

Tom reached across the table, taking Lotus-Flower's hand. "We're pregnant."

"*We* are pregnant?" Catherine paused to acknowledge Lotus-Flower. "Congratulations are in order then. Wong Foo will be a proud grandfather." She scraped the stew into large bowls.

"Father most angry."

"Your father is a proud man – and he will also be a proud grandfather." She passed them the food. "Bon appétit."

Tom devoured the beans hungrily. "He will have my guts for garters when he catches up with me."

"That you will have to negotiate yourself…follow my plan and the sergeant will call off the search. Nobody will know of your relationship until you choose to reveal it. If there is no shame brought to Wong Foo, his retribution will not be

503

required." She sipped her tea, "And you, Mr. Lennard, can resume your life without having to look over your shoulder."

"Why are you doing this?" Lotus-Flower enquired.

Catherine pondered, "I do not like fate playing cruel tricks."

Tom emptied his cup, studied the tealeaves and then slid the cup to Catherine. "What else can you see?"

* * *

Bycroft sat watching the folly unravelling at the front of the Advocate. Meg had appeared with a ladder and propped it up against the veranda. No sooner had she returned inside than Clarrie had emerged from the side laneway and removed the ladder. Meg reappeared with a bucket to find the ladder gone.

"Bycroft Holdings, John Bycroft speaking – yes Sergeant?" While listening, Bycroft returned to his viewing position. Meg and Clarrie were now having a tug-of-war with the ladder. "Well, I'll be buggered. Yes, that is good news." Bycroft tugged on his cigar, observing Meg's victory and Clarrie mounting the ladder with bucket in hand. "Tom Lennard? I don't know. I'll ask Clarrie – he's got his hands full at the moment." Clarrie had hung the bucket from the ladder and was swinging precariously from the guttering as the Advocate's sign received a scrubbing. "Yeah, you'd better let him out then. I don't know, you're the law; warn him to stop being a public nuisance or he'll get more of the same. He what? How many? That's one helluva confession list...naw, tear it up, Robinson's a liar too." In one movement, Bycroft swivelled around in the chair and slammed the phone down, catching Doyle again. "Sorry." he wailed, with a devious laugh. He looked to Billings. "I'll have to do something about this bad connection. I'm going out."

Bycroft strolled across High Street and stood at the bottom of the ladder looking up at Clarrie. "When you're finished there I've a few cleaning jobs that need doing."

"And pigs will fly too. I've got my hands full here, thank you very much."

"Yeah, I was just telling that to Doyle. He wants to know if Tom has turned up. Hey, watch out. If you're gonna fall off wait until I'm out the way," he stepped out of the fall zone, "I haven't made up my mind whether to sue Wong Foo yet and I don't..."

"...and you won't be suing me either." Clarrie regained his balance; his composure had disappeared the previous evening when darning socks to keep the peace. "I've got a missus on my back and I don't need you on my case. What do you want?" he snapped.

"Hey, just passing on a message from Doyle. He's thinking of sending out the constables to look for Tom." Clarrie's foot slipped on the rung as his knees buckled. He dropped the scrubbing brush and grabbed the ladder with both hands. "Is this part of the act?" Bycroft asked.

Clarrie could feel his world tumbling down around him, "Act?" he asked feebly.

"Yeah, Doyle reckons you and Houten are working on some kind of Tivoli act; if it's a balancing act, forget it – stick to your day job. By the way Lotus-Flower has turned up."

"Where? When?"

"She was at the whorehouse, the Madame's been ill and she was nursing her. There was some kind of communication breakdown – how 'bout that."

"How 'bout that." Clarrie repeated. "He *has* fallen down a shaft."

"You'll have to learn to project your voice – the cheap seats at the back won't hear you."

"What?"

"I'm not your manager. I've got better things to do than stand around coaching you," Bycroft jested.

"Clarrie." Meg's heavy footsteps approached.

"Bycroft looked at his watch, "Time I wasn't here." He spotted McSloy, "Paul, wait up."

"Clarrie…Lotus-Flower has been found alive."

"Bycroft just told me." He climbed down.

"That means…"

"They're going to put a search party together." He gave her a hug. "He'll be all right…"

"It's been two days?"

"He survived the Western Front, didn't he?"

Meg looked at the bucket and ladder, "Did you survive the…"

He put a finger to her lips. "Come on, it's over, let's concentrate on finding Tom." He removed the ladder.

"Hey Clarrie," Bycroft called from across the street.

"What?"

"You missed a spot."

"Don't give up ya day job," McSloy added.

* * *

That evening, news of Tom's rescue at the Yakka Dakka site soon spread courtesy of Betty at the telephone exchange. Ying Lee became a hero. The following day Catherine became the talk of the town as Ying Lee's acclamation of her psychic powers spread. Catherine had told him where to find the trapped photographer and the fake disappearance was accepted.

The following two weeks Catherine mixed with the others at the establishment during daylight hours and ate regular meals. Aware of her appearance again, she selected clothing to camouflage the small protrusion. Her gaunt, anaemic look was but gone and so too the rumours circulating amongst the girls of her opium addiction; however, the craving for the elixir remained.

Bycroft had reserved separate sleeping compartments on the train to Sydney as promised, although a door connected the adjoining hotel rooms at the Imperial. Catherine secured the key, locking it from her side. That evening they shared a meal in the hotel restaurant and each then retired to their own room. The following morning they breakfasted together and then surreptitiously went about their own business.

507

Catherine's Pitt Street check-up confirmed early May as the time of expectancy. She then strolled into Chinatown to visit Chow Lung. They conversed over tea while the elixir order was attended to.

"I was most saddened to hear of Chung Dow's death," Chow Lung commiserated.

"Oui, he is sadly missed; I am yet to replace him…it will be difficult."

"Would you consider employment of new gardener if I give family reference?"

"Merci, of course. I am most grateful that you found a position for Mademoiselle Lucile."

"Mademoiselle Lucile has many positions," he replied ambiguously. "She most popular lady at present, alas she is only employable for one season."

Catherine acknowledged his statement with a slight nod. "I hope to catch up with her before returning to Gunnadoo."

"I will have her informed you are in Sydney, she dances at the new Peacock Garden."

"A new restaurant, sacré bleu, she is doing well."

"Chinatown now becoming destination of bohemian Sydney," he declared, with an air of resolve in his voice, "much is changing."

"It is sad when authenticity is lost," Catherine empathised.

"I not worry about Chinatown authenticity…I worry about cat population; bohemian curiosity detrimental to nine lives," he divulged matter-of-factly while stroking Ming. The Siamese purred loudly.

"I guessed you were a cat lover." Catherine acknowledged another feline statue sitting pride of place on his desk. She leant forward to study the fine porcelain. "Is this a new acquisition for your collection?"

He removed the temptation from her reach. "I lover of this pussy-cat only," he informed Catherine. Ming received another tickle and then Chow Lung pushed the cat off the desk. "If cat population vanishes in Chinatown, rodents appear."

"Oui, the last thing you need is another plague."

"Or rat in recipe." Catherine clasped her chest and gasped. She received a wink from Chow Lung. "Peking duck at Peacock Gardens most unreliable, alas, fortune cookie not to be believed either," he chuckled. The turf war between two opposing families hadn't been foretold in the cookie; the Peacock Gardens had recently been rebuilt after fire had mysteriously destroyed it.

* * *

A prearranged lunch with Lockett was on the agenda for Bycroft. He first visited the gentlemen's outfitter to select a dinner suit for that evening.

"May I suggest a single-breasted jacket for a man of your stature, sir?" the tailor suggested having taken Bycroft's measurements.

"…and a cup of tea," Bycroft requested, "May I suggest you look after your customers and they'll look after you."

The unpleasable customer tried on every suit and tuxedo possible. He would select an outfit and then change his mind. The tailor ran back and forth, many times with the same suit for Bycroft to retry.

"I must compliment you on your choice, sir," the tailor advised him. "The cut of your jib is most becoming."

The words appealed to Bycroft, as did the outfit. He admired himself in the mirror. "I do believe I've lost weight." He was fishing for another compliment.

"I do believe you have, sir." The tape measure couldn't lie – the tailor could.

The brewery was in Ultimo, five minutes walk from Chinatown and the Peacock Gardens. In a private room, Lockett and Bycroft met for lunch to stitch up the final details of their new partnership; Lockett would provide financial backing to reopen Yakka Dakka. The bargain price investment would secure Lockett's vote for Bycroft when the board of directors met.

"You like house speciality," the waiter enquired as he cleared the table of plates and bowls.

"That wasn't duck," rebuked Bycroft, "it was too small."

The Chinaman's face turned pale. "What you saying?" he retorted.

Bycroft lifted a small bone from the plate and held it up, and then sucked on its remnants. "It should be called Peking Duckling." He flicked the bone into a bowl and licked his fingers.

"You correct." The man smiled dubiously. "Baby duck more tender. You now ready for fortune cookies?" he enquired. The men nodded and the waiter left.

"I believe Mr. Bastock's fortune is next on our agenda," Lockett suggested. He lit Bycroft's cigar and then his own.

"Mr. Kevin bloody Bastock won't know what hit him," laughed Bycroft, "his hotel launch is going to be a dry ol' turnout."

"I'll have a lackey in dispatch divert his shipment to…" Lockett paused to pick a piece of meat from between his teeth with the match, "…where's a good destination?"

Bycroft smiled. Many a time he'd used the same deceptive ploy. "Gundaroo – Gunnadoo; a simple mistake anyone could make."

"And get the sack for." Lockett chuckled.

"And get the sack for – that's brilliant."

"We don't want any loose ends to come undone, do we?" He flicked the match at the paper lantern overhead. "Of course you'll come to Bastock's rescue and make up his shortfall…so it won't be a dry turnout," Lockett advised Bycroft.

"And why would I want to do that?" Bycroft asked.

"The huge mark-up you can make for one thing, and most importantly, Cowper's will not lose a sale," Lockett replied. "Of course your Samaritan deed will not go unnoticed by the Admiral, I'll see to that."

"Not only are we gonna be good partners," said Bycroft, lifting his glass, "we're going to be fine shipmates – we thinks alike."

Glasses chinked as the men celebrated the alliance. Bycroft became absorbed in what his next move should be, having now secured Lockett as a partner. Lockett became absorbed in the silhouette performance projected onto a silk screen. The contortionist gradually discarded her costume, all but the dragon mask, and then the real show began. Bycroft lost concentration when she appeared from behind the screen and danced on their table delivering the fortune cookies in a most unusual way.

"Well go on…what does it say?" asked Lockett.

Bycroft crushed the shell in his hand and read the slither of paper aloud. "If monkey sees – monkey do." He screwed up the slither of paper. "What kind of fortune telling is that bullshit? What's yours say?"

Lockett made a display of eating the cookie and slither of paper without reading it. "I don't believe in mumbo-jumbo," he garbled with his mouth full.

That evening Judge O'Keefe's chauffeur escorted Catherine and Bycroft to the waiting motor vehicle and then on to the Admiral's private residence, The Keep, situated at Bellevue Hill. They were both impressed – Bycroft by its size and location and Catherine by the display of azaleas, wisterias and jacaranda, all within the confines of a manicured box hedge. Montrose showed them to a drawing room where they joined the five directors and their wives and one other couple, all in their finest regalia. Tanner's wife had long passed away and his private assistant, Nurse Shilling, now accompanied him everywhere.

No longer constricted or dictated to by early century fashion, Catherine had discarded corsets and layers of underwear. Her evening dress was straight and slender. The light chiffon enhanced her small belly. A simple string of long pearls fell from her graceful neck, directing attention to the small bump.

She looked stunning; her now glowing complexion and smile won Lockett over immediately. He felt her charisma and she commanded him with it.

"Thank you, Montrose," he said, stepping forward to greet them. "Ah, this must be Catherine. At last we meet."

"Enchantée," she replied, holding out her hand. Lockett bowed formally and kissed it.

He introduced her to Judge O'Keefe. After further protocols, the women surrounded Catherine for interrogation. Lockett then introduced Judge Paul Whittington, the other nominee for the vacant position on the board, and referred to him as the Commodore. The man was middle-aged and carried himself with an air of arrogance. Bycroft immediately took a dislike to him and his full head of hair, slicked down with Brilliantine.

Bryant introduced Bycroft to Larson, another company director. Small in stature, he could easily be identified as insignificant in Lockett's bigger picture. Bycroft looked long and hard at the man; his persona reminded him of Browning.

At the first opportune time, Bycroft pulled Lockett aside. "You didn't tell me Whittington was in the Boys' Club."

"We seafarers are aware of three bars – four if musically minded." He mimed playing a button accordion and then stopped. "Three bars," he held up three fingers. "One, sandbars, to be avoided at all times. Two, the bar you lean against and three, the bar you placate – lean with, if you catch my drift." He walked Bycroft out to the balcony. Simultaneously, both men leaned on the sandstone balustrade,

513

breathing in deeply. From their vantage point, they overlooked Rose Bay. In the distance, tiny lanterns hovered in the dark like fireflies as fishermen cast nets upon the water.

"Lovely, isn't it?" Lockett's smooth voice slipped through the salt breeze like a dolphin through water. "You're not a sailing man, are you John?" Bycroft wasn't allowed time to answer. "If you were, you'd know how important a lifeboat is – in business as on the sea." Looking straight ahead, he placed a hand inside his dinner jacket and stood in a Bonaparte pose. "Admiral O'Keefe is our lifeboat. Before he sails off into the hereafter to meet past colleagues from the Boys' Club, it would be prudent we get another lifeboat, don't you agree?"

Bycroft realised where the metaphor was going. "And Judge Paul Whittington owns one?"

"The Commodore is, let's say, in ship-shape condition." Lockett turned his gaze on Bycroft. "You keep an eye on Uncle Tanner; it's his berth you'll be getting," his gaze returned to the fishing fleet, "the Sway is another matter."

Bycroft hadn't forgotten about the Sway and he placed a hand over his eye. "Ah. Old Tanner's treasure…when do we be seeing that?"

"All will be revealed in good time, Mr. Bycroft. And now that you've met Mr. Larson, what do you think about him?"

Bycroft dropped his pirate stance and asked, "Is it a real moustache?"

Bryant stood in the doorway. "Is everything all right?"

Lockett's rigid pose vanished. "Ah. The Squatter. Join us on deck if you will, Mr. Bryant – yes, all is well indeed." The Bonaparte hand left the dinner jacket and Lockett cupped his mouth. "Prepare for sea." he shouted, and then turned to place a hand heavily on Bycroft's shoulder. "We should go sailing one day, John, you would enjoy that, wouldn't you? You'll receive a nickname once you come on board."

"After 'e walks the plank," Bryant added, his hand held over one eye.

"And I'z so looking forward to riding a goat," Bycroft countered. He missed the cronies and their sessions of tomfoolery and now joined in what he believed was horseplay, raising his glass to the Squatter and misinterpreting Lockett's sailing invitation. "Yo, ho, ho and a bottle of rum."

Montrose rang a tiny bell. An attendant stood either side of heavy cedar doors, the rustic hinges and adornments reminding Catherine of the Rookwood wrought iron. She automatically lifted her head to the drop arch and read, 'Ad majorem Dei gloriam'.

"To the greater glory of God," said Lockett, taking her arm. "May I?"

"Ladies and gentlemen," Montrose called with exaggerated British enunciation, "dinner is served."

The dining room ambience was that of a castle, including obligatory suits of armour with battleaxes ready and various heraldry hanging on walls. An armillary sphere representing an ancient universe took pride of place under the household banner. Every nook and cranny containing historical artefacts could be scrutinised; the electric chandelier overhead was brilliant. Somewhat taken aback by the atmosphere, Catherine was relieved to see a portrait of King George above the replica medieval fireplace. On pedestals either side of it, candelabras burned for show only. A long banquet table more suited to a sitting of the Knights Templar beckoned. The host sat at one end and his wife at the other; Mrs. O'Keefe commented how grand they all looked. To the right of O'Keefe sat Lockett and his wife Jean. The Commodore and Mrs. Whittington sat opposite them. Mrs. O'Keefe sat Catherine to her left – it being her good ear, she wanted to hear what she said when others asked questions of her. Bycroft took his place next to Catherine and observed the frail Tanner with Nurse Shilling sitting opposite. She appeared quite young for a position of such responsibility. Bryant and his wife sat with couples each side, and opposite them sat Larson and his wife.

O'Keefe tapped his empty glass and then bowed his head for the grace. "Benedicite omnia opera ... "

Servants appeared with the first course.

"Asparagus or...oyster soup," Montrose informed the guests with a drawl.

Whittington called to Bycroft. "Try the oyster soup, I collected them myself while sailing the Lady Olivia this morning."

Lockett jousted with him. "You said they'd be collected fresh this afternoon."

"The only oyster I saw this afternoon was in the Archbishop's Bloody Mary; he consumed it on the seventh before teeing off," Whittington responded with flair.

"Asparagus, it saved my life," Tanner shouted for Mrs. O'Keefe's benefit. Out of politeness, not because of his wit or humour, everyone gave him their attention while he told the tale. Tanner had made a fortune in the import business, asparagus being one source of his wealth. A shaky hand spilt more soup than his quivering lips received. Bycroft chuckled to himself when the bowl was finally taken from under the old gentleman's nose with very little consumed from it.

Montrose informed all, "Baked barramundi or roast lamb garnished with fresh vegetables."

"Try the lamb …"

Lockett interrupted Bryant. "You wouldn't know the difference between lamb and a mutton mallee root."

From an early age, Bryant had attended boarding schools and had never actually worked the land himself. His repartee of his father's dealing with lazy Aborigines on the family sheep station brought howls of laughter.

"How many head do you run now?" Bycroft enquired.

"Abos or cattle?" he enquired. Laughter rang out, then he answered, "None, I sold the property as soon as I inherited it. Let the missionaries deal with the lazy buggers."

O'Keefe agreed. "Missionaries, salt of the earth. Those black heathens need to be shown the Lord's path." Everyone displayed their solidarity with applause and Hallelujahs. Catherine felt uneasy but held her tongue.

"Speaking of heathens…" Whittington began tales of his adventures, from boarding school romps to expeditions in the Tropics. "Ah, New Guinea," he concluded, "deep, dark and impenetrable – I once landed a barramundi so large I'm led to believe it must have been a barramundi the Lord fed the masses with." The dinner guests supported Whittington's hypothesis by tapping their wine glasses lightly.

"Good show – landed the blighter." O'Keefe drained his glass, "Well done, Mr. Whittington, eh what."

The dining room staff began clearing the table for dessert. Bycroft observed Tanner sucking on a lamb's knuckle, and then conceal another meaty morsel in his Tuxedo pocket before having his mostly uneaten meal whisked away from in front of him. Nurse Shilling thoughtfully dabbed his gravy-sodden whiskers with the napkin that hung from his shirt collar.

When the flambé pudding arrived, Montrose lit it to whoops of delight from the men. The women likewise welcomed the chef when he unveiled his creation in a huge crystal bowl – layered on crushed ice were slices of tropical fruits covered in gelato and then layered again with freshly whipped cream. Strawberries adorned the top.

Antonio bowed humbly while reversing to the sanctum of his kitchen. "Grazie, grazie," he crooned.

Bycroft waited to see what anecdote the desserts would yield from Whittington. He didn't have to wait long.

"I was in the far north of Queensland, a botanical expedition. Sir David Kensington and I were collecting the seeds of rare tropical fruits. We had ventured to where no white man had when from out of nowhere we were attacked by the black heathens." The women gasped, Bycroft snickered and Catherine covertly kicked his leg. "The indigenous bearers deserted us, taking our supplies with them. We escaped, although Sir David received a spear wound to the, how shall we say, rear end."

The women fanned themselves, the men suggested what they'd have done if they'd been there. Whittington recaptured his moment. "There's only one thing more deadly than infection that I fear and that is…the bite of an Eastern Brown. Thankfully, it wasn't that." he chortled. "I've yet to meet a man who has survived one of those nasty buggers."

"What did you do?" Nurse Shilling enquired.

"I lanced the wound with a piece of shale I had sharpened, removed the spearhead and plugged the gaping wound with a large tropical seed, thus averting infection." She was impressed, as were the other listeners. He continued. "Seeds were collected on a return expedition; the samples were then cultivated." He speared a slice of fruit with a fork and held it up. "Ladies and gentlemen, I give you the Kensington Mango."

Rapturous applause followed. Whittington accepted the praise modestly. "Mr. Bycroft," he said pointedly, "you've not contributed to our repartee; surely you must have some small anecdote for our pleasure."

Bycroft felt all eyes upon him. "Ladies and gentlemen," he said quietly, "I have not been so fortunate to travel New Guinea nor have I fished for the great barramundi." He raised his head, "Lord knows how I pray for a fish that size to feed my flock; no, I'm a simple man, not an adventurer the likes of Mr. Whittington. My deeds pale into insignificance…"

"Come now, let's not be modest," said Whittington, leaning back in his chair, "there must be something?"

"Well, there is one thing." He paused.

"Speak up," cajoled the antagonist.

Bycroft's eyes continually moved around the table. "You are looking at a man who crossed paths with just such an evil serpent as described by our learned friend…yes, I faced Mr. Whittington's worst fear and…survived…I was bitten by an Eastern Brown." The women gasped, Whittington frowned and the men bade him continue.

As Bycroft told the tale, he played with two table napkins. "I was on a prospecting metallurgical expedition in the outback. We'd camped by a billabong. In the morning I was awoken by my colleague's screams. A snake seeking warmth had invaded his swag during the night; he couldn't move for fear of being bitten."

"What did you do?" enquired Nurse Shilling.

"I ever so carefully peeled back his swag…layer by layer, until the culprit was revealed." Bycroft took a drink, intensifying the suspense. "To my shock there wasn't one, but two coiled up, with their heads clearly visible." He leant back in his chair. All eyes were on him. "Unlike the King Cobra, an Eastern Brown can't be mesmerised, you only get one go at them. I assured my companion that should he be bitten, I would lance the wound and suck the poison from within him as Mr. Whittington did for his companion...only this was an Eastern Brown."

The tale clearly affected some women more so than others. Nurse Shilling got excited. Mrs. Bryant felt faint, Jean Lockett looked pale and Olivia Whittington continued eating unimpressed. Mrs. Larson, like a fish out of water, took the middle ground and looked to the other women for a guide as to how she should feel. Mrs. O'Keefe, like her husband, was off in her own world. Bycroft leant forward, his hands frozen above the rolled origami napkins lying curled on the table. "'On the count of three', I said to my comrade, 'Throw yourself as far as possible from where you're lying.' I counted, 'one, two', he yelled, 'three.'"

Bycroft's hands instantly flashed out, grasping the napkins by the neck and slamming them into each other, then tossing them. One napkin landed in front of the women at the opposite end of the table. Taken by surprise, Mrs. Bryant nearly fainted, Jean Lockett farted loudly and Olivia Whittington spilt dessert in her lap. Nurse Shilling had an orgasm and Montrose caught the second napkin as it flew past him. Like an experienced stockman, he twirled the napkin around his head once, and then brought it down like a whip. Crack. He hung the limp napkin over his forearm and then asked, "Baked or fried, Sir?"

"By Jove, good show all round," O'Keefe shouted, "You too Montrose. Well done."

"Bravo." Lockett shouted repeatedly while applauding loudly. The guests joined in his show of appreciation until Whittington's retort.

"You said you were bitten." Silence followed the accusation. "How could you have been if you dealt with them as your performance indicated?"

"Unfortunately, there was a third snake I'd not seen." Bycroft recommenced the tale to everyone's enjoyment and Whittington's resentment. "It lashed out, alas, while I had both my hands full – I took the bite for my mate."

Everyone asked the same question in unison. "Where?"

"The same place as Sir David received his spear wound."

"Are you saying your companion sucked the wound?" Nurse Shilling enquired.

"If only it had been that simple. No, my colleague had thrown himself with such force he'd rolled over the embankment and fallen heavily, breaking his leg; he was unconscious. I knew my wound required purging of the venom. If only the bite had been on an arm or a leg, I could have performed the necessary aid myself." Everyone contemplated the predicament and agreed on the untenable situation. Bycroft waited for Nurse Shilling's support.

"What did you do?" she enquired.

"Ah, what did I do? A leach saved my life."

Mrs. O'Keefe misheard. "Sow and ye shall reap, Praise the Lord for the humble leak." The women blindly followed suit.

"Asparagus saved mine," Tanner declared again.

"Not Leak. Leach," Bycroft stated, putting the derailed train back on the tracks. "In the wet undergrowth they reign supreme. I gathered up the blood suckers and placed them on the wound."

"Well done, eh what," O'Keefe was impressed, "that's taking the initiative."

"Yes, then I set and strapped my colleague's broken leg, built an a-frame stretcher from saplings and dragged him through the bush to safety."

Catherine was somewhat surprised at her response to the kudos Bycroft was receiving. She felt a confusing pride by being with him.

"And you have the evidence to verify your story?" requested Whittington.

Bycroft stood up. His hands moved to his waistline as though about to drop his trousers. The women gasped, Nurse Shilling had another orgasm and he had the last laugh on Whittington. He picked up a bowl of the trifle.

"Let me tell you, it was no trifling affair."

"No trifling affair." roared O'Keefe, "well said."

Bycroft sat graciously and received three cheers and applause. Never had his dessert tasted sweeter.

Montrose rang the tiny bell. "Coffee and tea is being served in the drawing-room."

Everyone complimented Mrs. O'Keefe on the fine meal. The dining staff once again whipped Tanner's desserts from under his shaky spoon. He consigned its contents to his pocket before Nurse Shilling took the spoon from him. She removed the napkin, wiped his whiskers and with the skill of a magician's sleight of hand replaced his dentures. Tanner patted his belly.

"I couldn't eat another thing," he picked at his teeth with a feeble finger, "that was a wonderful meal."

Montrose oversaw the serving of tea and pastries for the women, brandy and cigars for the men. Lockett pulled Bycroft aside. "Well?" he enquired.

"He can sure stuff the tucker away," Bycroft wisecracked. Both men chuckled deviously. "What's with Nurse Shilling?"

"She's employed by Cowper's Brewery to look after him. You could say...she's a part of the company's health benefits scheme." Bycroft was speechless at the contradictory statement. "I hope you don't mind but I've organised Tanner's chauffeur to drop you and Catherine off at your hotel. I thought you should see the bigger picture."

"What. There's more?"

"Oh, there's more all right," Lockett placed a hand over his eye, "If it be treasure ya eyes feast."

Bryant joined them. "Ah. 'ave ya told 'im 'bout the Sway then, 'ave ya?"

Three brandies and two pastries later, Bycroft heard Montrose's bell and his request for the guests to form a circle and join hands. The butler then placed a record on the gramophone, turned the handle and placed the needle in position. *Land of Hope and Glory* crackled through the speaker cone.

Bycroft called to Bryant who stood opposite him. "How are the bearers and joists?" He received a stern look.

O'Keefe began the final blessing.

524

"… and finally Lord, we thank you for the wonderful meal."

"Asparagus," mumbled Tanner.

"… and the new friendships formed this evening …."

Bycroft peeked around the circle at the guests standing with eyes closed, all except for Nurse Shilling – her attention was focused on him.

"Ad majorem Dei gloriam – Amen," O'Keefe concluded.

"Ad majorem Dei gloriam," chanted the gathering.

The fleet of gleaming motor vehicles lined the circular drive awaiting their passengers. Each guest was farewelled by the hosts like royalty farewelling heads of state. Nurse Shilling and Tanner sat with their backs to the chauffeur, Catherine and Bycroft opposite. The claxon horn bellowed as they departed The Keep.

"Would you prefer to change seats?" Bycroft asked politely.

"No, Mr. Tanner becomes ill if he sees where he is going," she replied. "Me, I know where I'm going." Tanner lay dozing with head back, mouth open and upper dentures dropping ever so slowly.

"I like to close my eyes and feel the wind in my face," Catherine confided. She opened a window. The city smells were alien; the sensation wasn't. "I much prefer summer to winter."

Bycroft relaxed into the plush leather. He closed his eyes, recalling the evening: the food, the wines, the conversations and his outstanding performance. He smiled, rubbing the copious amount of food and alcohol as it gurgled in his bloated belly; the purring engine masked the fermentation noises.

Horse-drawn traffic and pedestrians wisely gave way to the Daimler as it weaved along Oxford Street. The swaying motion was uncomfortable and Bycroft opened his eyes to Nurse Shilling's smile. He then focused on the top button of her white blouse rather than the moving streetlamps – the errant button was undone. It didn't help him. Beads of sweat formed on his forehead and he fumbled with his collar stud.

Nurse Shilling leant forward. "Here, let me help you with that." Catherine couldn't believe her eyes and neither could Bycroft. He was looking down the front of the nurse's blouse. Her breasts were swaying with the weaving of the motor vehicle as she assisted him to remove the bow tie and unbutton his collar. "That's better, isn't it?" she enquired and then sat back smiling broadly at Catherine and Bycroft.

Tanner's denture dropped into his whiskers and flip-flopped its way down to his lap. Mesmerised by the animated teeth, Bycroft lost his hard-on and Catherine her train of thought. Without hesitation, Nurse Shilling placed the offending denture in his pocket along with the food remnants Bycroft had witnessed Tanner squirreling away. The thought of what was in the pocket churned Bycroft's stomach and he began feeling anxious. They received a large smile from Nurse Shilling again. Catherine cooled her face in the breeze and shut her eyes, unsure as to whether the woman was flirting with her, with Bycroft or…with both of them.

At the Empire Hotel entrance, the chauffeur opened the door for his passengers and stood formally at attention. Nurse Shilling leant compromisingly forward to Catherine and placed a hand on her knee. "I know a little French – maybe there is more we can discover together."

"It all depends on what you already know?" Catherine replied apprehensively.

"Ménage à trois?"

Catherine was speechless at the woman's forthrightness but Bycroft naively believed Nurse Shilling wanted tutoring in the French language; this he could use to seduce her. His regurgitating Peking duck told him now was not the right time to take advantage of her thirst for knowledge. "It's been a long day …"

"I could come up for an hour," she persisted, "You could watch Catherine and I …"

"No, I must insist Catherine get her rest."

Catherine couldn't believe what he'd just said and that he had not taken up the blatant proposal. Befuddled thoughts now ran with abandon and she dismissed the incident as a minor irritation. Bycroft scrambled out of the vehicle followed closely by her.

"Another time maybe? Home, Anthony."

The chauffeur smiled, knowing his night's work wasn't over.

The door attendant greeted Bycroft and Catherine. The elderly gent toffed his top hat politely. "Mr. Bycroft, Madam. I trust you've had a lovely evening." He opened the door for them and received a tip.

"Look after the pennies, the pounds will take care of themselves," Bycroft advised him.

The elevator operator, restricted to his cubicle and a copy of *Variety*, chattered, thankful for the company. Meanwhile, the motion and his claustrophobia enhanced Bycroft's nausea. Catherine swam in a sea of confusion under the glare of a naked bulb and the realization that she may have had a little too much wine also.

"Gracie Field's at the Tiv', who'd believe it?" The trio watched the floor indicator arrow travel its arc. "My missus loves 'er, reckons she's tops ... " Bycroft's stomach rumbled loudly, though not interfering with the onslaught of chatter. "...listens to 'er on the wireless she does..." Catherine cleared her throat with a dainty cough. "Promised I'd take 'er to see Gracie for 'er birthday, I did, the missus' birthday, not Gracie's...it's a shame it is, a real shame ..."

"Pardon, Monsieur?"

"Don't think I can afford it, a couple of sick kids at the moment," he sighed, "Gracie may come back again...sometime."

"That is a shame..." Catherine empathised.

"We men never like to break a woman's 'eart but sometimes it's unavoidable, eh Gov, you know what I mean, don't cha? Here we are, fourth floor." He opened the gate grill. "A penny, that's right generous of you, Gov. 'ave a good night." He received no advice to go with the penny.

They alighted from the elevator. Wall lamps stretched into the distant yellow haze. Both stood looking at the long hallway, lurching as if in the passageway of a liner. Catherine took his arm to steady herself as they pressed on, each preoccupied in their own thoughts. At her door, she fumbled to find the key in her purse. "I enjoyed this evening…sacré bleu, where is it? Ah."

"Here, let me." Bycroft managed to get the key in the lock first go and opened the door. He stood back and politely gestured her through.

"Merci," she paused, and leant against the door, "I was impressed by your gentlemanly manner this evening."

Bycroft stepped forward, taking her hand. "I told you I had changed." Nausea overrode his lust, "and now I bid you goodnight." His kissed her hand, emulating Lockett.

"Will I see you at breakfast?"

The thought of breakfast was too much. He quickly pecked her forehead. "Lunch would be preferable."

27 – Tit for Tat

Retribution is the addiction
...the euphoric high
doesn't last

Catherine returned to Gunnadoo a couple of days before Bycroft. He returned in his usual condition – bags under the eyes, pasty faced and bloated, and spent the weekend at his property recuperating. Monday morning Billings vacated the chair, returning ownership of the office to Bycroft.

"Good morning, Mr. Bycroft, Mr. Robinson...would anyone like a cuppa?"

Robinson responded quickly, "Black, two sugars and no dandruff."

"Without curdled milk for me." Bycroft rubbed his indigestion and checked out his chair, "How many times have you swept the floor?" he asked cynically, resting his feet on the windowsill. He noted the newly painted sign above Houten's store and remembered Wally and the snake-oil mixture he used to guzzle.

Robinson sat opposite him laughing.

"What so funny, Sunshine?"

"I can't believe Bastock was so gullible," declared Robinson, "he practically opened the account books to you."

"He was convivial, wasn't he?"

They'd just visited the Plough and spotted Bastock at his near-completed complex. Bycroft had approached his opposition pleasantly and complimented him on the wrought iron around the balconies. Obligingly Bastock had provided them with a personal tour.

"Ego, it will bring you down every time." Bycroft lit a cigar. "Did you see it when he said he'd send me an invitation for the grand opening?" The belch destroyed the smoke ring. "It'll be a dry old turn without me to bail him out." He turned to face Robinson. "By the way, we'll be receiving extra booze with our shipments; I don't want it known to Bastock's spies."

"His drivers watch everything being unloaded."

"I'm aware of that. It won't all be coming in at once. The delivery will be spread out so as not to attract attention. My Samaritan gesture to Bastock can be accumulated with nobody being the wiser."

"You son of a gun." Robinson sat upright, "You pulled it off?" He received a wink. "Have faith and the Lord shall provide," he preached mockingly.

"Amen to that," Bycroft agreed. "Have it delivered to The Arms. It'll be further for them to carry." He carefully observed the surface of the spinning liquid in the teacup. "Leave the spoon," he told Billings.

Robinson dipped a finger into his cup. "Speaking of deliveries..." He paused to flick imaginary or otherwise bits from the end of it. "...I'm not quite sure how to go about this, er..."

"Out with it…" Bycroft scraped at the top of his tea with the spoon as though searching for archaeology, "…you know I don't like secrets."

"There's a rumour circulating, well actually there's a few. You're married."

"I am. And who is the lucky lady?"

"I heard, a socialite in the city."

"Billings, what have you heard?"

"Her father is a shipping tycoon," he responded from behind his desk.

Bycroft contemplated an information leak and wondered whether it had been Billings or the telephone exchange. This time it had worked in his favour, but in future, he would protect vital information by code or send it by post.

"Well," enquired Robinson, "are you a married man?"

"As mayor of this town my door is open but the door to my private life is shut. My personal business, as long as it doesn't interfere with civic duties or Bycroft Holdings, is my own. I therefore neither confirm nor deny the rumour. If there isn't anything else on the agenda, I'm a busy man."

* * *

Catherine concluded her business with Ying Lee.

"Missy, you look fresh as daisy," he confided. "You should take more holidays." He handed her the elixir, "And less medicine."

Tension had crept into the friendly relationship over her addiction; both were still wary and treading lightly. "Merci, I have cut back but it helps me sleep." He nodded. "Is it not a pretty dress I am wearing?" she asked, and he smiled in reply. "Bonjour Ying Lee."

Catherine smiled to herself as she crossed High Street; it was much safer than crossing the mêlée of George Street. The clatter of her shoes upon the sidewalk contradicted the slow pace of Gunnadoo. The spring of the wooden boards propelled her every step compared to the hard bitumen of Sydney streets. It felt good to be home; citizens took time for greetings, acknowledgements and even impolite snubs. She had enjoyed Sydney but the thought of living there, she now realised, wasn't so appealing.

"G'day, Luv, how was the holiday? You're looking better for it." Ruby studied her. "Actually, you're looking like the cat that ate the canary."

"Bonjour Ruby, it was very nice but it is good to be back."

"The kettle's just boiled, join me? Mr. Houten." she hollered, "A cup for Catherine also. We'll be out front…better still, bring the teapot."

The women sat on the courtesy bench catching up on the latest gossip. It was unusually overcast for February, but pleasant. "Sipping tea on the balcony, how refined," Ruby remarked. They noticed Bycroft's fleet of foot when skipping over puddles and then between two wagons passing each other. He bounded up the steps and saw the women watching.

"G'day, Mr. Bycroft. You've certainly got a spring in your step." Ruby's statement had the undertones of a suspicious journalist.

"Good morning, Mrs. Houten." He then acknowledged Catherine for the first time in public. "Good morning, Miss."

Immediately Bycroft entered the shop, Ruby stopped Catherine from drinking her tea. She held her arm. "I know what I haven't told you."

"I cannot possibly think what it could be." Catherine good-naturedly shrugged off Ruby's hand and sipped her tea.

"Mr. Bycroft is about to become a father."

Catherine coughed and the store moggy unfortunately got the spray. "Sacré bleu, a tea leaf is caught." Ruby slapped her on the back until she caught her breath. "Merci, merci, that is enough."

"I never met a person who has so much of a problem drinking a cup of tea." She poured her another cup. "Now I've forgotten what…"

"Monsieur Bycroft?" Catherine encouraged.

"Yes, how about that, who'd have thought ... "

"I did not know he was married?"

"Last year sometime – had to, if you catch my drift." She tapped her nose.

"And who is the woman?"

"A politician's daughter; some bigwig and she's his little princess, my sources tell me."

"She may be a very nice person." Catherine defended the mystery woman. "You should not listen to all gossip."

"Listen? I don't listen; I write it," she laughed, "…anyway I doubt we'll ever see her out here."

"Who won't we see out here?" Meg enquired.

She joined the women and Ruby brought her up to date.

"Well, I heard she was the daughter of a merchant banker and actually lives in Melbourne. Catherine, use your powers – who is it?"

The conversation was becoming uncomfortable.

"Who cares? As Ruby said, we will never see her out here, oui?"

"But it is interesting," Ruby tapped her nose, "I smell a juicy story for the column."

Meg agreed, "The ink gets in the blood, doesn't it? I think we should…"

Catherine shrewdly placed a hand on her chest, "Sacré bleu." she gasped, diverting the conversation.

"What?" both women asked in unison.

"No, it cannot be." She shook her head and looked at Meg, "Tom?"

Meg immediately went pale. Not knowing what Catherine was about to reveal she picked up Ruby's tea and drank it.

"What is it, Luv?"

"I see a marriage – interracial…" Meg dropped the cup in shock. It smashed. "It is gone," Catherine stopped the trance charade, "I am sorry."

"I wouldn't have believed it if I hadn't seen it with my own eyes," Ruby stated.

Meg sat silent, her heart pounding and her head spinning.

Bycroft left the store. "Good morning, ladies, have a nice day."

Ruby looked at Meg, "Mr. Bycroft marrying a wog…how 'bout that."

* * *

Intermittent reflections of lightning ricocheted off distant storm clouds. Catherine stood on the boudoir balcony knowing thunder would follow. She waited and then, as if carried on the warm breeze, the phenomena reverberated through her body and into the night. Her nostrils flared, like a hound's sniffing for a scent. *Havana,* she thought. As it approached, the red glow bobbing in the dark brought a smile to her face.

"Good evening, Miss Get-About-Town," he called from the bottom of the stairs. The suitor wore a scarlet vest and carried wildflowers. He bounced up the stairs.

"Bon soir, Monsieur Pimpernel," she greeted him, "Quick. Inside before you are seen on my balcony and my good name is ruined."

"All right, what rumour have you heard about me?" Bycroft followed her into the boudoir.

"Rumour, you?" she teased. "I have heard nothing about you. It is moi who is the daughter of a politician, and a merchant banker."

"And a shipping tycoon, and twins are expected." He kissed her politely on the cheek and sat in the easychair.

"I have not heard that one." She was amused and sat at the dressing table looking at her radiant skin in the mirror. "How was your sailing trip?"

The invitation Bycroft had misinterpreted from Lockett had eventuated and the men went sailing on Sydney Harbour. Whittington had got his revenge –

Bycroft hanging over the Lady Olivia's stern for a morning.

"Yo ho ho and a bottle of rum," he replied good-naturedly, using the ashtray supplied.

Catherine commiserated. "I am sorry you did not get the position you wanted."

"Not to worry, it won't be long, I'm next in line … I'm sorry you'll have to wait a little longer for the payout."

"There is no hurry," she smiled. "I will get you a drink and you can toast your mysterious woman."

"No, I'm on the wagon," he rubbed his belly. Her words rang like an alarm in his suspicious mind. "All joking aside, we've got to be careful."

"I agree. Ruby is taking her newspaper position most genuinely. It would be a pity if she was to find out who this *mystery* woman was, oui?"

Bycroft didn't know if he was hearing the beginnings of a blackmail ploy or not. "You don't think she'd get the Advocate to help her dig for information, do you?"

"It is possible." She paused and smiled. "But nobody will find my doctor or the birth record. I have already seen to that."

"A good detective can find out many things."

"Not if he is looking, how you say, up the wrong tree, oui?"

Bycroft's paranoia of everyone being out to get him was taking its toll. Catherine not only held the baby but also the ticket to his future with Cowper's Brewery; she held all the cards and he didn't want her to know it.

"If there is anything that you need or want just let me know," he confided to her. "Nothing but the best is good enough for you and the baby."

Catherine welcomed the attention. "You are acting like an expectant father, relax." She placed his hand on her belly. She felt a baby growing; he felt a piggy bank maturing.

Bycroft's attendance was requested on the twenty-fourth of April for the belated opening of Bastock's yet-to-be-named hotel complex. The week before the event, as planned, Bycroft departed for Sydney. The rumour quickly spread – it was for the birth of the twins. In Sydney, various superficial duties for Gunnadoo, appointments with banking officials and police working on the Sweaty Swindler case kept him busy during the day. At night, Bycroft partied with Lockett.

"More, more," insisted Bycroft, his double vision focusing on the rice wine.

"More of what?" slurred Lockett. He passed him a bowl of steamed rice and knocked over the bottle in doing so. Irene received the contents in her lap.

"More rice wine," Bycroft shouted, clapping his hands together sharply, "chop. chop." The waiter bowed, leaving quickly to fulfil the request yet again. "And chop chop to you too," he dabbed at Irene's wet lap with a napkin. Nurse Shilling's legs parted in compliance as she watched the naked silhouette dancer contorting behind the translucent partition.

"More, more." yelled Lockett.

A leg first revealed itself, and then the dragon facemask; the body followed. As if stepping onto a high building ledge, Lucy clung to the edge of the partition gyrating slowly.

"More, more." gasped Irene, her inner thighs wildly slapping together in time to Lucy's performance.

"Careful …" Bycroft lifted his hand, "I gotta sign a few cheques tomorrow."

Lucy focused on Bycroft, trying to remember where she'd seen him before. Nurse Shilling cavorted on the cushions, accidentally kneeing him in the groin.

"Mr. Bycroft has an injury, let me chop chop it better," she said playfully. Bycroft laid her over his knee. "I'm gonna do what should have been…"

"You're *gunna do* what Nurse Shilling tells you – spank me."

Gunnadoo – the penny dropped, as did Bycroft's hand. Whack. Whack.

Lucy immediately began eliciting information. Lockett's eyes widened as she mounted the table and commenced rolling in the remains of the late-night supper. He reached for the wine, sliding the bottle in front of himself. Nurse Shilling's eyes nearly popped out of her head when the slender neck of the wine bottle above which Lucy was now squatting disappeared. She projected herself above Lockett like the figurehead of a ships.

"There are many more sins than seven," she whispered in his ear. He massaged greasy food remnants on her breasts with one hand, the other still holding the bottle. "There are other worlds to be explored," she cajoled.

"Call me Cook, raise the mainsail," he yelled excitedly, "I'm all for exploring."

"A mainsail is not required in the jungle but your rope is…" she pinned his hand to the table, "travel in my company and your innocence is lost forever."

"Innocence." Lockett wailed, "Don't worry 'bout it – I've got a compass."

"Very well." She gyrated her hips, rising slowly on her haunches until the vacuum seal popped. "Your journey begins here." His fortune cookie dropped to the table. "Like *Karma Sutra*, many delights may be had from reading; do not eat it." Lockett had no intention of that – he couldn't figure out which orifice it had dropped from. She pressed her fingers against his lips to stop him from talking. "Not tonight. You – I do not share."

The following day, as though he was already a director, Bycroft laid a trail of cigar smoke as he strolled through the corridors of the brewery. The elderly secretary showed him through to her boss's office. He was on the telephone and motioned Bycroft in. "Yes, Mr. Bastock, I do understand your predicament." With only two days to the opening, Bastock was frantic as to why the shipment hadn't arrived. Lockett pulled the face of a drowning man and returned to the conversation. "Let me check and see what I can find out." He placed his hand over the mouthpiece, announcing innocently, "Mr. Bastock's shipment seems to have gone astray."

"What I'd give to see his face right now." Bycroft reclined on the leather sofa. "He pulls his dumbest look when he's angry…boy, you should see it."

"Are you still there, Mr. Bastock? Yes, I'm just checking with the shipping clerk, won't be long." He covered the mouthpiece again. "So what do think about the Sway?"

Bycroft exhaled a vertical smoke ring and poked his forefinger through the elliptical shape lewdly. "Aye, she be a treasure, she be."

"A femme fatal for Uncle she be. I don't think it'll be too long before you'll be receiving your title." Bycroft threw him a bemused look. "…nickname." Lockett returned to the telephone. "Mr. Bastock? Ah…we've found the problem. Your shipment has been delivered to Gundaroo by mistake." He held the receiver at arm's length until the tirade finished. "Yes, it would be possible to overnight it except for one problem…" Lockett placed a hand over his mouth to stop himself from laughing and composed himself. "There's a strike on the production line, and no shipments are getting out at present."

Bycroft hastily moved to the desk and listened in on the conversation, receiving a wink from Lockett. "Mr. Bastock, this is what I suggest. I've never met the licensee of…" he rustled papers on the desk, "…The Arms and…that's right, a Mr. John Bycroft. I've heard him to be a reasonable sort of a man. I suggest you have a word with him to resolve the problem. I'll have your shipment to you in three days." He gave Bycroft the thumbs up and then sank the boot into Bastock. "On behalf of Cowper's Brewery let me wish you every success on the forthcoming venture. We'll talk again, goodbye Mr.

Bastock." He calmly hung up. "Right. What's for lunch?"

Bycroft returned on the overnighter, arriving at the Dundee siding on the day of Bastock's hotel opening – as planned. The coach driver informed him that his boss wished to speak with him immediately. Bycroft rang from the stationmaster's telephone.

"Hello Betty, this John Bycroft put me through to Bastock." He watched as Robinson arrived with four men to take delivery of the three large packing cases he'd returned with.

"Yeah, Bycroft here…what's the urgency?" He sat back in the chair as if it was his own and lit a cigar while Bastock told him the situation. "Uh ha, yep…right, well I'll be buggered." He lifted the candlestick telephone from the desk, stuck the mouthpiece in his chest and then turned to the stationmaster. "Hey Sunshine, how 'bout offering me a cuppa, it sounds like I'm gonna be here for a few minutes." He returned to Bastock's pleading. "Yeah, I'm listening but it's no use. My publicans won't release any stock and they especially won't take instructions over the telephone. Billings can't do anything – they all have specific orders." Bycroft yawned and looked at his watch, "You of all people should have learned the lessons of hoax callers. You'll just have to wait until I get back this afternoon and I can personally give the directive…what time does it start?"

Expediency in delivering Bycroft to Gunnadoo was the driver's instructions but Bycroft had other plans. "Come on, put your backs into it," he shouted.

Robinson and the men grunted as they manoeuvred the heavy load onto the rear of the dray.

"Christ Almighty. What's in here?" Mick asked, "To be sure it weighs a bloody ton."

"A wigwam for a goose's bridle," Bycroft informed him and Paddy. "It may be heavy but it's fragile and so are the other two. I want all crates and contents arriving in one piece. If anything's broken…you don't get paid, got it?" He ambled over to the waiting coach driver, treating him like a chauffeur. "Right, that's it. Nope. Hang on." He returned to the platform and stuck his head in the stationmaster's window. "Hey Sunshine, ever smoked a Cuban cigar?" He selected a cheap imitation from his inside left pocket – the right one was for the authentic Cubans – and tossed it to the grateful recipient.

* * *

Mosaic floor tiles, indoor plants and polished timber impressed the invited guests gathered in the spacious foyer. Harrick had his fingerprints all over the décor. Clemet, Harrick and White posed with Bastock on the stairs below a covered sign. "Smile, gentlemen," Tom requested.

Catherine wore a straight tubular dress with an elegant sash; the fashion was accessorized with a cloche hat pulled well down over her eyebrows. As difficult as it was, her pregnancy could still be hidden beneath the stylish outfit. Wong Foo was resplendent in his richly embroidered cheongsam. They stood chatting.

543

"Bonjour Ruby."

"G'day Luv, nice hat. I like your skull cap too, Wong Foo, did you pinch it from a bellhop?" She nudged Catherine. "What'd you think of mine…a bit of alrighty eh? I made it myself."

Catherine studied it. "I think it is…"

"I'm actually wearing two," she interrupted.

"Pardon?"

Ruby winked and tapped her nose. "Pleasure *and* business."

"There is much to be heard for Advocate gossip reporter at a gathering such as this," Wong Foo acknowledged and tapped his nose. Catherine acknowledged him for his timely intervention.

"There certainly is alrighty." Ruby scanned the guests. Their impatience for the show to commence was becoming apparent. "I'd thought Mr. Bycroft would be here." She jotted down a couple of words in a notepad.

"Mr. Bycroft now father of triplets …" Wong Foo told her.

"Triplets." said both women in unison.

Ruby flicked to another page and began writing, "And who told you this, Mr. Foo?"

"Betty contain much information, she like directory."

Ruby scribbled a line through what she had just written; she knew of the telephonist's drinking problem. "Naw, it's becoming unreliable. I want to know who the new Mrs. Bycroft is. Whatever kept him in Sydney must be of importance."

"What is of importance?" Meg enquired.

Catherine didn't like where the conversation was headed and jumped at the first opportunity to change its direction. "Bonjour Meg, I like my hat better than Ruby's, what do you think, oui? Hers is, how you say?"

Being tactful, Meg interrupted, "It is an original."

"Sacré bleu." Catherine placed a hand on her chest and declared, "I see a wedding cake."

The offending headwear naturally drew Meg and Wong Foo's eyes straight to it as hoped, and then Ruby began defending her creation, thus forgetting about her quest to find Mrs. Bycroft. Meg, forewarned of the extreme adornment courtesy of Tom, had prepared her comment but not an exit strategy from Catherine's ambush. Wong Foo wisely bowed out of the heated discussion rather than become embroiled in it.

"Pardon," Catherine apologised to Ruby, "You misunderstand me. I did not mean…"

Meg interrupted her, "Did you have another premonition?"

"Oui…no, this is ridiculous. I am not psychic," she told the women.

Ruby opened her notepad. "Interracial, wedding cake…who?"

With cases of champagne purchased from The Arms at a marked-up retail price, Bastock began the official proceedings, much to the gathering's relief. "Ladies and gentlemen, on behalf of my esteemed colleagues…" After drawing out procedures for as long as possible, staff filled champagne glasses as Bastock concluded, "Ladies and gentlemen, I now officially open…" he pulled the shroud, revealing the hotel's name written Egyptian style, "…the Oasis." Tom snapped the shot as applause and cheers greeted the unveiling. The velvet curtain parted and Bastock gestured for the socialites to go through to the dining area where more refreshments awaited them. Bastock pulled White aside. "Bycroft is confirmed on the coach. How did you go?"

He shook his head. "I've tried again, it's no use; neither pub will sell us draft beer without Bycroft's consent. There's a good supply of champagne though. We'll just have to wait until he gets here."

"I see a disparity of agenda." Harrick's comment received no acknowledgment.

"At the retail price we're paying a bottle, an hour of this freeloading mob will bankrupt us," Bastock retorted to White.

Harrick reminded Bastock of the free shout in the front bar that evening for the locals. "They'll rip the place apart if the Oasis is dry," he concluded.

"Go and do something useful," Bastock chastised, "…entertain the ladies."

"I'll defuse their angst," he naively joked. "Coming, ladies…"

"So help me, he'll get another black eye if he keeps it up." Bastock was fast losing any remaining sense of humour.

"Come on," White grabbed Bastock by the arm. "Shelby's been told to have Bycroft delivered here post haste, there's a dray ready to pick up the barrels at a moment's notice, there's noth'n more that can be done."

"Except join in," Clement suggested, "we're paying for it, let's enjoy some of it."

Guests mingled in the ambience of a tastefully decorated room; ample sunlight shone through large windows. Landscape paintings broke up the wallpaper pattern and a large mirror hung over the mantelpiece. Bar staff accessed the kitchen through continuously swinging doors as the champagne flowed. Ruby watched inconspicuously as Bycroft received the royal treatment when he finally arrived. Bastock shuffled him into the office behind the reception desk. Minutes later the men returned to the foyer. Bycroft spoke loudly for any listening ears.

"Only too glad I can help out. I'll get it seen to straight away."

That was Robinson's cue to inform Ruby of the Samaritan deed. As hoped, she then mingled, gossiping about the news. Bastock did the honours and finally tapped the first barrel. Much to his indignation, Bycroft received the three cheers – he would only receive an outrageous invoice for the goods supplied.

Bycroft pulled Billings aside. "Is everything right for this evening?"

"It's all been arranged. The gate will be left unlocked."

"Mr. Bycroft," interrupted Ruby with notebook and pencil ready, "any news for the Advocate?"

"Actually there is a surprise but you'll have to wait until tomorrow."

"And what about the rumour of an interracial marriage pending," she asked deviously, "anything you'd like to say on that?"

547

Bycroft had no idea what she was talking about but wasn't about to let her know he didn't. Like any politician, he dodged the question, "Wong Foo is the spokesman for our oriental constituents, ask him."

28 – A New Tune is Played

...select your partners for the Coup d'état Polka

Cloud cover negated a luminous moon as the secretive operation unfolded in the early hours of morning. Bycroft waited at the community hall intersection.

"No problem." Robinson stooped with hands on knees, his panting quick and shallow. "We got the heavy rig...the padlock on Bastock's security gate was left unlocked."

Bycroft gloated. "Not by chance," he whispered. "Why didn't you come back with the men?"

Robinson stretched, filling his lungs deeply. "They picked up a few extras...there wasn't enough room."

"Well that's just dandy." The glowing cigar end flashed red, Bycroft's fury apparent. "I'll be locked up as an accomplice if they get caught." He paced back and forth. "We're doing a Samaritan deed here, not joining the bloody Kelly Gang. I'm the Mayor. The rig's going back after the job is done; they could have waited till then, bloody opportunists."

"I wasn't about to 'ave a barney with 'em in Bastock's yard."

"You've seen Bond at work…you should've known better."

"Here they come now."

Robinson's observation irked Bycroft. "Bloody hell," he whispered, "you can hear them a mile off. I told them to be quiet."

The men's chatter echoed down Main Street, gradually getting louder until the dray pulled up. "Top of the morning," Paddy delivered irreverently. "As you requested, all in one piece."

"Shut up you idiot or ya don't get paid," Bycroft hissed. The dray was loaded to the hilt with stolen goods; Paddy chose to avert the impending barney and said nothing. "Now get on with it. Robinson, keep 'em quiet."

They erected the lifting rig poles, set the block and tackle in position and then unloaded the first of the three packing crates in the centre of the intersection. "Break it open – quietly," Robinson directed. Each nail screamed when jemmied from the dry blanks.

"What is it?" asked Mick.

"Buggered if I know." Paddy stood back, scratching his head, "I can't see two foot in front of me nose."

"Shut up and get on with it," Bycroft snapped. Robinson heaved on the chain, lowering the second crate. The men opened it and then repositioned the pedestal from inside onto its dais.

"I know what it is," Paddy whispered, "it's a fountain."

"And what makes you think that?" Mick asked, while trying to read the embossed lettering as though it was Braille.

"It must be – and some idiot has filled it with water already."

"Ah to be sure Paddy…the world is full of idiots."

Bycroft froze as a wagon silently appeared from the dark. It pulled up beside the dray.

"Before ya be asking, it's a fountain," Mick informed Clancy.

The rogues quickly transferred the stolen goods to the wagon and it disappeared into the dark. Robinson dismantled the remaining crate on the dray and then swung the sculpture into position atop the pedestal.

Bycroft stood with his arms outstretched estimating an east west trajectory of the sun. "Turn it to the right a little more," he instructed.

"What's a wigwam for a goose's bridle look like Paddy?"

"I don't know Mick…I've never seen one."

"Clear up this mess and pull down the rig," Robinson instructed. He covered the Samaritan deed with a tarpaulin.

"No pinching anything else…and make sure you lock up when ya leave Bastock's yard," Bycroft added, "I don't want noth'n incriminating me. Robinson, you keep an eye on me fountain," he wisecracked. "You're on nightshift, I'm gonna get some shut-eye before church, I'll see you there."

It didn't take long for the rig to be dismantled and the site cleaned up. Diminishing stars in the east hinted at the arrival of dawn. Sitting on the dais, Robinson leant against the pedestal and lit a cigarette. He watched the dray move off.

"Ya know, I've been wondering, Paddy…could it be a sundial?"

"No, I don't think so Mick." Paddy sucked on his pipe, contemplating. "I think the statue be a dowser…"

Mick chimed in, "Of course, a wowser with his shillelagh," he scratched his head. "Now why didn't I think of that?"

"Not a wowser, I said a dowser, and he's got a divining rod pointing to the water below. That is what I think." Mick began laughing. Paddy looked bemused, "And what be so funny 'bout that?"

"'tis a fine joke Paddy," Mick slapped him on the back. "There be no tap to get the water out."

Paddy sighed deeply. "The world is full of idiots Mick."

"That it is Paddy…that it is," he replied all knowingly.

A crowd gathering at the obstacle unpleasantly surprised many a hung-over teamster; Main Street traffic came to a standstill. Parishioners attending the early service joined the perplexed gathering and they too began guessing. Robinson stopped the inquisitive from peeping under the canvas shroud.

"Coming through … coming through … good morning, Mrs. Tompkins," Bycroft toffed his fedora. "This will be most interesting for the children – history. Can't talk, the public awaits, excuse me, man on a mission, coming through." Breaking through the perimeter of onlookers Bycroft now enjoyed their attention. "Good work, Mr. Robinson. Now go and get yourself cleaned up. You look like ya been on the turps all night … the Advocate will want photographs. I'll hold 'em up until ya get back."

The Advocate team arrived and pushed their way toward the inner circle. "Make way for the press." Clarrie shouted. He helped carry Tom's equipment, Meg following with notepad and pencil.

Ruby and Houten joined the flow of pedestrians. "I don't know how you can go out in public like that, Abe," she chastised, while straightening his collar. Houten had slipped the suit over his pyjamas.

"Don't push," he requested. Ruby used him as a battering ram.

"Gossip columnist and entourage coming through." she bellowed.

Bycroft strolled around the dais gesturing to the onlookers.

Ying Lee and family, Mrs. Chang and the girls followed Catherine's instructions, "No, keep moving." She directed them to stand on the west side of the curiosity facing east.

Wong Foo sat observing the spectacle from under the Golden Dragon's veranda while partaking of tea. Pastor O'Dae and Sister Beth watched from the community hall steps. Doyle and his constables patrolled for pickpockets. Robinson bathed in the cold stream, his privacy disturbed by an early bird carrying her washing basket.

"How did he do it?" Bastock rocked back and forth, his hands in his trouser pockets. He stared up at the cloaked monolith. "How did he do it?" He looked at White, who shrugged. Bastock then looked warily at Dempsey.

"Don't look at me … I got no idea."

"I bet it's with the town's money," Harrick suggested in annoyance.

"How did he move it, you idiot, not how…ah forget it."

Bycroft held up his arms for silence while all the time moving in a circle on the dais. "Ladies and gentlemen, boys and girls, friends," he announced, "I shall not keep you waiting …"

"It's been thirty minutes already," White shouted, "get on with it."

The crowd followed his lead and began wisecracking too. Bycroft gestured to Bond for him to step onto the dais, hoping silence would follow – word had spread of the magistrate and his incarcerating gavel. "Thank you," called Bycroft, "without further ado I'd like Mr. Edward Bond to do the unveiling…but just quickly, before he does…"

"Here we go," whispered Clarrie. He gave Meg *the* look. "I reckon…"

"No way, I'm not betting – I haven't had a cuppa yet." She opened her notepad.

Bycroft reversed his direction on the dais. "…as Mayor of Gunnadoo I, and your council, make many difficult decisions …"

"What's so difficult 'bout buying a bird bath?" Clement yelled.

"It's a fountain, you idiot." Clancy's voice rang out. Many others followed with their own guesswork.

"Like – how to spend your taxes wisely…" Bycroft shouted. The mere mention of the word brought a tirade of jeers and booing.

"Get on with it, you're losing them," Bond advised.

"On behalf of Bycroft Holdings this donation to the Gunnadoo community ... " Bycroft stopped shouting. The dissonance was too great. He couldn't be heard so he motioned for the unveiling. Bond tugged on the shroud. Meg began writing:

April. Sunday 25th. The life-size statue of a soldier standing with head bowed and rifle at reversed arms silenced the sceptics…

"Soldier looks slightly familiar Missy?"

Catherine stared at the facial features. "You think so?"

"Ying Lee think so." He noted Catherine's slight smile and then deduced she knew more than she was letting on.

"So do I but it is our secret, oui?"

Protruding from under the helmet, the soldier's ears were larger than normal.

Bycroft believed the donation could be an impetus for a statue of the town's founding father: himself. Cedric Booth had fortuitously alerted Catherine to Bycroft's cenotaph enquiries. She rewarded the stonemason's discretion and commissioned the slight alteration. Booth received Tom's newspaper photograph as a guide.

"There is much I do not understand about Missy …"

"… and there will be more," she interrupted, "but whatever I do, do not hate me for it."

Ying Lee pondered the ambiguous statement and reached into his pocket. "I believe this is yours." He placed the marble-sized keepsake in her palm and then closed her fist. "No expectations – no disappointments," he replied apprehensively, "Missy will always find Ying Lee by throwing stone."

The Pastor and Sister Beth joined Bastock and his cronies as the moving mass slowly revolved around the dais inspecting the gift.

"I feel one of them wogs circling that wog place," Dempsey remarked sarcastically.

"This ain't Mecca," Bastock corrected, "that's the Trojan bloody horse."

Wong Foo stepped from the crowd. "It is not a work of beauty or of bronze, Mr. Bycroft," he twirled his moustache pondering, "and yet it still elicits respect. I bow to your penchant for immortality – your gift to Gunnadoo is…"

Bycroft clasped his lapel and stood tall. "Most honourable?" he announced conceitedly.

"Most shrewd," suggested Wong Foo, his fingernail stroking his cheek, "and what is to follow – grandchildren?"

"I'm working on it."

"Grandchildren?" Ruby sidled up him with her notepad and pencil. "Is this the surprise, Mr. Bycroft?"

"What surprise?" he snapped, and then pointed to the centre of attention. "What do you call that?"

"Editorial … I'm the gossip columnist." Ruby pursued Catherine's psychic charade of the previous day. "Yesterday we didn't finish our discussion on interracial marriages, did we?"

Bycroft vaguely recalled the conversation. "And what did I say?"

"Ask Wong Foo." She turned to him. "Mr. Foo?"

Ruby was lost in her own investigative journalism, as were her interviewees. Wong Foo's mind raced as to the right answer; the secret was out. He cursed Bycroft, he cursed Tom Lennard and he cursed Lotus-Flower.

"We got the answer," Meg informed the group. She and Clarrie joined the discussion.

"It appears everyone knows," Wong Foo chided.

Clarrie gave Meg a quick glance of apprehension, then she continued, "We believe this should be called the Anzac Parade intersection."

Clarrie supported her. "The answer to our unnamed streets; they could be given appropriate names from the battlefields."

"Battlefield here now," Wong Foo declared angrily.

Tom intervened from behind the camera. "One for the Advocate." he shouted. The group positioned themselves.

"Smile for future son-in-law," Wong Foo hissed.

Both Meg and Ruby's jaws dropped open; they gawked at the camera lens. Out of the side of his mouth, Clarrie whispered to Bycroft, "Have I missed something?"

"Buggered if I know, I'm running on three hours' sleep."

"Thank you," Tom gibed, "your photographs will be in the next edition."

"Pastor O'Dea," Bycroft called to him, "I believe now would be a good time for a blessing."

"I haven't prepared anything. I should have been told."

"What. And spoil the surprise?"

O'Dae delivered an unprepared blessing, not the commemorative service justified but long enough to have his photograph taken. He then summoned the faithful into the hall for his organised sermon. Bycroft opened one eye as Robinson sat down.

"I stopped the photographs from being taken for as long as I could....but once again you were too slow, Sunshine."

"Ooh, I dunno 'bout that." Robinson sat contentedly with arms folded.

During the service, the congregation regularly heard expletives from the street as irreverent teamsters acquainted themselves with the new icon.

* * *

Catherine had prepared the girls for her absence by telling them she was going on an extended holiday to Melbourne and Adelaide. The following Wednesday, she called on business associates and friends and let them know also. Bycroft received the news that night.

"You're leaving tomorrow?"

"I feel it would be wise to do so." She rubbed her belly. "Someone is becoming impatient and today I was told by an uncouth person I was getting fat. It is time, oui."

Bycroft held Catherine in his arms. "Our child has a beautiful mother."

"Can it be the leopard has changed his spots, oui?"

"What?"

"Never mind ... "

As prearranged, they would use coded words during telephone conversations and Catherine would at all times keep Bycroft up to date with her progress. The following day her luggage was loaded aboard the Ford coach.

Goodbyes were always difficult. The fine line they walked in their chosen profession was never spoken of at such times. Catherine and Mrs. Chang had met and farewelled many girls at the depot, never knowing if they would be seen again or, if they were, what condition they'd be in. It was all accepted as the downside of the game. Apart from the bitchiness and petty rivalries of many women living under the same roof, the girls had always bonded under Catherine's matriarchal attitude and Mrs. Chang's authoritarian demeanour.

"Madame Chang, I appreciate your not questioning my actions. No matter what happens, your position will not change. Monsieur Peck has instructions should there be any problems." She paused, contemplating. "There should not be any. I will keep in touch. Au revoir, Madame Chang."

The letter from Lucy arrived that afternoon, after Catherine's departure. Addressed as personal, Mrs. Chang put it aside for Catherine's return. Lucy had discovered the connection with Bycroft and Cowper's Brewery and the plan to stop Bastock's beer supply. Most importantly, she had discovered Judge O'Keefe's requirement for married men to be on the board of directors, and the fact that Bycroft's nomination was dependent upon his marital status. Lockett wasn't an easy man to coax information from and it had taken Lucy two sessions, but eventually all the information was revealed, except for the name of the unsuspecting woman of Bycroft's hidden agenda – Catherine.

Arriving in Sydney on the Friday morning, Catherine immediately checked into the private retreat at Vaucluse. She believed that the bumpy trip to Dundee and then the motion of the overnighter had instigated the labour pains. When Bycroft rang the Empire Hotel to confirm all was proceeding to plan, he discovered that it wasn't; Catherine had failed to check into the reserved room as arranged. He was beside himself with worry, believing a double-cross to be unfolding.

Her contractions began in the evening. Six hours later the doctors were considering taking the baby and prepared for a Caesarean. Catherine was becoming weaker; they feared not only for the baby but also for her. She moved in and out of consciousness. Reality and memories, enhanced by morphine, became vivid dreams of confusion as Danny, Wally and then Bycroft fused into one being – the instigator of her predicament. Catherine felt that she was about to split in half.

"Holy Mother." she screamed.

"Push," the doctor, demanded again, "it's coming – one last time, push."

The cry of her baby instigated an intuitive response but lethargy swept Catherine into an infinite darkness.

"Such big ears for such a small baby," he remarked, handing the infant to the midwife, "that's what the problem must have been. I'm glad a Caesarean wasn't needed."

She agreed. "The mother will be too; the scar would've been a beauty."

* * *

On Saturday morning, Bycroft had just replaced the receiver, having yet again been told Catherine hadn't booked in, when Lockett rang.

"The funeral will be on Tuesday afternoon, a small affair; Old Tanner outlived his family and friends. Can you make it?" he asked.

"I'll catch the overnighter on Monday."

"The wake will be at The Keep. The Admiral believes in giving the departed a right royal send-off."

"I had my money riding on Irene," Bycroft jested.

"And so did I," agreed Lockett. "We'll have to find her another position in the organisation."

Bycroft rang Billings, pulling him out of bed for the second time. Lockett had mistakenly rung the business number first. Still high from the previous evening, Billings wrote down the gist of the conversation, 'book a ticket'. Bycroft would use the Tuesday funeral as an excuse to hightail it to Sydney and find Catherine.

On the Monday, when Bycroft did leave, he was a bundle of nerves. He had not heard from Catherine. The rumour soon spread through

Gunnadoo, courtesy of Billings, that the fragile condition of Bycroft's wife and imminent early birth of the twins had instigated his radical departure.

"Good morning, Mr. Bycroft, we've been expecting you." The concierge swung the register for signing. "Your key, and two messages; we hope you'll have…"

"Yeah, yeah," Bycroft read the messages first and left the man standing with pen in hand. Lockett confirmed the funeral details at the Waverley Cemetery. The second message was from a Christine Wingood. "Bloody hookers," he mumbled, screwing up the note. He then tossed it over the desk at a wastepaper basket.

"Oh, bad luck, Sir – just missed," the concierge stated drolly. "Would you like another go? Your autograph, if you please," he requested sarcastically, albeit smiling graciously. Bycroft filled out the register; the procedure irritating him. The concierge placed the litter in the basket, returned to his post and watched until the task was completed. "We don't want anything going astray, do we?" He swung the register around and checked that Bycroft had completed the details correctly. "Will there be anything else, Sir?"

"Yes…another go." Bycroft gestured to the wastepaper basket.

The man flushed and retrieved the message. Bycroft smiled arrogantly when he handed it to him. The concierge returned to the basket and placed it where it would be impossible to miss, then stood compliantly behind it. "When you're ready, Sir."

Bycroft made him wait again. He opened the crushed note and requested a telephone book. "What do you know about the Bellvoir Retreat at Vaucluse?"

"Most exclusive, Sir…"

He held up the message, "This is it, nothing else?"

"I did not take the message, Mr. Bycroft; I can make enquiries if you wish?"

"No, don't bother." Bycroft screwed up the message again and took aim at the target. The concierge walked to the basket in a dignified manner, rolled his eyes upward and waited patiently. He didn't expect the telephone book to be thrown. "If Catherine Dunn rings for me I'll be back this evening; make sure she gets that message." He slammed the desk bell and bellhops came running.

"Will that be all, Sir?"

"Take care of my luggage."

"I certainly will, Sir."

Bycroft hailed a cab and left for his appointments. The concierge altered Gunnadoo to read 'Gundaroo'.

The cab stopped at the driveway entrance to the private Vaucluse retreat. "Good morning," the security guard welcomed, "your name please."

"John Bycroft, I'm expected."

Bycroft studied the ornate cipher on the wrought-iron gates as the man confirmed the details against his clipboard. Only then did the estate gates open. A winding driveway lined with poplar trees ran through manicured gardens, leading to the Romanesque columns and marble steps of the porte-cochere. The door attendant greeted Bycroft as though he was a luminary and escorted him to the reception desk.

"Christine Wingood?" he enquired.

"One moment, Mr. Bycroft, I'll ring."

Bycroft surveyed the opulent surrounds; there was nothing to suggest it was a medical facility.

"Thank you." The receptionist hung up. She gave instructions to an assistant and then informed Bycroft, "Revesby will take you to Miss Wingood's room."

The sun warmed Catherine as she stood reading a newspaper with her back to the bay window. Bycroft entered the room and was clearly surprised to see her. The black dress she was wearing, and no baby bump, sent a chill down his spine: "Catherine."

She folded the newspaper and placed it on the bed. "Bonjour, who were you expecting?"

"I didn't know. I've been worried sick; I didn't know where to find you."

"And neither would a detective, oui?" She peered out the window at a cat stalking a robin.

"Are you all right, the baby?"

"We are both fine."

"Whew. For a minute there I thought..." He gave her a kiss on the cheek and sat on the bed. "Using a fake name; that was clever. If I had known it was you, I'd have brought flowers."

"How sweet," she faced him, "thank you for the thought anyway." She then returned to watch the life and death scenario playing out in the gardens.

Bycroft was dancing with the ambiguities he was hearing from Catherine. He glanced down at the newspaper. The photograph of Tanner and the heading, 'Pioneer Dies', caught his eye. His tension heightened.

"When do I get to see my heir?"

"The baby is not your heir until your name appears on the birth certificate."

"Where is it? I'll sign on the dotted line."

"What you ask of Catherine, your business partner, I do. What you ask of Catherine, the mother of your child, I also do but do so knowing it is for the best."

"Nothing but. You know me."

"Yes, and if I am to hand my child over to you, there is more reading you will need to do first." The cat was within striking distance, stationary and ready to pounce, the tip of its tail flicking in anticipation. Catherine retrieved a document from the bureau drawer and handed it to him. "It is, how you say, an insurance policy."

Bycroft didn't like what he was hearing and began reading.

Benjamin Peck had prepared the legal document. Bycroft's deed of title, for his property outside Gunnadoo, was to be transferred into the child's name. Bycroft would hold the legacy in trust, either until the heir came of age or until his own death. He could never sell the property. Catherine demanded nothing for herself, unlike what he'd been expecting.

"Your secret will never be revealed," she assured him. "My name is not on the birth certificate and Christine will never be found; she no longer exists." He liked the sound of her words – 'no longer exists'.

Devious thoughts ran rampant – *leave no lose threads* he thought. "I have no problem with this," he informed her.

"I am sure you will receive much empathy from Gunnadoo when they hear your wife died in childbirth." Catherine picked up the telephone. "Thank you, we're ready for Miss Carter, and please prepare the baby." She walked to the window and observed the cat now feasting. "Do you believe a leopard can change its spots?"

"If you're asking me can an old dog learn new tricks? Yes."

"I hope so." Catherine responded to a quiet knock at the door. "Come in." Bycroft stood up politely. "Miss Carter will witness our signatures."

The woman smiled pleasantly. Her white uniform clung to her alluring figure. Bycroft liked what he saw and conveyed his innuendo to her as he unscrewed the fountain pen lid. "Well, let's do it shall we?"

"One more," said Catherine, after he'd signed the binding agreement and birth certificate. She slipped it in front of him.

"What's this?"

"The medical and accommodation bill, of course. Miss Carter, would you please get Mr. Bycroft's child."

Bycroft noted her shapely bottom and long legs; the woman left knowing he was eyeing her up. He lit a cigar. "And what name have you chosen?"

"You are the father of a daughter, 5lbs 3ozs. It is for you to choose."

"A girl, eh." He sucked hard on the cigar. "What would you like?"

"I have always been fond of Edith."

"Then Edith it is. Edith Bycroft...I like it." Catherine took his pen and wrote the name on the birth certificate. "The only problem I can see is, finding a qualified nanny prepared to live in Gunnadoo."

"That will be no problem; it has been taken care of." Miss Carter returned. "Come in. This is your daughter...and her nanny."

Bycroft didn't challenge the idea. "Welcome aboard, Miss Carter. Now, let's have a look at what we've got here, come to your old man." He lifted Edith from the nanny's arms, shrewdly feeling her up as he did so.

"Here, let me help, Mr. Bycroft."

She pulled the wrap back. Edith squinted through tiny slits and her tongue protruded as if blowing him a raspberry. A crocheted bonnet covered her abnormally large ears.

"Looks like her old man, what do ya reckon?"

Both women agreed.

"I'll gather baby Edith's things together."

"Here we go, Miss Carter...I don't want to wear her out." Bycroft returned the baby to the nanny; again, she felt his wandering hand on her breast.

"Thank you, Mr. Bycroft." She left the smoky room, having had Bycroft's interest confirmed.

"Miss Carter seems quite nice...where did you find her?"

"At an agency, of course," Catherine replied. She observed the cat skulking away with the lifeless corpse. "Well, let us be going, Mrs. O'Keefe is expecting us."

"What?"

"I rang her this morning. Better we see her at the funeral than she does us here, oui? Besides, you want to show off your daughter, don't you? I will enjoy, how you say," Catherine chose her words carefully, "seeing the wind taken from Monsieur Whittington's sail."

The thought was appealing to Bycroft also.

Nursing the bundle, the nanny sat with her back to the driver, the parents opposite. Closing her eyes and feeling the cool autumn wind in her face, Catherine smiled. Bycroft kept hearing Catherine's words, 'the mother of your child does not exist.' He looked at the piggy bank wrapped in the blanket. Miss Carter's eyes sparkled from beneath her blonde fringe. She smiled at him; he returned it.

The landscape stunned Catherine as they pulled into the Waverley Cemetery – the Pacific Ocean met the horizon and disappeared beyond. "Sacré bleu, it is such a magnifique view."

"Pity the residents are dead, they can't enjoy it," quipped Bycroft.

The late arrival of Bycroft and family upstaged the graveside service. Apart from the minister and gravediggers, all the mourners attended the dinner party. The Bryants and Larsons stood either side of Irene Shilling. Stylishly dressed in the latest fashion, her sex appeal oozed from beneath her black head veil, her appearance that of a widow, not a carer.

Lockett acknowledged Bycroft; he responded with a rolling of the eyes and then winked at Tanner's beneficiary. Irene observed the bundle and the nanny, as did Lockett; the smile he received from Miss Carter was both inviting and surprising. The Admiral and Mrs O'Keefe nodded approvingly to Catherine. The Whittingtons paid no heed to the brazen ploy to curry favour. Throughout the service, gestures, some ambiguous some obvious, were given and received by everyone.

The priest closed his Bible and reached down for a handful of soil. "Ashes to ashes, dust to dust," he delivered solemnly, as the breeze changed its direction and an easterly blew in.

Immediately the service finished the mourners became well-wishers, turning their attention to the new mother and arrival.

"The Lord giveth and the Lord taketh," preached O'Keefe. Mrs. O'Keefe held the infant and he poked at her. "Now let's see if Edith looks like her father." He began to remove the bonnet.

Catherine froze, her heart thumping.

"Excuse me," Miss Carter informed O'Keefe politely. "I am responsible for this infant." She wrapped the baby up again; Edith's tiny face was all that was observable. "We don't want her catching pneumonia, do we?"

"Let's hope she doesn't look like her old man," Bryant suggested. "He's an ugly bugger."

Bycroft handed out cigars to receive the congratulatory pats on the back. "Welcome aboard," Lockett whispered.

Miss Carter offered the infant to Olivia Whittington to hold. She refused, offering a cold as the excuse. Jean Lockett held out her arms.

"My turn – gimme, gimme, gimme." Lockett rolled his eyes.

Catherine took the opportunity for breathing space and walked to a bench. She sat there in a field of memories: cherubs, angels and Holy Mothers of sandstone, marble and granite mocked her. The salty wind tempted travel, but Paris could never be thought of without thinking of Danny, or the Middle East without remembering Wally. *Thrice knock the Reaper* invaded her thoughts.

From the abyss, Apollyon whispered, Fate sometimes plays cruel tricks.

Catherine heard Ying Lee's words but paid no heed. Her heartache enticed the elixir from her purse. She thirsted not only for the bottle's contents but also for Bycroft's blood and…the gold fob watch he had stolen from her.

"You still like the wind in your face." Miss Carter sat down on the bench.

The words shocked Catherine back to reality and she stared at the storm clouds approaching. "A storm is brewing," she replied enthusiastically, "and now for the coup d'état." She rose, secure in the knowledge she'd chosen the right nanny for the job, and returned to the gathering at the line of waiting motor vehicles.

Like a sailor drawn to a siren's singing, Lockett was drawn to Miss Carter. She could feel his eyes undressing her as he approached. "Miss Carter, may I sit?" He didn't wait for an answer. "I thought I'd take this opportunity to inform you what the Company expects. As you can see, we're a close-knit group."

"I did not know it is the Company I am employed by."

Lockett enjoyed his salacious fantasy as the cool wind teased her hair, breasts and nipples. She arched her back and gazed at a patch of sparkling water, mesmerised, her long legs twisting and curling beneath the bench like a mermaid's tail.

"Er…I…that is, the Company looks after those who do the right thing, Miss Carter."

Without turning, she responded, "Nurse Shilling seems to have done very well for herself."

"And what would you know about Miss Shilling?"

Lockett watched perplexed as she mimicked removing a mask from before her face. "Much can be learned by observation and listening. Much is to be heard when a man lusts for the ecstasy of pain." She bowed her head, feigning a bashful look. Recognition dawned on Lockett's face as he realised who he was conversing with.

"My God, it's you."

Without the black leather mask and with clothes, Lucy had been unrecognisable. He'd entered her jungle and now paid the price. "Mr. Bycroft and Nurse Shilling were very drunk; they will not recognise me either … but with a little encouragement they will."

Lockett's cocksure attitude deflated. "Your fortune cookie never predicted this meeting."

"The Peacock Garden is renowned for its debauchery, Mr. Lockett, not its fortune cookies."

He looked around quickly and then moved closer to her. "What do you want?"

"I have all that I want – a child to look after, respect and I believe Mr. Bycroft has a lovely property where I shall be living. For me, it is a new life and I want to keep it. If my secret is kept, your wife will never learn of yours."

"But why tell me in the first place, I'd never had recognised you?"

"Madame Catherine's wellbeing, of course." Lucy stared at the ominous clouds and whitecaps conspiring out at sea. "What do you see, Mr. Lockett?"

"There is stormy water ahead."

"Being a sailing man …" She paused, turning to stare him straight in the eye. "I'm sure you're aware of the dilemma faced by passengers on the Titanic."

"Not enough lifeboats," he responded unenthusiastically.

"… and?"

Like a pupil learning his lessons, he answered, "One could drown without a lifeboat."

"Correct, and Madame Catherine's wellbeing is *our* lifeboat," she tutored. "Until now, Mr. Bycroft has been at the rudder."

"Tiller," he corrected, "a lifeboat has a tiller."

"The point I am making, Mr. Lockett, is that…"

"There's been a mutiny."

"Let's just say there's a new Captain at the wheel."

"Helm."

Lucy closed her eyes briefly and breathed deeply to maintain her composure. "You, Mr.

Lockett, will make sure Mr. Bycroft does not rock the boat. I have been informed it is his life that is about to change, not yours."

"Informed … by whom?"

"The mother of his child," she replied indignantly.

"Of course," Lockett nodded his head knowingly.

Lucy's smile broadened, "Of course, but we won't be telling him, will we." A claxon horn sounded. She stood up and gestured they return.

"Baton down the hatches." Bryant shouted.

The gale front rushed from the shoreline below and up through the totems; Bycroft pulled down his fedora as the banshee wail threatened to relieve him of it.

Irene turned her back to protect the baby. "You is a beautiful baby, yes you are," she told the infant. Two brilliant starbursts from under her veil drew Catherine's attention to the obscured necklace she wore.

"Reef the mainsail, Mr. Bryant." Lockett gave a covert salute to Catherine and joined the men as distant thunder rolled in.

Irene smiled at the baby. "It is a fine day for a wake, yes it is."

She handed Edith to Lucy and, as she did so, the wind swept the veil up to reveal Roebuck's Misery; Browning had replaced the lost pearl. An overhead lightning bolt reflected in the abyss of the black opal's lustre.

Recalling the Sweaty Swindler's warning of time standing still, Catherine clasped her chest. "Sacré bleu."

About the author

Greg Davidson grew up in Victoria, Australia, and began working as a commercial artist. He then travelled through Europe and Scandinavia busking. Returning to Australia, Greg continued a musical path writing songs and performing with touring bands. In 2007, writing became his focus. He is a commissioned cartoonist, published playwright, and short story author. Greg lives on the Gold Coast, Queensland.

* * *

If you enjoyed this novel please 'like' Another Alias on Facebook; you are invited to follow the page and interact.
I would appreciate an Amazon 'purchaser review', and please inform your social network or book club of this novel.

The Facebook URL:
https://www.facebook.com/pages/Another-Alias-by-Greg-Davidson/489232107855186 can be accessed and clicked upon or copied and paste to your browser from my website: http://www.vacartistry.com.au

I thank you for your patronage – please communicate soon. Greg Davidson.
* * *

'Another Alias - Duty by Coercion'

The Sequel - Complimentary Chapters

Chapter 1

Late October 1941

The propaganda poster depicting the silhouette of a ship sinking launched itself into Catherine's face – 'Loose lips sink ships.' barked the red slogan. Scrawled over the ominous words, lipstick graffiti asked, "Where's the *Seventh* Fleet?" Catherine gasped as if she had received a sucker-punch below the belt. Her vague dream of the night before featuring the number seven had been a premonition. In her dreams, she had refused to acknowledge it. Now it was blatant; she *had* to.

A rolling motion united everyone in synchronised movement as the train rattled along the Edgecliff line to Sydney Central. For a change the conversation on passengers' lips was not about Churchill, Curtain or the fighting in the Middle East, Africa and Europe; the Melbourne Cup was next week and everyone knew a mate of a friend who knew the cousin of... Catherine smiled, not at the punters' conversations but at a young sailor who continually observed her.

Her trim figure was reflected in the carriage window. Blessed with an Aphrodite complexion, she did not show the signs of middle age. She often received wolf whistles from workers on building sites or unwanted attention from strangers on trains, as befitted a woman in her late twenties rather than one of thirty-nine.

"Would ya like a seat? 'ere ya go, Miss," he said, standing up, "put ya tail 'ere."

"Merci, monsieur but I am old enough to be your mother."

"And what a lovely mother you'd make."

The smell of stale beer slapped her face, reinforcing the intention of the ambiguous statement. The lurching train presented him with an opportunity and he pressed himself against her to whisper in her ear.

"No," she replied, "but I will gladly take monsieur up on the seat offer, merci." *What a pity; such a handsome young man,* she thought, sitting down and dismissing the lewd proposition more easily than the seven on the poster.

For nearly eight years, Catherine Bouvier, formerly Dunn, having relocated from the outback township of Gunnadoo, had resided in the moderately wealthy suburb of Edgecliff. With a fabricated image of respectability, she now enjoyed a stylish lifestyle that was as uncomplicated as her unconventional beginnings allowed.

"I should be on the *Sydney* with me mates." shouted the young lad. "When she comes back from the Mediterranean I will be."

"For Chrissake, shut up," a passenger rebuked, "ya loud enough to sink the bloody Seventh Fleet."

At nine-thirty in the morning, with only one cup of coffee under her belt, apprehension prompted by the omen and Chow Lung's request to see her urgently, Catherine knew the last thing she wanted was involvement in a public disturbance.

"Centraaal." bellowed a voice from the crackling public address system.

Catherine felt the shrill of a police officer's whistle more than she heard it and then déjà vu consumed her. From within a sea of faces, a voice yelled, "Stop that man."

"Stand back, stand back." the platform master shouted.

An overweight cop battled through the throng of shoppers to follow three plainclothes police. Resembling flapping capes, their mackintoshes snapped briskly as they pursued the villain along the station platform in what looked like the filming of a cinema melodrama.

Catherine raised her hand to the platform master. "Do not say it," she cautioned, "a pickpocket, oui?"

Upon hearing the accent, he gave her a suspicious look. "More like a spy...they're everywhere, ya know." His eyes moved in the direction of a wall covered in cinema advertising. The poster showing a black map of Australia stood out from the others. Australia's Fifth Column, a Rupert Kathner newsreel, had struck a chord with the platform master. "They're everywhere, ya know," he repeated.

Chinatown never changed; its inhabitants just grew older. Catherine's knowledge of Mandarin was comparable to her French. Her penchant for languages had been fruitful. The tiny bell above the door of Chow Lung Imports rang true.

"You are expected; please go through," said the shop boy.

Recent renovations had facilitated a new lift and it was no longer necessary to wander through canyons of merchandise to reach the old lift at the rear. The rank smell of mould still prevailed and so did the rats, no doubt. The lift doors opened onto Chow Lung's office foyer stylishly decorated with Chinese paraphernalia. An oriental beauty rose from behind the reception desk and bowed.

"Nai hao," she welcomed. Formalities completed, both women hugged. "It is so good to see you, Aunty."

There was no bloodline; when a toddler, Soo-Yee had given Catherine the 'aunty' title. She had attended Sydney Presbyterian Girls Grammar, as had Edith Bycroft, Catherine's daughter, although Edith believed that her mother had died in childbirth. Catherine taught French at the school to be near Edith. The girls were of the same age but not in the same classes and hardly knew each other, nor had they been encouraged to do so. The charade had been necessary, one of many successfully carried out by Catherine to conceal her past.

"My father awaits you. I am under strict orders to show you through straight away and not idly gossip."

"Then we best not keep him waiting."

Catherine proceeded along a narrow passageway that dissected another floor of merchandise. She knocked on an unpretentious door and entered. Although Chow Lung had transferred his office from one end of the long warehouse to the other, the office was identical to how it had been before the move. Catherine paid him no attention and wandered around studying the abundance of artefacts: porcelain cat statues, vases of dynasties past. Shelving lined the walls and all were all crammed with works of art. "I give up," she said, "I am looking at a reflection, a mirror image." She turned, getting her bearings and pointed. "That is east and that is west. I do not understand, why the move?"

Chow Lung clasped his cheeks with his large hands. "Catherine, would I not have good reason?" His dwarf stature and characteristics never failed to amuse her and she mimicked him. "Well may you mimic me, but look at this." He waddled to the side of the hanging tapestry, flicked a switch and a whirring noise began. The tapestry slid back to reveal a huge panoramic window that rose from floor to ceiling, the view taking in Blackwattle Bay, Ultimo and Chippendale. "This is why," he pointed to the expanse, "land value can only increase." He picked up the binoculars to observe the unloading of cargo from a freighter at Blackwattle Bay. "I always wanted to go to sea," he confided, "new lands and peoples of all persuasions, but alas," he lowered the binoculars, "it was not to be."

Catherine clasped her cheeks again. "I can only assume the world just wasn't ready for a miniature Marco Polo."

Chow Lung dropped his pretence. "Sometimes your remarks can be most cutting." He passed her the binoculars and sat observing as she surveyed the scene. "Well?" he enquired.

"Moi would need a machete to get through that thick hide of yours."

"The view…not me."

"Very nice."

"I will do the honours." Chow Lung poured the tea. "Congratulations are in order…again I am impressed by another of your hidden talents." He gestured to the open *Sydney Morning Herald*.

Catherine studied the photograph; it showed her receiving an award at the Brent Art Gallery. Her entry had won the amateur photographic competition – and ten pounds. The talent, gift or just plain good bluffing had also enabled her to attain work at the Presbyterian Girls Grammar School. Under the pseudonym of Catherine Bouvier and as a French teacher, although unqualified, she had successfully overseen Edith's education and her blossoming into a young woman.

He picked up the binoculars and again trained them on the freighter. "There is much anxiety on wharves…this is not good for business. I have much stock in Singapore warehouse and have difficulty moving it."

"What is of such interest to you?" Catherine's curiosity got the better of her and she playfully snatched the binoculars from Chow Lung and looked in the direction of Blackwattle Bay.

"The *Ocean Maru* is being unloaded. Cousin Weh has sent shipment and yet goods are not on my cargo inventory." He paused, deep in thought, and stared at the wharves. "This most perplexing."

Catherine adjusted the binoculars to focus on cargo nets swinging from a tall crane. "A telescope would be better, oui?"

"Yes, most observant but Singapore cannot be seen through telescope from window...as large as new window is," he added. Catherine lowered the binoculars and peered at him suspiciously. Chow Lung continued. "One must have eyes to see." He turned to face her. "I have need of...Madam Catherine's services."

The binoculars fell to the Oriental rug and Catherine stood stunned until she managed to shriek, "You what?"

Chow Lung smiled deviously and picked up the binoculars. "Please excuse my clumsy proposition." He motioned for her to sit back at the table. "Black market thrives, alas, thick as thieves doctrine does not – new tactics required."

"And what does this have to do with me or..." She began laughing and then caught her breath. "Two propositions," she looked at her watch remembering the young sailor, "and it's only just gone eleven. It's enough to turn a girl's head." She controlled her chuckling, "Madam Catherine is a bit too old..."

He cut in. "You not turn tricks, you turn informant – you be my eyes and ears. A socialite such as you will learn more with beauty and intelligence than…"

"A miniature Marco Polo with a meat cleaver."

He shrugged, grinned broadly and then sipped his tea, leaving Catherine to ponder the proposal seriously.

"And what is it you want moi to do?"

"Find my missing shipment."

"And what is the value of this missing shipment?"

"Commodity values fluctuate each day."

"Fluctuate indeed. Age has not diminished your cunning – you are still a scoundrel." Certain words surreptitiously teased the lilt of a long extinguished Irish brogue from Catherine. The cadence of a phrase would slip past unnoticed but to a trained ear. "Not a penny below five pounds," she demanded.

"Average wage only three pound for week. Two pound for one afternoon work most reasonable."

"Five." She paused to sip her tea, "Plus expenses. Being a socialite does not come cheaply," she added cheekily.

Both parties bowed politely. Catherine returned to the window. "I assume the treasure hunt starts at the *Ocean Maru*?"

"No treasure hunt, very simple." She turned to face him and he continued. "Shipping clerk will give you his copy of manifesto." Chow Lung's idiosyncrasy for secrecy preceded his next words; he touched his nose and spoke quietly. "You will give him envelope in return."

Catherine mimicked the gesture. "It all sounds very cloak and dagger."

583

"Imagination of cunning required – ingenuity most valuable commodity also." He winked and continued. "Tomorrow, *Ocean Maru* returns to Singapore. I will inform shipping clerk contact – he will give you documents this afternoon."

"Why don't you get the documents from the shipping clerk yourself?"

"This impossibility, all documentation accounted for at end of working shift, everyone who has dealings or works on wharves is marketeer suspect. Nothing go in or out without authorisation. Beautiful woman with imagination," he gestured to Catherine while picking up the newspaper clipping, "can succeed where other measures fail. War not always good for business." He passed her the clipping.

"I bow to your wisdom, Chow Lung is most wise," Catherine teased, but she knew he spoke the truth and his cajoling had already convinced her. "I could say I wanted to take a photograph but I don't have my cam…"

He cut in. "I have camera you may use…then we have deal, yes?"

Smiling cheekily, Catherine puckered her lips and then with an exaggerated accent answered, "C'est la guerre, Monsieur Polo."

Chow Lung excitedly clapped his hands together. "Such is war, *Madam* Catherine.

* * *

The boom gate at the Blackwattle Bay wharves only lifted after an inspection of the lorry had been

584

undertaken by the three Customs officers and authorisation given for it to proceed; as it trundled off another lorry pulled up for the same procedure. A dozen or so visitors stood in line beside the security office waiting for an entry pass to the wharves. The senior Customs officer folded the newspaper he had been reading and placed it atop a mountain of paperwork on his desk. "Next," he called in a surly voice. He did not bother to look up, holding out his hand instead. "Papers?"

"Pardon, Monsieur?" Catherine said coyly, "But moi have no papers." Her pronounced accent caught his attention, as did the camera case strap diagonally crossing her torso to separate her breasts. She could feel his searching eyes probing her silk blouse.

"Sorry, no papers no entry – orders from the top."

"It is so hot and I have been waiting for so long." She contorted her body to accentuate the heat and her figure.

"Say, do we know each other? You seem mighty familiar."

Confronted by the surprising statement and the man's intense scrutiny, Catherine felt her heart skip a beat. "I do not think so?"

"Naw, I never forget a face." He stood up.

Catherine immediately acted embarrassed and lowered her head to obstruct recognition. A multitude of possible scenarios flashed by, too many to comprehend.

"I've got it. I know who you are." The officer leaned on the desk and said no more until she looked up. "And we do 'ave something in common."

Catherine felt her knees go weak and her mouth dry up. She tried removing twenty years from his face and stopped abruptly. He looked about thirty-five so if he was a past client he would only have been about fifteen at the time. She stared at the smirking inquisitor.

"I'm a keen photographer myself."

His words rolled around in Catherine's head until they finally became coherent. "What. Pardon?"

"You're that woman." He opened the newspaper to the society pages and read aloud, "Catherine Bouvier wins Brent Art Gallery award." He showed her the clipping. "I told you I never forget a face."

The nausea in the pit of her belly disappeared and her confidence returned, her lungs filling with oxygen and clearing her confused brain. "Most fortunate. It was the first time moi have entered the competition." She seductively played with the leather strap, running her finger up and down it between her breasts.

"Now, now, don't be so modest, this award is quite a feather in your cap." His body language contradicted his words. "I like the way the newspaper photographer has positioned you in the foreground of your winning entry." Catherine felt her ego rise. He sat down to begin his critique. "Yes, I like the idea but whether you've actually captured the essence of comradeship...that *was* the brief wasn't it?" He rubbed his chin. "I dunno."

Catherine felt her ego deflate and defended the image. "That is a shrine and it is very dear to moi, comprenez-vous?" The silhouette of a soldier standing with bowed head and rifle at reverse arms against a spectacular Gunnadoo sunset was a fluky shot. She was a good photographer but not an expert.

"It's a bit ostentatious but I can see how it was an obvious choice for the judges."

"Sacré bleu. Everyone is a critic."

"Naw, I shouldn't be petty about these things." His demeanour changed as he folded the newspaper. "I've entered the bloody competition each year since it began and never got nowhere," he confided, "and you come along and win it first go. You understand what I'm sayin'?"

"But of course. You poor man, your feelings have been hurt. An artiste is fragile. We must be given our freedom," she clutched her breast, "to express our true emotions, oui?"

The man rose smartly to his feet and held out his hand. "Officer Topp. What can I do for you?"

"I wish to take some photographs of…"

"Nope, can't be done – restricted area."

"Of men hard at work, portraits, not locations, I'm aware of…"

He cut her off again and sat down laughing. "You've still come to the wrong place, this wharf is Union run and nobody works hard around here."

Catherine recognised his humour and laughed patronisingly. Topp shrugged and then continued, "You got no papers, besides I can't let you wander around by yourself." His demeanour changed again. "They're all a bunch of thugs, that lot. Stick a knife in

587

ya as soon as look at ya." He rose, walked to the window and looked out. "Who are the photographs for anyway?"

"The Salvation Army," she lied.

"The Salvos eh," he pondered, wiping the window with his fingertips. "I tell you what," he placed his cap on and adjusted it, "if I escort you we can bend the rules just this once."

There was no way out; refusing the offer was the same as throwing the five-pound fee from Chow Lung to the wind. "Merci."

Topp opened the door and gestured to Catherine to precede him, hollering, "Officer Brown." as he did so.

Officer Brown's boots clicked before him and a snappy salute followed. "Boss?"

"Take over and don't mess up or I'll 'ave ya guts for garters."

The smell of hot bitumen outside the bonded warehouses camouflaged the stench inside; men at work, rotting goods and carcases of decaying rodents made a rancid cocktail. Catherine had fortuitously not worn stilettos; the black tar squelched beneath her shoes as she tramped across the wharves. Topp insisted they begin in Shed 1.

"There's some bloody ugly mugs in here you can photograph."

What should have been a simple ploy for Catherine was turning into an epic photo shoot; Topp would not leave her side and she could not make contact with the shipping clerk.

"Merci. Thank you gentlemen."

"They ain't no bloody gentlemen," advised Topp, as the wharfies broke from their group pose and wandered off. "I wouldn't trust any of 'em. The only shooting of 'em I'd be doing is with Bertha." He patted the Smith and Wesson holster and then feigned drawing the weapon and shooting a victim. "Just give me half the chance." He blew on his pointed finger as though cooling a smoking gun-barrel. His eyes gleamed. "Half the chance, that's all I want."

Although perspiring profusely, her belief that the man was capable of anything chilled Catherine to the core; he had certainly displayed a multitude of personalities in the past ninety minutes. The five-pound fee no longer seemed such an attractive deal as she sensed the warped delight Topp took in putting her through this ordeal. It was time to get the better of the antagonist. The opportunity presented itself when a brawl started. Shouting from the far end of the shed alerted Topp and he quickly led Catherine to the shipping clerk's office. "Wait here," he said, opening the door and pushing her inside. She watched him sprinting off to join the fray through the opaque panel.

A series of photographs depicting the history of the Celtic Clover Line hung on the wall. Above the clerk's writing desk tucked into a sunless corner, a naked bulb tainted by cigar smoke emanated a yellow glow. The man looked up. "And w'at would it be I could do for ya?"

Catherine immediately recognised the accent and slipped into the dialect as easily as slipping into a pair of silk stockings. "Me Granny came from Belfast she did."

589

"Now tat be a fact." The cigar smoke rose: he did not. "And who be ya Granny?"

"Granny Dunn she be and no finer woman walked God's green earth."

"Hmm, Dunn?" He rose and moved to the counter and then enquired, "Who be ya t'en?"

"I be…" She hesitated briefly; a calendar with McCauley advertising caught her attention. "I be a McCauley and proud too I be. And who be you then?" she retorted. From lessons learnt well, Catherine knew how to turn the tables to her advantage.

"Shaun Cooney." Recognising a fellow Paddy, he smiled warmly and held out a hand. "Nice ta be meetin' ya."

Catherine refused his hand. "Then, Shawn Cooney, be so good as to direct me to the Orca Line office and stop leerin' at me."

Cooney stepped back from the counter. "You've got me wrong. I was only…"

Her raised voice abruptly cut short any forthcoming explanation. "I've a good mind to call a policeman, I have."

"Two sheds over and turn right, up ta stairs." Cooney slipped under the counter, opened the employee's door and pointed. "Tat is five; ya want number seven, take ta stairs on ta left – ya can't be missin' it."

Catherine checked she was clear of Topp and quickly crossed the busy thoroughfare to Shed 5. Inside, she endured the obligatory wolf-whistles and lewd suggestions from the men, likewise in Shed 6 and then the clerk's office at Shed 7 provided sanctuary. She closed the door and leaned against it as the bawdy calls faded. "Sacré bleu. How long have those men been at sea?" she questioned the astonished clerk.

"They're only the dock workers; they don't go to sea."

The Orca Line could well have been a replica of the Celtic Clover Line. Behind the counter, photographs of ships hung between maritime maps charting the progress of ships at sea. Musty reference books and dusty documents overflowed from shelves and assorted chandlery lay underfoot.

"Monsieur Willard?"

"You are alone?" The question sounded more like a statement of surprise. Willard moved from behind the counter and peered through the glass panel. "Nobody saw you come up?" Catherine's perplexed look told him otherwise. "Jeez, I'm making a right cock-up of this, aren't I?" He scratched his head. "And you are…?"

"In a hurry, I believe you have something for me?" While the young man watched, Catherine removed the 35mm Foca and from under a false bottom in the camera case retrieved the envelope. "Hurry up," she demanded, passing him the envelope. "I do not have all day."

"But I thought…"

"You thought what?"

He took the envelope. "I thought…naw, it doesn't matter." He shook his head and then proceeded to get the manifesto. "If you get caught, I didn't give it to you. I'll say you stole it when I had my back turned. It'll be my word against yours." He handed her three pages. "This is what you're looking for."

The folded pages replaced the envelope in the case and Catherine then placed the Foca inconspicuously on top. She swung the strap over her shoulder and left, saying as she went, "Bonjour, Monsieur Willard…it has been a pleasure doing business."

The knock-off whistle sounded and shift workers streamed from offices and sheds conveniently camouflaging her exit towards the security office gates. Within fifty yards of freedom, she immediately recognised the voice from behind. Her heart and mind began racing.

"You weren't thinking of leaving without saying goodbye?"

"I thought you may have been in your office. We seemed to have got separated."

"I asked you to wait."

"I was frightened when the fighting began and lost my direction."

"And if I lost you, I'd lose these," he pointed to the stripes on his sleeve, "and I'd have to track you down and shoot you with this." He patted Bertha.

Catherine was mortified; she did not know if he was joking or not. She stumbled. He took her arm and quietly cautioned her. "Mind your step; we don't want you getting damaged – but then again damaged goods are part and parcel of the business, wouldn't you agree?"

"The business? Pardon, I do not understand."

"Espionage."

Scenarios of what she could say in her defence at a trial for treason filled her head. Her instinct for self-preservation took over as she stepped spritely in front of Topp and collapsed. His hands immediately clasped her waist.

"Stop it." she yelled, conveniently painting Topp's compromising position as assault. One of the workers approached.

"ey, get ya 'ands off 'er or I'll…"

"You'll do what?" He removed his hands from Catherine and placed one on the holster and the other in the man's face, pushing him backwards and smiling nastily. "Mr. Brown." he shouted. Catherine felt the charade tumbling down around her feet as Topp's hand rested upon her shoulder.

"Five pounds – it wasn't worth it," she confided remorsefully. She lowered her head and stared at her flat-heeled shoes, contemplating making a run for it.

"Five pounds…I thought you won ten. If I won ten bob, I'd be over the moon." Again, he yelled for Brown. The surge of workers was uncontrollable at the exit gate and Brown had his hands full. "Well, come on then." He cleared a path through the crowd, pulling Catherine behind him. They didn't enter the office and she unexpectedly found herself escorted through the perimeter gate. Topp held out his hand. "I hope you got the picture you came for. "ave a good day."

The ploy had succeeded and Topp was none the wiser. Invigorated yet drained by the angst, Catherine shook his hand. "Bonjour, Officer Topp. I hope very soon you will get another stripe." She could feel Topp's eyes on her until she turned into Wattle Street, then she quickened her pace to match her racing heart. *Holy Mother, what I have done?* In times of dire stress, the Irish brogue instinctively came to the fore.

Catherine zigzagged through various streets and laneways hoping to evade any would-be pursuers, taking an indirect route to Chinatown. The tiny cottages and cobblestone alleyways evoked her memories as an eight-year-old living in the slums of Exetor Street at the Rocks. *Mother of Mercy, where am I?* She stopped as she realised the absurdity of being lost in the labyrinth. Above her thumping heart, she could hear the noise of shunting carriages in the Darling Harbour goods yard and was able to get her bearings.

Methodically making her way along the perimeter fence with blackberry bushes and weeds growing beside it, she found the hole marking the place directly opposite which was Chinatown. Sharp rocks between the railway lines tore at the soles of her shoes and a relentless sun baked her skin as her heaving lungs choked on soot. Working her way through the quagmire of steel, she took refuge from the hissing steam in a vacant controller's box as a locomotive trundled past. Although like a sauna, the small shed offered relief from the burning sun.

Catherine removed the pages from the camera case and stuffed them inside her knickers. She replaced the camera in the case but no sooner had she slung it over her shoulder than a voice from behind startled her.

"eh. What are you doing?"

She spun around in shock. The momentum of turning around propelled the camera in an arch and catapulted into the man's face. Such was the railway worker's shock he tripped over backwards, hitting his head and knocking himself unconscious. Catherine slapped the man's face and he groaned. "Thank God I haven't killed you," she said, picking up the camera case, "I'll be on me way then."

A hand clasped her ankle and she tripped. The momentum propelled her into the path of an unwitting co-worker who was just then entering the darkened space. The front-on tackle thrust him backwards and he fell onto the sharp rocks and writhed in agony, holding his back. *Mother of Mercy, I'll be shot at dawn,* she thought, and ran for her life leaving behind Chow Lung's camera.

A cacophony of noises smothered the distant wailing of the men as Catherine climbed up the ladder. Nobody took any notice of her appearing on the platform and she mingled with railway employees. About to enter a door marked *Ladies Washroom*, Catherine stepped back and gestured to a young woman to go first. Inside, the woman hung her smock on a peg and checked her appearance in the mirror.

Catherine observed her own bedraggled appearance and then that of the smartly-dressed woman.

"You look like you've had one of those days?" she said, smiling politely.

"Ah, to be sure indeed I have."

Catherine splashed her grimy face with cool water and her heart rate eased. She returned her gaze to the mirror and to her brunette locks that now hung like rats' tails.

"Betty's the name." The woman removed her headscarf and stuffed it in the smock pocket. "You must be new, I haven't seen you before."

"It be me first day, and Heavens to be, what a day it's been."

"Ah, they stuck you in the workshops then – it's an initiation rite, you won't be there long and then…" The rumbling from Betty's stomach stopped her mid sentence. "Excuse me." She dashed to the cubicle.

Catherine took off her blouse and tried to remove the oily grit but it only made it worse. "And how long have you been an employee?" she asked.

"Two years. I'm now what's called an executive cleaner, I get to wear a swanky uniform."

The starched and pressed smock was swanky. Catherine's pulse rate increased as she raised her head and looked heavenward. *Forgive me, Mother.* As she slipped out of her skirt and into the new fashion statement, a declaration of contempt startled her.

"You bitch."

Catherine froze, not daring to look in the mirror. A short silence followed Betty's tirade of expletives, and then, "There's no paper."

Catherine clutched her exploding chest to calm the erratic beating. She looked into the mirror and observed only herself.

"Excuse me? I never got your name," called Betty.

Catherine collected her faculties. "That you never, no."

"In the cupboard drawer under the washbasins there should…"

"I'll take a peek." Catherine kicked the cupboard door, and then began covering her rats' tails with Betty's headscarf. "No, I don't be seeing nothin' there." The door received another kick. "I'll try the other." She removed Betty's nametag from the lapel. Her appearance was now that of an executive office cleaner. "No nothin' there either – I'll get a roll from the storeman."

"Don't be long," replied Betty, "I start my shift soon."

* * *

The lift doors opened to a vacant reception desk. Catherine was glad; an explanation to Soo-Yee of the ordeal would not be necessary and Chow Lung could receive his tongue-lashing sooner. She pushed aside the double doors, crossed the empty room to open the door opposite and then shouted down the passageway. "I am coming Chow Lung – get out your chequebook."

There was no polite knock as Catherine barged in, and no let-up from the barrage of expenses she began rattling off. Chow Lung sat smiling broadly behind his desk as she approached with shoes in hand. "And you can double that for inconvenience, no triple it for the compromising position you put me in." she yelled.

"I observe change of dress since this morning, most flattering," he teased. "I also observe you do not carry camera ... where my camera?"

Catherine flopped into a chair and threw her battered shoes on the floor. "You have no idea what I have been through." She rubbed her feet. The silk stockings had soaked up the blood that the coal dust had failed to cauterise and blackberry welts now burned irritatingly. "And you can pay for my medical expenses also."

He shook his head. "I fear I may have lost camera and still not got manifesto."

"It was your idea to lend me it – chalk it up to expenses. Shut your eyes." She retrieved the pages from her knickers and threw them onto the desk. "Here. That is the wisest five pounds you have spent recently."

The whirring noise of the tapestry opening directed Catherine's attention to the window, the stream of light blinding her. Against a dazzling sunset, a man's silhouette stood rigid with arms folded. The surly voice was easily recognisable.

"So it was five. Black market or espionage, which is it?" Topp placed the newspaper clipping before Catherine and then produced identification from his inside pocket. He held out the wallet and flicked it open. "Shepard – C.I.O."

The acronym meant nothing but Catherine's complexion was that of the grey flannel suit he wore. "C.I.O.?" she queried.

"South East Asia Intelligence Organisation – you have some explaining to do."

"So do you, Monsieur Shepard…your acronym is incorrect." She stalled while trying to think.

"I have two colleagues down, one with concussion and the other with a slipped disc. Your overall actions suggest you're not who you'd like us to believe you are –Catherine Bouvier, or is it Catherine Dunn?" He moved behind her and bent over to whisper in her ear. She felt Shepard's hand upon her shoulder. "Is it Bouvier or Dunn, or could it be Wingood? Christine Wingood." The past flooded back to drown Catherine; her greatest fear, her true identity, Christine Wingood was discovered.

Wally Beaumont, Edith's blood father, had bequeathed shares in Bastock Transport to Catherine; it paid a tidy sum annually. Undoubtedly, the largest revenue earner had been the house of ill repute and Madam Catherine had made wise investments. The institution ran into less profitable times when Gunnadoo's gold-mining population dwindled; the commodity had run dry. The Depression was the nail in the coffin; the doors of the stately manor, Briarwood, closed. When the cuckold, John Bycroft, packed Edith off to boarding school in Sydney, Catherine followed. She left Mrs. Chang as the custodian of the property and made a new start by inventing another persona.

"There's some questions that need answering. We can either do it here," he paused and smiled, "or at my office. I'm afraid it isn't as comfortable as here." He opened a small notebook and scribbled the time and date. "Shall we get on with it?"

Chow Lung was no longer smiling.

Chapter 2

Yapsly Siding was a contradiction unto itself. Two large platforms and a majestic stationmaster's office suggested the siding had once played a significant role in the region's prosperity, but it never had. The big plans for a central junction had hit a snag when Gunnadoo gold resources began petering out. The depression was the last straw, dividing the consortium of financial backers, and the project fell apart. Weeds soon overran the idle platforms, and rust never had the chance to invade the steel rails to Gunnadoo as fettlers had never laid the rails. A cutting leading into the bush for two miles and abruptly stopping was evidence of incompletion. The stationmaster's building with its majestic façade had never opened. It now housed the local co-operative store, and the original 1890 stationmaster's office and platform still carried the rail traffic.

Lucy waved her handkerchief frantically as the locomotive and carriages shuddered to a stop. "Edie. Edie." she called as if she was on the platform at Central in peak hour rather than Yapsly Siding on a Thursday. In the region, locals said tongue in cheek that Gunnadooites measured time in days.

Upon stepping from the carriage, the object of Lucy's attention, Edith Bycroft, immediately felt the late afternoon sun upon her red hair and freckled complexion. Her skin tone had once been a bone of contention but she now accepted it, as she did Lucy's embarrassing show of affection. Edith shook her head and held out her arms to embrace her nanny of nineteen years. Lucy could no longer take Edith fully in her arms and she stepped back to announce, "Why, I do believe my late bloomer has blossomed."

"Stop it, Nan. You're embarrassing me."

Edith was no longer flat chested and stood taller than eight months previously when Lucy had last seen her. After leaving college, she had done a year's nursing at St. Vincents Hospital and when she turned eighteen, she joined the Australian Army Nursing Service. Her awkward persona had not changed until the training undertaken at Concord Repatriation Hospital; her deflowering by a randy intern there had helped.

"I can manage those," she said jovially and picked up the bags. "Come on then, let's get going, we haven't got all day."

Old Ted collected Edith's ticket and welcomed her home. The once thriving parking lot for travellers and commerce now lay deserted, except for the stripped carcasses of wagons and motor vehicles. Edith threw the bags in the rear of Bycroft's Daimler and then, with Lucy protesting, pushed her from behind the wheel. "Move over Nan, I'm driving."

Lucy slid across the leather seat. "Only if you drive carefully, I promised your father I wouldn't let you get behind the wheel." She gripped the door armrest and closed her eyes as the engine started. "Let's just have a pleasant chat, enjoy the scenery and…" The rear tyres spun on gravel and Spinifex tufts. Lucy swallowed hard as she felt the tyres grip and herself thrust into the padded leather.

Edith had displayed a penchant for excitement at an early age. For her eighth birthday, she received her own horse and could outride any boy her age – and then some. She had also soared in a Tiger Moth joy flight when a flying circus performed over Gunnadoo. That year, Amy Johnson had flown from England to Australia and she became Edith's goddess.

For her eleventh birthday, Edith pestered her father for a restored Harley Davidson, a Tiger Moth being out of the question, and she managed to all but fly on the motorcycle. The single-stroke engine was continually under repair at Bastock's Garage. For her twelfth birthday, she received an unpleasant surprise when Bycroft had packed her off to boarding school in Sydney.

Edith cut the usual two-hour trip by thirty minutes. Approaching Gunnadoo, she pulled the car over before the Bycroft homestead turnoff; the engine idled as she observed the fork in the road. "Don't you dare – your father is expecting you this evening," said Lucy. Edith gunned the engine and headed towards Gunnadoo. Lucy rolled her eyes. "I may as well talk to a brick wall."

"We'll ring him from the house."

"You mean I'll be doing the ringing and making excuses for you."

"No. No more excuses, those days are gone." Edith smiled cheekily. "I'll simply tell him I don't want to go out to the property tonight – I'd rather get drunk at his pub."

"You're not twenty-one yet, Missy."

"Get with the times, Nan, things have changed since your day. Besides, there's a war on, who knows what tomorrow holds." She blasted the Daimler's horn at a primary school classmate and yelled out the window, "Hey, Templar, have you been breeding any winners lately?"

Clyde Templar displayed a sloth-like reaction, his arm rising slowly with his middle finger extended.

"I swear he's dead from the neck up, always was. He wouldn't know one end of a horse from the other." Edith stopped Lucy before she could comment and laughed. "Don't say it – I was only eleven years old." The memory of being caught sharing one of her father's Cuban cigars, an incentive for Clyde to kiss her, brought tears to her eyes. The green-faced lad had thrown up in her lap and she had never received the kiss. That experience and other matters of the heart had shaken Edith's confidence until the intern got his way. "Here we are," she said, after pulling into the driveway and turning off the engine. "All in one piece – safe 'n sound."

Lucy relaxed her grip on the armrest and felt the blood return to her hand.

A mysterious fire had destroyed the parlour and front rooms when Edith was five, and Bycroft had had the cottage rebuilt. The volunteer fire brigade, established after the great fire of 1921 that had destroyed most of Chinatown, quickly dowsed the flames before it could spread. The Sergeant believed it arson, someone with a grudge against Bycroft. Edith and school friend Roger Lennard had barely escaped the flames. Roger's father, Tom, had taken the photos for the *Advocate*, making the front page.

603

The episode bonded the two kids together throughout their formative years and the close friendship still existed.

Edith threw her bags into her room, changed her clothes and then joined Lucy in the kitchen. "Why don't you ring your father, dinner will be ready soon. I thought we'd have a salad, it's too hot for a cooked meal."

Edith sat down at the table and studied the photo on the *Advocate*'s front page. "Roger certainly takes after his father." Roger's photo of the parade of volunteers showing their willingness to march off to war displayed his natural talent. Lucy looked over Edith's shoulder and began pointing out many of the boys Edith had gone to school with. "There's Tony." Ted White's son led the parade. "And there's Paul." The sole heir to Bastock Transport carried the banner displaying the Gunnadoo Volunteers emblem. "Look at..."

"Stinky Whitlock," Edith interrupted. "I can see." She removed Lucy's pointing finger from the page.

"His father's on the *HMAS Sydney,* you know."

"There's a rumour that it's coming back from duty in the Mediterranean."

"Ships in the night – they can wave to each other," said Lucy.

"Impossible. Basic training takes ... "

"You know what I mean." Lucy tapped the table to make her point. "They're too young, it shouldn't be allowed. They think it's a lark, an adventure, all of 'em marched down to the depot singing their fool heads off. I'm sure if they saw the shattered bodies you have of late they wouldn't be in such a hurry to get under a brown slouch hat." Lucy waited for Edith to support her comment but that did not happen. "Well?" she enquired, "I'm right aren't I…yes?"

Edith looked up. "Nan." She paused and took the woman's hand. "I've applied for an overseas posting." Lucy's face turned pale as Edith continued. "I'll know where I'm being posted in a week or two. This is what I've trained for – it's my duty."

"Duty." Lucy retorted, pulling her hand free of Edith's and walking to the sink. "What have you done child? I didn't raise you to see you get yourself killed in somebody else's war. Wasn't it bad enough to sign up and not discuss it with me? Now you tell me that. To hell with Curtain, Prime Minister for three weeks and he's packin' the boys off instead of bringing them home. Politicians. They're all tainted with the same war-mongering brush." She hacked at the tomato. "What will your father say?"

"I don't care what he thinks, it's my life. Besides, wasn't he once a politician?" Lucy sniffled and shrugged, not replying. The tomato was turning to pulp.

"Nan, I'm a big girl now, I've got to make my own way in the world and you can't go on protecting me from it." Lucy received a hug from behind. "You're the one I care about – that's why I told you first." Edith returned to the table and glanced at the *Advocate*. "I'm not hungry. I'm going to see Rog…don't wait up."

The slamming of the screen door echoed through the house. Lucy walked to the parlour, lifted

605

the telephone receiver and then replaced it, to sit staring at the wall opposite. The knowledge that Bycroft was a cuckold and that she had never met Wally Beaumont, Edith's father and Bycroft's original business partner, weighed heavily on her. Lucy had always resisted the urge to tell Edith of her mother's existence and had debated this with Catherine when she had visited recently. News of Edith's potential posting overseas now made it imperative that she meet her mother beforehand.

* * *

A brilliant sunset lit the sky as Edith strolled down Main Street. A cotton shirt casually tucked into khaki dungarees, and old riding boots, was her selected apparel. The six-o'clock swill had just begun when she popped into the Arms to deliver quick hellos to her father's staff before she continued south. She stopped at the Cenotaph at the Main Street and Flanders Lane intersection; the monument had always held a fascination since her first Anzac Day as a child when the schoolchildren attended the commemorative service. Now, under a flaming sunset, the lone soldier appeared more significant than ever.

"Boo." Roger yelled in her ear, grabbing her from behind.

"Christ, you scared the living daylights out of me, you bastard. I was just coming to see you."

"Saved you the trip then, didn't I." He released his hold. "Clyde told me you were back. Come on," he held up the camera, "I've got some developing to do."

At the *Advocate*, Edith shut the door of the darkroom and then joined Roger in the developing booth as she had done many times before. She loved to watch the methodical procedure, his hands conjuring images from the bath solution onto blank paper. It was in the red glow of the darkroom as kids that Roger had instigated the game of 'tell all'. Although Edith had, he had never done so although he'd claimed to.

"I've done it," she said quietly.

Roger sifted the developer tray, not looking up. "So did Dad – he's in Singapore. I reckon he did it to stop me from joining up. Mum received a letter last week. There were so many holes cut out of the letter by the censor it was hardly worth getting. He and Uncle Clarrie conspired and I'm stuck here taking baby photos – it's not fair."

Edith tried to make light of the situation. "Just as well, you'd probably have both sides shooting at you."

It did not go down well. The mixed marriage of Roger's parents had been a cross he had borne throughout his school years. Roger Tiang Lennard (Wong Foo had insisted on a Chinese second name), had facial features that were the envy of many females. The fine features and smooth skin of his mother Lotus-Flower's oriental lineage, which predominated over Tom's Caucasian, had instigated much taunting.

"Come on, buck up. I'm sure you'll get your chance. Your talents will be recognised and the army will send a staff car for you," she joked.

"It'll all be over soon and I'll have missed out."

"Is that you Roger? Who have you got in there with you?" called Meg.

"It's me Mrs. Radcliff, Edith Bycroft."

"Edith. I heard you were back dear, I've just put on a cuppa…"

Roger rolled his eyes. "See? Nothing's changed, everyone knows everyone's business. I'm drowning here and the world is passing me by." He pegged the baby photo to the line with the others for drying. "It's not fair, Dad's already made his name, it's now my turn." He flicked off the light. "Come on, Auntie Meg will soon be knocking…there's no such thing as privacy in Gunnadoo…except for in here."

Edith gave him a friendly push. "Well, what do you expect when you grow up in a township this size? Of course people are going to talk, it's called community spirit. I haven't been back thirty minutes and I bet the telephone lines are running hot. I told Nan I'd call Dad and let him know I've arrived…I know I don't have to."

Meg poured another two cups and gestured for them to sit.

"Hello luv." boomed another voice. "Just popped in for a chinwag with Meg." Ruby sat at the kitchen table with cup in hand trying not to be noticed staring at Edith's figure. "How long are you back for this time?"

"Three days, just a quick visit … "

Roger cut in. "And then she's being posted overseas – it's not fair."

Both women looked appalled. Meg sat down speechless; her son Michael was still posted as missing in action, his Spitfire shot down over

Dunkirk in 1940. Albert, the younger twin, was in the Middle East training with the 6 Division. He had the wild streak; of all the AIF divisions, the Sixth contained the highest proportion of larrikins. The 'Thirty-Niners', as they were called, took great pride in being the first division raised.

A tear trickled down Meg's drawn face.

"How's Albert?" asked Edith.

"He's fine. He was at Bardia, you know."

"It must've been some party after that victory," Ruby added.

Edith could not bring herself to give her condolences for Michael and just took Meg's hand, as she had done for many mothers who had farewelled dying sons at the Concord Repat. Meg sniffled and wiped her face quickly on her apron as men's voices approached from the back yard.

"If Abe is drunk I'll skin him alive," threatened Ruby. "Every November, when the Cup is run, it's always the same thing. I swear every man and his horse…" She paused to think about her pun and then joined the already laughing women.

Roger sat sulking, the dark rings around his eyes revealing his mood. Clarrie and Abe entered the room, their intoxication evident by the welcome that Edith received. She was surprised at how much Clarrie had aged. He appeared a man approaching sixty rather than fifty. The affection the respective husbands showed to Ruby and Meg confirmed the women's suspicions.

"You're drunk." Ruby hollered.

"And about to become a very rich man," slurred Abe, pulling a wad of notes from his pocket. "Punters are the soul of the earth, they are." The cigarette held in the side of his mouth jettisoned ash, which fell, rolled down the front of his shirt and dropped on his shoe. He immediately wiped it on the opposite trouser leg. "Da da." He placed the clean shoe forward, his hand circling twice while bowing. "Now you see it – now you don't."

Ruby reached out and secured the wad from his hand. "Da da. Now you see it – now you don't."

Clarrie raised his hands in surrender. "Not me, I'm not drunk," he declared to Meg, his swaying contradicting his words. "I only accompanied my good friend Abe to make sure he didn't overindulge."

Meg knew her husband of twenty-five years and the problem he had when drinking; Michael's disappearance weighed on him more than he let on and alcohol instigated depression. When they had first heard the news, his dark hair had turned grey overnight; the thick crop was now thinning.

He flopped into a chair, burped, smiled and then stood up again. "As proprietor of the *Advocate* please accept my formal apology and ... " He stopped as if he had writer's block, but it was an image he was unable to recall. An embarrassing silence ensued as he stood with tears in his eyes trying to remember Michael's features without looking at a photograph. Meg placed a hand on his shoulder and pushed him lightly so that his knees buckled and he sat. "Thank you my dear, I don't mind if I do."

Edith broke the silence. "Well, what's your tip – who's going to win?" Each man gave a different answer. "Well, I hear no joy from either of you, I'm afraid you've left me with no other option..." she sipped her tea as her audience waited, "I'll just have to ask Clyde." Howls of laughter rang out; even Roger smiled. Any subject that could divert attention from the war was welcomed. Their conversation started with the Cup and returned to it twenty minutes later. "What's your price on Skipton?" Edith asked Abe.

"Naw, Beau Vite," Clarrie said, "put your money on the Kiwi champ." He thumped the table to make his point and knocked over his cup. He calmly watched the liquid pour from the tabletop onto his lap.

"Come on," Meg helped him to his feet. "You can talk horses tomorrow."

"It looks like I pissed myself," he told her. "As proprietor of the *Advocate* please accept ... "

"Off to bed with you," Meg said.

Ruby nudged Abe in the ribs. "And you too, Mister." She checked her watch. "It's seven-thirty, you got a busy day tomorrow. Get a move on." The hardware store pre-Christmas sales were to begin.

"Goodnight Clarrie," Ruby called, "don't let the bed-bugs bite." She prodded Abe in the back and headed him to towards the rear door. "Call in and we'll have a girl chat before you leave," she said to Edith.

The flywire screen slammed shut.

"She's the last one I'd be chatting with," snarled Roger.

"What is *wrong* with you? That woman's been like a second mother to you." Edith noted the dark circles around his eyes; a mood swing was in progress. She made light of the situation. "Besides, she's the *Advocate* gossip columnist – it's her job to gossip." She thumped his arm, smiled and walked to the lounge room. About to call out her farewell to the Radcliff's, she stopped before a picture of Michael on the sideboard wearing his RAF uniform. The moustache he sported, characteristic of many air force pilots, was new to her. He cut a dashing figure. Faint sobbing emanated from the Radcliff's bedroom. She walked to the screen door without calling her farewell. "Come on, Rog, I'll walk you home, I'd like to see your Mum."

It was a humid evening and yet Main Street was quiet. The hardwood planks of the sidewalk, laid a decade before the street had received bitumen, clattered as a few townsfolk went about their business. Edith and Roger ambled south past the Cenotaph, all but in darkness; the blown streetlamp bulb needed replacing. Edith smiled. "Do you remember when they turned on the electricity for the first time?"

Roger began laughing and then abruptly stopped. "For Christ sake, of course I do. We were ten – you're only six months older than me."

Edith continued. "And all the bulbs popped. Pop. Pop. Pop. All the way along Main Street. I swear, Dad's face was so red he lit up the town. And do you know what else I remember?" She pushed him playfully. "I remember you being dared to walk on the bitumen when they first laid it. You had blisters the likes of which I'd never seen – you couldn't walk for a week." She stopped in front of the Palace cinema and read the coming attraction posters. "I'd have been the most popular girl in school if Dad had owned this back then."

She put an arm over Roger's shoulder, like a mate. He gave her a playful shove and crossed to the other side of the street. "Mum's at Grandfather's. Come on."

Wong Foo and his antagonist, Edith's father, were amongst the region's wealthiest but unlike many who had made their fortune and left they had chosen to stay and were now institutions unto themselves. Located on a large block of manicured land behind his four businesses fronting Main Street, Wong Foo's residence was palatial. A pagoda roof adorned the rambling weatherboard filled with Chinese artefacts.

Wong Foo was a traditionalist and still wore a cheongsam. "Ah, Missy Edith," he bowed his head politely and stroked his wispy chin hair, "I heard you were back, please sit," he gestured to her.

Edith gave Roger a covert wink. Lotus-Flower sat with her mother on the floor cushions at the low table. Mrs Foo, propped up by many cushions around her, sat rocking and smiling into space; the stroke had left her capable of little else.

"You will join us for tea," requested Wong Foo. His tone changed when addressing his grandson. He refused to call him Roger. "Tian is in bad books...go home," he told him sternly.

Black rings formed around Roger's eyes and he held his ground until Wong Foo repeated his words, then he stormed out of the room. Edith was again in an uncomfortable situation. She smiled at the smiling Mrs. Foo and then returned Lotus-Flower's smile as she poured tea into small cups. Edith reflected on the conversation at the *Advocate* and the respect the adults there showed her, despite their being from a different generation. Not residing in Gunnadoo played a big part in the acceptance, allowing her to communicate with them on the same level rather than that of the child they had known.

"My son is troubled, his father has been away too long," Lotus-Flower said to Edith, while wiping the drool from Mrs. Foo's chin. "The boy needs a father." Edith empathised. She could see the tiredness in the woman's eyes as she spoke. "My son is always angry, angry at me, angry at his father ... "

"And me," interrupted Wong Foo, "he show no respect to his Grandfather...he just plain angry with world."

Having listened to Wong Foo's whingeing about how he had to do most things for himself, because of his wife's inability, Edith finally tuned out. When he said that Lotus-Flower had been staying to care for her invalid parent, she could not decide who the invalid was, Mrs. Foo or her husband. She nodded her head and made noises of agreement while pondering Roger's situation. She looked at her watch. "Ooh. It's gone nine...time I was going." She stood, stretching her legs and back. Her face felt as though a fixed grin was attached to it and required stretching also. "I'm about ready for bed. I'll let myself out."

Edith strolled down the lane between the Chinese restaurant and Wong Foo's produce store. She muttered to herself while pondering Roger's situation and then stopped abruptly as she turned left on Main Street. *He doesn't need a father,* she thought, *he needs a woman.* She about-faced and her pace quickened, along with her heart, and she slipped past the saddlery into Dunkirk Street and up to Gallipoli Parade. The memory of being a child on late-night forays made her smile. Unbeknown to Lucy, Edith would sneak out, and unbeknown to the townsfolk or her friends, she had been the mysterious stone thrower. Many a house had had its roof rocked. She had been the bane of Sgt. Doyle's life, until he'd been recalled to Sydney to answer corruption allegations and had never returned.

As if on a foray again, she stealthily moved from tree to tree, always staying in the shadows out of sight of prying eyes and gossiping tongues. Stopping under Roger's open bedroom window, with the light shining down on her as the ABC news chimed nine o'clock, she tapped her watch and listened to the fanfare for the BBC World News. "Oh, Roger," she called. "Roger...I've got something for you."

* * *

Shepard had never let up firing question after question at Catherine. He had filled his notepad with scribbles and looked worse for the ordeal. With his suit coat removed, his sleeves rolled up, his collar undone and tie askew, the man looked frazzled. He had collected and pieced together information on Catherine as would a biographer and then laid it out before her like a book. She sensed the interrogation was nearing an end and squirmed in her chair. Snoozing peacefully on a couch nearby Chow Lung woke as the nine o'clock cacophony of chimes began. The noise from the collection of antique clocks stopped Shepard's questioning, as it had every half hour and hour over the previous four hours. He flipped to the front of his notepad and waited for the noise to finish.

"Let me summarise," he began, "your name is Christine Wingood and you changed it to Catherine Dunn ... "

Catherine interrupted him as she had done throughout the grilling. "I didn't," she protested, "I was eight years old and ... "

"For Christ sake shut up and listen, just nod yes or no or we'll be here all bloody night." His exasperation was showing. "You have an English heritage, the unrelated Granny Dunn, an Irish immigrant, changed your name when she took you in at eight years old." Catherine nodded agreement, he continued. "When you were eighteen you relocated to Gunnadoo, you find your fiancée is dead, you open a brothel, drop the Irish accent and become Mademoiselle Catherine."

"Oui."

"You learn French from a dictionary," his raised hand stopped the interruption, "you learn photography from Thomas Giles Lennard who works for the Gunnadoo *Advocate*." Catherine nodded agreement. "Wong Foo, Ying Lee, Mrs. Chang, your housekeeper, and Chow Lung are the only ones that know your true identity, yes?"

"Yes and no, it's complicated. Nanny Lucy knows."

Chow Lung removed his cap and scratched his head. "I not know you Irish."

"She isn't," retorted Shepard, "she's Australian with English parentage. Don't confuse me more than I already am."

Chow Lung looked to Catherine. "You very good, fool Chow Lung many years – many hidden talents."

Shepard continued, "Only these people, and..." he checked his notes and made an addition 'the nanny, know that Edith is your daughter, besides the father, John Bycroft."

Catherine sat in silence with a million reasons why she should lie running through her mind. Two reasons stopped her from doing so: Edith and Wally.

When she had relinquished her baby and given Bycroft legal custody, Catherine had made him sign Bycroft Station into a trust that Edith would inherit when she came of age. Edith and Lucy had lived at Bycroft Station until Edith started primary school and then they moved into Bycroft's town residence.

"John Bycroft is a cuckold," she confessed.

Shepard looked up, surprised, "A what?"

"John Bycroft is not the biological father of my child." She pointed to the newspaper clipping and the Cenotaph photo. "He is Edith's father – the late James Wally Beaumont."

Shepard scratched his head. "Gunnadoo erected a monument to Edith's father?"

"Without knowing, oui. I had the stonemason create a likeness and ... "

"Stop." Shepard placed his head in his hands. "Chow Lung, make a cuppa. I think we all could do with one." He began writing again. "Your story has more twists and turns than a *Henry Lawson* tale; continue."

She did and when Chow Lung returned with the brew Shepard was about as ground down as the lead in his pencil.

"I told you she very good." Chow Lung lifted the tray chest high and slid it onto the desk, asking Catherine to pour. To her surprise, he then gestured to Shepard to remove himself from the chair. "I apologise, Catherine, this is not of my doing." He climbed up into his chair regaining his lost authority. "And you will be compensated most generously, yes." Shepard was the one now nodding agreement. "There is no missing manifesto," Chow Lung confided. "Today an exercise and assessment."

Catherine stopped pouring the tea and sat down. Shepard took over pouring duties. "Sorry 'bout what we put you through, "ol girl, it was an exercise to see how my people would size up." The man's persona had changed from threatening to that of a grandmother at morning tea. "And they did bloody awful." he added, passing her the cup and saucer. He then held out the sugar bowl. "I do apologise, it appears our host is out of bickies...sugar?"

The Irish temperament of Granny Dunn exploded from within Catherine. "Mother of Mercy...ya be puttin' me through an afternoon of hell as an exercise." She gulped the hot tea and burnt her mouth. "Sacré bleu." She slumped back into the chair. "I don't know if I'm coming or going." She looked at Chow Lung. "And what have you got to say for yourself?"

"Chow Lung in same boat as you…I not Fifth Columnist, I am Patriot. Homeland ruined by Japanese, many deaths, much misery."

"And we're pretty sure the blighters will be heading this way. Fortress Singapore," he laughed, "is supposed to stop them from island hopping through the Dutch East Indies to Australia. Churchill has sent a symbolic gesture to boost defences but we, the Australian government, fear it is too little and quite possibly too late." Shepard spooned the sugar into his cup, "Two for mother," and casually stirred. "Nasty little devils, definitely not to invite for afternoon tea." He sipped and sighed, "But it appears they are inviting themselves: most disconcerting."

"I don't see how this has anything to do with me."

Shepard placed his cup and saucer on the desk and pondered Catherine's statement. He tapped the cigarette on the Craven 'A' pack and then lit up. "It jolly well will if you find yourself sitting across the table from Tojo at the Sydney Club." He picked up the newspaper clipping and studied it.

"I am not a member of your Sydney Club," she retorted.

"Chow Lung has never been invited to join," he confided, to anyone who would listen.

Shepard regained his thoughts and continued. "A socialite attends many elite functions and meets many people, and hears many secrets, information that could be very useful to certain people."

Chow Lung tapped the side of his nose and Shepard did likewise, and then continued. He placed the clipping on the desk before Catherine. "More photographic awards, an expense account and ... "

"More awards? You mean…"

Shepard tapped his nose again and this time winked. "C'est la guerre."

"Sacré bleu." Catherine shouted.

"C'est la vie," commiserated Chow Lung.

"We'll build your celebrity." Shepard's hands moved back and forth like a magician conjuring. "Sim Sala Bim and like Aladdin's Cave, the doors of the Sydney Club opened," he clicked his fingers, "or maybe the Members Bar at Randwick for the Melbourne Cup next week."

Chow Lung scratched his head again and looked to Catherine. "That pretty good trick."

"One question, Mr. Shepard or whoever you are." Catherine rose and placed her cup on the desk. "Do you do children's parties?"

Shepard was amused. "A car is waiting – the driver will escort you home."

"Am I under arrest?"

"I assure you this is a courtesy only, until we speak again, Catherine."

'Not if I have anything to do with it. Tut-tar, au revoir, hoo-roo and tootle-pip." She about-turned and then strutted to the door, which opened and a man gestured her through.

"Right you are, Stevens will see you home safely," Shepard called cheerfully, and then turned to Chow Lung. "Very impressive…very impressive indeed." He picked up the receiver, dialled and waited impatiently. He wasted no time on formalities when his call was answered. "Have these files on my desk first thing in the morning: Edith Bycroft, nurse, Concord Repat. John Bycroft, Mayor of Gunnadoo 1921 to '27. James Wally Beaumont, Gunnadoo, deceased WW1 veteran, served in Sinai and Palestine with the Camel Corps ... "

* * *

The quietness woke Edith and she slid her arm from under Roger's head without waking him. The experience had not been satisfying. Roger's enthusiasm and stamina were one thing but she felt cheated. Her breasts throbbed and her thighs ached. Getting out the window was precarious; stretching for the branch limb to step onto optimistic. The short fall did not break anything but her ego and she lay on her back waiting to see if the crashing noise had woken Roger. She need not have worried; it just woke Blackie the Labrador from next door, and he proceeded to harass her playfully as she limped from the yard. "Get off. Go home." she whispered. A handful of gravel convinced the mutt she was not playing. "Last time I do a virgin a good deed," she muttered.

Dawn broke the darkness and wildlife broke the silence. Shouts from the Chinatown district soon began calling out what could only be interpreted as commands and counter-commands as individual differences of opinion were defended rigorously. The ubiquitous barking of dogs followed. Edith hobbled past the Saddlery, her riding boots clattering on the sidewalk until she stepped down onto the bitumen road and proceeded in silence. A lone approaching

621

figure caught her attention, and she studied the man's outline until she recognised him. "Good morning, Mr. Dadswell."

"Good morning lassie, I heard ya was back, didn't think I'd be seein' ya at this hour." Edith did a couple of regulation star-jumps. "Ock. Now I see. Ya into physical fitness, good for ya. Tossed the caber I did when a bonnie lad, I'm a-ways past it these days...hardly got the strength to toss a saddle on a horse's back." The saddler let out a heavy sigh. "Ock. To be young again. Well I canna stand around chattin' all day, there's work waiting. Are ya attending the Cup? Ya father's running the favourite, ya know."

The Gunnadoo Cup, for the past decade, had run the weekend before the first Tuesday in November: the Melbourne Cup.

Edith smiled. "I heard a whisper that Clyde Templar ... "

"Ah, yes...Miss Jessie, she's a dark horse." Dadswell relit his pipe and drew on it hard remembering Edith as a skinny tomboy winning the inaugural Gunnadoo Cup. "Ya was a natural, lassie, if ya was riding on Saturday I'd be tempted to lay a wager on ya ... "

"Speaking of which," Edith cut in, "have you got a tip for me?"

Dadswell stepped back and studied Edith from head to foot. "I change me mind –ya a' might too big for a jockey these days." Edith laughed nervously, feeling a tad self-conscious. His pipe gurgled as he drew upon it again. "I've one tip for ya lassie. Get ya riding boots reheeled; they're makin' ya walk bandy-legged." His bushy beard parted as his tobacco-stained teeth flashed a smile of wisdom, "Ock. To be young again," he chuckled.

Dadswell's gift for witticisms embarrassed her and she felt her face glowing. The memory of when all the light bulbs had popped at the grand opening of the electricity grid returned to her and she recalled her father's red face. For the first time she felt a morsel of empathy for her father.

She stood watching the old man waddle towards the saddlery and boot maker's shop. It was he who'd shown her how to ride in shortened stirrups, to feel every muscle and sinew of the thoroughbred straining between her thighs and then balance the horse by changing the whip hand, and most importantly he'd shown her how to win. "I'll see you I before I leave." she shouted. He did not turn around or reply, just raised his arm in acknowledgment.

* * *

No sooner had Edith laid her head upon the pillow than she heard Lucy knocking softly on the bedroom door. "Edi, Edi, are you awake dear? I've got the kettle on…would you like a cuppa in bed?" The nanny's morning routine had never changed and Edith could set time by her.

"No thank you, I'll get up." The ABC's fanfare for the seven o'clock news emanated from the kitchen. She threw her legs over the side of the bed and sat up. "Good morning, Amy. Some things never change," she said to the framed picture of the aviator on the nightstand.

Amy, the first woman to fly solo from England to Australia in 1930, had died in January. Bad weather when ferrying a Royal Air Force plane for the Air Transport Auxiliary had forced her to parachute into the Thames Estuary. The search and rescue team never recovered her body.

Edith's reflection in the mirror indicated a late night but the bags under her eyes would pass off as the graveyard shifts she'd recently worked. She could not pass off her large ears as easily, they were inherited. She removed the elastic band tying back her hair. "I'll have a quick shower first," she said to Lucy as she passed through the kitchen to the bathroom. "Won't be long."

The mantle radio crackled, "And now to a report from ABC war correspondent Chester Wilmont..."

* * *

The Apian Valley, once heavily timbered with cedar and mahogany, had made a small fortune for Bycroft; most of that money had unfortunately been lost in the '29 stock market crash. At the time, his two pubs, the Arms and the Plough, competed for the dwindling clientele, as did the Oasis Hotel. Bycroft closed the Plough and leased the licence to a Sydney colleague. Catherine bought out Bycroft's share in the defunct brothel, and he used the cash to shore up his outstanding bank loans, recently converting the Plough into the Palace cinema.

The Apian Way road was in better condition than the main highway to Yapsly Siding. Many elitists had properties to the west of Gunnadoo and had continually harassed the council to have the road graded. The Gunnadoo racetrack committee had lobbied for the elitists and supported all the requests that the landholders put forward. Therefore, the drive out to Bycroft Station, now a sprawling sheep and cattle property, took twenty minutes instead of forty.

Edith had unfortunately run over a branch and it had punctured the muffler. "Slow down Edith." shouted Lucy over the roaring engine. "You'll kill us both." Dust clouds billowed behind them and then disappeared into the morning haze. The two-storey house loomed as large as ever as they turned off Apian Way onto Bycroft Station, the verandas and balconies of which had a panoramic view from their vantage point on the small hill.

Bycroft was standing on the front veranda. He removed the gold fob watch from his vest pocket and checked the time as the approaching dust storm travelled up the quarter mile stretch to the circular driveway. He walked through the open French doors to his study and set his large bulk behind the mahogany desk. He removed the watch from its Albert chain, placed it down in front of himself and waited. The car slid to a stop in the gravel and raised his ire. He grimaced at the gunning of the engine. It had never been an easy relationship; father and daughter had little in common but the love of speed. His mentoring on the importance of money had gone unheeded, as had most of his lectures.

Henderson's black face appeared to welcome the women. Edith was nine years his junior and at the age of ten, she had taken it upon herself to teach the

625

aboriginal how to read and write. Bycroft was not impressed with Henderson's literacy, and he blamed Edith for many of the disputes with the aboriginal workforce that eventuated when Henderson became their spokesperson and threatened him with litigation for unpaid salaries.

Edith smelt the sweet perfume from the rose garden in the air and then about-faced to survey the lower paddocks where the thoroughbreds grazed. The sparkling white of freshly painted fences divided the front twenty acres into four separate paddocks. The apple trees were bare but the plum trees bore succulent fruit. Edith was not sure if it was the fruit or the memory of playing hide-and-seek in the orchard as a child that made her mouth water.

Bycroft did not rise when the women entered. He picked up the watch and informed Edith, "You're slowing down."

Lucy rolled her eyes. Edith kissed the top of his balding head and then checked the fob watch. "I'll do better next time."

The timepiece had played an important role in her upbringing. She had always been in competition with it, whether it be riding time trials or fighting for her father's time. His idiosyncrasy of closing the protective cover with a flick of the wrist had been engraved in her brain like a metaphor of their relationship. Bycroft had passed off the words 'to JB love Catherine', on the inside of the protective cover as an engraver's error. Many times, Edith had fantasised stealing and smashing it.

"I was expecting you last night – I got at least a half dozen telephone calls saying you'd been seen in town." He observed Edith's apparel. "Why can't you wear a dress?" She observed the wrist flick as he shut the watch cover.

'I'm on leave…I wear a uniform … "

He abruptly cut her off. "What's this about an overseas posting?" Edith sat on the desk and pulled off her riding boots. He turned to Lucy. "Do you know about this?"

"I was informed last night, I don't approve." She left the study without saying more.

"Neither do I," he replied, and then looked at Edith, "but I can't stop you, never could. You take after your mother; she had a mind of her own too." Bycroft had delivered that statement many times and it meant nothing to Edith. She had never seen a photograph of her mother, had always been told that a fire at the property had destroyed all photographs. Memories planted by her father were all she could relate to. He lit up a cigar. "Do you know where you'll be sent?"

Edith straightened her legs and wiggled her toes. "Probably the Middle East, Egypt I'd say, things aren't too good there. Rommel is putting up quite a fight they say." She leaned across the desk, removed the cigar from Bycroft's fingers and took a drag on it, and then handed it back to him through the smoke ring she blew. "Auchinleck's forces are sustaining heavy causalities – we hear more in the hospital wards than the public hears on the BBC world news, you know."

Bycroft could not put his finger on it; not only was there a change in Edith's demeanour but somehow she did not look the same as she had eight months previously. The belated get-together to celebrate her nineteenth birthday had ended in disaster, as had her eighteenth when he ended up drunk and she hostile. It was then she had told him of her transferring from St. Vincent's to Concord. It was the last time he saw the awkward tomboy in her.

Bycroft moved to the liquor cabinet expecting abuse but it did not eventuate. He poured a shot of whisky. Edith observed a forty-eight year-old man drinking himself into an early grave, and now realised that she barely knew him. She had never taken the time and he never had the time.

As a child, she had spent hours in front of a mirror looking for resemblances. The attributes she had convinced herself with were nothing more than the optimism of a kid searching for her identity. The void had never been filled and the looking glass had revealed nothing of the growing rift between daughter and father.

Bycroft sat on the leather lounge. "How long before you go?"

She did not answer straight away, choosing to view the question as ambiguous and then delivering an equally vague answer. "It all depends…"

"On what?" he asked.

"The army of course."

"I meant Gunnadoo."

"Sunday."

"Fine."

An uncomfortable silence followed; they both played the game well. In the past, Edith had taken pleasure in watching her father squirm when she got the better of him, and he had done the same.

Somehow, the act now seemed childish but they still played it with enthusiasm.

"What are your plans..." he paused and then added condescendingly, "before you leave Gunnadoo?"

"I've got some personal things to do out here...clean up my affairs and ... "

He interrupted. "You should try cleaning up your room while you're at it."

She took the bait and bit. "If you've been in ... "

"I haven't been in your room since you were ten." He changed the subject. "Gallant Prince is running in the Cup tomorrow." He swallowed the remaining whisky and rose. "Are you staying the night?"

"If that's all right with you." She immediately wished she had not played the game. "I'd like to go riding later," she smiled at him, "refresh the memories. It may be a while before I get back."

He walked to the French doors and hesitated before exiting. "I'll see you at the evening meal then."

Chapter 3

Friday October 31

The freestanding terrace stood at the end of Victoria Street, Potts Point, as though balancing on an escarpment and ready to topple onto Brougham Street below. The prime position overlooked the Garden Island naval depot. A rooftop garden camouflaged communications antennas and a telescope housed in the garden shed could pan 180 degrees of Port Jackson from Millers Point in the west, five miles up the harbour to the half-mile wide heads at the entrance. Below the covert observatory was Captain Tony Shepard's apartment and below that on the second floor was the office of the C.I.O.

Blackboards with chalk scrawls, statistics and diagrams took up two sides of the large room. Photographs, maps and message-filled corkboards lined the other two. The shades were drawn and filing cabinets stood in front of the windows. Desks took up much of the floor space. Clocks displayed London, Paris, Singapore and local time. Shepard's office was in a renovated bedroom; off the hallway was the kitchen with table and chairs, a sink and a small two-burner stove. Behind the false wall in the bathroom, a door led to a room concealing the shortwave radio and Morse code and Typex machine; it coded and decoded sensitive material. Little Bo Peep Toy Importers, the C.I.O.'s cover, conducted business at ground level. Cartons of stuffed toys filled the basement garage where the Bentley sat behind closed doors with its nose pointing towards the Brougham Street exit.

Shepard clambered down the stairs still eating his breakfast; the stale corned beef sandwich filling out his throat like an enlarged goitre. Karen White, alias Betty, the unfortunate woman left to fend for herself in the railway cubicle, went into the kitchen and put the kettle on.

"Anyone for a cuppa?" she called.

Martin McGuiness, aka Shaun Cooney the Irish shipping clerk, sat at his desk perusing the Bulletin. Various newspapers lay in a pile before him; those already read lay scattered at his feet. "Is ta Pope a Catholic?" he replied.

McGuiness had arrived in Sydney having fled Seine Fein after a falling out. His expertise in communications was proven but his knowledge of explosives had never been tested. Just as well, the nearest he came to an explosion was firecrackers on Guy Fawke's night as a kid. For a decade he had lied his way through various cushy government jobs, and then with the outbreak of war found himself attached to the C.I.O. At fifty, he believed himself too old for active service of any kind except fishing, a passion he rarely had the chance to pursue.

Billy Windsor, alias Monsieur Willard, was a student mathematician from Sydney University. He connected lines and figures from a list of names scrawled on the blackboard. Hieroglyphic-like graphs showed numerals and percentages in unfathomable algebra.

Shepard looked at the hive of activity and shook his head as the civilians went about their business sheepishly; they were excellent office staff but hopeless field operatives. He knew that good field operators had to be naturals; logistics could be taught, the required cunning could not. Convincing his superiors of what was required had nearly cost him his commission when he went over the heads of a few people, but the top brass ultimately acknowledged that rogues *do* make the best agents.

Under the umbrella of the South East Asian Intelligence Organisation, Shepard had received the green light to assemble a covert team with the acronym C.I.O. Only after substantial background checks did he approach unsuspecting recruits. He soon identified Chow Lung as having a business that he could use and the manipulation began. For Chow Lung it was a choice of being supportive or sitting out the war in jail on trumped-up charges as a hostile alien, or even worse, being sent to an internment camp.

"Anything I should know about?" Shepard called to McGuiness.

McGuiness slid his hand into the pile, choosing a newspaper at random. "Friday ta t'irty-first of October. Germans advance on Russia – George Zhukov commands ta Red Army."

"Our own back yard thanks. Anyway, that news is a week old – get with it, man." Shepard checked the time. "1115 hours. Windsor, am I a happy man?"

Windsor did not turn around but continued scrawling on the blackboard at a manic pace. "On your desk," he replied. The lad's skill at getting things done, or rather, delegating the right people to the right task to get the job done was exceptional as was his IQ for problem solving. "Ten to one you're a happy chappie." His military etiquette was clearly lacking.

Shepard methodically laid out the folders on the desk. "Let's see, I think…" he rolled his fingers on the desk, "Mr. Beaumont." He settled into his chair and began taking in the information contained within the dossier. Until Karen spoke, he was oblivious to her entering with his cuppa.

'Here's the weekly summary." She held up the folder and then placed it on top of a filing cabinet. "Don't forget to sign each page."

"We'll have a briefing in an hour," he said, and returned to scribbling notes.

At ten o'clock, the subordinates sat around the kitchen table ready with notepads, blank sheets of paper, sharpened pencils and a heightened apprehension of what was to follow. Jenson and Blocker were military personnel, on assignment from another organisation; it now appeared that politics was playing a part and that the C.I.O. was lumbered with them. The humiliation that Jenson, who was as young and fit as a Mallee bull, had suffered was indicated by his black eyes and lacerated nose – the camera's point of impact. His broken jaw had resulted from spinning into the open door, and his chin bandage restricted talking. The bandages wrapped around his head and his overall forlorn look gave him the appearance of having been hit by a bus. He wanted to believe he had been. He and Blocker had recently completed a self-defence course and the training officers had pronounced them competent.

Blocker was now in a plaster cast at the Concord Repat.

Jenson wiped the dribble from the corner of his mouth and pronounced through wired teeth, "Za 'itch 'ook me 'y zaprise."

Shepard entered the kitchen and sat at the head of the table. He placed the folders within reach and did not address anyone in particular, choosing to look at the files. "Darn poor showing yesterday. One would like to think we could have done better." He sipped a freshly made cuppa placed within reach by Karen and then looked up. "Jenson. Good Lord man, what happened to you?"

McGuiness answered for him. "Ta bitch took 'im by surprise, she did. Isn't tat so?"

"She gave you the slip," Shepard pointed out to McGuiness. "The target had been in and out under your nose and you didn't even know. Explain man."

"I be expectin' a French woman."

The subordinates' chatter confirmed McGuiness' statement. Jenson struggled for volume. "Za itch 'ook 'im by zaprise."

Windsor took advantage of the lull. "Me too," he informed Shepard. "I was expecting you to be with her." The chatter began again, forcing Windsor to raise his voice, "I didn't know whether or not to give over the shipping manifest."

The banging of Shepard's hand upon the table redirected everyone's attention to him. "This is not a CWA meeting; it is a briefing, not a chance to chinwag." Immediately he apologised, "Present company excluded, Jenson." He then looked to

634

Karen, shaking his head. "Our last line of defence, what happened?"

McGuiness interrupted. "She got caught with 'er pants down, she did."

Shepard whacked the table again, quelling the men's laughter and Karen's shouts of protest. He raised his cup. "I've got one thing to say to you all – well done." Surprised faces looked at one another and then at Shepard. "It proves what I've been saying all along."

McGuiness concurred. "Good neighbours are more helpful t'an distant relatives." He lit a cigarette and sat back looking pleased with his comment.

Shepard contained his impatience. "Thank you for your pearls of wisdom, Mr. McGuiness." Jenson began laughing, slurping furiously for breath. Shepard removed his spectacles and massaged the bridge of his nose. "When you're ready, Jenson." He had recruited the man for his brawn, not his brains.

Windsor opened a notepad. "I've been doing some calculations and the odds of Catherine Dunn successfully carrying out that operation are ... "

"on the cards," Shepard interrupted. "Let's face it. We were not up to it. I repeat – rogues make the best thieves." He removed a cigarette from the Craven 'A' packet and threw it to Jenson. "Suck on one of those. Everyone relax. The operation went as I suspected it would…now you're all aware of what a field operator faces." He held out the burning match to Jenson and advised, "Expect the unexpected or ... " He blew out the match to make the point. Shepard then pulled the folders towards himself and tapped them. "Our job is to collate information." He paused to smile. "And from what I've read you've all done an excellent job, well done." He raised his cup in salutation. "Here's to our authorisation." The Ministry of Defence had delivered the C.I.O. the powers it required twenty-four hours previously.

"It's amazing what a bit of clout can do," said Karen, "I reckon there are quite a few blurry-eyed bureaucrats in City Hall and Canberra this morning." She had put a deadline on the defence clerks to collect the information overnight. "Anyone for another cuppa?"

All hands rose. McGuiness instigated a round of applause and Shepard continued.

"Righty-o, down to business at hand. General Percival has eight infantry brigades, with another two on the way to Malaya. He has no tanks, he has Indian troops at the front line who have never seen one – let alone been into battle against any if the Japanese land – all brigades are ill equipped and have little jungle training. Major-General Gordon Bennett and the Australian 8 Division in Southern Malaya are no better off; the tropical conditions and resulting diseases are hospitalising many soldiers and there's not a Jap in sight of the mainland...yet. Priorities are confused at all levels and lack of credible information is creating a headache at HQ. We're to oversee a special job. We need Catherine Dunn – she doesn't want us. Ideas?" There were no suggestions. "Come on, think like a rogue or a thief."

"Pilfer her bank accounts so she'll have no money and need the work," suggested Windsor.

"And her clothes, steal them too," added Karen.

636

Shepard smiled. "You're both on the right track but one should always try to be subtle and not draw attention to oneself."

"Steal w'at she values most," said McGuiness.

"Yes." shouted Shepard. "And what is that gentlemen...and lady?" he added as an afterthought. Faces stared blankly at one another other, ticking clocks filled the silence, Jenson stopped breathing, now self-conscious of his slurping and Shepard shuffled through the folders. He threw the dossier to the middle of the table. "Edith Bycroft – her daughter."

Loud chatter covered Jenson's gasping for air.

"Tat's kidnappin', isn't it?" enquired McGuiness. Jenson's heart rate rose even more when he heard that word. The thought of covert action excited him and the volume of his slurping increased. McGuiness made a cross with his forefingers and held it up to Jenson. "Shut up ya evil man."

Shepard smiled at Windsor. "The government doesn't kidnap; it 'seconders', right, Mr. Windsor?" He did not wait for an answer and continued, "No, subtlety is the name of the game. It just happens that Miss Bycroft is a nurse at the Concord Repatriation Hospital and has applied for an overseas posting. We are going to choose where she's posted to and Mother Duck will follow." He stubbed out the cigarette, "And we'll have our mole right where we want her to be." He placed the other folders on top of Edith's dossier. "It's all in here, learn well my friends – I won't be around to hold your hands forever. Karen, organise your people for tonight and make reservations for two at Romano's Restaurant. McGuiness, you look after the logistics. Windsor…" Shepard observed what now looked like Einstein's theory of relativity scrawled incomprehensively across two blackboards. "Carry on."

"Me?" Jenson enquired.

"Stevens will drive you." Shepard opened a notepad and wrote an address. "Pick up the goods and take them to Romano's, they'll be expecting you. After that, you get a long weekend. Carry on."

Shepard entered his office, picked up the receiver and dialled. "Good morning, Sir…yes, it's Shepard. We need someone posted to Singapore. When? As soon as possible. Next week? That will be fine. I'll have the details sent over to you."

He hung up and immediately picked the receiver back up.

* * *

Catherine had added Epsom salts to the bubble bath. Froth sat upon the water like a giant cumulus cloud, and she lay back soaking herself to relieve her aches and pains. The telephone rang. "Bonjour…Catherine Bouvier."

"Good morning, Catherine."

She recognised the voice and dropped her phony accent. "I've a good mind to sue you and your organisation. What do you want?"

"I was rather hoping I might make amends, let's say an apology for yesterday's inconvenience. Have you any plans for this evening?"

"My dancing lessons," she lied, raising a leg from the water and wriggling her toes, "and that is now very doubtful."

The previous night's ordeal had not finished when chauffeured home by Stevens. He had taken it upon himself to zigzag across the city rather than take a direct route to Edgecliff in case agents followed them. Her parting company with Stevens had been an impulsive decision when the vehicle had stopped at Taylor Square; Catherine absconded up Boundary Street. She had not planned the long walk home either – no taxicabs appeared for her to hail.

"My shoes are ruined and so are my feet." She raised the other leg and wriggled her toes. "I have been crippled," she said dramatically. "I will never dance again."

"Actually, I didn't have the Trocadero in mind. Not one for dancing myself, no; I thought a quiet meal and a chat at Romano's. Are you familiar with the restaurant? First-class I'm told."

"I'm all chatted out, Mister-whoever-you-are. There is nothing you can say or ... "

"I have a compensation cheque for you." Shepard listened to the silence and smiled. Having read the dossier on Catherine, he was forming a profile of her; what he saw he liked. The woman was not a femme fatal but she had the makings of one. What *was* immediately recognisable was her loyalty. "This cheque will keep you in shoes for ... "

"is this a bribe for my silence?"

"On the contrary, Catherine, without your assistance the flaws in...let's just say a new Bo-Peep line, would not have been detected as quickly. It is payment for a job well done."

"Romano's...I hear it is very expensive. I hope you have a fat expense account, Mr. Shepard."

"Shall we say...seven?"

"Shall we say...seven-thirty?"

* * *

At seven o'clock, Shepard turned into Cascade Road, switched off the car lights and engine and rolled to a stop, camouflaged in the shadow of a large elm. Allowing for the blown streetlamp bulb in front of her residence, he began estimating how far it was to Catherine's front gate. *Thirty-two yards,* he thought. He observed Catherine's Federation-style terrace and the surrounds as though through the lens of a camera, etching the image into his mind. *Top floor two bay windows, adjoining balcony accessible by large tree. Front yard estimated size half a tennis court, foliage, wrought-iron front fence.* At seven twenty-nine, he confirmed the estimated distance upon opening the gate. At precisely seven-thirty, the gargoyle doorknocker echoed his arrival throughout the house.

The veranda light immediately attracted a swarm of mosquitoes and bugs. Shepard slapped his neck and then began waving his trilby, although he waited patiently for the door to open. Catherine stood in the dark passage watching him through the opaque glass panels of the door, testing his patience as much as her own was capable of being tested. He finally knocked again. She opened the door and stepped out smartly, pulling the door behind her. Dressed in a satin couture evening gown she looked a picture of elegance. Her perfume wafted on the warm air, attracting him but more importantly, repelling the plague of mozzies.

"Good evening, Catherine."

She took him by surprise by slapping his face. "That was a big one," she said, "the mozzies will eat you alive at this time of year."

"Yes, quite. Shall we?" He gestured her forward and followed, rubbing his cheek, undecided whether she had got the better of him. He skipped ahead to open the gate and motioned her towards the Bentley. "Perks of the business," he informed her before she asked.

"And exactly what business are you in today?"

"Toy manufacturing." He handed her a business card.

* * *

Shepard parked in the grounds of Parliament House and they walked across Macquarie Street to Martin Place. Romano's was busy. Catherine distractedly returned the polite smiles and nods of acknowledgement from other diners as the maître d' escorted them to the VIP table overlooking the dance floor. A pianist was tinkling softly on a baby grand. The subdued lighting from small lamps on each table enhanced the elegance of the exclusive restaurant. A waiter presented the wine list to Shepard and a menu to Catherine and then formally welcomed them both.

"On behalf of Mr. Romano, I Carlos, welcome you."

Catherine studied Shepard's face as he studied the wine list. A slightly bent nose and strong jaw made even more pronounced by a five-o'clock shadow indicated strength. His wavy hair, a little longer than normal, gave the appearance of rebellion or that he was a busy man and could not find the time for a haircut; she could not decide. Although only twenty-four hours old, the small moustache cultivated on his top lip already gave him the look of a dashing air force pilot. The devil-may-care guise suited him.

Shepard closed the wine menu. "Your best champagne, garçon."

"Sacre bleu. Your fat expense account must be obese, Monsieur Shepard."

The austerity of the times had even affected Romano's cellar; there was no champagne. Carlos raised an eyebrow at Shepard, retrieved the folder and then explained the situation, recommending instead the sparkling white. Shepard agreed. Carlos then turned to Catherine, lifted her hand and kissed it. "And the beautiful Senorita…may I take your order?" Catherine felt a warm flush upon her face and fanned herself with the menu.

"She'll have the sparkling white too."

Carlos displayed his contempt by ignoring Shepard. Gesturing to a nearby waiter for attention, he continued his intimacy with Catherine. "May I recommend an oyster entrée, the steak Diane and fresh vegetables and for dessert, a Pompadour pudding with a chocolate fluff topping." Catherine agreed, her taste buds screaming for the chocolate;

another scarce commodity. He looked to Shepard, "And monsieur?"

"I'll have the same too, Don Quixote."

Carlos directed the waiter to take the order before they both disappeared into the kitchen.

"Are you going to address me as Monsieur Shepard for the rest of the evening? It's Tony." He tapped a Craven 'A' packet.

"Then Anthony," she smiled cheekily and leaned forward, "tell moi who you are."

Her low-cut gown distracted him and he fumbled to light the cigarette. "There's not much to tell really." He composed himself to draw back on the Craven 'A', then blew smoke from his bent nose. "I originally came from New Zealand but was educated at Melbourne Grammar."

Catherine gestured to his nose and he smiled. "The boxing club, middle light-weight...I could hold my own but I preferred rowing on the Yarra actually." She nodded and he continued. "My father was with the diplomatic service. When he and my mother divorced, we stayed and he went back to New Zealand. I graduated from Melbourne University in 1927 and ended up in Canberra's bureaucracy for ten years." He related the boredom he had experienced in Canberra and then added, "And that's about it."

"That is it? You are a very dull man, Monsieur Shepard." She recognised the smile of a bachelor and the fake wedding ring. "How does your wife put up with you?"

Shepard smiled coyly. "You're not buying it, eh?"

Carlos returned with the sparkling white wine, his colleague following with the entrees. Shepard tasted the wine and gestured to Carlos to fill Catherine's glass. She raised it.

"Let's see if the bubbles will loosen your tongue."

They did, and after the first glass of claret, which arrived with the main course, Shepard proceeded to tell her of his adventures backpacking through the outer provinces of China in 1937 and then escaping Shanghai just before the four-month siege and eventual surrender. He did not elaborate on Nanking and the horror suffered by its populace, although he did demonstrate he knew what he was talking about. "Now you know why I'm not particularly fond of the Japanese," he concluded, as the waiter arrived to clear away the dessert remnants.

"Sacré bleu, moi has had sufficient." Catherine placed her spoon neatly beside the empty bowl, placed a hand upon her chest and burped quietly. "Pardon." She smiled cheekily at Shepard.

As they finished their port and coffee, he told of his travels through Malaya, Sumatra and the Dutch East Indies and his return to Darwin. Catherine was pleased with herself, believing the man had loosened up and revealed more than he had intended. She dabbed her lips with the napkin. "I believe there is one last thing you have for me?" He frowned. She smiled. "My cheque. Of course moi would much prefer cash but if we cannot trust the government, who can we trust?"

"Ah, yes…the cheque." Shepard paused to drink the last of his port. "Of course you realise the government must not be seen to be involved."

He stood up, patted his pockets as though searching them and then sat back down. The pianist immediately stopped his rendition of *Tea for Two* and began playing a fanfare. The subdued lighting rose and Romano, sporting his trademark pencil-thin moustache, white tie and tails, entered from the kitchen and walked to the piano as the diners applauded. He bowed flamboyantly until the applause died down.

"You are all too kind. Tonight it gives me great pleasure to introduce Monsieur Davenport." Davenport entered, followed by an assistant who immediately set up an easel and returned to the kitchen with Romano.

"Good evening, ladies and gentlemen. On behalf of the Davenport-Jones Foundation, welcome." Davenport waited for the applause to stop. "I shall not make a long speech; we all know why we are here." The assistant returned carrying a covered frame and sat it upon the easel. Davenport moved to the mystery display. "I am very happy to unveil the winner of the inaugural Davenport-Jones portraiture award." He removed the shroud to reveal the face of a toothless wharfie smiling proudly. Catherine had taken the photograph at the Blackwattle Bay wharves. Shepard had retrieved the camera from the rail yards and had the film developed and the negative blown up.

He stood applauding along with the other patrons. "Bravo, good show." he called.

Catherine was stunned and sat trying to comprehend the situation. Shepard cajoled her to stand and ushered her onto the small stage. "There's your compensation cheque," he told her, "accept the award, receive the cheque." He stood back as cameras appeared from under tables, bulbs popped as flashes of light lit the subject. "Speech, speech." he called, offering a catalyst for the other patrons to follow.

"Merci. I am, how you say, speechless, merci."

The crowd called for her to continue. Catherine floundered for a couple of minutes and then pleaded her case to sit down. "Merci...au revoir." She returned to her seat and sat watching the patrons quickly leave the restaurant, realising Shepard had set her up again. *Very well,* she thought, *if that's the way you're going to play it.*

Shepard returned to the table from the kitchen. He skipped up the three stairs and leaned on the balcony railing. "Just giving my regards to Romano, truly a master impresario he is." Catherine camouflaged her rage, bit her tongue and let him continue. "Well..."

"Well?" she repeated, and sat waiting until the awkwardness of the moment instigated his next move.

"Shall we?" he gestured towards the exit.

She placed the inane trophy in his hand. "I'll just powder my nose first."

* * *

Catherine wound down the window of the Bentley to feel the warm breeze upon her face.

Shepard observed her while she was not looking. The nape of her slender neck was as intoxicating as the perfume now swirling upon the current of air that passed teasingly under his nose. She kicked off her shoes and wriggled her toes in the stream of air from the ducting under the dashboard. Out of the corner of his eye, he saw the satin gown slide aside to reveal the white of an inner thigh.

"Er…I think this evening went very well…most enjoyable if I do say so…myself." Catherine ignored his attempts at conversation; he sounded like a nervous teenager on his first date. "The food was all right…wasn't it?" The more he tried not to sound inane the more his self-consciousness rose.

He parked under the elm again and bounded from the car to open Catherine's door. "Thirty-two yards," he said. She looked surprised but said nothing. He shook his head. "Never mind." As much as he tried, he could not shake the feeling of being like a lap dog, leaping around the feet of its master or in this case, mistress. "Let me get that." He pushed the gate open and let her pass first.

Catherine spoke for the first time since leaving the restaurant. "I hope you don't think I'm leading you up the garden path." She smiled at the pun and held out her hand for support as she stepped up to the porch landing. "My, my, what strong hands you have Mr. Shepard, must be all that rowing you did on the Yarra."

"Tony…call me Tony."

She put the key in the lock and then leaned with her back against the wall with her knee bent and her foot sliding up the sandstone. Under the radiance of the porch light, her white gown glowed as it again opened revealingly. With shoes in hand, she smiled alluringly and whispered seductively, "Come here, Anthony."

Her moist lips were inviting and he moved closer, all the time aware of the bent knee and the damage it could inflict, but he closed his eyes. She pushed his trilby back on his forehead and slowly ran her finger down his forehead and crooked nose, and then without warning she plucked a hair from his moustache. The blinding pain sent him reeling backwards, and she had the door open and was inside before his eyes had time to water.

"I am so sorry," she called through the letter slot, "I thought it was a fake moustache – forgive moi."

Shepard rubbed his eyes, nose and face, and then slapped at the mozzies. "What about your award?"

"You keep it – moi will keep the cheque."

"I'll ring you tomorrow."

"My business hours are nine to five, Monday to Friday only. Adieu, Monsieur Shepard."

The porch light went out along with any aspirations he might have had for the night. ... To be Continued in 'Duty By Coercion'

* * *